LESSER DEMONS

ROSE CARD-FAUX

MAMMOTH CREEK

MAMMOTH CREEK

ISBN: 978-1-961245-00-6 (hardcover)

For questions and comments about the quality of this book, please contact us at Admin@MammothCreekMedia.com

To anyone who has ever doubted whether they were enough.

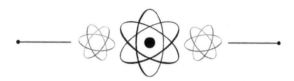

Note to readers:

LESSER DEMONS has a large cast of characters and an intricate story universe that includes some terms you will probably find unfamiliar. For your convenience, both a list of characters and a glossary have been included toward the back of the book.

Additionally, LESSER DEMONS touches on some heavy/difficult topics. I have tried to handle them with respect and care, but, before reading, you may still wish to be aware of some things that you will find in the book. Namely, that there will be depictions of violence and killings, mentions of the deaths of loved ones, representations of grief, allusions to and discussion of addiction, and brief references to kidnapping and the deaths of children. There is also a short description of someone being held down by their throat and feeling powerless against their assailant. This attack takes place in the middle of a battle, but it may be difficult for anyone who has experienced physical assault.

LESSER DEMONS

Our old Chevy truck rumbles and rackets in complaint over the ruts frozen into the snow as I drive down the winding roads that run between our mountain valley farm and the highway into Flemingsburg. The sky's clear at the moment, but the evergreens crowding the sides of the road are heavy with last night's storm. My breath comes out in cold puffs, freezing the lip gloss onto my lips.

The sun's barely a hint of light over the mountains. Other than the noise of my truck, everything's real still and kind of otherworldly with the way the snow glows blue in the dark.

I've got this thing I do where I close my eyes tight and then flash them open and pretend I'm in another time and place. Blinking my eyes now, I send myself to the pilot seat of a WWII-era plane. One of those with room for only two people but lots of cargo space. I've got a co-pilot who's real handsome. Like, as handsome as Matthew Wolfe, this actor I'm sort of into. It's stormy outside and dark, and we're bouncing heavy in the turbulence, and it's all I can do to hold the plane on course.

"We can't see where we're going!" shouts my co-pilot over the noise of the engine. "We have to turn on our lights or we might crash!"

"We can't do that, Harry!" I shout back as loud as I can. "We can't risk being seen. We've got to get our cargo to the drop site by morning or the whole plan will fail. We'll just have to trust our instruments tonight. Old Jinny's gotten us through worse than this."

I pat the dash all tender with one palm but have to quick grab both hands to the wheel again to stop from losing control of the plane.

"It's not Old Jinny I trust," Harry says. "It's you." And the look he gives me makes me feel proud and warm all over. Like the way you imagine a kiss is supposed to make you feel, but then it doesn't.

Mrs. Hermans, who owns the general store in town, likes to say I have a "wild imagination." I take it as kind of a compliment, even if she claims daydreaming's not a positive trait in a girl of eighteen. I mean, other people spend their time wishing they had what they don't or that their lives were different. If I want something, I just imagine I've got it, and then I'm basically happy enough.

Today is the second morning of Swedish Days, the big Founders Day festival, and I'm headed into town to sell some of our greenhouse produce and meet up with my friends Sylvia Álvarez and Logan Jacobsen. This is our last Swedish Days before we graduate and they leave for college, so we're planning on making the most of it.

Generally, I try not to think much about the fact that they're leaving. Or the fact that I'm staying behind. Sylvia tried to get me to apply to the same university as her, but when I mentioned it to my mom, she just said, "Oh, interesting idea," in that way that means she doesn't find it that interesting.

Mom's probably the only parent I know who hasn't drilled into her kid the importance of higher education. I mean, she's always expected me to do well in school, but whenever anyone's mentioned anything about college, she's jumped in with, "There's no need to rush into it," so quick you'd think they'd asked me about some embarrassing secret. Then, when I told her last fall that I was thinking about not going to college this year at all, she wrapped me in this weirdly intense hug and said, "Okay, honey. That might work out for the best." So, that's where things stand now.

When I get to the smooth asphalt of the snow-plowed highway, I blink myself into a spaceship. I'm on a leisurely scenic flight through the Jupiter region. I stare out my windows at all the moons, greet them by name like they're old friends. Only, I don't actually remember any of their names. So, I just make stuff up.

"There's Gorgilon," I say with my cell phone to my mouth like it's a space-age recording device. "Its reds are looking particularly vibrant this year. Like the old historian wrote, *The blood spots of Gorgilon seem to pulse, like cavernous windows into the heart of the fiery moon."*

A couple times, cars pass going the other way, and I turn them into asteroids. Saying into my recorder, "The asteroid count is low right now, but they may just be outliers from a larger field. I need to keep my eyes open."

My stomach's a little upset. This buzzy sort of static behind my belly button. Probably because of all the jostling of the truck after such an early breakfast.

"I can feel the forces of Magnitronius tugging at my innards, but I'm keeping my distance. Many a traveler's fallen victim to the power of that giant moon."

Traffic picks up the closer I get to Flemingsburg. Swedish Days happens right in the middle of February, and it's always cold in our part of Idaho at that time of year. Like, it snows pretty much every day. So, you'd think there wouldn't be much of a turnout. I mean, Flemingsburg isn't the biggest town around. Definitely not the most exciting.

Over this one weekend every year, though, people flock in from all over. Maybe it's because, in spite of having both Valentine's Day and President's Day, February's one of the most depressing months of the year and people need something to brighten up their lives a bit. I've come pretty early, and I'm barely able to find space to pull up alongside Fleming park, where most the activities happen.

Before I get out of the truck, I take some hand warmers and scrunch them up to get them working. I put them in my boots and in my coat pockets so I can shove my hands in there whenever they get cold. Then I step into the chilly morning to pull out the crates of produce and set them up on the snowbank by the sidewalk. Across the side of the truck, I stream this big sign I spent pretty much all night on.

When I was first making it, I planned for it to say just, *ROOT VEGETABLES!* I put my heart and soul into that thing. Painted pictures of beets and potatoes and happy people with their mouths open getting ready to eat everything. But, like most my artistic efforts, the thing failed pretty bad. Turned out looking more like people screaming and being attacked by giant slugs.

I didn't have time to fix it, though, so I just added some words at the bottom to make it seem like I did it on purpose: *ROOT VEGETABLES ward off giant slugs.*

I call out to people as they pass, "Watch out for the giant slugs! Protect yourself with these sweet potatoes!"

Some people go out of their way not to look me in the eye, but a lot of others stop to go over the selection. Our produce is pretty good, so most of them buy something too. I've sold out close to all the crates by mid-morning when Logan texts me to say he's gonna be here soon.

Mom's into what people call "subsistence living," and she always says, "We don't own this farm to make money," like it's a badge or something. So, I take her at her word, and I start giving out that stuff for like ten cents a pound. After a group of older ladies gets done picking through everything, I've only got one beet left.

I pack the crates back into the truck and fold up the sign. Then, after a quick peek in one of the sideview mirrors to readjust my beanie and fix my unruly curls, I start off toward the center of the park where Logan and I are supposed to meet up with Sylvia.

As I move through the growing crowd, I watch for Logan's scruffy red hair and his goofy cowboy boots. Nobody our age wears those things, and kids tease him about it. But they were his grandpa's boots, and he's proud of them no matter what anyone says, and I like that about him.

Logan's not exactly the most handsome guy in the world. It's not like Flemingsburg is full of gorgeous guys anyway, and Logan falls right about in the middle of the Flemingsburg scale. But he's real nice, and he's funny, and he likes to listen to my stories.

That fuzziness in my belly has spread to my arms and my left leg right under my skin, like the weird sort of tickle you get if you stand too close to the screen of the old TV Sylvia's dad keeps in their basement. I jiggle my arms a couple times, kick out my leg like I'm shaking the snow off my boots, but the feeling won't go away.

The morning's pretty far gone now, and the park is full. Everybody's squeezed inside these narrow, freshly shoveled lanes that are sandwiched between three-foot high picket fences, and, even though it's probably only ten degrees above freezing, I start to feel pretty hot. Hot enough my scalp's all sweaty and my fingers feel about twice as thick. For a second, my vision even starts to swim a little.

Snatching off my gloves and hat, I swerve quick off the path so I can rest. I lean with my elbows tucked between the wooden peaks of one of the picket fences and try to act like I'm not having to struggle hard to breathe.

The fence itself runs along the side of one of the big event pavilions, where some sort of performance is about to start. People are packed into the white folding chairs that've been set up in rows, and anyone who couldn't find a seat is crowded along the edges. My eye is drawn to this older, brown-skinned man standing there. He's got a luxurious, silver mustache that drips down way past his waistline, and he's dressed in a distinguished wool trench coat and bowler hat. His whole vibe reminds me of some old-timey gentleman from a BBC period drama, except for his bright pink and purple, tie-dye socks that peek out from under the hem of his trousers.

He's focused on the performers lining up on stage—a mismatched assortment of old women and little kids who make up the town's traditional Swedish folk-dance team—but as I'm watching him, his gaze shifts to scan the stream of people moving by on my side of the fence, and then he zeroes right in on me. Stares me straight in the eyes. And I get this feeling in my chest like this man knows me. Not like I've met him somewhere before and just forgot about it, but like he's always known me. Like he will always know me.

You don't go around having feelings like that about people every day. So, when he steps away from the pavilion and starts in my direction, I'm not sure what to do about it. He's smiling sort of tentative, like he's begging for a smile in return. And, honestly, he seems innocent enough with his bright-colored socks and his cheerful eyes. With that face of his that makes me wonder if he's somebody's grandpa and what would it be like to be that kid.

I can't help thinking about how many times Mom's warned me about strangers, though. About anybody acting strange. Living in a place like Flemingsburg, it's not a concern I've ever taken too serious, but—and maybe it's all that tickling under my skin right now—suddenly this whole day feels real odd. Like the sort of day when you just know odd things are going to happen.

With a jolt in my stomach, I turn quick from the fence and slide back into the stream of people squeezing their way through the park. Throwing a glance over my shoulder as I try to disappear, I see that the man has stopped. He's looking around the crowd, searching for someone else now, like he needs to find them fast. I try to crane my neck to see who it might be, but the momentum of the people around me is doing a pretty good job of swallowing me into their flow. So much so that I don't see the other girl until I'm nearly crashing into her.

She's standing there, tall and sturdy, in the middle of the path, as if this is exactly the place a person's supposed to be standing. Like the rest of us are being rude by jostling her. She's turned away at first, but as I try to find a path around her, she looks down at me all sudden, with this glare so forceful I freeze in place, just staring back at her. She's pretty, in a furious sort of way. Like every day of her life's been one bad joke after another, and she's just waiting for this day to be the same.

"Sorry," I apologize, even though I haven't actually done anything.

Her eyes go narrow, and she lets them travel down to my toes and then back up again, nice and slow like she's deciding if maybe she'd like to eat me.

I get this awkward grin on my face, stiff and lopsided and probably showing exactly how intimidated I am. Shuffling to my left, I inch back into the stream of people without my eyes leaving her face. My instinct right now is to take off as fast as possible. But with her gaze still steady on me, I can't make myself look away until I've been swept around a curve in the path and there are enough people between us to block me from her view.

My stomach's beating as if it's taken over the duties of my heart, and I've got this weird tightness at the back of my throat that makes it feel like I'm going to puke pretty much any second. Probably, the run-in with that girl has something to do with it, but maybe also my blood sugar's off. It has been a while since I ate.

I know there's got to be a food truck around here somewhere, and while I look for one, I play this focus game Mom does with me. "You're a secret agent," she says, "walking the streets of Paris, looking for your contact. Everyone around you could be your enemy. You have to watch for any possible sign that something isn't normal. Tell me what you see."

I start listing everything in my head. An older woman moving along the fence with a thin, hollow-looking face and a glazed expression to her eyes. A couple boys my age near the ice sculpture display, arguing about something under their breath. A guy wearing shorts and this forced grin, like he's pretending it was a smart clothing choice. Though, that's not exactly strange behavior. There's always someone like that at Swedish Days.

When I see the hot chocolate stand, I figure that's close enough to actual food. You can get these Swedish-themed flavor add-ins like cinnamon lingonberry and stuff, and the owner of the place always dumps in loads of marshmallows. But the truck's a pretty popular one and, with this many people, there's never a proper sort of line.

If the sidewalks seemed packed, waiting in front of the hot chocolate truck is like being suffocated to death in other people's breath. I'm regretting deciding on hot chocolate as soon as I'm far enough into the crowd to make it more trouble than it's worth to fight my way out again.

The buzzy tickle's all over my body now, even my tongue. When the people in front of me shuffle forward a few inches, their steps make them sway in a way that makes me think maybe my vision's gone swimmy again.

Then I notice the guy next to me is standing way too close. He's dressed like some sort of lumberjack, in this hunting cap and a flannel coat and a cowboy shirt. Like someone wearing a hick-town costume as a joke. He's got lots of dark brown facial hair, but he's real good-looking, with blue eyes and lightly tanned skin. Probably I wouldn't be bothered at all by him if it weren't for how interested he seems to be in me.

Not like he's staring too hard or something, like he thinks I'm cute. I don't think he's actually looked at me even once, but it's like I can just feel the weight of his attention. Like if this were a cartoon, he'd be leaning way into me, and his ear would've gone all big and listeny, and it'd be right in my face.

Maybe my imagination is getting the best of me, but Logan's always digging up these news stories about perverts rubbing up against girls in public and stuff like that. "It's a sick world out there," he likes to say, as if Flemingsburg isn't even on the same planet as the rest the world. Which, I guess, it practically isn't. But who's to say none of those creeps would ever come to Swedish Days, and who's to say this guy isn't one of them? Right now, I'm really not in the mood to let some guy get his kicks by rubbing himself all over my arm or leg or something.

In fact, with my head so fuzzy and my guts topsy turvy and my sense of reality a little foggy maybe, it's easy to make myself believe that's exactly what this guy's trying to do. Even if there hasn't actually been any rubbing. The creep's just waiting for the right opportunity, probably.

Which is why, when we get to the service window of the truck, and I see him stretching his hand out toward me, I realize a second too late he really might just be reaching for some napkins. My reflexes are pretty quick, and my hand is around that guy's wrist before either of us knows what's happening.

He's obviously startled by it, but not as startled as I am because, as soon as I touch him, something happens that's definitely not my imagination. Where my fingers are wrapped against the bare skin of his wrist, there's this feeling like static electricity biting and jumping between us, pushing into my hand and crawling up the inside of my arm.

I look up into his face and see his eyes've gone as wide as I bet mine are. Then, with the force of an explosion, the electricity's just torpedoing through my whole body. All these tiny shocks surging in my veins and, at the same time, a thousand images rushing into my head at once. Shapes and colors jumbling together into these visions of people and places, none of them things I recognize and none of them lasting any longer than the switch of a light.

The guy doesn't look shocked anymore. Instead, he's staring at me with all that interest I thought I might just be imagining before.

I wrench my hand away from the guy so fast. And, as soon as I've broken my grip, that rush of electricity stops, and the images die away.

I may've been startled when I first grabbed onto him, but I'm outright scared now. I start moving before my brain's even registered it's time to go. Jogging in a retreat backwards, bumping through the people behind me until I come out into the open and I can turn to run. But looking where I'm going is not exactly the first thing on my mind, and the man I crash into now is so solid he stops me dead in my tracks.

This guy is all leather and tattoos, and these real black eyebrows like turned-over checkmarks. He grabs tight onto my arms, grinning into my face as that rush of electricity starts through me again. Only this time, it hurts. Bad. And now it's like something being pulled out of me. Dragged like barbed wire through my veins.

"It's you," the guy's purring with hungry eyes, his fingers digging into me like he's never going to let go. "You're not so hard to find."

I'm panicking, looking all around me for help, but nobody's paying attention. Other than that lumberjack guy, who's pushing toward us through the crowd, his eyes set on me and his face intense. A scream goes off in my mind. Only somehow, I can't get it to come out of my mouth.

Now my vision really is swimming, and I'm thinking I'm about to learn what it's like to faint, when I hear Logan's voice behind me call out all cheerful, "Alexandra! Alexandra Monroe!" Saying my full name like he does because he thinks it's charming.

Some people turn to look at the sound of Logan's shout, and the tattooed man let's go of me. The other guy—the lumberjack one—is already gone. I mean, he was striding at me one minute, and now he's just not there.

I'm not sticking around to give him or the tattooed man another go at whatever they're trying to do. I book it over to Logan's side, surprised my legs are still working.

"We've gotta get out of here." It comes out all cracked, like my vocal cords have gone dusty.

"Huh?" Logan looks around, surprised.

He doesn't pick up on things too quick sometimes, so I grab hold of his hand and just start pulling him away. Glancing back, I see the tattooed man starting after us, and I pick up speed. Dodging through the crowd as fast as I can, zigging and zagging around people until I'm sure the man can't see us anymore. The whole time Logan's chirping, "What's going on? What's going on?" as if someone set him on repeat.

When we get to Main Street at the far end of the park, I pull him down a narrow alley that runs between the general store and Rhoda's Pawn, and I don't slow down until we've come out behind the buildings, where no one else can see us. I stop then, trying to catch my breath.

"Alexandra Monroe," Logan says, "are you gonna tell me what's going on here?" He's got his hands on his hips, looking for all the world like his mom when she gets upset with him.

In response, I slump down into the snow. It's not a conscious thing. Just one minute I'm standing, and the next I'm not.

"What the—" Logan grabs hold of me, hoisting me over onto an old bench that sits against the back of the general store. He looks legitimately worried now. "Zanny, for real. What's going on?"

The bench is covered in snow, and I can feel the cold wetness seeping in through my jeans. It's a nice contrast to the heat burning up my body.

"There were these guys." I look up at him. "They must've had tasers or something."

"Tasers."

"They must've had something. I felt all this electricity inside me." I remember the rush of images. "And my head went weird."

Logan stares at me a good long minute, reaching his hand up his coat sleeve and scratching his arm. I think maybe he doesn't believe me, but then he asks, "You think they were going to kidnap you for illegal science experiments?"

I should've guessed he was just imagining up the worst possible explanation. But then, for all I know, whatever it was they were trying to do is actually worse than that.

Another thought occurs to me.

"We've got to tell Sheriff Álvarez. Before they go after someone else." I pull out my phone and call 911, but all I get is static. When I try to call the sheriffs' station directly, I get the same thing.

"That's odd." I sink back against the wall, unsure of what to do now. "That's real odd."

Logan's got his phone out too, texting. "I'll see if Sylvia knows where her dad is. We can have her tell him."

But Sylvia doesn't text back.

"We're going to have to go find Sheriff Álvarez ourselves." I try to stand up, but it's like the earth's folding in beneath me. Logan grabs my arm before I fall and helps me back onto the bench.

"I don't think you're going anywhere," he says, kind of pushing his beanie back so he can pull at some tufts of his bright orange hair.

Leaning my head against the wall, I look up at him with one eye. "You'll have to do it."

"I don't want to leave you alone."

I don't want him to either, but I can't really think of anything else to do. We can't just let those guys run rampant through Flemingsburg. "I'll manage."

He keeps staring at me. Then he reaches down to pull this knife out of one of his boots and hands it to me. I shouldn't be surprised he's got something like that on his person. It's a pretty simple thing, with a black wooden handle and a switch-out blade about the length of my palm. If it turns out I need a knife, this one sure isn't going to do much damage, which is probably what Logan's thinking as he stands there eyeing me some more.

"How about I just step into Rhoda's Pawn for a minute and see if I can use her landline? Then we can figure it out from there."

It's not ideal, but I can't think of a better option.

When he disappears down the alley, I let my eyes fall closed, and I don't know if they're like that for fifteen seconds or fifteen minutes before I hear footsteps in the snow. Someone's coming, quick and light on their feet. Just about the opposite of Logan.

I stand up fast. Or I try to. Really I just end up flopped forward on the bench, with my elbows propping me up on my knees and my hand gripping the knife and trying to point it in the alley's general direction. I'm hoping it's the sheriff, but I'm scared it's one of those creeps who tried to electrify me. I'm not at all expecting it to be that guy from the event pavilion, his mustache trailing graceful behind him as he strides into the backyard.

"O, *hridoy jole*," he says in some other language, "you can sense your flaring from half a mile away. I can't imagine how it must be affecting you."

That last part was English, but I've still got no idea what he's saying. When he sees the knife, he stops short, eyeing the way it's quivering in my hand.

"It doesn't seem polite to mention it," he holds his pointer finger up in an apologetic way, "but in your current condition, it's doubtful that blade will be of much use to you."

It wouldn't be much use to me in any condition, but he's right. It's not real nice to say.

His face breaks into this sort of repentant grin, and again I'm picturing him with some grandkid on his knee. I mean, you could wrap yourself in the warmth pouring out of that smile. Still, I'm not going to forget the feel of the electricity dragging through my body anytime soon, and Mom's warnings about strangers seems a whole lot more relevant now.

I keep the useless knife pointed at the old guy, even if it is mostly on principle.

"I can help you," he says. "You've had an upsurge of energy that your body is not yet equipped to handle. If I syphon it off, it should provide relief for a time."

He takes a step toward me, all careful and soft, with his hands held out like he's trying not to startle a scared animal.

"Don't worry. I've set up a temporary barrier. No one else will discern that you're here."

The words coming out of his mouth still don't make much sense to me, and, with the way I'm feeling, I can't be too sure it's not me that's the problem. I squint at him, willing my head to stop buzzing.

When he takes another step, on instinct I try to back away, but with all the snow on the bench, I only manage to slide probably half a centimeter. The man takes the hint, though, and stops where he is.

"I am Rishi Mitra. Does the name mean anything to you?"

Again, I get that sense of knowingness, like when I first saw him. Only this time it's like maybe *I* know *him* too. Or like I'm supposed to know him. Neither makes any sense.

I watch him without saying anything, trying to figure out what to do with this situation and wishing he'd just go away.

With a sigh, he says, "It appears I have some explaining to do."

He bends down with his hand an inch or so above the snow, then straightens again. And, as he brings his hand upward, this wooden stool rises beneath his palm like an enormous mushroom growing in fast forward. He sits down on it real casual, as if fully formed wooden stools just grow out of the ground every day.

If I thought my brain was playing tricks on me before, now I know it is.

He sits there with his back straight and his hands folded neat in his lap, and he looks at me. "I come from the city of Deffro," he says. "I'm a reader, and—"

"How'd you do that?" I cut him off, waving the knife at the stool.

His head does this little tilt, and he studies me out of the corner of his eyes.

"It was painting, simple enough," he answers with a question in his voice. "You don't know what painting is."

I should probably be working out a way to get away from this guy, but also, I figure if he was going to hurt me, he wouldn't have made himself so comfortable on that magical stool of his.

"I know what painting is. That," I wave the knife again, "is not it."

He manages to give a smile at this, but mostly he just looks tired all of a sudden.

"You know nothing of Painters," he says more to himself and in a voice that makes me feel like I'm a disappointment.

"I know what painters—"

He holds up his hand. "No, no, no. The Painters I refer to are quite different. Our physiognomy allows us to sense matter on a sub-atomic level. This is not something your parents have discussed with you? Seeing cells, molecules, atoms, particles even smaller than that?"

"Can't remember Mom ever mentioning it."

At this point, it's occurring to me that, either I accidentally got high on something, I'm dreaming, or I've completely lost it. And the thing is, I'm not that bothered by any of these options. No matter which one's true, it means I'm not really in danger. No one's actually trying to fry me up like some Twinkie on a stick. I can relax and ride this buzzy wave of hallucination until it fades.

Plopping the knife onto the bench beside me, I lean back against the wall again and eye the old man, just daring him to do something else unbelievable.

"We don't see it with our regular vision," he explains, still with that tone like at any minute one of these things is going to ring a bell for me. "It comes to us through our bodies and our minds, and we can interact with it. Give it a tug, a pull, change the shape of it."

"Yeah?" I say, all cheerful and encouraging. He may just be a figment of my imagination, but I might as well be polite. "That sounds like it could be real useful."

He seems to think that's funny, stroking his mustache like he's wiping away a smile. "You're humoring me, but it's true. I will show you."

He holds his hand up, his fingers pressed together, and, after a second, this tiny sprout of green rises up between his fingertips. Flopping this way and that. Growing leaves as it gets taller. Then a cluster of buds appears, breaking open and spreading out slow into white, delicate flowers with centers of orange.

If he'd done anything else, I'd probably just keep thinking this was my imagination, but I know about someone who used to do this exact thing, and that person was very real. Of course, if I were hallucinating, that's exactly the sort of detail my brain would use.

"That's an optical illusion," I tell the man. "My dad used to do it."

"Yes, probably your father can do it too, but it's not an illusion. It's painting, or particle manipulation. Observe."

He holds his hand over the ground beside him and, as I watch, the snow there melts into a small pool of water and then solidifies into clear blue ice.

Leaning forward again, I look close at his hands.

"You've got something up your sleeve," I say like I've just guessed the right answer in a game show. "A tiny machine or something."

My whole face has gone tingly now, so I'm not totally sure, but I think I might be smiling pretty big. I'm kind of impressed with myself, having a brain that can make up a mind game like this inside a hallucination, which is basically a sort of mind game.

The man raises his eyebrows, looking like he can't decide if he should laugh or cry at this point.

"There's no device. It's all done with the force of my mind. Shall we try again?"

This time he tucks his hands nice and tight against his body like he's showing me he's not playing any tricks. Then, while he's staring me right in the eyes, the snow at my feet starts to do this shimmy, and a clump of white pulls apart from the rest. It floats up into the air about a foot and starts to change form in a series of shivers, stretching and shrinking and rounding in on itself until there's a little snowman floating there in the air. Some lumps of coal grow on its face. A mini carrot extends out as its nose.

I look at that thing, and then I look at the old guy. It's not that this stunt's any more believable than the other stuff. I'd probably be giving him a round of applause if it weren't for the fact that I've seen this before.

When I had hold of that lumberjack guy in the hot chocolate line and all those images were rushing through my head, I saw this exact moment. And now that I'm seeing it again, I'm filled to overflowing with this almost crushing feeling, all warm and absolute in my chest, that I'm exactly where I'm supposed to be right now. And that, even more, this is real. Very, very real.

The old guy's saying, "Your father told you all this is simply magic tricks?"

"No," I shake my head. "Mom did. Dad died when I was a baby."

Despite the buzzing, my mind's real clear now. I think I knew all along this wasn't any dream. But if it's not a dream, that leaves me with some pretty pressing questions.

I look the man full in the eye. "Why are you here? What do you want from me?"

"Well," he says, with this almost-smile playing at the corners of his mouth. "Not to sound overly dramatic, but you're going to save the world. Or, at least," he qualifies, "significantly change it."

It's hard not to think the guy's joking. Like any minute now some actor is going to jump out shouting that this is all a prank. I do a quick check around the yard. You know, just in case. But I don't see any hidden cameras. What I do see, when I look back toward the old man, is that lumberjack guy standing at the mouth of the alley where he definitely wasn't two seconds before.

I'm on my feet without even meaning to be, that knife in my hand again and my legs very nearly what you'd call steady.

"What are you doing here?" I snap at him, trying hard not to look like a big gust of wind could probably knock me over any second, but the guy doesn't even respond. Just looks me over, his eye traveling past the knife as if it isn't there.

From this angle, the whole shape of his body is telling me it wouldn't take much for him to hurt me if he tried. Then, in this voice like someone who's genuinely concerned and not at all treacherous, he blurts out in some sort of British accent, "*Calon tân*, you can barely stand," and he's moving toward me with a speed that's totally unnatural. I flinch away, but the old man's standing up too, and he stops the guy with just a gesture of his hand.

To me he says, "Dylan's with me. He won't hurt you." And you can tell the man really believes it.

"Except that he already did try to hurt me."

The lumberjack guy's reaction is immediate and earnest. "That was an accident," he says, leaning around the old man to talk to me. "I never meant to touch you."

With him looking me full in the face like he is, it's hard not to believe him. He just has the kind of eyes that make you want to believe. Plus, he's got a point. I was the one who touched him first.

"The other man that hurt you is a different story, however." The guy steps sideways so he can look at both me and Rishi at the same time. "And, I'm sorry, but we don't have time to hash this out because he and all of his friends are already on their way to your house, and there's no telling what they might do to anyone they find there."

"Mom."

I get this image in my head of her alone and in danger, and that's all it takes to make whatever doubts I still had about the guy disappear.

"How far ahead of us are they?" Rishi asks.

"Far enough."

"Then we must—"

"We've got to talk to the police," I cut in, taking some trembly steps toward the alley, but Rishi grabs my arm to hold me back.

It's not like he grabs hard. There's barely any pressure at all, but there's just something about his grip—some sort of instinctive authority—that makes me stop in my tracks.

"Your police can do nothing to help you against these people, but Dylan and I can. If you take us to your house now we will keep you and your mother safe. Will you trust us?"

I think about what it might mean to take them to my house, to my mom. What if this is all a trick, and he and this Dylan guy are really the ones I should be worried about? I stare at the old man, look up into Dylan's eyes, and I get that warm feeling in my chest again. That certainty. If it had a voice, it'd be purring at me, telling me the answer is yes. That trusting them is exactly what I should do.

I hear Logan coming down the alley, then. The clumsiness of his footsteps in the snow so unmistakably him that even Dylan has no trouble guessing who it is.

"Your friend cannot know about any of this," he says in a quick whisper. "It would put him at terrible risk."

I look between him and Rishi again. What's most important to me right now is getting to my mom, and Logan's just turned into a huge distraction.

I head him off a few feet into the alley, and he's surprised to see me up and walking, however wobbly.

"Sylvia says Sheriff's at the sleigh rides," he announces. "But he's not answering his cell. She went to get him, and I came to check on you. I called Eddie at the station and told him to have the rest of the force on the lookout."

I can see a sheen of sweat on his forehead like he gets when he's worried, and for some reason this moment feels suddenly like it's a goodbye.

"We don't need the sheriff," I say, closing his knife and handing it back to him. "I'm okay. Everything's okay."

He squints hard at me like he's got a whole load of questions he's about to ask, and, just like that, I lose my patience. I don't have time to do this properly.

"But you said those guys—?" he starts, and I cut him off.

"I was wrong. Turns out it was just weird hormones making me feel funny." I say this because I know it'll shut him right up. "I guess I started my period. I gotta go take care of things before, you know, anything's *showing*."

When I move to step past him now, he's happy enough to let me go. Even shifts away from me a little, like maybe I'm contagious. He's lived his whole life on a functioning farm, but he still gets real uncomfortable about female reproductive stuff.

I'm already at the end of the alley when he calls after me, "You okay to drive?"

I just give him a wave and keep walking as if I'm actually okay to be doing anything right now. Rishi and Dylan meet me on the sidewalk, and I don't know how they got there so fast, but at the moment I don't care. I follow them across Main Street and down a residential road to a dark gray, generic sedan of a make I don't recognize.

As soon as I'm settled in the backseat, I try to call Mom, but no one answers. I try again with the same result. So I text her not to open the door to anyone. Or better yet, to get out of the house completely. *You're in danger*, I write but get no response.

There are a lot of people out. The festival will keep going until pretty late, and, with the evening creeping in fast, the lights around town are starting to turn on. Snow-covered Flemingsburg is at its best at night, lit up by the blue moon and with the snow sparkling like fairy dust under every patch of lamplight. As we pass Fleming Park with its hanging lanterns strung from tree to tree, it's looking extra magical. A place where nothing bad could ever happen.

I'm glad that Dylan guy drives fast. Like break-the-sound-barrier fast. As urgent as if it's his own mom he's rushing to save. But, when we pull off the highway onto the mountain road and we're barreling toward the end of the plowed pavement, I sort of panic. Even in my truck, I couldn't handle the ridged and frozen snow of the dirt roads going this fast. Their flimsy sedan will probably just disintegrate.

"The road isn't plowed," I shout. "You can't take the snow at this speed."

The old man's unbuckling his seatbelt and moving his chair back as far as it'll go. He looks at me from the passenger seat.

"We have a secret weapon," he says, holding his hands up and sort of twiddling his fingers. Then he crouches under the dashboard with his palms against the floor and closes his eyes in deep concentration. I don't know how the guy even fits down there.

"What're you doing? What is he doing?" I ask Dylan, but he's too focused on driving, and he doesn't answer. Just keeps steering the car straight down that road toward what's probably about to feel like a sheer wall of ice. I throw myself against the back of my seat and try to brace for the shock, but then there's barely even a bump. Like, we'd probably feel it more if we ran over a trail of ants.

I sit up again and lean forward as far as my seatbelt will let me, trying to get a good look out the front window. Lit up in the headlights, it's all blue-tinged icy dips and ridges coming at us so fast they should be completely murdering the car's suspension right now, but out the back window we're trailing a winding ribbon of fresh-looking snow, packed just soft enough for the speeding car to leave shallow tire marks.

I guess this isn't too different from anything I've already seen Rishi do today, but it's the scale of it that surprises me. And the speed. I mean, he's instantaneously transforming whole stretches of snow without even touching them.

"Who are you two?" I ask Dylan, mostly rhetorically. "Wizards or something?"

His lips twitch, so I know he's close to smiling when he says, "It's not magic," like he's pretty sure I should already know this. "It's painting. Rishi's fiddling with the molecules."

His British accent's extra pronounced when he says this, but I'm not appreciating that because I'm thinking that if this old man can do what he's doing to the snow, what'll those other people be able to do to my mom?

"Turn here," I remember to say just in time, and Dylan takes the corner kind of sharp. Down on the floor, Rishi bumps against the bottom of the dashboard, but he doesn't react.

"How'd these people know where I live?"

"Your boyfriend announced your name loud and clear. Might as well have handed them the directions," Dylan says like Logan couldn't be a bigger pain, which is pretty unfair. We're in Flemingsburg, probably the safest town in America. Just what was Logan supposed to be afraid was going to happen?

Plus, Logan's not my boyfriend.

"Who are they? What is it they want from me?"

Dylan's expression barely changes. It's not like he flinches or does anything remotely dramatic. He doesn't even take his eyes off the road. There's maybe the slightest tightening in the muscles around his jaw, but that's enough to make him look like some sort of shadow's passed over his heart.

"They're called takers. They live off of death and pain."

It's not exactly an answer to my question. It's terrifying, but it's vague. I already figured those guys weren't headed to my house to talk to Mom about Jesus. But the way he says it, it's like he's sent that shadow of his stabbing straight through my chest. Again, I'm picturing Mom alone in the house, the nearest neighbor miles away.

"Turn," I say one more time, and the closer we get the tighter my throat feels. Whatever that buzzy-ness is that I've had all day, I'm barely aware of it now. I'm a pillar of adrenaline, a ball of anxiety seconds from detonating in one giant blast.

After the next turn, we're sliding up the long drive to our farm and, in the dusk, I can see the shadowy shape of the house. The front door's wide open, letting the light from inside beam a beacon across the snow-covered field. A snaky black body, all winged like a giant bird, rises up behind the house for a minute and then shoots down into the evergreen trees.

"What was that?"

"I don't know," Dylan says, and I can't tell from his tone if he's as spooked as I am, or if monster sightings are just an everyday thing for him. Me—it's like my heart's right up in my throat, pounding against the back of my tongue so hard I can practically taste it.

We're slowing down, coming up to the front of the house, and the old man's quietly unfolding himself from his spot on the floor. There's a strange car in the yard. A four-door sports car, all severe and dark. Dark windows, dark hubcaps, dark headlights. It's more like a weapon than a vehicle, and it looks real out of place against the rustic homeyness of our log house.

Rishi's already out of our car, almost before it's stopped.

"You stay here," Dylan commands me, but I don't. There's no way that's going to happen.

I fumble a little with my seat belt, but I'm not too far behind them when I enter the house. The front door's broken clean off its hinges. It's lying across the foyer several feet from the wall. Rishi and Dylan are disappearing into the other room, and I hurry after them.

Our kitchen's a mess. Seems like everything we ever owned has been smashed across the place. There are scorch marks all over, and one of our butcher's knives is imbedded in the wall by the hall. The back door has been blown off its frame too and is lying in the snow in the backyard. Rishi's looking out there with this worried expression on his face, and I can hear Dylan moving through the next room over.

There's a U-shaped set of wood counters at the far end of the kitchen, and the island that's usually in the middle of that is sitting askew, backed up against one of the counter corners, like it was thrown there by the same explosions that blackened the walls. The countertops are burnt, and some tomatoes that were sitting out by the sink have been cooked through, their red juices still spreading slow across the ruined wood and dripping onto the floor. It's like a scene from a horror movie, except there aren't any bodies.

Please, please, don't let there be any bodies.

The only place in the room that's nearly untouched is the nook between the refrigerator and the wall, where there's a little pantry. You probably wouldn't notice it if you weren't looking, it's tucked back there so tight. I'm staring at it because we never keep the pantry door closed unless guests are over, and the door's definitely shut now. Mom's steel meat tenderizer is on the ground beside it, partly hidden underneath the edge of the refrigerator and reflecting the room's light in a sort of signal.

I bend down and grab it off the floor, gripping the handle in my left hand like it's Thor's hammer. Everything in my body's gone still. As if there's no heart pumping blood through my veins, no breath passing in or out. I wrap my fingers careful around the pantry doorknob like I could break it if I squeezed too tight, and, with a tilt of my wrist, it turns.

I don't know what I'm expecting to see in there. Mom's broken body maybe. Somebody else's. Based on the rest the kitchen, I'm definitely expecting something gross. Instead, I see my mom standing there very much alive, her hair wild and her eyes wilder, a gun in her hands that's pointed at the pantry door like she's absolutely going to use it.

At the sight of me, she lets out this whoop that sounds half like a sob, and she flings herself at me, wrapping me up in her arms so tight I can hardly breathe.

"Zanny, Zanny," she's saying into my hair, and I'm mumbling back at her with just about as much relief in my voice. Although, I'm having a hard time concentrating on anything except the gun that's currently being pressed grip-first pretty hard into my spine.

Then Rishi's beside us and Dylan right after him, and they're both asking Mom if she's all right, and she's swinging me around behind her and pulling her gun hand free.

"Who're you?" she demands in a voice I've never heard her use before.

"Mom! Geez!" I grab for the gun, but she's not actually pointing it at them. Yet. "They're here to help."

She stands there, still holding me a step behind her with one arm.

She's staring at those guys like she's the god of war and they're lowly worms she'd have no problem squashing to death with her almighty feet.

"Ms. Monroe, what happened here?" Dylan asks in this quiet voice. "How'd you drive them away?"

Her eyes fix on his face, bore into him like, if she looks hard enough, she might be able to read his soul. Then—and maybe it's that sense of calm about him, or maybe it's those eyes of his—but she just sort of descends. As if every muscle in her body's unwinding at the same time and shrinking her back down to her normal size.

"You're Zanny's guardians, aren't you?" she says, suddenly real tired, and she sets the gun down on the counter. "Daniel told me what you'd look like."

"And you are not a Painter yourself, I gather," Rishi says, smiling kind of gentle.

What I'm wondering is what exactly Mom means about Dad telling her she'd know these guys? Why is she acting suddenly and absolutely not at all surprised? Just looking out the window like she's found some intense memory out there, in the dark.

"I haven't heard that term in ages," she says.

"Your husband was a reader?"

With a nod, she pulls something out of her pocket and holds it dangling from her fingers by its chain. It's the locket she's worn around her neck for as long as I can remember. I recognize the twisting dragon etched on the front even though the locket itself looks like someone's tried to smash it to smithereens.

"This is how I got rid of them. Daniel gave it to me before he left." That's the way Mom talks about Dad's death: leaving. "He told me they would come for her, but he didn't know when, and then it started to feel like a fairy tale. Until they showed up at my door and caught me off guard. I threw half my kitchen at them before I remembered this."

"The zoetic," Dylan says suddenly. "That dragon. He programmed it into the locket. And it chased the takers away?"

Mom raises her eyebrows at Dylan and shrugs. "Daniel was always turning things into dragons. I should've known his idea of protection would be something like that."

My whole world's shifting. Like the Earth's orbit doesn't apply to me anymore, and I'm being left behind. Mom's always talked about Dad's "complicated family history" and about his little magic tricks, but this was not part of that. Conjuring dragons was never part of that.

I see it now, though. She knew all along they weren't tricks. She knew all along about all of this, and she never told me.

"Dragons?" Rishi asks with his head tilted to the side like some sort of broken bobble-head.

"Is that strange?"

"Oh, no, no. It's merely…an interesting choice."

"How many zoetics were there?" Dylan asks Mom.

"Three, I think. They flew out of the locket so fast, it was hard to know exactly what was happening. There was suddenly fire everywhere, and then the dragons chased those people off."

"I can't sense anyone anywhere close. But, even with three zoetics of that size, we can't have much time. We'd best be off."

"Already?" Mom turns to Rishi with this question on her face that I get the impression he understands real well.

"It must be now," he says, apologetic. "Pack lightly, only what you can fit into one bag. Alexandra will need warm clothes for camping."

For a second, Mom looks about as lost as I feel. Then she grabs my arm and links it with hers. She has to set aside the meat tenderizer that I was still gripping, but then she squeezes her fingers through mine and starts marching us out of the kitchen, with Rishi and Dylan trailing a few steps behind.

The hand thing is something she's done since I was a kid, to help me be brave. Only right now, I'm pretty sure it's as much for her as for me, and that's when I realize we're not coming back here. That, when we walk out our door tonight, this place'll stop being our home. I've spent my whole life in this house. This is all I know, and the thought of leaving it for good makes me wish I could dig in my heels and refuse to go.

We're almost to the foot of the stairs, when mom lets out this breath of surprise and stops walking. She pulls the necklace out of her pocket where she must've been holding onto it with her other hand, and, when she opens up her fingers, the locket falls open across her palm. Which is a thing it never could've done before. As a kid, I played with it enough to know it didn't have working hinges.

Staring at her hand, Mom's got a weird expression on her face, with all her muscles tight and her mouth pulling down in this tiny frown. Sliding her arm out of mine, she takes a square of paper from inside the locket.

"I think this is for you," she says, and hands it to me.

It's an old photograph of a man, probably in his mid-twenties, with this head of tight, curly hair that borders on the totally dorky. Still, he's handsome, all strong jaw and broody eyes. The Greek heritage is a lot more obvious in his features than in mine, but there's something about him that reminds me of me. Something in his half smile that's so familiar, it hurts.

Mom told me all her photographs of him had been destroyed, so staring at this one now, it's like someone's lit a fire in my chest. And crawling up the back of my neck is this sensation like two points in time colliding. I feel as if I've just been given back something necessary that I didn't even know I'd lost.

I've had barely enough time to get a grasp of the face, when the photograph suddenly disintegrates into dust in my hand. Just crumbles away like ashes. Then it's rising into the air, melding together and growing until there's a tiny dragonfly hovering in front of my eyes, all shimmering greens and blues. It's wings, which look more delicate than glass, start whirring so fast you can barely see them. Then the thing goes veering away from me and out the open kitchen door. In a matter of seconds, it's gone. He's gone.

This is pretty much the last straw in this whole mind-boggling day, and I think everyone knows it. My eye falls on Dylan, who's watching me with this sympathetic expression that about pushes me over the top. I cram my hands into my coat pockets, balling them into tight fists, and will myself not to cry.

Mom thinks swear words can actually alleviate pain. She likes to say I should save them up until I really need them. This is definitely one of those times.

"Damn it," I say, real quiet. "Damn it to hell."

Upstairs, in my room, I just start shoving stuff into my backpack, taking my frustration out on anything I happen to have in my hands. Jamming in as many pairs of underwear and socks as I can fit. I know we're in a hurry, but, if we're going to be camping for a few days, I'm absolutely going to have clean underwear.

I'm trying to stay calm about all this. Trying to remind myself there's no use flipping out about things I can't change. But that's the type of thing my mom would say, and right now, I'm more than a little mad at her.

The adrenaline's wearing off, and my body's giving in again to that buzzy tickle, which is just another thing that makes me furious. I've just found out my dad was some sort of mutant or something, and that my mom's lied about it my whole life. I'm having to say goodbye to my home, my friends—pretty much everything I've ever cared about—without actually being able to say goodbye. And to top it all off, my body's turning itself into a human static machine.

Basically, my whole world's turning upside down, and somehow I'm the only one who doesn't know what's happening.

When I go stomping back downstairs, both the doors have been fixed, and everyone's already outside. Dylan's doing something to the car the takers left behind, and Rishi and Mom are standing by the gray sedan, Mom looking about as white as the snow falling soft around her.

"It would be best, I think," Rishi says to me as I walk up to them, "if you were to contact your friends now, and tell them you're going on an extended vacation." The snowflakes are catching in his mustache and the brim of his bowler hat, turning him into a steam punk-ish Father Christmas. "Your continued absence from town will eventually cause suspicion, but the longer we can put that off, the better."

"You can tell them you're visiting family in Oregon," Mom says, only sort of looking at me. "It's a place I've mentioned to people before."

She's trying real hard not to give away any emotion, which usually means she's chock-full of it. Which also usually means I'd be trying to comfort her. Right now, though, it just feels pretty unfair to me that she's the one retreating behind her emotional force field when I sure could use some comfort myself.

"Oh, all right," I say as I pull out my phone, and I don't even try to stop the sarcasm from blistering up in my voice. "*Do* we have family in Oregon? Are they vampires maybe? Werewolves? Lizard aliens in disguise?"

Mom doesn't answer, and Rishi just takes my bag from me and puts it in the trunk. I send a message to Logan and Sylvia telling them we'll be gone. Then I turn off my phone because I don't think I want to get their responses at the moment.

As I'm slipping it back into my pants' pocket, Dylan comes striding over to us. It's like the only way that guy knows how to move is to stride.

"If they come after us, it'll have to be by their own strength, at least," he announces. "No taker is going to waste their energy fixing that."

I glance behind him. Where the sports car used to be is just a blanket of what looks like ash on the snow. A layer of dust as black as the car itself. With everything I've seen today, it probably shouldn't surprise me, but considering he disintegrated a whole car in mere seconds, I have to admit it does.

I turn my eyes toward him, and he must be able to see how impressed I am because, I swear, for a second, he's on the verge of breaking into a smile. Then he glances away, sort of pulling at the bottom of his jacket like he's re-situating something that's out of place.

Once we're all inside Dylan and Rishi's car, I think maybe now I'll get some explanations about everything that's happening, but nobody breathes a word. Other than the sound of the snow rolling away beneath us, it's quiet as a church as we drive back down the mountain. That's got to be one of the loneliest feelings in the world, on a winter night with the snow falling noiseless against the windows and everything around us as motionless as a corpse.

When we reach the main road we turn the opposite direction from Flemingsburg to head out toward the freeway, away from home. In the backseat beside me, Mom looks like she's thinking at once of all the saddest things she could possibly imagine. As if this, right now, is the worst moment of her life.

Obviously, I hate that we're leaving too, but the expression on her face—this goes way beyond homesickness. This is a sadness that makes my whole insides go hollow just looking at her, and for the first time today it occurs to me that those takers we're running from may not be the scariest thing about all this.

"Do you think—" my voice sounds sharp, breaking into the quiet, "now might be a good time for some explanations?"

That heavy silence continues for a few more long seconds, and then Rishi twists around in his seat and looks at me like he's trying to decide where to begin. But he's not really the one I was talking to.

"You first," I point at Mom, and, as if she knew this was coming, she gives this tiny nod and sits up a little straighter.

"I'm sorry," she tells me, looking me straight in the eye for the first time since she found Dad's picture in the locket. "I was going to tell you everything soon."

Soon obviously wasn't good enough. She should've told me before a bunch of strangers chased us out of our house and we found ourselves on some bizarre road trip with a real-life Gandalf and Frodo.

"I wanted you to at least have a normal childhood. Then it became a habit, keeping it from you. We were so happy—*you* were so happy here that I didn't want to end it."

"So, what is it you were going to tell me?"

Kind of agitated, she brushes some stray hairs out of her face, then runs her other hand down her pant leg to smooth away imaginary wrinkles.

"Your dad was...very special."

"That much I figured," I say, but it feels lousy as soon as it's out of my mouth. Anyone who knows my mom'd be able to tell how much she's struggling right now, and, seeing it so clear on her face, I can feel my anger dying away.

"He used to have these visions," she continues, deliberate. "He called them sightings. After you were born, he came to me and told me he'd seen you when you were older, and that you were going to be—"

She glances at the front seat.

"Well, Mr. Mitra would be better at explaining that, but Daniel said you were going to be very important. 'Necessary,' was the word he used." She tries to smile, but it's so strained, it just ends up looking like a grimace. "He said there would be people who would want to hurt you, but that you would have two guardians—these two—that would keep you safe and teach you what you need to know."

She's staring me so hard in the face that her brows have pulled together and her lips have gone tight. For the first time ever, I notice she's looking older, and it scares me a little.

She finishes in a rush, her words spilling out of her. "He told me your life would be difficult—that you'd feel the weight of impossible responsibilities—and I wanted to protect you from that for as long as I could."

It sounds like a plea. Like this is her way of asking for forgiveness, but even though I'm not so angry anymore, I'm not quite ready to give her that. Not when I'm apparently careening pretty helpless toward some enormous and mysterious fate.

In the rearview mirror, I catch Dylan watching me, and it strikes me that he's got the eyes of someone who knows. Like this guy has been through some things, and, whatever miserable emotions I might be feeling at this moment, he gets it. And, for just a second, I feel that much less alone in all of this.

Still, when I look at Rishi, I'm not sure anymore that I want to hear what he's got to tell me. Seems like life has been a whole lot easier not knowing it.

"Your turn," I say, halfhearted.

He's more eager to explain than Mom. With a businesslike clap of his hands, he shifts almost completely backward in his chair and pulls his legs up in front of him so he can look at me more easy while he talks.

"Under the circumstances, I will have to give you simple explanations for incredibly complicated situations," he warns.

"That'd be more than I know right now."

He nods and grins kind of rueful.

"I've explained already that we—" he gestures toward Dylan, "that Painters—can interact with the world on a sub-atomic level. A small percentage of us, called readers, can also sense knots in the particle patterns. Clusters of particles that hold information about events that are distant from us in space and time. Our minds interpret these in the form of visions, which, as your mother mentioned, we call sightings."

"So, my dad was one of these readers."

"Yes. And so am I. Then there are the ones we call Way Readers, whose connection to the particle world and to the universe itself is so intense that their abilities far, far outstretch that of any other Painters. Way Readers come to us only once every century or so, when the balance of forces in the universe threatens to bend too far toward destruction.

"A few weeks ago, readers across the globe had the same sighting— a very rare occurrence—in which they saw that the universe had chosen a new Way Reader. A girl with dark, curly hair. At a festival in a mountain town in the northwestern United States. Not much to go by. However, I had a more specific sighting. I was told to find this new Way Reader and guide and protect her, with the help of my friend Gweneth's son, young Dylan here. I was given the Way Reader's name, her location. I knew what I was to be doing when I found her. I saw her face. I think you know where I'm going with this. Alexandra Monroe, the new Way Reader is you."

He's staring at me real sober now. They're all looking at me. Waiting for me to respond. And I don't know why, but I start laughing. I mean, I do know *why* I'm laughing—this whole situation is ridiculous. I just wish I was expressing that with a bit more dignity.

They don't know what to do with my reaction. Mom leans away from me like she's trying to get a better look at my face, Dylan's eyes in the rear-view mirror go all narrowed, and Rishi's head tilts to the side again, his eyebrows raised.

The looks on all their faces make me laugh even harder, and it's a few minutes before I get ahold of myself.

"I'm sorry, I'm sorry," I say with my hand up to my mouth to hide my smile. "It's just—I'm not that type of person."

"It's very seldom the sort of person you'd think it would be. Any storybook can tell you that."

"No, I mean, I'm not able to do any of those things you've said. There's absolutely nothing even half special about me. I'm not like you."

"No Painter can do those things when they're young. Your body must go through the transfiguring, the maturation."

"Maturation." It's a word with too many fifth-grade health class connotations.

"Yes, when the body finishes developing the necessary organs for painting. You're going through it now. The last phase, if I'm not mistaken. That sickness you're feeling is due to the final formation of your essence, the place where all humans store what we call essensal energy," he holds his hand over his chest to show me where it is. "Yours is now different than the average human's, and it is currently excreting waves of electricity through your body and out into the particles around us. This flaring process seems to have been intensified when you touched Dylan as you did. Your flaring is so strong now that it's growing quite distracting."

He's almost cheerful as he says this last part, but I'm sinking deeper into my seat.

"You...can feel it?"

I get an urge to wrap my arms around myself like I could maybe stop this stuff from coming out of me. Stop my body from *excreting* anything. I know I poked fun at Logan for being awkward about menstruation. And, if that was the topic right now, maybe I wouldn't feel so uncomfortable. At least a period is a private thing. At least no one else has to actually feel it.

"Once the flaring is done," Rishi continues, "your essence will be fully transformed and you'll be, for all intents and purposes, like any other Painter. Then it will simply be a matter of training and practice."

"You mean I'll be able to, what do you call it, paint with matter?"

That part? Well, that could be pretty okay.

"And much, much more," he says like it's something to celebrate, but this is the part that's not okay. I don't want much, much more. Much, much more sounds like it comes with a whole lot of extra baggage.

"What does it mean to be this Way Reader person? What is it I'm supposed to do?"

"We're nearly there," Dylan interjects.

"Yes, indeed," Rishi nods. Then to me again, "Every Way Reader has their own peculiar calling to fulfill. Definitely, it will involve working against evil, trying to bring more good into the world. Your task, I believe, relates to the takers, some of whom your mother chased away from your house tonight. Takers are Painters who, to put it shortly, feed off of essensal energy, which they can only access through the destruction of human life. These particular takers belong to a cult called the Sons of Morning. Named after Lucifer in the Christian scriptures. They have been terrorizing the Painter community, and we have reason to believe they have already, in some part, infiltrated the Painter government. If they are able to solidify their stronghold in our government, their reach will be long. Perhaps the entirety of the world, Painter and Particle-Blocked alike."

"Particle blocked?"

"Humans who are not Painters. We are not yet sure what the takers' exact ambition may be, but it most definitely means the end of many lives. I will be blunt with you and tell you that, as Way Reader, a terrible weight will be on your shoulders. If the takers' plans continue, you will likely have to use your abilities to fight very powerful, dangerous people. You will come to know death, see it first hand in manners you may never have imagined."

I hear Mom suck in her breath real quiet, like a stab. The sound of it frightens me in a way Rishi's words haven't.

"But," he goes on, "as Way Reader, you will also be able to save many lives. You will bring hope to people who have lost it. You will come to understand the most intricate details of the universe."

Dylan takes an exit off the highway onto a small unpaved road, pulls over next to some snow drifts under a small cluster of trees, and turns the car off. Rishi talks into the silence.

"If you accept this calling, we will take you with us. It may be months before you see your mother again. Dylan and I will be by your side, though. We will train you and support you and protect you. There will, eventually, be others to help you too. You will not be alone."

"What do you mean I wouldn't see Mom?" I look over at her, but she's staring hard out the window. "Wouldn't she just come with us?"

There's a long pause before Rishi answers.

"We've tried to devise a scenario which would allow us to safely bring your mother along. We're headed to Deffro, the capital city of the Painter Republic. It's usually a peaceful place, but there are dangerous people around these days. It is the best location for you to learn everything you need while maintaining the strongest protection, but to add your mother to the equation makes it much more dangerous for you both. It is not unheard of for Particle-Blockeds to live in Deffro, but there are so few, she would draw a great deal of attention. We could attempt to hide her identity just as we will hide yours, but we cannot disguise the fact that she is not a Painter. We would need to arrange a separate place for her to go."

I study the back of Mom's head, the rigid huddle of her usually graceful shoulders. I understand now why she looked like her heart was breaking earlier.

"If I choose not to go with you?"

"We will conceal you and your mother. Keep you safe. However, the takers will continue looking for you as long as you are alive. You will still become a very powerful reader because it's who you are, but without real training and support, you will find it difficult to develop abilities strong enough to protect yourself for long. We will try to protect you, but if we are waging a war against the takers, our resources for you will be limited. I don't say this to try to scare you but to give you an honest idea of what I think you will be facing. I wish we could give you more time to decide, but we cannot stay still for long. It's time to make your choice."

I'm pretty sure I'm not emotionally mature enough to be making these types of decisions.

As if she knows what I'm thinking, Mom glances at me. Takes my hand and squeezes it, but doesn't say a word. She doesn't have to. I know what she means. She's saying I'm the only one that can make this choice, but what I keep thinking about is that moment before I turned the doorknob to the pantry, that moment when I thought maybe I'd lost her for good. I don't want to lose her again.

"People have already died," Dylan says, soft like he's not so sure he should be saying it. "They're dying every day, but you can stop it."

I see Rishi touch his fingers gentle to Dylan's arm, maybe quieting him, maybe for comfort.

It isn't Dylan's words that get to me. It's the tone of his voice. He isn't just telling stories. He knows what he's talking about first-hand.

There's only one person I've ever known too well who's been killed. This girl who sat next to me in kindergarten. She was one of those girls whose hair was always half falling out of its braids and who always had something to say when the teacher asked a question. She and I used to play hopscotch together at recess, and she'd laugh the whole way skipping through the squares.

There was an accident on their farm, and Mom took me to the funeral. The way her family was crying, I was worried they'd shrivel up and disappear themselves, losing all that water. What I'm saying is, even though I haven't experienced much with death myself, I do know it's awful.

Dylan saying I can save people's lives—I'd like to do that, but I'm really not sure I *am* the type of person who can.

Dylan's still watching me in the rearview mirror. Rishi's turned toward me with that grandfatherly kindness on his face. Mom's not looking at me at all again, which shows how much this decision really means to her. They all expect an answer, but all I can think is how scared I am. How small and incapable.

This time, I don't notice the warm feeling in my chest until it's practically erupting out of me. At the same moment, a weird sort of tickle starts nipping at the back of my neck, spreading through my body.

It's different than the awful static. This feels like I'm growing, outward and upward and downward. Like I've got roots stretching in all directions, reaching into everything around me. Becoming a part of the fabric of the world itself. I'm powerful. Whole, as if before I was just a hollow shell.

I'm not so scared anymore. I know what I've got to do.

"Okay," I say, and Rishi's eyebrows rise.

"Okay...you'll come with us?"

"Well, I'm going to try to be this Way Reader thing. So...okay to whatever that means, I guess."

Up in the driver's seat, I hear Dylan let out a breath as if he'd been holding it in for years.

"Well, then," Rishi snaps his fingers. "We have no time to lose."

He swings himself around in his seat more quick than a man his age and length should be able to. Then he and Dylan get out of the car and move to the trunk to start unpacking whatever it is they've got in there.

Mom's looking like she's been turned to stone. A human statue. All bent forward with her head against the seat in front of her, her right hand resting on her knee and her left hand cold in mine. She's still as still as still. For a second, I'm sure I made the wrong decision—that she thinks I'm making a huge mistake—but then she's turning toward me, and grabbing my other hand in hers, and pulling me around to face her more direct.

"I'm so proud of you," she says, her eyes real fierce. "You are so kind and clever and strong."

She tucks my hair behind my ears, cups my chin in her hands like she's trying to memorize me.

"You are everything you need to be to succeed. When things feel hard, remember that I know this about you, and remember that I love you, and that we'll be together again soon."

She opens up my hand and presses the broken locket into it.

"Remember that your father also loves you, even if he's gone. He saw into the future, and he knew what he had to do to protect you. You're not alone in this. You're never alone."

Over her shoulder, I see Rishi approaching her door, but she beats him to it. Rips her hands from mine and launches herself out of the car before either he or I can say anything.

The cold air rushes in at me, stabs at my skin as I sit there suddenly vulnerable and alone. I'm trying to recapture some of that certainty I had a few minutes ago, but it's hard to say goodbye to your mom and still feel like some all-powerful being.

When I get out of the car, Mom's talking quiet with Rishi off to one side. The snow's still falling, and it's cold enough that, with every word they speak, their lungs puff out steam like tiny ghosts in the night. Rishi asks her if she's got somewhere she can go where she can hide for a while.

"I have a brother in Arizona," she says, which is news to me. She's never talked much about her family, and she's got to know this comes as a surprise, but she doesn't even glance in my direction. I guess she's retreated back into her forcefield.

Real quiet, Dylan steps up beside me and hands me my backpack. I look up to thank him but have to snap my eyes back down again right away. His face is so full of sympathy, you'd think he was trying to make me cry.

"The car's number plates are changed," he tells Rishi, who nods and walks over to the sedan without looking away from Mom.

"You can take our vehicle," he says, placing a hand on the hood. I watch as white pigment spreads away from his fingers and across the surface of the car like a never-ending milk spill. "It's practically a non-entity, and they shouldn't be able to track you."

"You'll need to lend me your cell phones too," Dylan says to Mom and me. "I'll make sure they're untraceable, and I'll hold onto them until you're not in hiding anymore."

He hands Mom a new one that's simple and black.

"Turn this on once you reach your brother's house, but don't use it until you hear from me. We will contact you as soon as we're sure it's safe."

He takes our phones over toward the tree line to a pile of things he and Rishi have pulled from the trunk. I'm wishing now I'd left my phone on during the car ride to see how my friends responded to my text. To say goodbye to them in a way that actually counts.

"It might take us some time to reach our destination," Rishi's telling Mom. "Probably a few days. Possibly more than a week. The distance is not so large for us, but there will be people looking for her, and we will have to weave our way around them."

After everything they say, Mom just nods. Then Rishi's handing her the car keys and wishing her a safe journey, and the time for her to leave is suddenly staring me right in the face.

She turns to look at me finally. Only, now I don't know what to do with it. When she comes toward me, opening her arms, I'm afraid I won't be able to hug her back. Afraid my own arms'll just hang limp at my sides and my tongue won't be able to tell her I love her. It's an instinct, though, wrapping my arms around Mom. A reflex programmed into me by years of doing that exact thing. And even if the only word I can get out is a goodbye, I think she knows what I mean.

I follow her around to the driver's side and watch as she gets into the car. The sound of the engine starting up is jarring in the quiet night. We lock eyes through the window, put on brave faces for each other so we both don't break.

"I love you," she mouths through the glass, and then, with a tight-lipped little smile, she faces forward and puts her foot to the gas.

It doesn't take long for the nearest bend in the road to swallow up the lights of the car, but I keep standing there staring after her for a while. The wind's gusting snow around my head. With a blink of my eyes, I imagine it sweeping me up and taking me along with her.

Rishi steps up beside me, puts his hand real gentle on my shoulder and considers the point on the horizon where Mom just disappeared.

"We have to leave now," he says. "We have a long way to go, and we should get started before the takers have a chance of finding us."

I just nod. The things going through my head are not the kind that feel better by sharing them.

Over by the line of trees, Dylan's messing with a tangle of straps that looks a lot like a harness.

"We've got to go by foot," he says, looking over at me. "But you can't do it the way we do yet. You'll have to ride on my back."

He holds up that harness thing, and it takes me about one second to figure out what he really means by that.

"Oh no," I say. "There is no way."

"You won't be able to keep up with us on your own. No matter how hard you try."

"I'll hang on tight. I'm not riding in some baby backpack."

Again, there's this moment where I could swear he's going to smile, but then he doesn't.

"Having you ride on my back is not exactly the most exciting thing for me either, but it's the best option we've got right now," he says in a voice that does not make me any more eager to comply.

"We will be going for hours at breakneck speeds," Rishi chimes in. He's methodically slipping items from the pile into a hiking backpack. I see a few silver emergency blankets folded up, a long-nozzled electric lighter, and what looks like a tiny brick of slate or something. "I'm afraid your flaring—your discomfort—is only going to grow worse for you, and holding tight will not be an option for long. Dylan needs to focus on his movements rather than on making sure you don't fall off. I know the situation is quite preposterous, and I would certainly feel similarly, but this is the best solution."

I don't know how to argue with Rishi on any of that. I don't think he's the sort of person you do argue with. Still, I feel about two years old as Dylan packs me into that harness. It doesn't help that, as he's doing it, I notice again how, even with that tacky beard, he's annoyingly handsome.

"Why were you rubbing yourself all up against me at the hot chocolate stand?" I ask him, and for a second, his hands go still.

"There was no such thing as rubbing," he says. "I was simply attempting to confirm that the flaring was coming from you."

He's got to know I'm only goading him but, still, as he moves up to work on the strap running right under my bust line, he keeps his eyes real carefully leveled on a point just around my belly button and not a centimeter higher. From this angle his lashes are almost startlingly long, and I can't help relishing the idea that I've managed to make him a little uncomfortable. He's so pretty, it'd be easy to forget he's human.

Once I'm in the harness, he's got to strap it on himself. There are some loops hanging off the front of me, and he crouches down a bit and backs up to me to slip his arms through, buckling the harness across his own chest and waist. I stare hard at the sky the whole time he's doing this and try to pretend like it's not actually happening.

Then he stands up and lifts me into the air, and I'm pretty sure this is the most embarrassing moment of my entire life. I'm dangling off his back as stiff as a board, trying to touch him with as little of my body as possible. And I sort of hate Rishi for looking over just now and so obviously wanting to laugh at us.

"If you don't relax, it's going to make things rather difficult," Dylan says.

I can see what he means. He has to bend far forward just to keep the balance right between us.

"If you wrap your arms around my neck, it might help," he prompts. But when I do, it brings my face right up next to his, and boy, does he smell good. Kind of sweet almost, and also kind of musky.

He grabs my legs at the knee and pulls them forward around his torso so he can stand straight while bearing my weight. Wrapped around him like that, real aware of the unsettling solidness of his body against mine, a new electric tingle ignites all down my arms and my legs—pretty much anywhere I've got skin. And I pray to any power that may be listening that, unlike the flaring, this is not a thing Dylan can feel.

Rishi pulls the hiking pack closed and slings it onto his back. Then he steps over, explaining that he's going to paint an energy barrier around my body to make sure the takers can't detect my flaring. He moves behind me, and I can't see what he does, but after a couple seconds I get the distinct impression that the air near me is a little thicker, a little closer.

"It'll keep the energy in for now," he says to Dylan as he steps away. "But it may also increase the transfiguring's negative effects on her, so we will want to cover ground quickly."

Dylan nods, accidentally bumping his cheek against mine, and I pull my head back quick so he doesn't think I was trying to get too cozy.

"Let's go, then," Dylan says.

Rishi takes off running, and Dylan starts after him with such a jolt that I nearly fall off. Which means those straps are actually good for something. We're going so fast that, for a second, it's like the whole world stretches out around us. Then it snaps back into focus, and I realize that what Dylan and Rishi are doing isn't really running at all.

Up ahead, Rishi looks like he's wading through water. Or, more like gliding across ice. His movements are graceful and kind of dreamlike, not the sort of thing you'd associate with speed. But, more importantly, I'm pretty sure the man isn't even touching the ground.

I try to look down over Dylan's shoulder, then crane around behind me so I can see below us. His legs are moving, stride after long stride, but there's no impact to his steps. From up here, I can't tell if he's actually touching down at all. We definitely aren't leaving even the hint of footprints in the snow. Perched where I am, the sensation's as gentle as the rocking of a boat, but all around us the world's just whizzing by.

The wind isn't as strong as you'd expect going at this speed, but it is cold. Just enough to be bracing. It's pulling through my hair and singing against my cheeks. This is how I imagine flying feels. I want to throw out my arms and scream like a little kid, but I'm guessing Dylan wouldn't appreciate that. Instead, I open my mouth wide and pretend I'm a giant cloud animal swallowing the wind, gulp by gulp.

I don't realize I'm making any sound until Dylan asks, "What are you laughing about?"

"I wasn't laughing," I say, even though I was. Right out loud.

"Don't do it anymore. It's distracting."

I clamp my mouth shut and, for a long time after that, do my best not to make any noise, even when I breathe. We pass through fields and forests, glide along the edges of mountains. Minutes merge into each other, stretch into hours. Until I can't even guess how long we've been going anymore.

I try to stay awake, but Rishi was right about the buzz in my body getting worse. It's whirling in my stomach and all up behind my eyes.

I try to focus on the scenery going by, but the sickness in my body keeps demanding all my attention. When a real troubling queasiness starts in my belly, I figure it's not worth it to be conscious anymore, and I give in to the sleep pressing at the backs of my eyes. The last thing I remember is my head slumping down onto Dylan's shoulder and me hoping that maybe he won't mind.

The next time I wake up, I'm lying on my stomach on a flannel blanket under a canvas-looking lean-to. Dylan's lying next to me, and my nose is only inches from his face. He's picture perfect, with his dark brown eyelashes, and the sunlight soft on his cheekbones, and his lips parted just enough to make them look extra full. He reminds me of some classic fairytale, all delicate and serene. Even his breath smells fresh as it whispers warm against my cheeks.

He hardly makes a sound as he sleeps, but me—just the buzzing of my body feels loud enough to wake the forest. At least I'm quieter than Rishi, whose snores are drifting over to me from Dylan's other side.

I can't say I'm feeling great. Sleep seems to have helped a little, but I'd gladly lose myself to unconsciousness again, if it weren't for the fact that my bladder's probably ten times more full than it ought to be.

It's about all I can do to get to my feet. Our lean-to is at the edge of a small clearing, and I'm surprised by how trembly and weak I feel as I head for the pine trees on the other side.

There's thick snow on the top branches of the trees, but it's warm and dry in the clearing itself, even though it's totally open to the sky. I'm guessing this was also covered with snow before Rishi and Dylan got to it.

As I walk into the shadow of the trees, it feels like passing through a sheet of mist or something, all tickly and cold. I stop, and take a step back again. That same sensation moves over my body in the other direction. I try it a couple more times, back and forth, and the feeling gets stronger with each go.

"That's the energy barrier," Dylan's voice cuts through the air, and I spin around to face him. He's still under the lean-to, propped up on one elbow with a sort of ease that makes him look like he owns the place. "As well as keeping unwanted guests out, it's the only thing preventing your energy from beaconing to every Painter in a mile radius. You should probably stay inside it."

I glance around the clearing. It's not exactly a private place, and my bladder situation's getting worse by the second.

"The barrier only covers...here?" I indicate the tree line with a twirl of my finger.

Dylan considers me for a minute, and then stands up and stretches and starts walking toward me. It's easy to see the smile playing at the corner of his lips now, and in this setting, his lumberjack look actually works.

I mean, it really, really works. Like, that electric feeling's suddenly going wild all over my body again, and the closer he comes to me, the worse it gets. By the time he's standing beside me and looking down into my face, I'm pretty sure I'm about to say or do something real embarrassing. I'm wondering if maybe an increased libido is part of this whole transfiguring thing, but that's not a question I want to ask him right now.

He holds his hand up in the air for a minute, at about where I'm guessing the barrier is, and says, "It should follow you now, but don't go far. You don't want to stretch it too thin."

I give him this little nod and try to walk off real nonchalant, like I'm just going for a stroll and not at all heading out to take care of a urinary emergency.

"You might want this."

When I look back at him, Dylan's got a bundle of crisp tissues that I'm guessing he made by painting. He's holding them up in this taunting way, and the smile on his face isn't playing around anymore even if it is kind of wry and lopsided.

He looks so unfairly cool.

I snatch the tissues from his hand and spin back toward the trees.

"It'll disintegrate when you're done with it, and there are sensors set up to alert us if anyone comes too close," he calls after me. "So don't worry, your only audience will be the squirrels."

I shoot a quick glare back at him, but I just keep walking, stomping a bit for emphasis.

When I come back, Rishi's alone in the middle of the clearing, cooking something in two pots over a small fire. It must be pretty obvious I'm feeling quivery and nauseated because the first thing he says is, "You look like you could use some food, and a relief from your energy build-up. Sit down, and I'll siphon it for you in a minute."

It looks like he's got some type of porridge cooking in one of his pots, and a creamy stew in the other. I can smell the spice of them as I pass by, and I realize I haven't eaten anything since yesterday morning, which has got to be over 24 hours ago. My stomach makes a sound like a lion in a cage, and Rishi looks up and smiles.

He's got a pile of green pine needles and other vaguely organic tidbits and, as I sit down on my blanket under the lean-to, I see him pinch out something wet and limp and probably moldy. He holds it between his hands for a second and then drops it into the pot in the form of some herbal-looking leaves.

I try not to gag at the fact that the man's making our food out of compost.

"Where are we?" I ask. The forest here is similar to the one back home, but everything seems darker, bigger, closer.

"At the top of Montana, near Canada."

"Canada?" I'm floored. "We were really moving that fast?"

"Particle sailing," Rishi raises his eyebrows with a flare, "is my favorite way to travel. Both quick and tranquil. Dylan is better than I am, better than most. He's been known to hit speeds well over one hundred miles per hour, but he had a little extra weight last night," he winks at me, "so I had no trouble keeping up with him."

I make a face. "Right. And where's this place we're going?"

"Deffro? It's hidden in the mountains of North Wales, in the United Kingdom."

I've got a mostly vague sense of geography outside Idaho, so this doesn't mean a whole lot to me, but I'm pretty sure the United Kingdom is a highly populated place.

"There's a whole city of people like you just hanging out in the Welsh mountains and I've never heard about it?"

"We have ways of hiding ourselves. Illusion barriers, similar to the energy barrier Dylan and I created here. It doesn't let people through unless their unique essensal energy code is in the city's system, and it tells Particle-Blockeds that the only thing their eyes and their sensors are seeing is more mountains. Or, in the case of some of the other city-states, more desert or forest, etcetera."

He finishes adding ingredients to the stew and pulls out that little brick of slate-looking rock I saw him pack up yesterday. Sliding his hand across it, a steel serving spoon appears between his fingers as if it's being pulled out of the stone itself. He gives the stew a few quick stirs, then gets up and comes over to me, telling me to hold still. He places his hands on either side of my head, and soon the buzz and the nausea and the heat grow more bearable.

When he's done, he says, "One benefit of your excess energy is that we can use it. Perhaps I'll make some fresh naan to go with the shorba."

I'm not sure I love the idea of energy that's come out of me going into my food, but he digs some twigs out of his garbage pile and holds them up to me so proud I have to smile.

"Back in Flemingsburg, you made a flower out of thin air. Why're you using that stuff to make the food now?"

"It takes less energy if you use something with a similar molecular structure. Proteins to make proteins, that sort of thing. Essensal energy will replenish itself if you give it time, but it is possible to overtax it. So, we conserve whenever we can."

He stretches the slate brick into a long flat board and places the sage twigs on top. With a pass of his hand, the twigs turn into a fine powder that looks like it's maybe flour.

"In order to paint anything, you have to know its particular pattern. And when I say *particular* now, I'm referring to particles. There are some things in the particle world—especially for those of us who are readers—that each brain may interpret a bit differently, but particle patterns manifest the same for every Painter. It's something you will learn once we reach Deffro."

Placing his hand flat against the ground, he pulls a palm-sized globe of water out of the earth and adds it to a small bowl where he's already painted a few other ingredients. His brain must be completely filled with these particle patterns. It's a wonder he's got room in there for anything else.

"What am I going to do in Deffro, exactly?"

He's kneading the dough, and he doesn't look up when he answers, "You will be staying with the Lucases—Dylan's family. You will go into his home as the daughter of an old friend of his mother's, on the pretense that you are there to prepare for painting academy. Something similar to Particle-Blocked university, which all Painters attend after their transfiguring. You'll not, in fact, be attending, since you'll most certainly be fully engaged in your Way Reader duties before the semester starts. However, this will give you an excuse to be in Deffro. Additionally, interacting with Dylan's family—especially his younger sister Eilian—will teach you something of the Painter ways."

I'm not real sure how to respond to any of this. Not sure what I think about living with Dylan and his beautiful face. I'll probably just go around feeling tingly and foolish all the time.

"You mentioned something before about training me?"

"Yes. Dylan will train you in self-defense, and I will train you in your specialized Way Reader skills. But you and I will have to do it secretly. In Deffro, I train readers. Have done so for years, and many people believe the most obvious person to train the Way Reader is me. I will be closely watched by all interested parties, so it's important that we don't appear to be connected in any way."

I get this pang of anxiety.

"What about that sighting you said all the readers had? And the takers who found me in Flemingsburg. Won't people guess I'm the Way Reader?"

He's pulled some more particles out of the slate board and is partway through shaping them into a cast iron skillet, but he stops and points at me like he's got just the answer.

"Ah, yes. Well. Dylan works for our republic's Global Intelligence Bureau, which is probably one of the reasons the universe chose him as your other guardian. He's arranging for an air-tight secret identity for you. You will be Sophie Warren, from a small farm outside of a small town in Wyoming. Dylan says the two most important things about selling a lie are to keep it very close to the truth and to act as though everything is normal. Therefore, most of the details of your identity will be similar to your actual life. We cannot avoid the probability that both the takers and the Painter Republic's government will have you on their radar as a possible Way Reader, but they will most likely have many other girls on that list as well. You'll not stay in hiding forever. We simply need time for you to develop your skills."

There's one detail in all this that's really sticking out to me.

"Dylan's a spy?"

Geez, I really can't live with that guy. I'll never stop tingling again.

Rishi busts up laughing. Then leaning forward a bit, he says, "Cool, right?" And then he busts up laughing again, so that I've got to laugh along with him.

That's the scene Dylan walks in on when he comes back to the clearing, his arms full of long branches and sticks and his hat covered in a light dusting of snow. He eyes the two of us kind of skeptical, but Rishi waves him over, announcing that the meal will be ready soon.

Dylan dumps his sticks in front of the lean-to. "There's no trace of anyone for miles around," he says to Rishi. "We should be safe to take the route we've planned. Still, we'll want to leave as soon as we've eaten."

Flopping down on his back on the blanket, near me, he throws his arm over his eyes for a minute and then shifts onto his side so he can peer at me around his elbow.

"How're you feeling? Your flaring seems better."

He's so comfortable looking lying there, I can't help smiling. With a nod toward Rishi, I say, "I had some help."

"Thought as much."

Dylan sits up and absently reaches a fist around to thump his shoulder blade a couple times like it's sore, which I'm guessing is because of hauling me. Then he opens his fist and lays his palm flat on his back, closing his eyes in concentration. He's obviously doing something Painter-y, but I can only guess what it might be. Loosening his muscles up, maybe? Applying heat?

When he opens his eyes again, he gives his shoulders a few rolls like he's working out kinks, and then he leans forward and starts going through the sticks he brought back.

He finds a long one that's probably a little thicker than my thumb, slides his hand down the length of it three times, and then tests it for flexibility. He does this over and over again, the stick getting thinner and flatter and bending more with every swipe of his fingers.

Once he's happy with its spring, he pinches one end and draws a thin bit of twine out of it. Pulling it tight toward the other end of the stick and fastening it there, making it so the stick itself bends into a graceful bow.

I know a bit about bows. Mom was always asking Logan's parents to take me on their family hunting trips even though it was not exactly my thing. She said it was an important skill to have. Mrs. Jacobsen's favorite way to hunt is to sit high in the trees and wield a bow instead of a gun because she says it takes more finesse. She only ever uses those high-tech compound bows, though. The type that look like some kind of robot skeleton. So, maybe I'm not expert enough to judge the thing Dylan just made. But, as elegant as it looks, I'm guessing you wouldn't want to be on the other side of it.

He's standing now, aiming the bow and testing the draw. Looking like he definitely knows how to use it. When he sits down again, he starts working on the rest of his bundle of branches, turning them into arrows.

"Are you going to hunt as we go?" I ask, teasing. "When you make a kill, you'll just sling it on your back right beside me?"

"These arrows aren't for animals," he says in a grim voice. "In this situation, we're not the hunters."

Geez, he knows how to ruin a mood.

Actually, Mom wanting me to learn hunting has a whole new meaning now I think about it. Lots of things she's done. All her little focus games, her hypothetical situations. Asking Sylvia's dad, Sheriff Álvarez, to show me self-defense moves, how to use a handgun. Even having Logan's brother teach me how to throw knives. Not that I took that lesson too serious.

Mom must've been grabbing at even the most remote opportunities to prepare me for this, all without telling me a word. It's like my whole life has been one blind road toward violence.

Geez.

When Rishi slaps his hands together, I about jump out of my skin.

"Our meal is ready," he announces, sweeping his arm out in front of him to indicate flat bread and cups of rice laid out on these little stone trays, bowls of stew and porridge set into the corners.

The food looks appetizing, no matter what rotting plant matter may've gone into it. When Rishi brings me my tray, the smell of it—savory and sweet and fresh—is real good too.

My over-empty stomach probably wouldn't care if it was made out of pig spit right now. I practically shove that stuff in my mouth, and the taste of it on my tongue washes away any remaining concerns about its ingredients. It's got some new flavors for me, but it's pure comfort.

When I'm done, Rishi gives me seconds, and I don't complain. The sun's shining down at an angle, glancing soft off the tops of the trees and washing over us. Rishi crouches at his cooking station, preparing what looks like granola bars for the road. In between bites of food, Dylan's shaping more arrows. It bears in on me, as I watch the two of them, that this new life I've agreed to is still a total mystery.

"Who are you, really? Painters, I mean. Where do you come from?"

"Same place as you," Dylan says with his hint of a smile. "You're one of us."

I don't feel like one of them. "You know what I mean."

"We're a sub-species of human," Rishi responds. "We've always been a rather small portion of the human population—never rising above fifteen percent—and because those aspects of our bodies which make us Painters do not last long after death, our origins are still rather vague. We do know that all the Painters alive today come from common ancestors. Most likely from the Western or Central Asia regions. As far back as, at least, the 14th century B.C. They eventually dispersed throughout the world, mingling with Particle-Blocked communities."

"So...from Earth."

Rishi grins. "We believe so."

"If you—we have been around for so long, why doesn't anyone know about us?"

"Oh, we maintain a low profile in the Particle-Blocked world. History has shown that when we don't, the consequences can be dire."

"Witch trials," Dylan cuts in with this caustic tone, "have always been rather destructive for us."

"It can be bad for Painters and Particle-Blockeds alike. Many lives have been lost to takers throughout history."

"And what is it takers do, exactly?"

Dylan and Rishi look at each other, as if deciding who's going to be the one to answer this one. Then Rishi puts down the half-formed granola bar in his hand and gives his full attention to me.

"We've told you about your essence, here." He holds a hand over his chest. "There are still many things even Painters don't know about it, but what we do know, is that it's the source of essensal energy inside each of us. We also know that it is itself made out of a shell of densely packed essensal energy.

"We also have something called a shadow. What Particle-Blockeds might refer to as an aura. The essence and shadow together are foundational to who each of us is. The DNA, you could say, of what people think of as their souls. The essence and shadow exist before our birth and continue after our death. All humans have both. Though, no Particle-Blocked technology has so far been able to detect them with any reliability.

"When someone dies, their essence and shadow pass on. We have evidence to suggest they go to a different dimension. However, that process requires energy. When someone dies of natural causes, the shell of the essence holds firm, allowing the shadow to use the necessary essensal energy to cross over first. Then, the essence uses the remaining energy to cross over itself.

"However, when a death comes violently—purposefully—it can cause a tear in the essence, and the energy begins to spill out. If this spillage happens too quickly, the essence itself may cross over first, leaving the shadow behind.

"It seems a cruel fate, to be not fully in one place or the other. So, it's our custom, in the case of violent death, to give the shadow time to pass by stemming the flow of the essensal energy. We cannot stop it entirely. So, we must guide it slowly out of the body and take it into ourselves. This is called the rite of crossing, and the energy is meant, then, to be used for something positive, constructive. A way to honor the life to whom the energy belonged."

"You use it like you used my energy earlier?"

Rishi smiles and nods. "Essentially, yes. While you're alive, I am able to take in your energy only because your body is shedding it, and what you're flaring now is a great deal. However, to take the whole of someone's essensal energy is an indescribably powerful thing, and that is where the problem begins. Some Painters become addicted to essensal energy. The Republic offers support to anyone trying to fight that addiction, but there are Painters who willingly give themselves up to it.

"The word 'taker' is a colloquial term that has come to mean a person who preys on others in order to harvest their energy. One of the mysteries of the essence, though, is that you cannot receive the essensal energy of a person whose death you have purposefully caused. Either the energy will not flow to you, or your own body rejects it, we don't know.

"It means, however, that takers tend to band together and do their killings and their takings in turn. Either that, or they get others—often Particle-Blockeds, who don't know their ways—to do the destructive work for them. Takers have learned to sow the kind of hate that leads to violence. In battlefields and dark alleys, all over the world, you'll find takers lurking, manipulating to their own advantage. Many of the world's greatest wars were secretly engineered by takers."

Rishi's speaking in these soft tones, all lilting and even pretty. It's totally incongruous with the things he's saying. You'd think it'd mellow their impact a little, but instead, it just makes the takers seem that much darker.

"These are the people I'm supposed to stop?"

Dylan glances up at me real quick, and the expression on his face doesn't seem much like a vote of confidence. I must look about as small as I feel. Probably the exact opposite of what a Way Reader should be.

"You'll have us by your side," he says in this voice that's trying to be reassuring even if his hands are moving so sharp across the length of his current arrow, you'd think it was the actual enemy. "You're not alone in this."

"The universe wants to help you succeed," Rishi chimes in. "All you need to do is let it."

He watches me until I meet his gaze, like he wants to make sure I understand what he's saying, that I believe it. The thing is, though, he's got a conviction that's been built over years. I've only known about this stuff for maybe eighteen hours.

Dylan stands up and drops his last arrow on the ground with the others.

"We can't stay still much longer. It's time to take down camp."

"Yes, yes," Rishi nods and starts bundling away his cooking utensils. "I'll clean up all of this."

"I can help," I say and start to stand, but Dylan shakes his head.

"You need your rest."

He pulls down the lean-to by himself, shrinking the pieces to fit into the hiking backpack. Then he folds up the silver emergency blankets, grabs hold of the flannel ones where he and Rishi slept, and shrinks them down too, tucking all of it into the hiking backpack.

Over at his station, Rishi's absorbing the silverware and cookware back into that slate brick, gathering up his granola bars, and packing everything away as well. Both of them are focused on their work. Busy as little bees, while I just sit here twiddling my fingers.

Then Dylan's pulling out the harness again and approaching me with it kind of apologetic, although this time I don't complain. I don't even get too embarrassed about his hands being all up in my personal business as he tugs the straps around, because, right at the moment, my mind's pretty occupied with one question: What've I gotten myself into?

Rishi creates an energy barrier around me like he did yesterday, and then dissolves the larger one around our campground. Dylan rigs up a quiver for the bow and arrows that ties like a belt around his waist and somehow doesn't get in the way even with my legs wrapped around him.

When we set off again, the sun's high and almost blinding in the sky. And, when we hit some meadow valleys all blanketed in untouched snow, the whole world seems to shine balmy and bright in the winter sunlight. It's not exactly like the valleys in the mountains around Flemingsburg, but there's something so instantly familiar about them, it sends memories like photographs flashing through my mind.

In the spring, our mountain meadows at home are so spread with golden wildflowers, it looks like a piece of the sun itself fell to rest there. Sylvia and Logan and I like to trek out for picnics before it's technically warm enough to be inviting, so we can be sure to have the meadows to ourselves.

Things like that—they'll only ever be memories for me now. No more day trips on Sylvia's horses. No more spreading blankets out and lying down among the flowers to daydream together about the things we want our lives to be. No more Logan and Sylvia.

I wonder where Mom is now. On her way toward a place of heat and sun, to the brother I never knew she had. What other family have I got out there? Maybe more uncles and aunts and cousins. Maybe grandparents. All I know is that, right this minute, the only person that's ever been family to me is driving steady in the opposite direction from mine, and I've got no idea how long it'll be before I see her again.

If I ever do.

"Tell me about your family," I say to Dylan, and the sound of my voice is a little too loud after probably an hour's worth of silence. He hardly reacts, though, and I think maybe he didn't hear, but then he lets out this sigh that seems about as homesick as I feel.

"What would you like to know?"

I rest my chin on the back of his shoulder, not real worried at the moment about being too much in his space.

"How many of you are there?"

He takes a long time to answer this question, and, when he does, there's something kind of spare about his voice.

"There are just five of us left now. My sister and me, my aunt Nia and her husband Uri Jacoby, and, much less often lately, my cousin Gwilim. My uncle Hiarwar's son."

I try to get a look at his face, try to figure out what's in his voice that he's not actually saying, but all I can see are his dark eyelashes and the line of his cheek where it disappears under his beard.

"What do you mean by five of you being *left*?"

Again, a pause. Then, "Mum's gone to the Philippines, where her da is from, to take care of her parents for a while. Da is—Well, my da's in jail. For a crime he didn't commit."

He doesn't look like he'd have a grandparent from the Philippines, but I'm not too focused on that right now because I think I can guess what he's not saying this time.

"That's got something to do with the takers, doesn't it?"

"It has everything to do with them."

"What's your dad to them?"

"A threat," he says, and it's not quite bitterness he's feeling. It's worse. Something deeper and stronger and more lasting. "He was researching their organization, writing a book about how they're infiltrating the government. He's a well-respected journalist. They must've realized how close he was to the truth and knew that if they killed him, his story would still come out. They decided to ruin his reputation instead, ruin him. So, they got him charged with treason, and now he's sitting in a cell in a high security prison, and we only get to see him once every few weeks. And Mum's had to run off to the

Philippines—not really because of my grandparents, but because she was afraid the takers might come after the rest of the family unless she seemed to be backing off."

"Was she a part of your dad's investigation?"

"We all were. Well—" Dylan tilts his head up a bit like he's looking at the sky. "Well, I was. Because of my work. We tried to keep the rest of the family out of it, other than Mum. She's a member of the Keepers of the Way, and she was helping Da with his work. The two of them often work in tandem."

"What are the Keepers of the Way?"

"Oh, right," he says as if he's forgotten I'm brand new to practically everything he's ever known. And, on reflex, he turns his head toward me so fast I don't have time to dodge out of his way.

His face goes grazing against the side of my lips and cheek, all smooth skin against smooth skin. Quick as a switch, he's snapping his head back around to the front, and I'm yanking my own face away from his.

Then it's a couple seconds of this crawling silence while the two of us try to figure out how to handle what just happened. Him staring straight ahead and me completely fixated on what I can see of his face, trying not to think too much about the feel of his skin against my lips. Or even the feel of his beard, which was sort of soft and strangely pleasant.

You'd think I'd never even kissed a guy before, the way my body's reacting. I tell myself nothing actually happened, but that doesn't make much difference. I can feel that now familiar electricity lighting up right at the nape of my neck.

When Dylan starts talking again, though, his voice is real pointedly neutral, as if things absolutely did not get weird just now.

"The Keepers are an ancient order," he says, calm and collected. "They champion the forces of good in the world. One of their biggest roles is to protect and support the Way Reader, when we've got one. Right now, Rishi and Mum are the only Keepers who know who you really are, and we feel it's safest to keep it that way. But, once you're viable—once we no longer need to hide your identity so closely—the Keepers will be an important part of your life."

I'm listening to him, I really am. This Keepers of the Way thing sounds like it could be great. Someday. After I've had a chance to figure out all the other new and enormous things coming my way. Like fighting an energy-sucking army. Or learning how to live in a world that, a few days ago, I wouldn't even have imagined could exist.

Or just figuring out how to be around Dylan without turning into a total mess.

I mean, I cannot make myself stop getting distracted by things like how cute it is when he says words like "mum," or how his whole British accent is really doing it for me right now. I'm totally mesmerized by every movement of the muscles in his jaw as he talks, fixated on the line of his neck at the edge of his facial hair. The thought of what it'd feel like to just run my finger along there is doing things to my body I didn't even know were possible.

We barely even touched each other, but every centimeter of my skin's gone tingly and real aware of how close it is to his skin. Or more, the idea of his skin, since there are at least a few solid layers of winter clothing between us. It's all I can do not to lean forward and just bite his earlobe a little, or nuzzle my nose against the back of his neck.

I don't know how he can act so casual. Except that, obviously, I'm not having the same effect on him as he is on me, and I know why that is too. It's because his body isn't completely out of control. This is definitely one of the effects of this whole transfiguring process. It's turning me into a hormone-ridden sex-fiend or something. I couldn't hate this harness any more than I do right now. I mean, geez, I could really use some physical distance from the guy.

When Rishi pauses and turns back to us, I think maybe we're stopping—that I'll be able to get that physical distance—but he just says he senses someone else out there, and we'll have to take a detour to avoid them. Then we're on our way again, and all I can do is stare hard into the snow-covered trees streaming by on either side of us and wait for the annoying tingle to die.

Only, when it finally does, the queasy buzzing comes on again instead and, honestly, I think I'd rather be dealing with the out-of-control libido because this time it's like my stomach's gone nuclear.

I try to fight the sick feeling for a while until it's all I can do to hold my head upright, to keep my eyes open. Finally, I just give in. Sliding my arm up against Dylan's back to act as a personal space preserver, I rest my head down on my wrist, and pretty soon I'm swinging in and out of consciousness.

Flashes of strange lights and colors and patterns start flaring in my mind like some defective, old-timey film reel. With every flash, my stomach turns, and my skull throbs.

Eventually, from outside all the disorientation, I hear Dylan's voice as if it's behind a closed door. He sounds concerned and reassuring and steady, and I hold on to that steadiness, try to locate the source of it in all this fog in my brain. Then I'm opening my eyes with almost as much confusion as if I were doing it for the first time ever, staring bleary at the winter landscape tinged pink and purple with the setting sun.

"Alexandra," Dylan's saying, "you don't sound well. Can you speak to me about what's going on? Alexandra?"

We're still moving quick—maybe even faster than before—and everything's sort of blurring into everything else as we pass. It makes my head, my stomach—everything—feel worse. Especially since, on the edges of my vision, those unfamiliar lights and colors are still twitching along.

"I'm seeing things," I tell him, and my voice sounds weak. "Weird patterns and shapes."

He's quiet, and I can hear that his breath is coming more heavy than it was earlier in the day, like someone who's been running hard for a long time.

"You're starting to see the particle world," he says, and the concern in his voice is sharper, more anxious. "That's your brain learning how to interpret it. Everything's progressing too fast for you. I'm sorry, but there are people near us again, and we can't tend to you. We'll stop as soon as it's safe. Can you hold out a bit longer, Alexandra?"

"You can call me Zanny," I say, because for some reason that's what seems important right now.

I'm already drifting back into the stormy confusion of my brain, and this time, I'm pretty sure it'll be a while until I find my way out of it. At some point, I think I feel hands on my back, Rishi's voice all gentle in my ear, and I'm aware of the nausea fading and that the sky's dark and filled with stars.

Then time warps. It could be days that I'm swimming through brain fog, or maybe minutes. Now and again, I catch moments of the real world. Things like, recognizing that I'm sitting on the ground, that I'm propped up in someone's arms—probably Dylan's—and Rishi's spooning something warm and brothy into my mouth.

Mostly, I'm so lost in the frenzy inside my head that it begins to feel like it's the only world I've ever known. Especially once other images start coming along with the particle world. Strange faces and dark forests and gaping holes in the ground. And vampires. Lots and lots of vampires.

Only, instead of sucking your blood, they whisper awful things into your ears until you can't stand it anymore, and you try to take your own life just to stop it. But before you actually die, they ever-so-painfully sip your soul from your body. There's only the tiniest prickle at the back of my mind reminding me it's a dream.

Some time later—maybe days, maybe months—I wake up enough to realize I'm lying on the ground between Dylan and Rishi, beneath a cover of towering pine trees. Or at least, I think I'm awake. When I look around, everything seems to pulse in my vision. Dylan and Rishi —and all the trees near us—go sliding away from me and then rush back again, and again. It makes me sick to try and focus.

The buzzing's in the core of my bones now, as if I'm just a block of energy and nerves and a nausea that's like some demon creature inside me, swirling in my stomach. Trying to jump out of my throat.

Dylan and Rishi themselves start to change, their faces turning into the vampires from my dreams. They're gnashing at me, up on their haunches and ready to pounce. From one side of the clearing, I see other figures, hazy and inky black, creeping toward me. Promising in hissing whispers to end my pain.

Fear shoots through my veins, and I manage to get myself upright. Then I'm stumbling forward into the snow and the trees. Somewhere in my mind there's a voice saying, *pay attention to where you're going*, but that voice is like the squeak of a mouse compared to the roaring of my other impulses.

I'm not sure how far I've gone, when the bile that's been churning in my stomach starts rising up my throat, and I know I can't hold it anymore. I'm realizing, too, that I must've been hallucinating back at the camp. And that now I'm out in the open without any protection and without any idea how to get back.

I drop to my knees in the snow, and I barely have enough time to pull my hair up out of my face before toxic waste erupts out of me. I haven't thrown up that much maybe ever, and as the vomit's coming, so are the tears. They're just streaming down my face and onto my neck.

At first, I'm crying because I feel awful, but then it turns into a teary sort of relief, because the buzzing is dying away, finally. Flowing out of me along with probably everything I've ever eaten. I feel empty and thin. Almost nonexistent. But at the same time, it's like I'm being renewed.

When it's all over, I stay crouched there, spitting the taste of vomit out of my mouth. My body's starting to feel more substantial again, as if it's slowly wrapping itself back around me in a series of shivers. Then, at the back of my neck I get a sharp spark. Not that oversexed business Dylan keeps activating, but something more piercing and more to the point. It ignites my mind and chest with that sense of knowing. Knowing there's someone there with me, edging toward me, and that this is no hallucination.

Standing up shaky but fast, I stumble a few feet over to clutch onto the limb of the nearest pine tree, and I spin around to look toward the intruder. When I see him, my lungs seize.

It's that tattooed man from the Flemingsburg festival, and he looks real pleased to see me.

"You make it so easy," he says, with this laugh like he can barely believe his eyes. "I thought it was supposed to be a punishment, making us patrol so far out of the way. In the end, you practically walk into our arms."

I can feel someone else too, behind me, and I inch around so I can see both of them at the same time. It's that tall girl from Flemingsburg. The one I thought was going to bite my face off when I nearly ran into her. She's approaching real slow, her expression a whole lot more cautious now, maybe even scared.

"Lidi," the man calls to her, "I guess your sour face wasn't such bad luck after all."

He's moving with less caution than the girl is, but he's still wary of me, like he's not sure what I might be capable of.

"You're going to come along nice and easily, aren't you?" he says with this vicious little smile and a voice that makes my skin creep. "You're outnumbered, you see. And, though we will have to bind you, we would prefer not to cause you pain. You'll have to come with us, one way or another."

I can't run. My body's spent, all trembling and flimsy. I don't think I even have the strength to scream, and I don't know how far away Dylan and Rishi are. Don't know if we're close enough to the campground that the security alerts would trigger. I set my brain speeding through my options, playing one of Mom's focus games that she calls "I Will Survive."

"You're alone in the forest and you're cornered by an angry bear. All you've got is the clothes on your back."

Only this time, it's not an angry bear. It's two takers who, I'm guessing, have the ability to do things to me I can't even imagine.

And me? I can barely stand.

The man's about six feet away now, and it's about as close as I can handle. I go with the only solution that's popped into my brain. I pull a cheesy wizardy pose on him, swinging my arm up and thrusting it forward as if I'm casting some deadly spell.

It's meaningless, obviously. I don't know what in the world I'm doing. But it sure startles him, and he responds on instinct, swinging his own arm up in defense. Only, something happens when he does it. This bundled mass of flame and sparking air comes flying at me so hot, I can feel it practically as it leaves his fingers.

It's such a surprise that I'm frozen in place. I'm pretty sure I'm about to die, when this huge burst of cool wind slams into me from the side. Knocks me clear of the ball of fire and sends me sprawling into the bushes underneath the tree. A second later, that girl lets out a terrible scream.

She's spinning all over, clawing at the air by her face and shoulders.

When I stretch around toward her, I see that the top of her body's been seared, like someone just melted her skin clean off. My own body snaps into some new instinct, and I'm scrambling to get up and help her. To do something to stop the horror scene in front of me. But that tattooed man suddenly grabs my arm. Yanks at me, sending me stumbling back to the ground.

"Look what you did," he shouts and slaps me across the face so hard it rings an echo through my skull. Then he catches me by the collar and tries to haul me to my feet. "Get up, you gindge! You better believe you're coming with me now."

I try to push him off me, but I don't have the strength, and the world's gone slanted with the force of his blow.

"Please," I hear myself saying over the sound of the girl's screams. "Please." I don't know if I'm asking more for her or for me.

The man wraps his hand so tight around my throat that I can't tell if he's still trying to lift me or trying to kill me. I grasp his wrist and kick at whatever part of his body I can reach with my feet, but even though I know I make contact, his grip just gets tighter until I can barely breathe.

"You worthless piss!" he spits in my face, and my vision's clear enough now I can make out every bright red vein in the whites of his frenzied eyes.

Then, over his shoulder, I see Dylan coming toward us through the forest like a movie star hero, bounding through the pines, all swift and serious. He's nocking an arrow to his bow and pulling the string back. Striding sideways, he dodges off the trunk of a tree, springs himself up into the air, and lets the arrow fly.

There's a sickening sort of thwap, and the man's body seizes. This broken gasp spills from inside him, and his eyes go wide, checkmark brows creased. For a second, he's still looking at me. Then his gaze unfocuses and, slow like a tree that's just been felled, he slumps heavy and limp across me, his oiled hair pressed against my cheek and his shoulder jabbing into my jaw.

Two people are screaming now, and it takes me a second to realize one of them is me.

Dylan's by my side. He's dragging the man off me and onto the ground. Then he's leaning over me.

"Are you all right, Zanny? Talk to me."

I hate that I'm screaming. Hate that I've just completely lost it. I manage to make myself stop, but then I can't turn off the shuttering gulps that take its place.

Dylan looks me over quick for any injuries and turns back to the man to check for a pulse. Then he places his palm between the man's shoulder blades, where the arrow's still stuck in his back. Based on what Rishi and Dylan've told me, I'm assuming he's checking the man's essence. It should be just inside there, under Dylan's hand. Dylan sits still for a few seconds, quiet, like he's listening, and then he sort of shakes his head and turns away.

I can guess what it means.

Either when he fell or when Dylan moved him, the man's arm has somehow gotten twisted at an angle no living person should be able to stand. The skin of his hand already looks a few shades too pale, his fingers a little too inert. Dylan must notice my tears because he crouches beside me again, pulling me up to him and pressing my head against his shoulder.

"The girl," I whisper into his coat, but I can hear Rishi with her.

"Please stop moving," he's saying, urgent and kind. "I'm here to help."

But her screams die off in this wet, guttural scratching and, as we hear her body fall heavy to the ground, Dylan pulls me to him tighter.

Rishi coos over her, so quiet I can't tell what he's saying. Her tortured breathing slows and stops, leaving this silence that's way too pressing, that throbs in my chest.

Dylan's hand goes to the back of my head, his face against my bangs as if he can somehow shield me from what's happened. All I can think is how that man and that girl were standing there alive and dangerous only minutes before, and now they're simply gone. All that's left of them just empty shells of meat and bone.

So, this is what death is. It's terrifyingly final.

"You must take her quickly and go." Rishi's bending over us, his face bleak, his mustache and hands spotted with something disturbingly wet and reddish. "We can't risk there being more takers nearby. I'll clean up here."

"And then?" Dylan asks.

"I'll catch up to you."

Dylan pulls away from me and looks me in the face.

"Can you walk?"

I'm not sure I can. My tears are gone, but I'm numb all over. I nod anyway.

Dylan's not convinced. He unslings his bow and quiver of arrows and hands them to me.

"Put these over your shoulder. You're just going to have to hang on this time."

When he pulls me by my arms up onto his back, I wrap myself real tight around him.

"The bags?" he says to Rishi.

"I'll get them."

"See you soon, then."

When Dylan takes off sailing, there's no danger of my falling asleep even though I wish I could. I've got too much in my head that I'd really rather wasn't there. The image of the life falling from that man's face, the silence after the girl stopped breathing.

Being there for their last moments, I can't make myself believe they deserved it even though they definitely meant me harm. Seeing death in movies is no kind of preparation for what it's really like.

I wish I could talk to Mom. Feel her warm arms around me and just forget everything, but I'm stuck here clinging to Dylan's back, with nothing to do but think over all of it, again and again.

I have to keep re-adjusting my grip around his neck. The wind that's rushing against us is pushing bitter cold into my face, and even inside my gloves, my fingers are numb. My arms are hurting. I feel empty inside. I'm weary to my bones, heavy as stone. But I'm trying my best not to let on that anything's wrong because I'm aware we need to keep moving. I want to get as much distance between us and those bodies as we can.

I manage to hold on for a good long while before I lose consciousness for a second and have to snap my hands back together to stop myself from falling.

Dylan grabs my hands too, for more support. Holds them tight against his chest, and his fingers are soft and warm on the skin of my wrists.

"You're frozen," he says with this note of guilt in his voice. "I was too focused on speed and forgot you can't fight the cold."

Then heat like a warm breeze starts to seep from his hands over my body.

"We can stop soon. Do you think you can hold on a bit longer?

"Mm," I say in a sort of affirmation, but the warmer my body gets, the drowsier I become. My head's already slumping down against his back.

With a real effort, I manage to stay coherent for the next few minutes, but, before I can even feel it's happening, my fingers just slip away from each other—pull out of Dylan's grip—and I fall backward.

On reflex, Dylan's hands swing to my legs, and his momentum forward falters. Then he's stopping completely and spinning around to grab at my flailing arms.

By the time he catches me, I'm already so far down, it throws us both off balance, and he falls right along with me. I feel this puff of air balloon up beneath us, which I figure is Dylan's doing. It's not enough to completely break our fall, though, and when his body hits against mine, the pillow of air bursts, and we smack into the snow with a thud.

White powder ruptures around us like a firework. The quiver and arrows crumple beneath me, but what really hurts is the simultaneous impact as my body absorbs the force of the earth from one direction and Dylan from the other.

He's off me in an instant, but I still can't breathe.

"*Nefsakes*," he says as he bends over me all worried. "*Nefsakes*, are you broken?"

I've got no air to speak, so I just stare at him with my mouth gaping fish-like, waiting for my lungs to fill again while his hands are running all over me, checking for anything damaged.

"*Calon tân*, can you speak to me? Zanny?"

Maybe it's just a relief not to be thinking about death for a minute, but this is when it gets to seeming pretty funny to me. Dropping off him without warning like I did, the two of us scrambling at each other mid-air. Him flattening me.

The laughter comes out in these wheezy gasps at first, and Dylan obviously doesn't understand what's happening.

"*Calon tân*," he breathes again, "Show me where you're hurting."

When my air comes back and my laughter starts sounding like what it really is, Dylan sits on his haunches and stares at me. Then a smile pulls at the corners of his lips, and his face slides into a wry, lopsided grin. He lets out this sigh of relief and starts laughing too.

Flopping onto his back next to me, he flings out his arms like a snow angel and lets his laughter grow deeper and free, as if he hasn't laughed like this in a long time. Like he loves the feel of it in his chest. When he turns his head to look over at me, the smile on his face is so wide and contagious, I start laughing even harder myself.

"Shh," he says through his own laughter, rolling up onto his side and clapping one hand over my mouth. "Shh."

But he doesn't seem too urgent about it, so I figure he doesn't sense anyone close. After a second, he gives up and rolls back into the snow. The two of us lie there with our heads together and laugh until we've used up all the humor and we drift off into a friendly sort of silence.

The problem with silence, though, is it gives you time to think. And right now, there aren't too many pleasant things to think about.

"What's a gindge?" I ask, turning up onto my side to look at him.

My question has an immediate effect, his expression going real sour. "Did those takers call you that?"

I nod, and he looks away, drawing in this long, tense breath.

"It's an ugly term for a body once the essence and the shadow have left it. A detestable word."

"What are the words you use? The ones that sound like 'nev-sakes' and 'cah-lone tahn?'"

He almost smiles again and glances at me.

"It's Painter slang, minor expletives. The first one's a mash of Welsh and English. We do that sort of thing a lot. *Nef* comes from the Welsh word for 'heaven' and *sakes* is just 'sakes,' in English. As in, 'heaven sakes.' *Calon tân* is Welsh too. Translates roughly to 'heart of fire' or 'fiery heart.'"

I think of that warmth in my chest when I knew to trust Rishi and Dylan and when I decided to follow them and leave my mom.

"There are going to be more, aren't there?"

Dylan slides his gaze over to me again. "Hm?"

"People that're going to die because of me."

Turning toward me completely now, he props himself up on his elbow so he can look me full in the face.

"Those two did not die because of you."

"Yeah, but they did, though, really." I try not to sound petulant about it. "I'm sorry, by the way."

He raises his eyebrows, questioning, and I pick at my sleeve a little, suddenly not sure how to proceed.

"I'm sorry that you…had to do that."

Kind of sighing and dropping his head back, he scratches at the hair peeping out the front of his hat, and even in a moment like this, I can't help noticing how cute he is.

"It's not the first time," he says without any bravado. "It won't be the last. The takers are hurting people. Whether it's to protect you or to protect someone else, we'll have to do harm. You're meant to save lives, and that you will do. If you're to make it through all of this without breaking, you'll have to focus on the lives saved instead of the ones lost."

At the moment, I don't feel like the sort of person who saves lives. I don't know what that's like. Right now, all I know is the death part.

"How far until we reach Deffro?"

"A day, maybe, until the portal that'll take us across the Atlantic Ocean. You'll like that part. It's one of the more common ways Painters travel around the globe. After that, it's a few hours to my house."

It's hard to know what to think about that. On the one hand, reaching Deffro could mean a bit of rest, but it also means more change.

"We can't keep lying here," Dylan says, getting to his feet. "The day is almost over. Let's make camp."

He helps me stand, then gathers the pieces of sticks that used to be arrows. We head into the trees to find a good place to stay for the night, Dylan erasing our tracks as we go. Even though my flaring seems to be gone for good, I feel pretty weak, and Dylan has to hold my hand and help me along until we find a workable clearing.

He makes me sit down while he builds a makeshift lean-to out of pine boughs and prepares dinner, saying, "You haven't eaten all day. I should've thought of food earlier."

He sets up another invisible barrier around our lean-to, "to keep the heat in," and with that and some good food in me, I do feel a lot better.

Dylan must not think so, though, because he studies my face and says, "You're tired. You'd best sleep while you can."

Normally, this'd be a pretty appealing suggestion, but right now, sitting cozy with Dylan in our bubble of warm air, the last thing I wanna do is close my eyes and invite nightmares.

When I start to protest, Dylan says, "I'm not sure when we'll have to be on our way again."

"What about Rishi?"

"He'll find us. I've left particle clues for him along the path."

He grabs a bunch of pine needles from the foot of the nearest trees and throws them in a pile near the lean-to.

"We don't have our supplies, so I'll have to make do."

He holds his hands over the needles, and they start to shimmy against each other. Changing shape and melding together until they transform completely into a brown pillow that looks inviting enough, even if it is real plain.

He makes another of these and then two big wool blankets. With a signal from him, I move out of the way so he can throw one of the blankets across the floor of the lean-to and then the pillows on top of that.

"Do you mind if we share?" he asks, holding the second blanket. "I'm too tired to make more of these, and we'll stay warmer that way."

He does look like he's about ready to collapse.

"That's fine."

"Choose your side," he says, and I crawl onto the blanket.

"How does painting work exactly?" I ask. "I mean, if even normal people—sorry, Particle-Blockeds—have an essence and a shadow, what makes you—us—different from them?"

Throwing the second blanket over my legs and crawling in next to me, he says, "Painters have another set of nerves in our nervous systems, and an additional component to our brains, which is called the ignus. You've probably already felt it prickling back here."

He waves his hand toward the back of his head.

"Here?"

He's leaning across me now and pulling at the blanket to give more leeway on my side, and I don't think about it before touching his neck at the point he's indicating—the same spot where I keep feeling that weird tickle myself.

As soon as I touch him, though, there's this flash of energy that passes between our skin, through my hand and right up my arm to my chest like an electric shock. It's a surprise to me, but it's Dylan that's jerking away so fast you'd think I'd tried to stab him to death. The look on his face—all dismayed and violated—makes me feel immediately and totally embarrassed, even if I've got no clue what it is I've actually done.

"I'm sorry," he says, recovering quick. "You caught me off guard. For Painters, touching someone there is very…intimate."

My face flares as hot as a furnace. "I didn't know."

He waves it away, lying back and settling onto his pillow.

"There's a lot we'd better prep you on before we arrive in Deffro. You'll see that when family members or very close friends greet each other, they use *ramu*—palming the nape of the neck—as a sign of endearment. But people also use it as a way of expressing, you know, romantic affection."

"Oh."

Trying to decide if I now feel more embarrassed or rejected, I slide all the way up to my nose under our shared blanket. Making extra sure not to bump against him or crowd his space in any way, while at the same time trying not to make it obvious that's what I'm doing.

He's not even aware of me, though. His breathing's already gone steady and soft, while I'm left wide awake.

Lying on my back, I stare through the boughs of the lean-to up into the star-dusted sky, and I wallow in the mountain nighttime. The sounds, the smells—even the quality of the air—are real close to what I've known all my life, but it's the subtlety of the differences that makes it so lonely.

I'm finally starting to fade off into sleep, when I get a tickle of energy at the back of my neck, in what I guess is called my ignus. I'm barely aware it's there before it explodes, bursting through my entire body and burning at the ends of my fingers and across my palms. It's scorching and alive, like lightning coursing through my veins.

Then, with the stroke of a slap, my world changes.

A flood of shapes and colors goes tumbling through my head. Some I know from my recent delirium, but none of them are things I have a name for. Through my wide-open eyes, I realize I can still see the towering pines rising up to frame the deep purple sky. All these other images bombarding my mind are getting to me by some other means, and they're coming in bigger and more hurried waves.

My body's lit up like a star with all that energy, and pretty soon, I lose myself so completely in the rush of chaotic patterns, I can't even make out the earth beneath me. It's like I'm pitching down a never-ending water slide, speeding topsy-turvy toward some unknown destination until with a jolt—I arrive.

The shapes and colors swarm into one fluid shape. With this hot, hot heat in my chest, I know I'm sensing some*body*. Somebody moving fast, right toward me. It's only a matter of minutes before they'll be here.

Bolting upright, I push all these new senses to the back of my mind. I'm grabbing hold of Dylan, shaking him. Hissing at him to wake up.

He rises like someone poised to attack. "What's wrong?" he hisses back at me, gripping my shoulders.

I must've been shaking because, at the pressure of his hands, I feel my body try to go still.

"Someone's coming."

My throat's tight with the reality of it.

Dylan's moving instantly, scooping up the arrows and the bow that were still lying bent and broken at the edge of the lean-to, his silhouette against the moon turning into some prickling monster thing.

"Which way?"

I point in the direction we came from, and he doesn't ask how I know.

"Get behind those trees," he tells me.

One by one, he's repairing each arrow with a touch of his hands, his motions quick and instinctive. I'm scrambling to hide like he's told me to when something else burns into my chest like a fact.

"It's Rishi."

Dylan's hands freeze. He stares at me like he's not sure he can breathe, and I wonder if he was as scared as I was.

My eyes flick to some movement in the forest behind Dylan, and he twists around to see where I'm looking. It's as if Rishi's just melting into existence there, the way he comes sailing through the dark shapes of the trees and glides graceful to a stop in the middle of our clearing. His wiry frame's practically overflowing with the two backpacks, and his mustache is hanging limp from his face.

He looks half dead, but at the sight of the two of us still tense and paralyzed, he smiles wide and laughs like he's as relieved to see us as we are to see him. Striding forward, he grips Dylan at the back of the neck, pulls his head against his own and touches foreheads in greeting. Then he's coming toward me and wrapping me in a big, grandfathery hug.

"You're okay?" I ask, searching his tired face as he steps away from me.

"At the moment, could barely be better. Hungry."

Dylan's already set to work concocting something in the handmade pot he used to cook dinner, and the smell of it makes our little clearing feel a bit more homey.

"It'll be ready in a minute. Sit down and rest," he commands, and Rishi laughs again.

"Indeed."

The way he slides onto the blankets, it's almost involuntary. Like he's only been staying upright by sheer force of will. I sit down next to him, keeping my eyes on his face, a part of me disbelieving he's here and in one piece.

"What happened?" I ask. "Did you run into anyone else?"

"Almost," he nods. "Some people came near soon after you left, but they didn't see me. I believe they were companions of the other two. We'll need to be more careful going forward."

His giddy energy seems to be fading away. He slips the packs off his shoulders and leans against them like a back rest. Closing his eyes, he lets out this huge breath that flutters the stray hairs at the edges of his mustache in a way that'd probably be funny if it weren't for the solemn set of his facial features.

With his eyes still closed, he says in a quiet voice, mostly to Dylan, "I performed the rites of crossing and returned their bodies to the earth."

Dylan pauses in his work and glances up at Rishi, his lips pulling tight, but his only response is a soft sound of affirmation. When the food's ready, Rishi eats it quick and efficient, then hands the bowl back.

"We're about a day away from Deffro," Dylan says.

"Mm."

"We have things to prepare."

Rishi looks at me, his eyes kind of smiling even though his mouth isn't. "He means you, you know. We have to turn you into Ms. Sophie Warren. Teach you about Painter culture and change your appearance."

Something occurs to me that I hadn't thought of before, and my heart drops a little. "Like—like my face?"

Dylan's mouth twitches, and I think maybe he's about to laugh, but he just gives me this nice, lopsided smile.

"Couldn't do that even if we wanted to," he says. "As long as the shadow and essence are intact, we can't use painting to make permanent changes to the human body without inflicting actual damage. And, even that—harming the structure of a body on a particle-level—requires a great deal of energy and skill. Besides, as far as we're aware, no one in Deffro knows what you look like to easily recognize you, so there's no need for extreme measures. However, the sightings that announced your existence offered vague descriptions of you, and we don't know what those two takers might have told others about you. So, to be safe, we'll dye your hair, change your clothes. Nothing big. Still, it'll take some energy."

"Energy neither of us has right now," Rishi says with this yawn so big, it's impossible for Dylan and me not to copy.

Too worn out to make any other arrangements, the three of us just pile together between the two wool blankets. This time, with the warmth of both of them on either side of me and my head full of Dylan's scent that never seems to go sour, I fall asleep pretty easy. The whispers of new particle shapes and pigments dancing at the back of my mind and reminding me my life has changed forever. I've changed forever.

In the morning, Dylan asks if I've got a preference about how my hair looks, and I just stare at him because, yeah, I've got a preference, but I didn't think I'd have a say.

I've been wanting a particular hairdo for months now, ever since I saw it on a character in one of my friend Sylvia's graphic novels. Mom said it was too high maintenance, though, for someone with hair as curly as mine, and she wasn't about to spend money on something so frivolous. So, I'm not expecting Dylan to be all that excited about it either.

"What if," I say, trying not to sound like I'm bracing for Dylan to reject the idea outright, "we straightened it, and did a long a-line sort of bob that starts back here and comes forward just below my shoulders with, like, bangs that cut across like this."

I motion with my hand, and keep on talking as if I definitely believe what I'm about to say is totally reasonable.

"And maybe we could do it in, say, a dark purple-y blue with, like, some lighter blue tones that sort of, I don't know, shimmer when the light hits it?"

Dylan's lips pull into this poorly suppressed smile.

"Thought about it much?" he asks, and right at that moment he looks pretty adorable and, even though all those extra hormones from transfiguring don't seem to be there anymore, my pulse still skips a beat.

I give a shrug and say, "Maybe a little," totally failing to repress my own goofy grin.

He studies my face, and I think for sure he's trying to find a nice way to let me down, but then he says, "I think it could work," as if he really does think so. Looking at Rishi, he asks, "Suppose it'd do the trick?"

"Oh, yes. Brilliant colors are quite the thing in Deffro these days."

"Though they're uncommon enough to leave a strong first impression."

"While still being sufficiently playful to suit her well."

Dylan considers me for a minute more. "Yeah, I think you could pull it off."

He doesn't say this like it's supposed to be anything more than an objective observation, but I feel kind of flattered anyway, because, I mean. Well, it's Dylan saying it, and also because this hairdo's maybe the coolest thing I've ever wanted for myself.

He finds a loose log for me to sit on, and then he stands behind me and places his hands on my head.

The particle world's fully with me now, and as he begins to work on the color of my hair, I can sense the changes he's making like little tickles at the back of my mind. It's all swirling shapes and soft lights. Real pretty.

I can't imagine what it'd be like growing up knowing someday this whole extra vision of the world was going to be available to you.

Knowing everyone around you could already see it, could change it. What kind of a life would that be, when this is just part of your everyday?

"What's it like in Deffro?" I ask out loud.

Rishi, who's crouched a few feet away from us absently decomposing our bedding into some unappealing looking sort of mulch, glances up with a smile.

"Now, that is a difficult question to answer. What the city is to me may prove quite different for you. I come from Samagra, a Bengali Painter city tucked away in the Indian Himalayas. That will always be the home that defines me, but Deffro is now the home of my heart. It's where I live with my wife Yvette, and she colors everything in the city for me. Even without that connection, though, I believe anyone would find it beautiful."

"The city of the sun," Dylan offers from behind me. "The light in the mountains."

"Yes, yes," Rishi's nodding. "That's what some call it. People say it's because of the way the buildings downtown reflect the sun's rays, but the city went by names similar to these long before those modern structures existed. Since the time when the valley was first settled, by a group of Painters who broke off from the Celtic peoples who lived in the region. They named the valley Deffro, which means 'to wake up,' so it's not difficult to imagine that the city has always been associated with light. A special place."

"If it isn't obvious to you yet," Dylan says with a smile in his voice, his hands dropping from my head as he steps around beside me, "in addition to being a highly skilled reader, Rishi is a rather formidable historian."

Rishi smiles at this, shrugging a little. "I like to have a sense of where I fall in time and space."

Dylan leans down and starts working on the cut of my hair now. As pieces of it scatter in feathery tufts, I can feel his fingertips brushing against the back of my neck here and there, quick and soft and obviously unintentional. Still, the electricity in my ignus sparks every time, as if it's trying to jump out of my skin to reach him. And when he starts talking again, his voice is almost right in my ear, his breath distractingly warm against my neck.

"Deffro is a city with a rich history," he says. "The Welsh welcomed other Painters in from early on. They, along with my Filipino ancestors and a few other groups, were among the first Painters to introduce the idea of a global democracy, and much of the negotiations happened in Deffro. To me, it's like a tapestry of the story of the birth and growth of the Republic. Or really, the story of all Painters as a whole."

You can hear the pride in his words, this unexpected freedom of emotion that makes me want to turn and look at his face.

Rishi's voice has that same pride when he says, "It's a city of many stories, of many people. It's also currently the capital of the Republic— a tenure that lasts ten years before cycling to the next city-state—so the richness of the cultural experience there is all the more magnified."

As Rishi stands to use one of the pots from breakfast to scoop up the mulch he's been making, Dylan steps in front of me to work on my bangs, leaning down for a better angle, his face suddenly real close and his eyes so focused on the line of hair right above my eyebrows, that it's hard not to feel like he's actually staring into my eyes themselves.

I try not to act too awkward about it, but that's not easy because the whole atmosphere in the clearing feels pretty intimate right now. The way he and Rishi talk about Deffro, it's like the way you'd describe the love of your life or something, all raw and reverent. Makes me feel kind of homesick. I mean, I don't suppose too many other people'd wax poetic about Flemingsburg, but I've always loved the place.

"We're done," Dylan says, taking a step back and looking at me like he's pleased with his handiwork.

"Already?" I tug at the front ends of my hair to try and get a better look at the color.

"Use this," Rishi says, painting out a rectangular sheet of mirror and stepping over to wave it at me. He scans my hair and face, and he gives me a big, appreciative grin. As I take the mirror from him, my chest cramps with an excited, jittery feeling, but when I see the new me for the first time, I just go still.

Play it cool, I'm telling myself, suddenly feeling uncomfortable about having an audience for this moment. Don't make a fool of yourself.

But honestly, I don't think I'd care too much even if I did do something totally ridiculous right now, because I look amazing. I mean, Dylan got it exactly right. Better than I'd even imagined. The color is rich and sleek, and everywhere the sun hits it, my hair shines so blue it's practically sparkling. The way it frames my face, I do almost seem like a different person, and this girl—this girl might actually be able to save the world.

"I look...awesome." I breathe out as I grin, giddy, up at Dylan and Rishi, totally ruining whatever coolness I might've been faking before. But Dylan's grinning too and trying his best not to look too proud of himself.

"In Deffro, they'd call you alpha," he says.

"As in a dog?" I raise my eyebrows, and he and Rishi laugh.

"As in the first. An original."

I've never thought of myself as an original before. Of course, I don't think I've ever known enough people to have that be a thing anyway.

"We do still need to do something about your clothes."

I look down at my white T-shirt and blue hiking pants I just changed into this morning. First time in days I've been able to wear something clean.

"What's wrong with them?"

"In our current circumstances, it's mostly the fabrics. Once we're in Deffro we'll set you up with a wardrobe that's more fitting for Painter fashion, but for now we'll just have to do something about the way your clothes are formed."

"They're too obviously Particle-Blocked fabrics," Rishi chimes in from where he's now disintegrating all the cookware. "If anyone stumbles onto you before you reach Dylan's house, it could make them unnecessarily curious."

I look closer at the clothes the two of them are wearing, and I can't tell the difference between theirs and mine, but when Dylan takes the cuff of my shirt in his hands and starts to change the particle patterns of the fabric, I see what he means.

I may not understand much about the particle world yet, but even I can tell the new patterns probably make for a better fabric. Stronger and more flexible, even prettier as far as the particle patterns go. It's smooth on my skin, breathable and sturdy. Like if you created the ultimate fabric for every situation, this'd be it.

"When people meet you for the first time, we want to solidify your new identity in their minds as quickly as possible," Dylan says, crouching down to pinch at the hem of my pants and start the changes there. "We don't want them wondering about who you were before Deffro, about there being a difference between you then and now. The hair will help with that. It will dominate their impressions of you, make it hard to imagine you as anything else. Having the right clothes will help too."

He's started changing the color of my pants to white, and, like he can feel my question before I've even asked it, he explains, "We'll be moving slowly enough now that we'll be more easily visible to others. We're heading into a territory that's sufficiently populated to make particle sailing too risky, so it's worth expending the energy to help us blend into the scenery a bit. Don't want anyone to notice us if we can help it."

He finishes transforming my pants and then moves to my boots, his long fingers all slender and tan against the grey leather. Then he straightens up and glances around as if he's looking for something. I stand too, twisting my head back and forth to feel the brush of my hair against my shoulders. Dylan steps over to grab my hat off the ground where I left it this morning, and he turns it white as he brings it back to me.

"It's a pity, but we'll have to cover your hair for now," he says. Then, as if it's just instinct for him, he's sliding the beanie onto my head himself and starting to tuck my hair inside it.

It's such a personal thing to do, getting into my space like that without any warning, and the surprise of it makes me look right into his eyes.

His hands pause for a second, and then he's pulling them away from me again and saying real casual, like nothing's at all unusual, "I'll go change the color of your other things."

He strides off, and I'm left standing there with my heart still going a few beats too fast and my ignus buzzing. It's going to take me a long time to get used to having that little generator back there, always so ready to send its electricity down the back of my neck.

Not sure what else to do, I just hang out in the middle of the clearing for a while until Dylan's whitened his own clothes and he and Rishi take down the lean-to. Then I trudge over to my now white bag and sling it over my shoulders, watching from a safe distance while the two of them finish erasing the signs of our having been here.

When everything's ready to go, I have to climb onto Dylan's back again, and, as I wrap my arms around his neck, it's about all I can do not to think about his hands on the side of my face and his eyes looking right into mine.

We particle sail a little ways from the camp. Far enough to make it hard for anyone to follow our trail. Then I get off Dylan's back, and Rishi and Dylan paint out wooden snowshoes for each of us so we can walk side-by-side. After days of almost a hundred mile-per-hour travel, moving at a regular pace feels painfully slow.

Rishi fills the time by expounding on the history and customs of Painter life. He gets real into the weeds on history, especially, explaining that the seven Painter groups that originally founded the Republic were from the regions now known as Wales, British Columbia, New Zealand, the Philippines, Syria, South Africa, and Ecuador, and that they still have a lot of influence in The Republic today.

"For instance," he says, "once you've been revealed as the Way Reader, you will be presented to the Seven Elders, who represent the original seven city-states. This ceremony is called the Aykar, derived from the Aramaic word meaning 'honor.' If you pay attention, you will find that the languages and practices of the original seven states, as well as others, have woven their way indelibly into all of Painter culture."

I get the impression the man takes a lot of pride in knowing all the things he knows. And the truth is, I like listening to him. It's like Sylvia talking about her horse-riding competitions or her comic books, or Logan with his conspiracy theories. You end up loving it a little yourself because of the way they do.

After the history lesson, Rishi goes in depth into Painter greetings, explaining that Painters don't normally shake hands unless it's with Particle-Blockeds. Instead, they do something called *pono*—derived from a Maori word meaning "honest"—where they place their hands together, fingers against fingers and palms against palms.

He has me take off my glove and exchange *pono* with him, our hands bumping against each other with the swaying of our snowshoed steps. Little swells of electricity jump between us each time we make contact.

"Some of the most sensitive essensal nerves are in our fingers and palms," he says. "When you touch another Painter's palm like this, you can feel the connection, can't you? It's a sign of respect to allow this connection. It's like saying, 'I will share myself with you.' In other words, it's a promise of sincerity."

When he starts talking about *ramu*, that greeting that involves touching the back of the neck, I can't help glancing kind of guilty up at Dylan. But if he's remembering how I accidentally touched him there last night, he doesn't give any sign. Doesn't so much as look in my direction, which, actually, is just a little disappointing.

"The word *ramu*," Rishi explains, "means 'to love,' and it's derived from the ancient language Akkadian." Glancing over at me with an eyebrow cocked and a confessional kind of smile, he adds, "Of course, that's a fact even most Painters don't know."

I smile back, and on the other side of Rishi, I can see Dylan's got a hint of a smile on his face as well.

"To greet someone with *ramu* and a touch of foreheads is to count them a very dear friend, someone for whom you have great affection and care. Lovers, however, exchange *ramu* with a kiss, and when you have the chance to experience this you will see it is one of the best feelings in the world. Which," Rishi waggles a finger at me, mock serious, "is a good reason not to do it with just anybody."

My face flashes hot and probably red, but at least I manage not to look at Dylan this time.

About mid-afternoon we start having to duck out of sight of other travelers, who particle sail by so fast I don't really register them with my eyes so much as with my particle sight. And every time we dive for cover, Dylan gets a little more sober and distracted, like his mind's clocking in somewhere else and like that place is not pleasant.

After a while, Rishi seems to notice it, and he offers to take the backpack from Dylan.

"We'll reach the portal by midnight, I think," he says. "There, we'll have to part ways. This close to the travel hubs, I'd best move up ahead of you so I can sense anyone coming from further away. It will only give you a few extra seconds to hide, but every second counts."

Dylan nods. Says he'll keep his mind open for anyone coming from behind. Then Rishi starts off ahead of us, and Dylan and I walk side by side in a silence that's practically pulsing with whatever's on Dylan's mind. The absence of Rishi's cheerful stream of trivia makes our own quiet all the more obvious, and I watch him ahead of us, moving in and out of trees, his head angling up every once in a while, as if he's listening for something.

"How do you and Rishi know when someone's coming?" I ask after a while, as interested in shutting off the silence as I am in getting the actual answer. "How'd I know it was Rishi last night?"

Dylan presses his lips together as if he's considering my question. From this angle he's framed almost perfect against the sun, his face thrown into a sort of sepia-toned shadow.

"Painters can sense each other's essences. That is, some Painters can. Most Painters are only able to sense another's essence when it's actively shedding energy, in the case of violent death or a transfiguring. If you want to be able to sense essences in a general way, you have to train for it. Well," he glances at me, "most of us have to. The current theory for how this functions is that our essensal energy is drawn to other essensal energy in much the same way a magnet works, but that you've got to open your mind to the pull of it in order to recognize it's there. Rishi is much better than I am, but recognizing an essence as belonging to a particular individual, as you did—well, as far as I know, that's strictly Way Reader territory."

"Like, Spidey senses or something?"

Dylan nearly smiles then, cocking one eyebrow at me in a question.

"As in Spiderman, the superhero?" I offer, and he gives me this look that's exactly one step away from rolling his eyes.

"I do know what Spidey senses are," he says. "I simply wouldn't have thought to compare the two."

"What other Way Reader powers am I going to have? Flight? A lasso of truth?"

Now the smile flashes through despite himself, and I like the feeling that I'm the one that made that smile happen.

"Couldn't tell you. It's different for every Way Reader. Rishi can give you a long list of possibilities, if you like."

We fall into silence again, and if it's not quite so heavy as it was, it's still not as comfortable as I'd prefer.

After a while of that silence, I blink myself into my imaginary world, to a magical land ruled by ice trolls. I've stolen the seven-league boots from the troll prince and escaped from their frozen castle, where they were going to roast me and eat me for dinner. Every step I take rushes me away from them, dozens of miles at a time. Every evergreen tree we pass, is a mountain peak marking the distance. Every chirp of a bird in the woods, is the sound of the trolls coming after me.

My heart's not in the daydream, though. Not with Dylan storming along beside me. He's walking fast now too. Focused. I think maybe he's in a hurry to be home, like maybe being this close makes ignoring his own homesickness harder.

"Tell me more about your family," I say, skipping forward a bit so I can see his face.

He just gives me this sidelong glance with his eyebrows raised like he's wondering exactly what I'm expecting him to do with that request.

"Like, how about your cousin. You said he lives with you?"

"Mm," Dylan slides his hands into his pockets and turns his face up to the sky. "Gwilim's lived with us since we were both about four years old, he and I. Since his mum died. All of us kids were close, but Gwilim—well, it was always the two of us. Like twins almost."

The way he says it, it's like something that's not the case anymore, and I squint up at him, trying to get a sense of his expression.

"What changed?"

It's a few seconds before he answers, and I'm thinking maybe my question crossed some sort of line. But then he says, all tired, "I'm not sure. Gwilim's always been...moody, I suppose."

I almost laugh at this. Because right now, at least, Dylan seems pretty moody himself.

"When Gwilim's mum Cerian died, he came to live with us. His da
—well. My uncle Hiarwar is president of The Republic now, but even
back then he was an ambitious politician, and I suppose he thought he
didn't have time to raise a kid. Gwilim's careful not to show it, but he
feels things strongly, and his da's letting him go like that has always
bothered him. The idea that he could be sloughed off so readily, that
people you care about can just disappear—"

Dylan stops talking real sudden, his jaw clamping shut and that
same lost look washing over him.

I'm still trying to figure out if he really just said his uncle is
president, though—as in *the* Painter president. So, it takes me a second
to register something's changed.

When Dylan starts talking again, it's like every word holds a special
pain for him and if he doesn't maintain absolute control of his
emotions, one of these words might just break him.

"Last year," his voice hangs in the air all sour and spare, "my older
brother Padrig died. Then came Da's imprisonment, and then Mum
left for the Philippines. Gwilim's not been the same since. None of us
have."

Calling Dylan moody a few minutes ago—well, that seems pretty
inappropriate now. I'm thinking back to that look in his eyes in the car
outside Flemingsburg, when he said people were dying, in that way
like he personally knew it. And then to that moment when I was trying
to decide what I should do, and I felt sure he understood exactly what
I was feeling, and how that made everything just a little bit easier for
me.

I'm not sure I can do the same for him right now—not sure any
understanding I've got could even come close to what he's actually
feeling—but after having stood in my ruined kitchen wondering if my
mom was dead, there's at least something I think I might understand.

"Is it hard?" I ask, glancing kind of tentative into his face. "Having
so many people you care about?"

The look he gives me then—out of the corner of his eyes and real
sharp, as if he's only now properly seeing me—makes my heart take
this little leap and my breath just sort of pause.

"You care about people too," he says—almost dismissive—before looking away again.

I nod and shrug, feeling extra out of my element.

"Yeah," I say, "but other than my mom I don't think I've ever felt all that responsible for anyone else."

Until now, of course. Until, apparently, the whole world's supposed to be my responsibility.

Then Dylan, with his voice low and disarmingly gentle, says, "Your da—programming the locket with the zoetics and his photograph like he did—that's some powerful painting. He must've been an incredible man."

I've got no idea what to say to this. On the one hand, it feels like a thing I've been waiting my whole life to hear. On the other hand, having just learned that Dylan lost a brother he knew and loved, it's hard to feel like I've got any claim on a man I've never truly met.

"Thank you," I say, quiet, because even if I'm not sure I've got much of a right to feel it, Dylan's words have made me pretty proud.

We're silent again after that, the rhythm of our snowshoes keeping time as the seconds tick away. The mountains here are a lot taller than back home, with long peaks as harsh as icicles. The sun is falling behind them. Turning their silhouettes into razor-sharp, angry teeth, and covering everything in a blue-hazed, unsettling dusk that makes it harder to pick Rishi out of the mosaic of snow drifts and trees ahead of us.

The towering mountain walls catch the echoes of our footsteps and bounce them back to us, transformed into a sound like weird, distant laughter. It's exactly the sort of setting to turn my thoughts about as dark as the shadows around us.

"What do we actually know about these takers?" I ask Dylan, trying not to sound as petrified by the idea of them as I absolutely am.

He's clearly been lost in his own thoughts, and it takes him a minute to answer.

"Not a great deal that's useful," he says finally, with this strange, caustic laugh. "We know they've infiltrated the Republic government, but not to what level or to what purpose. We know they have a network of strongholds in Deffro, as well as across the world, but we don't know where any of the important ones are located. My department at the Global Intelligence Bureau has entrenched agents in their organization, but the taker leaders have set up so many safeties against infiltration that the information we've gained is sadly piecemeal."

He stares up into the dimming light of the sky, his footsteps falling heavy on the snow.

"What makes it worse is they believe themselves to be guided by a supposed higher moral purpose. That history has taught humans false mercy—taught us to be weak and soft—and that they, the Sons of Morning, have a duty to make us strong again. That the whole human race will die out without them."

"The Sons of Morning think that killing loads of people and gobbling up their energy's somehow part of them saving the world?"

Dylan gives me a rueful smile.

"A means to an end, they say. They need the essensal energy to do whatever it is they're trying to do. And they claim their victims deserve it. It's one of their recruiting strategies. Offering to help dispense justice against the people who've wronged you, sort of thing."

"That's messed up. They've got to know that's messed up, right?"

"You'd be surprised what you can get people to do when you give them a sense of purpose. Especially when the leaders know how to make good use of it."

"Who are the leaders?"

"The second in command—the only one any of our agents have seen —goes by the name Beelzebub, but he always wears a full-headed mask, so we don't know his real identity. He's bad enough, on his own. Known to enjoy inflicting pain, even on his followers. He appears to have left Deffro a couple weeks ago, though. On some special mission. There's another leader—an apparently more powerful one—going by the title The Angel, but as far as we know, no one but Beelzebub and a select few from the Sons of Morning inner circle have ever seen him. He gives his commands from behind a mysterious cloud of anonymity, while Beelzebub and the other higher ups manage the day-to-day leadership and bring The Angel victims for his takings."

I'm realizing that bringing up this topic was not a good idea in our current surroundings. I find myself searching the darkness between the trees, my skin crawling with this feeling like someone's watching us. Like they're barely out of sight themselves.

I tell myself it's just my overactive imagination, which almost helps. But then, just as the sun gets swallowed completely behind the mountains, a blast of particle sight slams forward in my brain. Rushing images in with such a shock of warning that, for a second, I lose all sense of where I am. I go stumbling forward, feel the world dip topsy-turvy around me.

Dylan grabs me by my elbows, pulls me upright before I hit the ground.

"What is it?" he asks, his eyes fierce on mine, locking me back into the tangible world.

"Something's coming." I think my fingers are digging too tight into his arms. "Something bad."

Up ahead, Rishi spins around toward us, the look on his face making it obvious he's sensed something too, and he knows he's not going to get back to us in time.

Dylan gives a sharp wave to show he's got the situation in hand, and then he's moving. Hauling me over to the nearest tree, pushing me up against the trunk of it, more concerned about speed than comfort. He dissolves our snowshoes in an instant, and then steps up right against the front of me, placing his arms on either side of the trunk.

With the softness of a whisper, the bark surges outward around us. I can see it with my eyes and sense the multiplying of its particles at the same time. There's something sort of pretty about it as it rolls forward, surrounding us in a pillar of fresh smelling wood that tapers as it bends upward to leave just this tiny circle of purple sky peeping through the top. It feels like a totally incongruous thing, to be noticing the beauty of this moment at the same time that I'm real aware of the danger in whatever's coming.

It's two shimmering, clamoring pinpoints of hate. Approaching so fast I barely have time to breathe before they're stopping feet away from us. Then comes the muted sounds of people moving cautious through the snow, and, in my mind, I sense their essences. See a darkness inside them. Writhing around as if that darkness itself is a living thing. A nebulous, inky parasite at the heart of each of these people's essensal energies. Black tendrils twitching and stretching outward like poisonous roots.

Low voices come thick through the living wood of our hiding place.

Their owners so close that if it weren't for the bark surrounding us, I bet we could reach out and touch them.

"I thought I saw something," a female-sounding voice says.

"Doesn't seem to be anything now."

I wonder if they can sense us like I can sense them. If they listened close enough, they could probably hear the sound of our breathing.

Dylan's still pressed against me. So tight I can feel his warmth even through our coats, feel the heat of his bearded chin against my cheek. Can even feel the beat of his heart all heavy and quick like mine.

Then the takers—I'm sure they're takers—are moving off again, launching into a particle sail and speeding away. Dylan and I keep standing there as fixed as if we're frozen, searching our senses for any sign that danger might still be close.

He begins to shift just as I feel someone else approaching. I grab his coat real fast, pulling at it to keep him still. But then, again, I somehow know it's Rishi. Can sense his essence, familiar and clear and bright.

"It's me," he whispers into our hiding spot. "It's safe to come out."

As if on cue, Dylan and I sort of relax against each other, and then Dylan's straightening again, letting the bark recede back into the tree and opening us up to the chilly night air.

Rishi's face shows relief when he sees us. A relief still tinged with the remains of his alarm.

"I got too far ahead," he says, apologetic. "They could've sailed right into you. How did you know—?"

"Zanny sensed them," Dylan says, and Rishi's eyes shift quick to mine.

"You're already at that stage?"

I don't know what that stage might be.

"It's more dangerous than ever to stay still now," Dylan says, painting new snowshoes for me and him almost as fast as he dissolved them before. "We've got to press on."

This time we walk close together, moving with caution as Rishi and Dylan concentrate on scoping for signs of human life. It's excruciating, going so slow, afraid every sound we hear signals danger or that every sound we make is going to give us away. The moon's out in its full strength, splashing light over us like a spotlight. We're the only moving figures in a world that's totally still.

Then Rishi stops without warning. He turns to face us, and something about his expression tells me it's time for our goodbye.

"The two of you must be on your way," he says, offering a gentle smile as he steps over to give me a hug in farewell.

"Zanny," he says, looking at me with his warm brown eyes. "It is safest if I am not seen in Deffro until a few days after your arrival. Remember that my thoughts are with you and my mind aware. For now, I leave you to Dylan's expert care."

He exchanges *ramu* with Dylan, and in the moonlight, with their heads together like that, they look like brothers, the difference in their ages just melting away.

It's a scene I remember from that first rush of images that came to me back in Flemingsburg, when I had my hand clamped around Dylan's wrist. I guess Rishi would call it a sighting. Recognizing this moment should comfort me. Should make me feel like this is all supposed to be happening right now, but it doesn't. After the darkness I saw inside those takers—after everything that's happened in the last few days—the world has just become too big and scary a place.

Rishi steps away from Dylan and turns toward me again. With this forced, comical smile, he waves goodbye and goes sailing off into the snow and the trees and the darkness.

"This next bit's going to be tricky." Dylan says. "The portal we're using is a secret one, known only to the Keepers of the Way. The path to it is steep and rocky. Are you ready?"

He holds his hand out to me, and I take it, his grip strong and bracing through my glove. We head up the side of the mountain at a diagonal for a while until we come to a sort of fissure in the snow. It's tall and narrow, as if a giant came along and pinched the mountain together there, leaving a deep and dangerous-looking crag.

You wouldn't think a person could fit in it, but Dylan pulls me right inside, and suddenly its abrupt walls are towering above our heads, blocking everything else from view and giving me the sensation that I'm being swallowed alive.

Tired-looking evergreens are hanging haphazard off the upper edges of the embankment, and great big puffs of snow twirl down through their spare branches to disappear against the white of our coats and the ground. I can feel the flakes falling on my face. Cold little kisses that send shivers of crystalline patterns through my mind.

Somehow everything's quieter in here. Even the sounds of us struggling up the snow-covered, rocky bottom of the ravine are muffled and ghostly. My breath gusts out in front of me, then brushes back, both hot and cold on my face.

It's all so dreamlike, I almost don't realize when we've come out at the top. Don't register at first that I'm staring straight down the gaping edge of a sheer cliff. When I do realize it, though, my instincts kick in. I clench tight on Dylan's hand and take a sort of jumping step backward, my snowshoes entangling and almost sending me stumbling to the ground.

Dylan laughs and says, "There's nothing to fear." Then he lets go of me and steps right off the cliff into nothing.

He doesn't fall. He's just plain not there anymore. My heart goes leapfrogging inside my chest, and I drop down on my knees to look over the edge, calling out his name as loud as I dare.

"Don't worry," he says, as he steps back onto the ledge, materializing as if he's walking out of a waterfall or something. He leans down, kind of laughing, and offers a hand to help me back to my feet.

"It's the portal." His smile plays at the corners of his eyes and mouth. "It, essentially, folds space so that you can move between two disparate places instantaneously. To get through, you'll have to come with me. Your essensal code isn't in the system yet."

My heart's still hammering from shock, and, just at the moment, I wouldn't mind giving him a good, hard punch. But he's already grabbing my hand again and, before I can say anything, he pulls me off the ledge along with him.

I gasp as I feel the tickle of the portal pass over me. Then, with a thud, my foot hits solid ground and the world around us has changed completely. The sheer drop-off has been replaced by a gentle snowy slope, and beyond that there's an ocean of lights spreading across a gigantic valley. One vast city just sparkling away in the night, where before it was total darkness.

Dylan looks over at me and bursts out laughing, and it's such a nice sound I can't even be mad.

"You like it?" He gives a nod toward the city.

"Is it real?" I ask in response, and I'm only part joking. "That's all Painters that live down there?"

"It is."

"And there are more cities like this all around the world?"

"As well as the Painters who choose to live permanently among the Particle-Blockeds."

I'm not even sure how to describe how I feel. "It's real pretty," is all I manage, and it comes out kind of hushed like a prayer.

The trip into the city takes a couple of seconds, maybe less. With our snowshoes dissolved again and me on Dylan's back, he takes us particle sailing down the mountain to the city's edge and into this dark, damp avenue.

Apparently, it's illegal to particle sail within city limits, so we have to go at our regular pace, inching through black alley after black alley. The dim glow of lights in windows gives a sense of buildings unlike anything I've ever seen. They seem to stretch off each other like piles of giant pick-up-sticks, and I strain my eyes trying to pin down the actual shapes of them.

We've got to stop sometimes, huddle in shadows to avoid being seen by other people. After traveling most the day and not eating a real dinner, I'm pretty tired and I'm not paying attention to where it is we're going. Just following Dylan. Stopping when he says to stop, going when he says to go, while I try to take in everything we're passing.

We've been walking for well over an hour, when Dylan pauses in front of a long wall that looks exactly like any of the other dozens of walls we've passed. He presses his hand against the stones there until a doorway opens where there was definitely not a door before. Then he steps through it and holds the door open for me to follow.

On the other side, it's a tunnel of evergreens so thick I can only get brief glimpses of what might be beyond them. They arch over us with their tips twined together at the top.

When we reach the end of the tunnel several minutes later, we step out into a well-manicured and enormous garden. The moon's swallowed up in clouds now, and it's snowing hard enough that everything's blurred, but I can make out the shapes of winding sculptured hedges and many dozens of trees all covered in white.

We're right up against the side of some sort of huge building. I think there's a window or two off to my left, but they're just darker shapes against the flatness of an already dark wall. Dylan presses his hand against the building, and another invisible door melts into being there and swings open, soundless and slow.

There's something kind of creepy about it in the middle of this already weird night and, when we step into the pitch-black hallway, I try to stay as close to Dylan as I can without being creepy myself. Another door opens onto more pitch black. Then Dylan hits a switch, and the place explodes with light so sudden I wince.

We're in a curving, seemingly endless corridor—and it's definitely a *corridor*, not a hallway, if you know what I mean. Dylan's already moving down it, and I hurry to keep up with him, staring around me as we go.

The walls are a warm, polished sort of wood, all marbled with dark graining that winds around itself in pretty vine-like patterns and every once in a while, erupts into a flurry of delicately-lined flocks of sparrows in flight.

At the end of the corridor, we step into an elevator that, from the outside, looks like a big trunk of a tree growing right inside the wall. Dylan waves his hand in front of the bark, and two hulking panels slide away from each other to reveal a glowing interior that's plastered with gold chipping. There's a sliding knob on one wall, with intricately carved numbers running vertical alongside it, from zero to six. Dylan explains that in the United Kingdom, the ground floor is numbered as zero instead of one. Which, I realize, means the sixth floor is actually the seventh.

"It's the first elevator that was put into our house. One of the first in Deffro," Dylan says as he pushes the knob up to the number two, and the walls around us rumble into motion.

It's weird enough to me that he's got an elevator in his house—especially, an elevator like this—but it's the number of levels that really gets to me.

Seven floors, I'm thinking. *Who lives in a house with seven floors?*

When we get out, the corridors are the same warm-colored wood, this time with graining in the shape of elaborate peacocks. I touch my fingers to the wall as we pass, dipping down into the particles there. I note how the particle patterns in the graining are different from the patterns in the wall itself. How both are a little more fluid than the patterns I've seen in the snow and the rocks outside.

We pass several thick, old doors covered in engravings of flowers and animals and trees. Then, before I know it, we've stopped in front of one, and Dylan's opening it and switching on a light inside and gesturing for me to walk in.

It's clearly meant to be a bedroom. I mean, it's hard to miss the jumbo canopy bed squatting toward the far end. But the size of the room—well, I've never seen a space like that in anyone's house before. It's the sort of place where I imagine princesses probably slept back in the olden days, with lush, golden draperies over the windows and walls and bed, and elegant wardrobes and dressers scattered around.

Dylan steps over to the nearest wall and opens a door onto an ensuite bathroom that's about as big as my bedroom back home. There's a tub I could probably swim in and thick violet rugs that look as soft as downy fur.

"Once you've got the hang of your painting, you can control everything with these sensors on the walls," he indicates a panel lit up in a soft blue, "but it also works like a Particle-Blocked bathroom, so you should be comfortable here."

As if these weren't the most extravagant surroundings I've ever encountered in my life.

Dylan steps back into the bedroom and asks for my driver's license, saying he needs the information on it as a reference to finish creating the Sophie Warren identity.

"We breakfast at eight in the morning. I'll fetch you a little before then, take you down to meet everyone. Remember, the only person in my family who knows who you really are is my mum, so be careful not to give yourself away to the others. It's for their safety as much as yours."

He's walking to the door now like he's going to just leave me here, and I have this little burst of alarm. Like, the more steps he takes, the stranger and smaller I feel in that huge room with the huge bed and the army of wardrobes.

But once he's got his hand on the doorknob, he turns back to me. Studies my face for a minute while I try hard to hide the fact that I'm totally panicking.

"You going to be all right in here alone?" he asks, and for some reason I about lose all my cool. This weird little laugh comes out of me. A sound I'd definitely rather not have made.

"Truth is I am kind of anxious," I admit, while at the same time I'm trying to sort of wave my words away with my hand.

He smiles. "You get ready for bed. I'll be back in a few, and I'll stay with you 'til you fall asleep."

The relief's almost more embarrassing than the fear, but I hurry to get ready like he said. I hop in the shower, and I don't know whether to cry or laugh, it feels so good to have that hot water rolling down my body.

Putting on my pajamas for the first time since leaving home, it suddenly strikes me how real childish they look, with these big cartoon cows all over, grinning goofy grins. Mom always gets these sort of things a couple sizes too big too, because it "keeps you warmer," she says. They hang loose off me, which makes me look even more like a kid. So, when Dylan knocks on the door again, I jump quick into bed before telling him to come on in.

He's clean shaven and washed, and with that tacky beard gone, he's even more handsome than before. He's wearing these kind of jersey pants and a short-sleeved T-shirt, and for the first time I get a sense of how he's actually shaped. My pulse starts pounding, and I get that annoying tingle in my neck and all over, and I suddenly feel real shy about him being here at all.

He doesn't seem to think it's weird, though. Just sprawls next to me on top of the covers with his hands behind his head and looks over at me out of the corner of his eye.

With a sympathetic smile he asks, "You ready to become someone new tomorrow?"

The anxiety leaps in my chest. "Honestly, maybe not?"

He laughs.

"You're ready," he says. "Ready enough. I'll help you, and it'll be easy with the others. They'll expect you not to know much about life in a Painter city. Simply be yourself. Though, not *entirely* yourself."

He laughs again, and I can't help smiling back at him.

"What's your sister like?" I ask, and a different kind of smile springs up on his face.

"Eilian is…ionic."

"What's that?"

"Unpredictable. Energetic. A bit chaotic?"

I raise my eyebrows. "Good chaotic?"

"Wait and see. I expect you'll find she's the best sort of friend."

Saying goodnight, he props himself up on some pillows against the headboard, opening a book he's brought with him and settling in. I slide all the way under the covers and lie there watching him read, my pulse gradually slowing until all I'm thinking is how nice it is not to be alone.

I fall asleep like that, the blankets pulled up to my nose and my mostly lidded eyes turned on him. And, just for that little while, I don't feel so impossibly scared.

After a night full of dreams of my own room and my own house with my own mom in it, waking up in that strange bed covered in its billowing golden canopy feels like stepping into another dream rather than out of one.

Dylan's gone, but I've barely had a chance to bathe and clothe myself before he's knocking at the door again. He comes in real brisk and purposeful and, with a glance at my outfit, says kind of apologetic that I'm going to have to change into Painter-made clothes. He leads me over to one of the huge wardrobes, but, when he opens it, the thing's completely empty.

I watch, curious, as he taps his thumb against a black ring that I'm pretty sure he wasn't wearing yesterday. A holographic, rectangular screen made of dark purple light appears over his upturned palm.

"This is a helcom," he explains, glancing at me as a I peer over his shoulder. "Or a com for short. It's the Painter equivalent of a smartphone. Though it can do much more. For instance—"

With the slightest flick of his finger across the holographic screen, a whole closet-full of clothes materializes inside the wardrobe seemingly out of thin air. Everything already hung on sleek, wooden hangers or neatly folded on the lower shelves.

"How the—" I step in for a closer look, my eyes wide and my mouth open. A hint of Dylan's self-pleased smile hovers over his face, and I pin him down with a mock glare. "Don't you think it's a little early for your magic tricks?"

His smile quirks even deeper.

"The com holds something in it called light matter, which you can program and turn into other things. It's also what the com screen itself is made of. There's a limited amount of light matter available in the com at any given time, but it comes in handy. I've got a com for you too, but, first, you'd best dress in something more Deffro-appropriate."

He tells me to choose what I like from the wardrobe, saying it's organized into separate outfits, but that I can mix and match as I please. He adds that he selected the collection based on what's trending in Deffro now and what he thought would go with my new hairstyle. Then he takes up residence on the edge of my bed to wait for me.

I feel kind of self-conscious with Dylan sitting right there, so I just grab pretty much the first things I see and disappear into the bathroom to change.

I immediately wish I'd been more choosy. There's a leathery black bodysuit that fits, admittedly, as comfortable as my own skin, and this thin, asymmetrically hemmed tank top to go over the top of it. With dark red combat boots that look a lot heavier than they actually are. And then, to top it off, a short black, lacy biker jacket. The whole outfit's much more effortless and cool than I'll probably ever feel.

When I come out of the bathroom in the thing, it must be pretty obvious how skeptical I am because Dylan looks amused and says, "Don't worry, it suits you."

He has me sit next to him on the bed so he can show me how the helcom phone thing works before giving me my own. Apparently, even though the ring part of the com stays snug on the finger during a call, you can hear the other person's voice in your ear as clear as if they were actually in your head. If you get notifications or text messages, the com screen shows up automatically on your palm when you turn your hand toward you. A flick of your thumb against the ring projects the screen any time you want it, and you can disconnect that screen from the ring and use it totally separate. You can even stretch the screen to be about any size you want.

There's also a sensor on the palm-side of the ring and on the front of the expanded screen that, when you've got your thumb pressed over it, responds to your brain synapses, through the essensal nerves in your fingertips. So, once you know how to, you can control the whole thing by painting.

"You can access just about anything with your com," Dylan says. "Things you're probably used to, such as movies, books. The helix, which is what we call our version of the internet. But also, a lot more. You'll see, the longer you're in the city."

He pulls a small, black jewelry box out of his pocket, and opens it to reveal a glowing white, light matter ring suspended inside it. When he takes it out and has me slide it onto my pointer finger, I can sense how the particles of the thing are in constant motion, dancing around each other in complicated waves and rhythms. Pulsing with an unleashed, eager energy.

"Let me show you how to customize it." Dylan leans in, his shoulder bumping accidental against mine as he indicates where I should tap my thumb against the ring to bring up the com screen. And then, where to go on the screen to find the helcom gallery, which shows a list of probably hundreds of different options for how the ring itself can look.

Dylan lets me look closer at his own—a simple band, made out of a dark black stone that seems to glow from somewhere inside—and then points out his sister Eilian's ring in the gallery. A white gold, Celtic-looking tree, which doesn't exactly match the chaotic personality he described yesterday but is real pretty.

I think, with so many options and with Dylan staring over my shoulder, it's going to be hard to pick out the com I want, but I find it in about five seconds. A delicate dragonfly, all sparkling blues and greens, uncannily like the dragonfly that formed out of my dad's photograph back in Flemingsburg. I know it's the one as soon as I see it, and there's a hint of something in Dylan's expression that tells me he can probably guess why.

He has me hold down the dragonfly's image on the screen for three seconds, and then I feel the ring begin to change on my finger. The light matter starts to shimmer and shift and then, faster than a blink, it's transformed into the metal dragonfly ring from the gallery. The particle patterns through most the com itself are now more docile and stable, while there's still a clump of compressed light matter that I can sense in the core. I look over at Dylan in surprise and delight, and he grins back at me.

He shows me how to select the color I want my light matter screen to be. I choose blue, like my hair. Then he says, like it's nothing more than a passing thought, "I got hold of your mum, by the way," and my response is immediate.

"You *talked* to her?" He'd have to try real hard not to hear the million-and-one follow-up questions in my voice.

"First thing she asked was if she could speak with you," he says. But, when he sees the reaction on my face, he's quick to add, "Which we can't allow yet. There's more I have to set in place before I'd advise any contact. I need to be sure no one else is able to monitor her or is able to tap into your calls."

Trying not to act too disappointed, I ask, "Is she safe, then?" and Dylan nods, reassuring.

"Said it's nice to be with her brother again and get to know his family."

I don't say it, but this just makes me feel worse, picturing Mom happy without me. Reestablishing ties with some family I've never known.

"I'm still working on tightening up any loose ends with her situation," Dylan says, standing and looking down at me. "I'm setting her up in protective custody. She'll have security watching her at all times, discreetly. They won't know who she is or why she's in the program, and her brother won't be able to tell that they're there. Most of those arrangements should be finished by tomorrow afternoon. In the meantime," he holds out a hand to me, and this keen little smile flashes across his face, "let's introduce you to the rest of my family."

The house seems brighter today, even though there aren't any windows in the hallway. There's a fresh, alive smell to the air too, as if it's been pumped in straight from the garden outside.

Dylan leads me down the corridor to a wide set of marble stairs, all bright white and curving gently downward. Again, it's the sort of thing I'd expect royalty would use, with whole throngs of servants straggling behind them and trumpeters at the bottom announcing their descent. All we've got to accompany us is the heavy echoes of our shoes against the stone.

At the bottom, the staircase opens up onto a room that's literally the size of a small amphitheater. The blue stone floor is marbled with veins like enormous waves spreading out from our feet. Massive pillars the same white stone as the stairs rise up to an angled ceiling, which has got to reach at least three stories at its highest point. It's made of white marble too, with these big, lacy-edged sheets of stain glass inset all over it, showing Painters doing things like shooting light from their hands, or spinning flowered vines through the air around them, or joining palms in the *pono* greeting.

All the scenes are made of eye-popping colors, and they filter light through in shafts of softly diffused rainbow.

Dylan's already several strides into the room before he notices I'm not following. Turning to see what's wrong, he takes in the stunned look on my face and is immediately and annoyingly entertained.

"This is the great hall," he says, as if that explains everything.

"Who *lives* in a house like this?"

"As of last night, you do. Come on. Uncle Uri has probably already set the table."

The dining room, which Dylan calls the "family dining room," as if there's maybe another, is in the furthest corner from the stairway. It's lined with huge, arching windows and so many hanging potted plants you'd almost forget you were indoors. Most the room's taken up by a dining table that could probably fit upwards of twenty people, but in a far corner there's a smaller, round table set with just five plates and a spread of food that'd give most of mine and Mom's Thanksgiving dinners a run for their money. The inviting smell of it seems to fill the entire space.

There are three people sitting there—a girl about my age and a middle-aged man and woman. When Dylan and I step through the door, the three of them look around toward us all wide-eyed and curious.

The woman, who I'm guessing is Dylan's aunt, Nia Lucas, makes this excited noise and pops up out of her seat to scurry over to us.

"Oh, it's so *good* to have you here," she says, wrapping me in her arms as tight as if she actually knows me. Her hair's in my face, and she smells like flowers, and her hug's so full of exactly the kind of warmth and welcome I need this morning that, for a second, I'm afraid I'm going to cry.

Then she's pulling away and smiling at me like I'm just the sort of person she likes the most. Gripping my shoulders, she says, "Dylan's mum's told me all about you. Well, I suppose, about your mother, but I'm sure the apple doesn't fall far from the tree. Do come and eat, my dear."

She takes one of my hands and pulls me toward the table.

"No doubt you've had no proper meal while you've been traveling. And, no slight meant to our Dylan, of course, but even his culinary skills can't compare to my Uri's."

She's a short woman, sinewy and as sun-wrinkled as if she'd never spent a whole day indoors in her life. She smiles easy, and almost constant, but somehow it still feels like something special every time she flashes that smile at me. She tells me to call her Aunt Nia, like Dylan and Eilian do because, according to her, I'm officially part of the family now.

Her husband Mr. Jacoby—who she introduces to me as Uncle Uri— is a stocky man with a bald head and bright eyes and a noticeable pooch to his belly. He's gotten out of his seat to greet me, standing there with his hands behind his back and his feet slightly apart, looking real solid and imposing.

I feel pretty out of my element about now, but I hold my palm out sort of tentative for *pono,* like Rishi taught me. The man's lips twitch at that, though, and he takes a quick step forward and pulls me into a hug. His arms are substantial and strong, in the way you'd expect from someone who works with his hands on a regular basis. He and Aunt Nia, with their weathered skin and that air of hard work about them, seem like they shouldn't belong in this grand, opulent old house, but somehow, they just really do.

The girl—who I'm thinking must be Dylan's sister Eilian—stays in her seat through all of this. Eyeing me kind of critical with her head cocked to one side and her arms draped across her chair, all casual and somehow dignified.

She's dressed in loose orange pants with a green silky tank top and a sun hat, her mess of gold curls tumbling out around the bottom of the hat and framing her peach-toned face like a halo. She's pretty and petite and pixie-ish, but there's something intimidating about her too. At least, the way she's staring me down right now is more than a little disconcerting.

When she's sure she's got my attention, she leans toward me as if she's trying to get a better look. Real blunt, she says, "You don't look like a farmer," and I'm pretty sure Aunt Nia about dies.

"Eilian!" she says like scolding her niece is a regular necessity, but I catch Uncle Uri's hint of a smile, and I remember the way Dylan described Eilian last night.

"I left my overalls upstairs," I say, "and the straw hat blew off while we were traveling."

She looks at me for a few seconds.

"Careless of you," she responds as if she's totally unimpressed, but there's a smile peeping out at one corner of her mouth and, just like that, I know we're going to be friends.

"Leave off, Eilian," Dylan says, affectionate, pulling out a chair for me next to her. "We're starving."

He takes the seat on my other side while Uncle Uri dishes mounds of food onto our plates.

Aunt Nia asks about our journey, and I let Dylan tell her it was fine, that we took it slow and leisurely, and that the only difficult thing we encountered was a little too much snow. He's a real good liar. It probably shouldn't impress me, but turns out, it does.

The food's delicious. Like to the point of maybe actually blowing my mind. So, I'm content to sit there eating slow, letting the flavors develop on my tongue in ways I didn't know food could do even, and I just listen to the others talk. The conversation's mostly about their close friends and family—cousins living halfway around the world sort of thing—and it's interesting to watch how they all interact with each other.

Uncle Uri mostly sits and listens, but Aunt Nia talks in an almost stream of consciousness that's accentuated by these exclamations of "Oh! Did you know that...?" and "Ah! Have I told you...?" in varying levels of excitement, all while Dylan grins at her and does his best to respond appropriately.

Every few minutes, Eilian leans forward to deliver some imperious commentary on whatever Aunt Nia or Dylan's just said. Then she punctuates her statements by thrusting herself back into her chair again, her arms folded smug against her chest and her whole demeanor radiating a playful self-satisfaction.

They're all energized by each other, having fun. It's the most noise I've heard in days, and I'm loving it. But then the conversation lulls, and Dylan totally ruins the mood.

"Where's Gwilim?" he asks, soft and unexpected, and you can tell his question makes everyone pause.

At least, everyone except Eilian.

"Who *knows*?" She gives the nearest table leg a good, sharp kick. "He's been gone since before you left and he's not been home once. At least not that I've noticed."

"No. Nor have we seen him," Aunt Nia agrees, kind of subdued.

"Franny Demirci said she heard he's been staying at young Tom Cameron's," Uncle Uri speaks up, his eyes on Dylan and his voice sounding like he knows this is definitely not good news.

Dylan stares back at him, stony-faced. Then he looks down at his plate again and starts picking at his food with his fork, suddenly real done with a topic he brought up himself.

After breakfast, Dylan says he's got to pop into work for a while, and he asks Eilian to give me a tour of the house. She agrees, but says that, since Dylan's leaving anyway, we can start with something called the hangar. We follow him out to this huge garage where three car-sized vehicles shaped like raindrops caught in a heavy wind are just hovering there a foot off the ground, as if they're mini spaceships or something.

"They're called emvees, or electromagnetic vehicles," Dylan says with a smile in his voice as he watches me crouch down and look under one of them to make sure the thing really is floating in mid-air. "They're powered by the push and pull of electromagnetic forces. Not, like it appears you're thinking, by magic."

Eilian suggests I try out the passenger seat of Dylan's emvee, which is a soft silvery sea-foam color. Inside, it's a whole lot roomier than you'd expect from its flattened outer profile. All sleek and comfortable, with captain's chairs in the front and a bunch of light matter screens spread across the dashboard, like some alien control panel.

When I sit down, the cushioning of the chair actually sucks in to conform to the back of my body, and it's such a shock, I let out this squawk of surprise that makes Eilian burst out laughing.

She climbs into the backseat, demanding that Dylan give us a ride before he leaves. "Just around the neighborhood. To give Sophie a taste of what a Painter city's really like."

Dylan agrees and, as the emvee skims silent and gently swaying out onto their long driveway, I notice Eilian leaning forward in her seat, trying to get a look at my face. So, I know something's up.

There are loads of tall, dense evergreen trees lining the drive, and I can't see much of the garden beyond them, but I start scanning what I can see. Trying to figure out whatever it might be Eilian's so sure is going to get a reaction out of me. Other than the sheer size of their yard, though, I don't notice anything too out of the ordinary.

Then, as the line of trees drops away, I get a clear view of the outside of their house for the first time, and, at this point, I'm pretty sure my jaw drops.

"You live in a tree."

It comes out all monotone and disbelieving, and Eilian about loses it.

"It's a great big, hulking tree," I say again and look around at them, as if maybe this time they'll appreciate how weird that is. But Dylan just smiles, and Eilian laughs even harder.

I crane my neck to get a better view. Most the side and top of the emvee is a huge window, so even though their house—a weeping willow, from the looks of it—is as tall as a large office building and probably as wide, I can still see most of it. It's dotted by windows that look like hollowed out, giant knots in the trunk, with little balconies here and there and flowering vines growing all over it, and grains of something sort of silver and shimmering running in the grooves of the bark. It should look like something straight off a Keebler Elves package, but it doesn't. It's magical and charming and even kind of stately.

"Back in the early days of the Republic people took a lot of pride in shaping houses out of living plants," Dylan says. "Out of things that already existed in nature. This house has been in our family for generations."

I stare at him for a second and then jab my thumb back toward the tree. "Did you just say that thing's still alive?"

Eilian goes off in another peal of laughter, but even though Dylan grins, he answers without any hint of teasing.

"Aunt Nia cares for it. We call her the plant whisperer."

We've pulled out onto the street now, and, as we drive down the road, I see a lot of these kinds of houses. Huge trees of all varieties, towers made out of what looks like stacks of giant stones, hill houses like humongous hobbit mansions.

They're interspersed with buildings that are more recognizably man-made, built out of bricks and stone and cement and wood. Though there's always something unusual about them. Turrets jutting out at unexpected angles, walls bulging into the air where you'd never think a building should bulge. As if, even though they're manmade, these houses were still built to look like the things you'd find in nature. Made to loosely resemble mountains and plants and animals and things.

There are a lot more people out on the streets than I'd expect to see in such a residential area. People from all over the world, wearing clothes that throw together styles from all over the world, too. From probably every time period since humans started dressing themselves.

There's a dark-skinned woman dressed in knee-high riding boots, metallic leggings, and a cropped jacket and midi dress combo that's made out of bright green and yellow African-looking traditional cloth, with a dozen layers of gathered, shimmering tulle underskirts that sparkle in the morning light and make the dress puff out tutu-like. A man with long, black hair who's wearing one of those Sherlock Holmes-style cloaks printed in a neon rainbow block pattern. A kid about my age sporting a gray newsies hat and a full-length puffer jacket that somehow has an anime-style animation of a rainstorm playing across the whole surface of it. With splashing raindrops and flashes of lightning bolts and shifting clouds and everything.

After a few minutes, we hit an even busier area that seems like some sort of city center, and we have to stop at a traffic light. The lights themselves are the usual red, yellow, and green, but they're cased in decorative copper, and they hang without support, apparently just floating in the air.

Dylan's explaining to me that Painters use the same traffic signals as Particle-Blockeds because it makes it easier for people to transition back and forth between worlds, when a huge figure looms up on my side of the emvee. And, after one glance at that thing, I start to scream.

It's like something straight out of a nightmare, all long and lanky, with half a dozen tentacle-like arms and a face of shining metal. It's bent down toward my window, and it's staring at me with stone cold, pupil-less eyes.

I'm twisting around in my chair, scrambling at the seatbelt with no other thought than that I need to get away from this terrifying monster thing. It takes me a couple seconds to realize Eilian's practically cackling now and that Dylan, through his own fair share of laughter, is trying to calm me down.

"It's just a zoetic, Sophie," he's saying, his hand steadying on my arm, and it's weird to hear him address me by that name. "They wash the windows while we're stopped. It's nonsensical and unnecessary, but people find it charming to mimic the Particle-Blocked world in these little ways."

I notice the metal bucket on one of the thing's arms now, and the yellow rags in its other hands. Dylan waves the zoetic off, and it turns away and ambles back to the side of the road, its six arms hanging loose like some sort of homemade insect costume, its movements real creepily smooth.

My heart's still beating twice as fast as it should be, but I can feel my breath starting to slow down. Eilian scoots forward and flops across the shoulder of my seat, and there's still laughter in her voice when she says, "You've really never heard of steel faces?"

"If that's what that thing's called, then no. I've definitely never heard of those."

The light turns green, and Dylan starts the emvee moving forward again, saying, "They're basically service zoetics, biological machines performing whatever tasks they've been programmed for. They're used all over Deffro, as well as most other cities in the Republic."

"They give them the metal faces so that they don't make people uncomfortable," Eilian offers as if this makes a whole lot of sense.

"That face is supposed to *not* make people uncomfortable?"

They both laugh.

"It's supposed to make them less humanoid," Dylan explains.

"Right. Well, they definitely hit that nail on the head."

As we head back to the house, I notice all sorts of those things around. Tall ones and small ones, with any number of arms and legs, moving up and down the sidewalks right alongside the real people. They all have those shining steel faces, and it gives me the jeebies every time they so much as glance in our direction.

After Dylan drops Eilian and me back at home—which they refer to as "Lucas House," as if that's its official name—Eilian continues my tour of the place. Though, to call it a *tour* would be really stretching the meaning of the word. It's more like a game of hide and seek, the way she's already disappearing around corners or into another room every time I so much as pause to get a better look at something.

The hallways are maze-like, and most the rooms aren't much better. Every space is filled with family heirlooms and antique Painter artifacts. Eilian says each floor of the house was built by a different Lucas generation, carved out of the inside of the tree as it grew big enough to allow for it.

In addition to an army's worth of bedrooms, the place has loads of spaces no normal person would have in their house. Like, on the ground floor there are two entertainment rooms Eilian calls the blue and red salons as if she's stepped straight out of some old romance novel. And, on the fourth floor, there's a full-on ballroom just dripping with chandeliers and golden sconces.

Eilian says this is where they'll be holding something called an introduction party that Aunt Nia and Uncle Uri are throwing for me. Which is, she explains, a traditional way to welcome friends to Deffro for the first time. Dylan mentioned something about it on our trek through the city last night, but I pictured it as something small. Just family. When Eilian announces that at least a hundred people have already confirmed they're coming, I'm guessing I look exactly as horrified as I feel.

"Mum bought you a dress," Eilian says, already on her way out of the ballroom and completely oblivious to the effect her words've had on me. "And jewelry. Aunt Nia's got it hung up in her room as inspiration for the party design."

I groan and make another face that Eilian doesn't see. In my place, my friend Sylvia'd probably die of happiness over a party like that, but mostly I just feel overwhelmed.

One wing on the third floor of the house seems a little mustier than the others. A little less commonly used, with all sorts of extra weird oddities and stuff stashed away. Things like a huge, Gothic-style mirror or an antique Particle-Blocked printing press. With all the dust and cobwebs that've gathered, everything sends strange shadows crawling along the floors and walls.

Eilian has even less time to give this part of the house, as if she thinks whatever might be here isn't worth our attention. But it's exactly the sort of place I bet some ominous, ghostly figure would be roaming around. So, maybe I'm already a bit primed for a haunting by the time we pass the nook at the end of one of the corridors.

It's not an inherently creepy nook. There's a comfortable-looking, cushioned bench seat and a shelf with a few books on it. What makes it creepy is the snarling brass dog's head that's hanging on the wall right smack above the bench.

There's no light on in the nook and the dim light from the hallway falls across the dog's features at just the right angle to make it look pretty downright terrifying.

"What is *this*?" I ask, kind of laughing and stopping in the arched entryway in fascinated disbelief.

But, as usual, Eilian just shrugs and keeps walking, barely looking over her shoulder to say it probably belonged to one of her long dead ancestors.

I can't turn away from the thing. I mean, despite the fact it's made from brass, it's mesmerizingly life-like. I wouldn't be surprised if any second now it turned its metal eyes down on me and made a quick lunge for my jugular.

So, that's where I am—rooted in that dim hallway, staring at the dog, with the sound of Eilian's footsteps disappearing around the corner again—when I feel suddenly sure there's someone else in the hall behind me. Someone standing real still and real close.

I turn around. Moving slow as if whoever's there can't really exist until I'm actually seeing them. No one *is* there, though. It's just the empty hallway and the soft swishing sounds of Eilian's steps as she abandons me.

Except, I can still feel the energy of a person there, even though I can't see anyone. Not an essence, but a sensation so strong, I'm pretty sure if I reached my hand out, I'd definitely make contact with some physical being.

Just a few seconds ago, all the spookiness was kind of fun. Like the harmless thrill of scary stories at a slumber party. Now, I'm thinking about the fact that there are real people in this world who want to harm me. People whose powers I know way too little about and who, for all I know, could be standing there right in front of me, invisible to my eye and trying to decide how best to kill me.

The unseen person—or thing, or whatever—isn't moving, and I can't make myself move either. Part of me wants to reach out and touch it, to find out if there really is something in that pocket of energy hanging in the air. The rest of me wants to run.

The sound of Eilian's footsteps abruptly stops and, for a heavy three seconds, I hear nothing from her at all. There's just this terrible quiet that makes me sure the same ominous, invisible force has gotten hold of her too. Then her voice sounds out, loud and clear down the hall.

"Are you coming?" she calls, and her tone of teasing impatience totally breaks the spell.

Of course, no one else is there with me. It's so suddenly obvious no one ever was. I probably just let the setting get to me—let my imagination run a little too wild again—and now, standing here in a glaringly empty hallway, I'm feeling pretty foolish about it.

Swearing, sheepish, to myself that no one else will ever hear this story, I hurry after Eilian, shooting one quick glance behind me as I go. You know, just in case.

Dylan comes home for lunch, and afterward he takes over the house tour, saying there's only a couple places left to see. We use the main elevator, which runs up the center of the tree house. The inside is covered in the same golden gilding as the other elevator, but with hundreds of little odd-shaped mirrors too, so no matter where you look, your own reflection's staring back at you many times over.

Dylan waves his hand across one of the mirrors, and the elevator controls appear as a golden white light matter panel. Elaborate, glowing designs wrap around the numbers zero through six, coming together in a Celtic knot at the top.

He takes us to the fifth floor first, to show me where his room is, in case I ever need to find him. To get there, we've got to pass through a gym that has a tall, domed ceiling and pegs and ledges all over the walls. It's pretty big—at least as large as the gym in Logan's church building back in Flemingsburg—but after everything else I've seen in Deffro today, I'm not all that surprised the Lucases have a space like that in the middle of their home.

Dylan's bedroom is about as different from mine as a room could be. It's modern and sleek, and from the ceiling right down to the threading in the quilt on his bed, everything's a bright, crisp white with just a few pops of color here and there.

The only thing about the place that seems at all disorderly is the built-in bookcases lining one wall. There are so many books in there, it looks like some kind of literary explosion. Books are squeezed in at every angle, double- and triple-parked on the shelves. And they're nearly all real well-worn like they've been lovingly and frequently handled.

"We'll want to train every evening, when it's feasible," he tells me. "And this is probably the best place to do it, since we've got the gym outside, and no one else's rooms are near mine."

We head back to the elevator, and I think he's going to take us to the sixth floor, but instead he taps on the Celtic knot at the top of the control panel. I thought the thing was just for decoration, but as soon as he's touched it, the elevator starts moving.

"This takes us to the aerie," he says. "It was my parents' pet project until—" He pauses just long enough for me to notice. "Until they had to stop working on it. The part I want to show you, though, has been there for a few generations."

We ride the elevator up for what must be at least six more stories, and when the doors open finally, I'm not real sure what I should expect. There's a hallway, a bit narrower than on the other floors. It's still made of that sunny-colored wood that's all over the house, but up here there aren't any of the bird designs in it. The hall leads to a small reading room that's lined in cushioned benches, with a few other loungey chairs and strategically placed side tables.

The far wall's made almost entirely of glass, and Dylan walks straight over, opening a couple French doors and waiting for me to step through. They lead to a balcony, so high up it almost feels like we're flying. The house's huge willow branches drape in front of us, framing the Deffro cityscape in a way that makes me stop dead in my tracks.

All those jumbo tree houses and green hill mansions rising up next to monumental desert buttes—that was pretty amazing to see from the ground, but from up here it's something out of a dream. Even more eye-boggling, off to the left are skyscrapers that I'm guessing must mark downtown Deffro. I've never seen anything like them. There's a fifty-story orca bursting off the ground as if out of water, a jumbo-sized bird poised like it's just landed on feet that seem way too delicate to support an entire building.

Most of the other skyscrapers aren't inspired so directly by real-life things, but they're still much less buildings than they are works of art. Every surface is smooth as still water and wears the light of the sun like a cloak, softly shimmering as though the city itself were made of quivering candles, and I understand now what Dylan meant when he called Deffro a light in the mountains.

As a backdrop to all this, the towering, snow-covered peaks sit like kings against the dusk-tinged slate blue of the afternoon sky. I can't come up with a single word to say. I'm just standing there, staring at it all and thinking that I couldn't imagine a better version of heaven.

Dylan steps over to the balcony's edge, leans against the carved wooden railing and looks back at me with a gratified smile, as if my appreciation for his city is somehow a compliment to him.

"Deffro shows its best from up here, doesn't it?"

As an answer, I just move to the railing next to him to stare over the side for a better view. We're so high right now, I can actually smell the cold. Dylan takes a tiny step closer to me, places his hand on the railing next to mine, and I can sense him heating the space around us. Sense more movement in the particles in the air. It's cozy and kind of intimate.

"Well," he straightens and turns toward me, grabbing for my hand.

"What're you doing?" I ask, taken off guard by the sudden flare of essensal energy that sparks between our fingers and reverberates up my arm.

"Helping you call my mum," he says, pushing my thumb against the back of my dragonfly ring to bring up the com screen. Then he takes the screen in his own hand like you would a cell phone, typing some numbers in and hitting send. When his mom answers, he says a string of words in what I'm guessing is Welsh. Then he's handing the com to me, and any cozy feeling I might've had before is gone in a snap.

I take the screen from him, but not because I want to. My insides feel suddenly like something's in there that's alive. I mean, what is he thinking, springing a conversation with his mom on me like this? You've got to give a person time to prepare.

But turns out his mom's got the same knack as Aunt Nia for making you feel worthwhile. She tells me to call her Gweneth, like I'm just any other friend of hers and not a kid.

"I'm sure Dylan will do his best to make you comfortable in our home," she tells me. "Cadfan's sister Nia, and Uri as well. But if you find you're in need of anything they can't provide, do feel free to contact me. I've asked Dylan to put my number into your com, and I hope to come for Gathering Day in a week or so. It's a holiday we celebrate much like Christmas, and I wouldn't want to miss your first experience with it."

We don't talk for too long. She says she's got to help her parents ready themselves for bed.

"Maybe someday you can visit us here in the Philippines. From everything Dylan's said, I think my parents would really like to know you."

When we say our goodbyes, Dylan grabs for my com screen again and starts entering a new number. "I'm adding my com to your directory, as well as my secure line. Never text me anything that could hint at your being Way Reader, and only use the secure number in the case of emergencies. If anyone were to hack into your com somehow, we don't want it to be a frequent contact."

He hands my screen to me and reminds me how to shrink it back into the ring. Then he reaches into his pocket and pulls out a small gray envelope.

"Here's your new Wyoming driver's license," he says. "And a Sophie Warren passport, to add further credence to your identity."

It's weird to look at those ID cards and see my own face, framed with my shining blue super-hero hair. Dylan clearly just altered the photo from my actual driver's license and put it on this one, but he's made my hair a bit shorter, even, than it is now. To give the impression time's passed since the IDs were issued, he tells me.

Looking down at those things, holding them in my hands—for the first time in days the idea of living this secret identity actually feels kind of cool. I smile up at Dylan.

"This makes me an official spy now, right?" I ask, and he lets out a soft laugh.

"You still need more training. Which," he glances around the balcony, "we might as well do now."

He pulls a couple of the smallest chairs out of the reading room inside and sets them up facing the balcony railing.

Looking at me over the top of the chairs, he says, "I can't teach you much about how to be a reader, but I can teach you self-defense and how to control your sightings, so that they don't keep sending you stumbling to the ground. Won't take long for people to suss you out if they realize you're already getting sightings at this point in your development."

He has me sit down while he sets up another bubble of heat around us, so it's almost as warm as if we were inside the house. For some reason, I'm kind of nervous as he sits in the chair next to me. Like maybe I'm not going to be able to do all this painting and reading stuff after all. Like maybe I'm just a dud.

"Today's focus will be meditations," he says. "They'll help you learn how to channel your essensal energy and receive sightings without giving away visible signs."

Digging into his pocket, he pulls out a book and hands it to me. It's about the size of a notecard and less than a quarter-inch thick. The pages are curled at the edges, and most the cover's torn off, as if the book's been carried around in his pocket and read every single day.

"It details a variety of effective meditations," Dylan explains. "I'll teach you a few today, and you can look over the rest later. But, before you can understand what's in the book, you'll need to know the basic principles behind particle painting."

Propping his feet against the wooden rungs of the balcony railing in front of us, he slumps all casual in his chair in a way that reminds me of Eilian.

"You're probably getting well used to seeing the particle world now. Tomorrow, we'll teach you how to interact with it, but for the time being, all you need to know is that intent equals force. You simply will your mind to reach out and make matter do what you wish it to do."

He expands his com and pulls a set of notes up on the screen. As he scrolls through with one hand, he taps sort of absent at his temple with the other, running his fingers through his hair every once in a while, in a way I find just a little distracting.

"So, for instance," he glances up from his notes, "the easiest interaction is to make something hotter or colder, which is why one of the most common Painter weapons is fire. It takes little of your own energy. Just a bit of heat and some molecular kindling."

He pauses to reference something else in his notes and then continues.

"You've likely noticed particles are usually in motion. If they're moving slowly, that typically translates to a lower overall temperature for the material they compose. More movement means more heat, except with light matter, where the particles are always moving quickly without generating noticeable warmth."

I turn my attention to the book in my hand, look down into its particles to see what Dylan's describing. Most of them are moving slow except around where I'm holding it with my fingers, where my body heat must be speeding the particles up.

"So, the idea is that if you want to make something warmer, you'd simply will the particles to move faster and—"

Before he can get any further, this burst of flame ignites in my hand, shooting skyward and pretty nearly singeing my eyebrows off. I drop the burning book on the balcony floor and jump backwards in my chair. At the same time, Dylan's springing to his feet, his com screen disappearing in the grip of his tight fist and his eyes fixed on me.

He's positioned as if ready for an attack, but his mouth's gaping open in such comical surprise, I can't help if I start laughing. It only takes him a second to recover, and then he nearly smiles too and drops down to the ground where the book's still burning. With a quick movement of his hand, the flames are gone, and he's looking up at me with a sort of bewildered expression.

"Was that you?" he asks, like he almost can't believe it.

"Think so." I nod, still doubtful myself. I glance at the book on the ground in front of him. It's barely more than a burnt binding now. "Me and your beloved book of meditations, I guess. Sorry about that."

"I can always print another," Dylan says, sitting back on his haunches and studying me, this strange little smile growing across his face. "Well, that was unexpected. Looks like I'll have to reevaluate the pace I'd planned for your trainings."

I've never had anyone look at me that way before—like I'm a surprise to them and like that's a good thing—and I really don't know what to do with it. Dylan gets back into his chair, leaning forward with his forearms on his knees and his eyes still turned toward me, considering.

"I wasn't planning on it today, but why not keep working on

painting, then?" he says. "We can do the meditations after."

He pulls some light matter out of his com and turns it into something that looks like clay. He calls it a practice ball, and he shows me how to influence the speed of its particles in a more controlled way, trying to get the temperature of the thing where I want it.

Every once in a while, he reaches over and wraps his fingers around my wrist. To get a better sense of what it is I'm doing on the particle level, he says. And every time he does it, I can feel my ignus start to light up at the back of my neck and my pulse beat a little quicker.

He keeps commenting on how fast I'm picking up painting, but it'd probably be a whole lot faster if he'd keep his pretty hands to himself.

When he thinks I've got the hang of heating and cooling, he has me practice making fire, for self-defense. Using particles from my shirt sleeve as a sort of controlled kindling and shooting flames off into the air beyond the balcony.

After that, we run through a few meditations he says should help me with channeling my sightings, and with painting in general. Then he takes my com again and downloads an electronic copy of the meditation book, telling me that before I go to bed tonight, I should look through it.

We've been training for hours, and the sun is hanging low in the sky when Dylan gets a text message from Uncle Uri saying that dinner's ready. The message also says that some of Eilian's friends are joining us. I'm not sure how I feel about meeting even more people today, and Dylan must see it on my face because he says, with a heavy dose of apology, "I suppose it *will* help establish you as Sophie Warren in Deffron society."

I try to keep that in mind, but it's one thing to play act that I'm Sophie Warren with Dylan's family, who seemed pretty primed to accept me from the start. I've got no idea how Eilian's friends will react to me. So, when we step off the elevator on the first floor and we're met with the sound of voices and laughter, I feel my whole body go tense with nerves.

Along with Aunt Nia, Uncle Uri and Eilian, there are three other people in the great hall, near the front door and the bottom of the big marble stairs. One of them is probably the tallest girl I've ever seen, who looks exactly how I imagine a real superhero would look. With wide, strong shoulders and thick, strong legs, and muscles that stand out on her arms even when she's not moving. Her skin's a warm, medium brown, and she's got lush, black curls that tumble down the length of her back, accented by shimmering gold streaks. As we approach the group, she makes some sort of joke that I only half hear, but it must be funny because everyone bursts out laughing.

The kid next to her is only slightly shorter, with light brown skin. Even though I don't know the Deffron fashion trends too well, I'm pretty sure he'd be considered real stylish. He's got a precise, black pompadour hairdo, bright white sneakers, and a black leather bomber jacket that has shoulder pads for days. He stands with a subtle swagger, his hips pushed forward like he's purposefully highlighting the pooch of his belly as another feature in his overall look.

He's got his arm around the shoulders of another kid, who's all soft and tentative and almost shockingly adorable. With big, amber-colored eyes and bleached, wavy blond hair, and an openness to his round, copper-toned face that makes me feel like I could safely tell him my most personal secrets.

Dylan and I are only a few feet away when Aunt Nia notices us, and she couldn't be more excited to introduce me to Eilian's friends, calling them "some more of the family" and practically pushing me into the center of the group. She says the tall girl is Leti Moeaki, the pompadour-haired kid is Min-suk Holm, and the other kid is Min-suk's boyfriend, Rafael Silva.

"He moved here from Refúgio, Brazil only a few months ago," Aunt Nia says. "So, Sophie, you aren't the only transplant among us."

When I exchange *pono* with Rafael, he flashes me a shy smile. And the fact that a kid that cute also has that cute a smile seems pretty categorically unfair. Exchanging *pono* with Leti is more than a little intimidating, since, despite her huge, welcoming smile, her eyes bore into me like they could literally pin me in place where I stand.

It's *pono* with Min-suk that causes the problem, though. As soon as our palms touch, I'm unexpectedly washed over with the feeling of a sighting coming on, and I have just enough warning to throw my mind pretty desperate into one of the meditation methods Dylan taught me.

Luckily, even though it takes about all my will power, I do manage to channel the energy of the sighting in a somewhat controlled way.

As in, I don't fall over or anything, but I do go real still, just trying to hold myself together while the thing moves through me. Which is difficult, because my mind's suddenly filled with an image of Min-suk in a dark room by himself somewhere, weeping wild and grabbing in desperation at the skin of his own face.

When I come out of the sighting, I'm staring at him. Blank-faced and startled, our palms still together and his eyebrows furrowed in a curious kind of concern.

"Still getting used to *pono*," I'm quick to say, smiling rueful, as if my behavior was simply a reaction to the tiny spark of energy that our hands exchanged, and as if I hadn't just done *pono* with Leti and Rafael without a problem.

I'm not expecting Min-suk to buy this explanation. But maybe he thinks it's none of his business because all he does is give me a polite smile and a nod. Then turns back to the conversation with the rest of the group, unburdened by the knowledge that I, like some psychic peeping Tom, just intruded into what I'm guessing must be one of his most private moments. If he knew what I'd seen, I doubt he'd be too happy about it, and I try to imagine what could make someone as self-possessed as he seems to be feel that much anguish.

The others are all so caught up in each other, that nobody seems to have noticed my weird reaction to Min-suk. At least, nobody but Dylan, whose eyes are on me, narrowed and unsettled. He moves in closer and leans his head down like he's about to say something quiet in my ear, but then the doorbell rings. A chiming arpeggio coming from somewhere up near the great hall ceiling.

"I wonder who that could be?" Aunt Nia says, starting toward the door, but Leti holds her back by sliding in next to her and putting her arm over her shoulders.

"Yeah, who knows?" she asks, her voice performatively loud as she exchanges a knowing glance with Min-suk.

"Dylan, maybe you should go see," Min-suk adds, similarly performative.

Everyone looks at Dylan then, who looks, in turn, between Min-suk and Leti.

"Shall I?" he asks kind of skeptical, but when they just look back at him real innocent, he shakes his head and decides to humor them.

"This had better not be a prank," he calls over his shoulder as he walks to the door.

It seems like the only people that know what's going on are Min-suk and Leti, so I don't feel too bad about feeling completely in the dark. That is, until Dylan opens the door.

From where I'm standing, I've got a clear view of the person waiting on the other side, and she's gorgeous. With radiant, dark skin and thick, black coils of hair cascading around her head. Dark eyes so brilliant it's like they actually sparkle when the light hits them.

Dylan's stunned to see her there. I can see it in the slackness of his jaw, in the sudden stillness of his arms as they hang at his sides.

The girl hesitates on the doorstep for just a second, and then she steps into the house, smiling at Dylan like he's a bright light after a long night. Each move she makes is a little piece of poetry. Like she's in precise control of every muscle in her body.

She reaches up toward him and slips her hand around the back of his neck for *ramu*. When she kisses him on the mouth like she's done it a hundred times before, his whole body pulls in to meet hers, and my heart just sort of sinks.

Don't get me wrong. I know I'm not in love with Dylan or anything. I mean, he's gorgeous. But, really, I think it's just that he's the only one in Deffro right now who I'm allowed to be myself with, and I guess I felt like I had some sort of claim on him. Like he was, in some small way, kind of my territory or something.

Seeing him with this girl now, though—seeing the way he looks at her as they pull away from their kiss, the way his hands linger on her body as if they've always just belonged there—I'd be pretty dense not to realize the only person's territory he's probably ever been is hers.

"Teresa!"

Eilian's eyes are fixed so dumbfounded and happy on this new girl that, with her blond curls falling around her face, she looks about as bright as the sun itself.

She lets out this squeal so unlike anything I'd expect to come out of her and takes off running. She ploughs into the new girl's arms, and they exchange *ramu*, laughing and talking at the same time.

Eilian's as giddy as a schoolgirl, and for some reason that kind of hurts.

Aunt Nia joins them too, Uncle Uri right behind her, and their pleasure at seeing this Teresa person is only slightly more contained than Eilian's. They offer their own hugs, their own *ramu*. Aunt Nia, in that way she does, is talking about a mile a minute.

"I didn't know if you'd ever be back," she repeats about every other sentence, giving Dylan these little side hugs as if half her excitement's really on his behalf.

"I just got in this afternoon," Teresa says.

Leti and Min-suk, and Rafael with them, also move to greet Teresa, leaving me standing there, not sure what to do with myself. Seems awkward to step forward and butt in on everything, but it'd be weird to just sit here and watch them too. I'm thinking maybe I could sneak into the dining room and wait for everyone there, but then Uncle Uri mentions dinner's on the table, and he asks Teresa if she'd like to stay.

She does this thing where she touches him all affectionate on his arm and smiles with her beautiful eyes, and says, "I've been *dying* for some of your home cooking," as if she really has just been wasting away somewhere without it.

Then they're all turning back toward the dining room, and I've lost my opportunity to sneak in before them. On reflex, I step closer to the wall below the marble stairs and do my best not to be seen, but Aunt Nia catches sight of me. She blurts out my name like she's only now remembered my existence, and I freeze, trying hard not to look like someone who's been lurking this whole time.

As everyone else turns to look at me, Aunt Nia's already bustling across the floor with her arms outstretched, so I feel like I've got to meet her halfway. She takes me by the shoulders and spins me around in front of her, holding me out toward Teresa like I'm some sort of life-sized doll.

"This is the newest addition to our family," Aunt Nia proclaims over my shoulder, while I pretend to myself that I'm not entirely uncomfortable with this situation. "Sophie's the daughter of one of Gweneth's old friends, and she's staying with us in preparation for painting academy."

Teresa graces me with a smile, but it's real mechanical and polite. As if she's trying to figure out what sort of person I am before she decides how to treat me. Still, faced full-on with that magazine-worthy face of hers, it's hard not to hope she's at least a little impressed by my alpha-blue hair.

"Welcome to Deffro," she says, and even though the way she says it is friendly, I still end up feeling like she's doing me a huge favor just by acknowledging me at all. "I'm starting my last year at painting academy next term. It's so nice to meet you."

She steps forward to do *pono*, but somehow the greeting doesn't feel so much like an exchange. Her eyes pierce mine with a cold sort of scrutiny. Then, as soon as politeness would allow for it, she's already turning away from me and slipping her hand back into Dylan's.

The only other person who seems to notice anything strange about this interaction is Rafael, who meets my eye with a surprisingly impish grin, like the two of us are sharing some private joke. What that joke may be, I couldn't say for certain, but the kid has the sort of smile I can't help but return.

All through dinner, Teresa laughs with everyone, flirts harmless with Uncle Uri, asks Rafael and me exactly the kinds of questions you're supposed to ask new acquaintances. But, the whole time, I get the feeling all her energy's focused on Dylan. Like, I'm willing to bet she's real keenly aware of about every breath he takes.

And he's aware of her, watching her like she's some unaccountable blessing that's just come blowing into his life and might go blowing back out of it again any second.

I understand his feelings. I mean, everything about her pretty much demands she be adored. And it's not just her looks either. There's an energy to her that's hypnotizing. A vibrancy that, the more I watch her, makes me think I'd be hard pressed not to fall in love with her myself.

I've ended up seated opposite her, with Rafael and Min-suk on one side of me and Leti and Eilian on the other, and I have to say that Eilian's friends are pretty great. Leti, for one, seems to have an endless supply of jokes and laughter. Just about anything anyone says, she finds some comedy angle to it. Especially when it comes to Eilian and Min-suk. The banter between the three of them is like something out of a book or a movie.

It's only made better by how much Rafael clearly enjoys it. If I thought he had an adorable smile, it's nothing compared to the laugh on that kid. It's the bubbliest sound I've ever heard come out of a person. Add to it his habit of clapping his hand over his mouth like his laughter is a physical thing that's at risk of spilling out of him.

It's no wonder Min-suk is openly delighted by everything Rafael does, but he's not alone. Leti and Eilian sometimes seem to be competing to make Rafael laugh, and I get the impression that even

Teresa's enchanted with him. Which, just based on my first impression of her, is kind of saying a lot.

Turns out, she and Min-suk are cousins on their mothers' sides, and that Teresa's staying with Min-suk's family while she's in town. The two of them couldn't be more different, though. Min-suk definitely acts more sure of himself than I will probably ever feel, with the way he lounges in his seat, his arm stretched over the back of Rafael's chair like he'd be completely at home in any space and with any group of people.

But Min-suk also seems genuinely interested in others. Like, every few minutes, he's bending around Rafael to ask me about myself. Looking me in the eye and listening intently to whatever vague tidbit I feel is safe to share without giving myself away. He's not the only one who makes an effort to draw me into conversation, but out of everyone, he and Rafael seem the most instinctively sincere.

In fact, every time Min-suk talks to me, Rafael turns his attention on me too, and the combined effect of the two of them is something else. They've apparently only been dating a few months, but they seem like they just belong together. Like some natural law of physics must've brought them to each other, and it'd take an act of god to tear them apart.

Actually, the rapport between all four of the friends seems like something concrete and everlasting. So much so that, despite everyone's efforts to include me, I can't help feeling like the odd person out. It doesn't help that watching them all interact reminds me of my Flemingsburg friends, which makes me feel increasingly homesick as the meal wears on.

I wonder what Sylvia and Logan are doing right now. If they bought the premise that Mom and I left on a sudden vacation, or if they're stressing out because we disappeared.

After dinner, everyone heads upstairs to the family den to eat cookies and sit cozy together by the glowing fire. With our chairs pulled in close and warm blankets tucked around our legs, Aunt Nia starts probing Teresa about what she's been doing for however many months it is she's been gone.

Apparently, Teresa's reason for leaving in the first place had something to do with Dylan and Eilian's dad, Cadfan. Or really, the fact that, after Cadfan was convicted of treason, Teresa's stepdad didn't want that same shame to leak over onto her. So, he carted her off to his old family home in Minnesota, and he wouldn't let her come back until her painting academy threatened to rescind her position at the school. Almost wouldn't let her come back even then, which I guess is why her being here is such a surprise to everyone.

"When he finally agreed to allow it, I didn't want to give him a chance to change his mind," she explains, her gaze flicking over toward Dylan as if she can't help herself. "So, I left for Deffro without letting anyone here know I was on my way, as soon as I could get my things together. I thought it would be a fun surprise."

"She showed up out of the blue this afternoon," Min-suk says. "I've rarely seen my sisters so excited."

It's practically a modern-day Romeo and Juliet scenario, with Teresa and Dylan as the main characters. I look at him—at the way he's looking at her—and if she's someone that can eat him up inside like that, it kind of gets to me that he hadn't mentioned her even once.

I'm trying not to be mopey about all this, about the way Eilian's friends and Teresa being here has put some special light in everyone's eye. The way the four of them seem to complete the whole family picture, while I keep feeling like a fly on the wall.

Probably their arrival hasn't actually changed anything. Probably it's just highlighting a truth that was already there. That no matter how much the Lucas family may like me, that doesn't mean I belong yet. Simply being here doesn't make me one of the family like Teresa and Leti and Min-suk—even Rafael—clearly are. No matter how many times Aunt Nia says otherwise.

The conversation eventually changes to other things. Talk of mutual friends and family. Stuff happening in Deffro and throughout the Republic. I've got nothing to add to any of it, so I just sit and listen.

At one point, Eilian breaks the cheery mood by mentioning something about people with troubled minds being found wandering the streets lately. There are murmurs of acknowledgment from some of the others, but Dylan seems as much in the dark on this topic as I am.

He had been talking in low tones with Teresa about something they both apparently found amusing, but now he turns his full attention on his sister and asks, "What's this about troubled minds?"

Eilian gives a little shrug. "They started showing up out of nowhere. Most of them seeming not to have bathed in weeks. Complaining of headaches and unable to remember their own names."

Teresa, I notice, has gone real quiet. Her eyes are on Eilian with a guarded sort of intensity, and her mouth's shut tight and tense.

"With all of them appearing over the last several days and the increase in people disappearing, the entire city's getting antsy," Minsuk says, and, from the tone of his voice, I'm guessing that by, "the entire city," he particularly means himself.

"Some people are saying it's all the work of the Sons of Morning." Leti catches Dylan's eye with an uncharacteristic seriousness, and I swear there's some sort of understanding or message in that look. Some shared worry or knowledge. Something below the surface that neither of them seems to want to say out loud.

In fact, I'm getting the impression there's a whole lot of unspoken somethings simmering under everything right now. Safely shielded, secret thoughts behind every pair of eyes in the room.

Even Aunt Nia's gone surprisingly quiet, and she and Uri are watching the rest of us like they're seeing the unspoken somethings too and they're worried over it.

The laughter and cheer from just a few minutes ago seem ages away, and I feel even more out of my element than ever, not knowing what's going on.

Then Rafael, his voice coming out in barely more than a whisper, murmurs, "This is what the Way Reader's supposed to be for," and every muscle in my body goes taut.

Dylan real pointedly does not look at me, but I can see the added tension in his face too. Everyone else is silent, and I don't even dare to breathe. Don't dare to do anything that'd draw attention to me.

"Let's hope she begins her work soon," Uncle Uri says finally, and it sounds to me like some sort of prayer.

Dylan lets that thought resonate through the room, and then quietly changes the subject, mentioning that his mom Gweneth said she's wanting to come soon for Gathering Day. His eyes meet mine then, just for a second, and I do my best to welcome in the reassurance he's trying to convey.

Eilian demands to know when he talked to their mom, and Nia and Uri press him for more details. Then the conversation moves on to Gathering Day in general and who else will be having family travel in for festivities.

Somehow, things move from that to the subject of transfiguring, and the mood grows slowly lighter again. Apparently, Eilian, Leti, Min-suk and Rafael had their transfigurings within the last couple months, and they've got a lot to say. Pretty soon, everyone else is talking about their own experiences too.

I'm surprised by how nostalgic they all are about it. They go over every detail as if they're reliving some charming memory. Even Uncle Uri laughs about having his transfiguring during his family's celebration of Rosh Hashanah, saying something about it being symbolic because of the holiday's themes of creation and renewal.

All the while, I sit and listen and think that their transfiguring experiences sound like a series of minor annoyances compared to my nightmare days.

It's only Eilian that's having none of the sentimentality.

"I don't know how you all can be so cavalier about it. I thought it was rubbish. All my life, I heard talk of it as some quaint spell of feebleness while everyone cosseted and cooed over you, but there was nothing quaint about it."

Everyone laughs, but Eilian's not finished.

"No, really. Didn't you think it was miserable?" She turns to me for support—maybe because I'm the only one who hasn't spoken up yet—and I'm surprised at how gratifying it is. How glad I am for a chance to join the conversation.

"Um, yes," I say, real emphatic, and my eye catches Dylan's long enough for me to notice a hint of a smile tug at the corners of his mouth.

"Like, the nausea went straight through to my bones," Eilian continues.

"Right." I could barely describe it better.

"And that tickle to your skin you just can't be rid of. Drove me half mad."

I nod some more.

"Then there were the raving hormones. It was like…it was like…" She pauses as if she can't quite conjure up the words, and I don't even think before diving right in to help her.

"Like you wanted to jump on pretty much any guy that came near you?"

When Dylan bursts out laughing—this full-bodied thing without any of his usual reserve—I realize too late that obviously he'd guess he's the only person I could really be talking about.

My cheeks go hot, and my eyes flash over toward him, but then Aunt Nia—almost as if she can't help herself—blurts out, "Oh, it's so *nice* to hear that sound again," and Dylan's laughter just dies in his throat.

He looks like he was caught stealing or something. As in, there's actual shame on his face. Aunt Nia too—she clamps her jaw shut tight, raises her hand halfway to her mouth as if she's horrified with the words that just came out of her.

The whole atmosphere of the room's gone awkward. And, from everyone else's expressions, I'm willing to bet I am, yet again, the only one who doesn't understand why. Even Rafael seems to have some sort of clue.

It's Teresa that saves the day. Real quiet and unobtrusive, she takes Dylan's hand in hers and leans around him to look at Aunt Nia.

"You almost didn't make the transfiguring deadline for your first year at academy, isn't that right?" she asks as if nothing at all weird just happened, and Aunt Nia couldn't look more grateful for the escape.

"Yes. Exactly," she nods, shooting a quick glance at Dylan, who's already trying his best to act normal again too. "And if I'd started even one term later, I might never have met Uri."

Back in my room half an hour later, I can't help feeling just a little sorry for myself. I mean, after Teresa's quick recovery, everyone was eager enough to save the mood, but they couldn't fix it totally. That unspoken uneasiness was still there in the air, making me feel weirdly left out. Just another thing that ties them together and keeps me on the outside.

Standing with my back against my door and looking around my bedroom that still feels so big it could swallow me, what I want to do most of all is talk to Mom. Or Sylvia or Logan. Or Rishi. But I can't talk to any of them right now. So, after washing my face and getting into my pajamas, I flop onto the top of my bed and just lie there, staring at the huge canopy above me.

After a while, I doze off, my legs hanging part off the bed and my head sandwiched between two of the huge pillows. My mind drifts through half-familiar images, things I recognize from the first rush of sightings I had when I touched Dylan's skin back in Flemingsburg. I keep trying to make sense of them, trying to organize everything in a way that might mean something. But, when I start to come back to consciousness again, I can't hold onto any of it. The images go falling haphazard away until I can't even remember what most of them were.

What's there instead is an eerie, familiar feeling. The sense—growing slowly stronger—that I'm not the only one in the room.

I sit bolt upright, tucking my legs under me and pushing myself flat against the thick wooden headboard of my bed. Just like this afternoon, I don't see anyone there and I can't locate any essence, but at the foot of the bed—right where it just *feels* like someone is—there's a deep impression in the quilt, as if it's being pressed down by the weight of something unseen.

In the morning, I'm the first one at the breakfast table, after Aunt Nia and Uncle Uri. That's because I've been awake ever since the sun came up. And that's because I didn't exactly sleep much, on account of my mysterious invisible guest.

I tried to talk to the thing. At least, I asked who it was and what it wanted, but it didn't respond. What it did do was disappear. As in, both the feeling of its presence and the weight of it on the bed just faded away. Which means it's not only invisible. It can teleport.

You can bet I didn't wait around to see if it was coming back. I booked it out into the hallway to the central elevator, and I found Dylan's room after only a couple wrong turns and several moments of panic. Just as I was about to knock on his door, though, I heard Teresa in there laughing a bell-like little laugh and, turns out between her and a ghost, I'm less afraid of a haunting.

I spent the rest of the night locked in my own bathroom, trying to sleep in a nest of blankets and pillows I'd piled on the floor even though I was well aware the closed bathroom door was no real defense against that ghost thing. Which is, of course, why sleep wasn't exactly forthcoming.

So, I'm antsy this morning, waiting real impatient for Dylan to come down to breakfast and hoping I can get a moment to talk to him alone before he heads off to work. When Dylan does come into the room and there's no sign of Teresa, I feel kind of guilty at how much a relief that is. I guess I'd been picturing her as an unavoidable constant in my life.

Dylan's in a good mood, greeting everyone cheerily and humming quiet to himself as he fills his plate with food. Aunt Nia and Uncle Uri notice it, and they exchange their own smiling glances. When Eilian comes slamming into the dining room, though, everyone's mood changes quick for the worse.

Her expanded com screen's gripped tight in her hand, and she's got a terrible look on her face. We watch as she stalks over to us and tosses the screen onto the table, as if she can't let go of that thing quick enough.

It's playing a video, and I glance down at it just as someone—in this heart-wrenchingly high-quality footage—slices a knife across the throat of a bound and terrified-looking man.

I snap my eyes away so fast, let out this involuntary gasp that comes from way down inside me. Without a word, Aunt Nia reaches out and quietly turns the screen over, her face about as pale as I feel.

"They've done it again," Eilian says, her eyes traveling to each of us in turn, boring into us with a terrified sort of fury. "Another public taking."

After that, there's no real chance to talk to Dylan about my personal haunting. Eilian describes the rest of the video in awful detail. As if there's something compelling her to relay each horrible thing the takers did as they harvested the essensal energy from the man they killed. Then Dylan has to go to work, and I'm left trying to decide if the ghost thing's enough of an emergency to warrant texting him on his secure line.

Last night, Eilian and the rest of the friends made plans to show me around downtown today. With the shock of the public execution, there's a question of whether we should go anymore, but, in the end, they all decide we could use the distraction. I wouldn't say that a distraction is what I need at the moment, but I can't think of a way out of it. So, not long after breakfast, I find myself walking with Eilian to the nearest town center to catch something called the Magnix, which is an underground train that, like the emvees, runs by electromagnetism.

Leti and Min-suk and Rafael are already waiting outside the station for us, and there are loads of other people around too, moving in and out of the station doors or striding by on their way to wherever else they may be going. It should be chaotic and noisy. Instead, it's real subdued. Suffocated by a quiet apprehension that seems to hang in the air.

As I follow Eilian along the sidewalk, staring down the fear in the eyes of everyone we pass, I keep thinking about the fact that I'm supposed to be doing something about the Sons of Morning. That a man died at their hands today, and yet, here I am, heading out for fun with friends.

I know Dylan can't miss work to train me after being gone nearly a whole week while we were traveling, and I know he and I are supposed to train this evening. I also know that Rishi thinks it's important for me to spend time getting familiar with everyday Painter life. But I can't help feeling like I should be doing more than roaming around the city right now.

Eilian's friends are talking in low voices as we come up to them, grim looks on all their faces, and before we have a chance to greet anyone, Min-suk's already asking if we saw the video.

Eilian gives a short nod. "First thing that came up in my feed this morning."

Min-suk is wearing all black. A black, nearly sheer t-shirt embroidered with lines of metallic black threads. Black wool coat. Black gloves. Black jeans. Black, heeled boots. I don't know if he did it on purpose, but he looks like he's dressed for a funeral.

"People shouldn't be sharing it," Rafael says, his amber eyes even bigger than usual. "It's exactly what the takers want."

He and Min-suk are standing close, their fingers entwined, as if grounding themselves in each other's proximity. Leti towers beside them, her easy smile traded for a solemn expression that looks more natural on her face than I'd have thought.

Eilian asks if anyone knows anything about the victim in the video, and I notice a flash of some bleak emotion cross Min-suk's face. So quick I almost doubt I saw it.

"My dad says it was one of the partners at Mountain Vista Property Management," he answers, his voice carefully neutral.

Leti lets out a humorless snort. "Biggy Argyle? Partner at Mountain Vista he may be, but what he's *really* known for is an enormous list of shady dealings down in Stranger's Hollow."

I've got no idea what that means, but I see Min-suk's lips press together and the hint of a crease appear between his eyebrows. I notice, too, that Rafael glances up into Min-suk's face as if instinctively checking on what emotions might be visible there.

You can almost taste the tension. Like, yet again, there's a dozen unspoken things filling the empty spaces between us.

"I don't understand why the takers care about that place," Min-suk says, and when Eilian responds, I get the impression she's trying to offer some sort of reassurance.

"I doubt they *do* care about Stranger's Hollow. It's the same old story. They're trying to set themselves up as the good guys. All their 'watching out for the downtrodden' rubbish."

"The takers," Leti's voice is low and careful, "said Biggy Argyle was making money off the backs of Stranger's Hollow residents. That he represents the corrupt establishment that they claim the Way Reader is here to serve. Killing Argyle was a challenge to the Way Reader to come out of hiding and prove them wrong."

This aspect of it is not something Eilian mentioned when she was detailing the video this morning. This is also definitely not the conversation I want to be having. A sense of alarm starts up inside me. Like, on some instinctive level, it must be obvious to everyone that I, the Way Reader in question, is standing right in front of them, doing exactly nothing to make their world a safer place.

I want suddenly to be anywhere but here. I want to pretend the taking—and its message to the Way Reader—is in the same category as one of Logan's conspiracies. Something far removed from myself and, probably, not even real.

It's very real for these kids, though. I can see in their eyes how their fear of the Sons of Morning is a weight hanging on each of their shoulders. Probably every person moving in and out of the Magnix station feels that exact same weight. And none of them have the luxury of ignoring it.

Then Rafael asks, "Why *is* the Way Reader in hiding?" with an entreaty to his voice that I feel like a punch in the gut.

"Perhaps she's still unaware she is the Way Reader," Eilian suggests.

"Or maybe she's still in training," Leti adds. "Maybe she'll reveal herself soon."

I appreciate the unwitting votes of confidence, but I also don't think I want to see where the conversation might head next.

Before Min-suk can jump in with his opinion on the Way Reader, I blurt out, "What's Stranger's Hollow?" Changing the subject as offhanded as I can. And the way they all look at me, you'd think I'd just announced I thought the world was flat.

"You don't know?" Leti asks, something close to her usual laughter flickering across her face. "Rafael here never left Refúgio City until three months ago, and even he knows about Stranger's Hollow."

"Give her a break," Eilian injects, half in my defense and half kind of teasing. "She grew up on a minuscule farm in the mountains of Wyoming. Of course, she's never heard of Stranger's Hollow."

The rest of them laugh at this, in an appreciative way. Like I'm in on the joke and not the butt of it. I manage to join in, but my laughter's cut short when I see Teresa hurrying toward us from across the street. I'd figured maybe she wasn't coming today, and I cringe internally at the realization that, since she's Min-suk's cousin, she probably *is* going to be a regular fixture in my life.

When she comes up to the group, she's a little breathless, like she sprinted the whole way here. She says something about thinking she was going to be late, and when Min-suk asks where she was coming from, she says she had to take care of something on her dad's behalf. Min-suk accepts this without question, but I can't help noticing she didn't look him in the eye when she answered. Which is one of those things my mom was always telling me to watch out for.

If Teresa's hiding something from her cousin, though, it's none of my business. And, if I am going to have to be around her a lot, I'm sure not going to stick my nose where it doesn't belong.

With Teresa here now, we all head into the station. I've never been on a commuter train before and I'm not at all prepared for the sheer number of people. It's a constant flow of bodies bumping and jostling each other, and by the time we've gone down the light matter moving stairway and gotten on the train itself, I'm already frazzled. When Eilian takes the window seat, I'm grateful to get the aisle so I have the option to bolt toward the doors if I want to, but then I notice there are a whole lot of people crowded there too.

So, there's no escape.

When I sit down, my seat conforms to my back the same way Dylan's emvee did, and it's such a surprise that I again make a sound like a squeaky toy being strangled to death, which delights Eilian, along with everyone else. Everyone except Teresa, who just looks around at me from the seat in front of Eilian, a veiled but clearly unpleasant expression on her face.

My first impression of the Magnix train is that it's way nicer inside than I would've expected for public transit. Everything looks new and clean. Every seat has its own light matter screen set into the back of the seat in front of it, which can produce things like drinks and snacks and magazines. Basically, the most high-tech, futuristic vending machine I've ever seen. The windows display a 3D projection that makes it look like we're passing through sprawling mountain meadows, and there's a scent to the air that reminds me of spring.

I'm just thinking I might enjoy the ride, when I hear an older couple in the row behind us talking about that Sons of Morning video again, wondering where the Way Reader is, exactly like Rafael did.

Letting out an internal groan, I drop my head against Leti's seat in front of me.

"Nobody answered your question about Stranger's Hollow," Min-suk's voice comes from across the aisle, and I open one eye to look over at him.

He's watching me with an inscrutable expression on his face, his back stiff and his hands clasped a little too tight in his lap. Rafael's on the other side of him, perched with one leg pulled up on his seat and his back against the train window. He glances between Min-suk and me like he already knows where Min-suk's going with this.

Sitting up straight, I say, "Eilian mentioned something about the downtrodden?"

"One thing you'll learn the longer you're in Deffro is that most Painters don't indulge regularly in things like drugs and alcohol because they mess with your ability to paint." There's something grim and kind of disquieting in Min-suk's voice. "But we're just as susceptible to addictions as Particle-Blockeds. We have programs meant to help—programs that work, when people are ready to use them. But when people aren't ready for that type of help, they often find their way to Strangers Hollow. It's a district on the outskirts of the city that's full of conmen and murderers who feed people's addictions in order to prey on the vulnerable, and you should avoid it at all costs."

I'm not sure how to respond. I mean, I definitely get the sense he's told me this with a purpose. And he's speaking loud enough I'm pretty sure everyone around us can hear. At least, Leti and Teresa have turned in their seats to look, and there's a guy a few rows up, in a professor-like wool sweater and a wide-brimmed fedora, who gives off the distinct impression of listening in.

"*Calon tân*," Eilian says from my other side, half laughing and reaching across me to slap at Min-suk's arm. "Don't spook her. She practically had a hernia the first time she saw a steel face. After what you just said, she'll never sleep again."

I roll my eyes hard at this, and everyone laughs. Even Teresa. Sort of. At least, the hint of a smile definitely pulls at the corners of her lips.

"Stick with us, Farm Girl," Leti says, grinning big at me. "We'll teach you everything you need to know."

And they do. Throughout the rest of the train ride and as we wonder through the city, they give me all sorts of information about Painter life. Like how most Painters spend some time as kids in the Particle-Blocked world, then gather more permanently in the Painter city-states around middle-school age or later, as a way to prepare for their transfigurings and, after that, painting academies.

They also tell me heritage is real important to Painters. Everyone tries to stay connected to the cultures of their family lines, beyond just the Painter world. Leti, for instance, lived in New Zealand until she was about nine, but her family would visit her mom's parents in Ecuador for a few months every year. Min-suk split his time between South Korea and Sweden. Eilian's family goes between Wales and the Philippines a lot. Teresa spent time with family in South Africa and South Korea, as well as at her stepdad's house in Minnesota, though she doesn't seem too eager to talk about that.

Apparently, when the Republic was formed, and it reconnected all these Painter communities that had existed separately in Particle-Blocked nations, people started forming cross-cultural relationships pretty early on.

"It's not uncommon now for Painters to have at least some form of mixed ancestry," Eilian explains.

In fact, Rafael's the only one in the group whose family all comes from the same place.

"It's one reason why we never traveled much," he says. "Or at all," he adds with a flash of his impish smile. "My parents did talk about going places. It just never happened. Would've gotten in the way of building their manufacturing empire, which I sometimes think is more their child than my brother Gabriel and I are. I'm lucky my grandma talked them into letting her bring us here this year or we'd probably never have seen anything outside Refúgio."

As shy as Rafael seems, once he gets talking, he's pretty open. It sounds like his grandma's been more of a parent to him and his younger brother than their actual parents have been. He doesn't say it with any bitterness. Just shrugs and laughs it off, but there's something in his face that makes me think it might be a bit of a sore spot for him.

"My family could probably do with a little less involvement," Leti says. "Almost nothing happens in my life without all my cousins immediately knowing."

"Your parents still don't know about that time Eilian and I helped sneak you out to see that singer you were obsessed with," Min-suk says kind of dry, and Leti spins on him, pointing her finger in a mock threat.

"And they never will, will they?"

As the conversation goes on, I learn more about all their families. Min-suk's dad, for instance, used to be a prominent reader, and they'd have loads of important people coming in and out of the house every day, seeking sightings from him. Min-suk doesn't specifically say it's not like that anymore, but the way he talks about it is definitely in the past tense.

He also mentions that his mom—half-sister to Teresa's mom—died a few years ago, so I wonder if that has something to do with his dad not working as a reader anymore. Per usual, there's a lot that Min-suk seems not to be saying, but I get the impression he's had to cover most of the care for his two younger sisters ever since his mom's death.

Teresa, I notice, doesn't say a word about her own family. She adds a few comments about Min-suk's life, and she clearly adores him and his sisters. From stuff Min-suk and Eilian say, I learn that Teresa's an only child, and she's been living with her mom and stepdad for the last eight years, ever since her biological dad died. But she's apparently got nothing to share on the topic herself.

Eilian's plan for me this morning was that I get a taste of downtown before we stop somewhere for lunch, so we've been wandering kind of aimless. If I were doing this alone, I'd definitely be feeling overwhelmed. People are bustling by on either side of us. Emvees crowd the streets, moving silent and sort of ghostly. There are steel faces all over the place, helping in shops we walk by, or just moving with the rest of the foot traffic.

Everywhere, there are other little signs that this is the world of Painters. Like the man who notices a scuff on his shoe and bends down to paint it away. Or a couple that parts ways at an intersection, where one of them blows a flurry of tiny flower petals to the other the same way someone would blow a kiss.

I keep feeling like I've fallen through a mirror into Wonderland. Especially when it comes to the architecture of the buildings. Walking at the feet of the shimmering, impossible skyscrapers is a whole different experience than seeing them from the Lucas House aerie. I find myself staring up at them wide-eyed, stunned a place like this can even exist.

Once, I catch Eilian's eye, and she gives me a big, appreciative smile, but she doesn't laugh. Probably no matter how long you live here, you never stop thinking it's amazing.

I have a passing thought that Mom and my Flemingsburg friends would probably love it here, and it threatens to throw me straight into a raging bout of homesickness. So, while the others reminisce about some event or other from their past, I blink myself into a daydream where I transform into the glass waterbird building and I'm launching off the ground and into the sky. For a second, I trick myself into believing I'm actually starting to lift off the earth, but then I notice Teresa watching me out of the corner of her eye, and any sense of buoyancy disappears in an instant.

When it's getting near lunchtime, while everyone's talking about what type of food they want to eat, Min-suk paints out a gum ball-sized bubble of water, and he and Rafael take turns floating it over their palms. Playing with the size and shape of it as they walk. I'm not paying attention to them beyond noticing how cute it is when Min-suk sculpts the water into the shape of Rafael himself, and Rafael lets out a ripple of laughter as he bumps his shoulder into Min-suk's arm.

I'm not at all ready for it when Min-suk then turns toward me, saying, "Catch, Sophie," and tosses the bubble of water my way. I lurch forward, my hands stretched out, but it slips right through my fingers and splashes across my shoes and the bottom of my pants.

There's this moment of silence, where I'm staring at Min-suk in surprise and the rest of the friends have frozen in place, all staring at me. Then laughter ripples up out of Rafael again, and he claps his hands over his mouth in that way like he just can't help himself, and the rest of us start laughing too. Teresa even laughs for real this time.

Eilian steps over to paint my pants dry, making a big show of it as if I can't do it myself, which makes everyone laugh even harder. When Leti makes a comment to Min-suk about it not being friendly to "biff things at Farm Girl," I'm pretty sure my nickname's going to stick. And, all at once, this feeling washes over me like maybe I'm actually starting to belong, and I have to try hard not to show on my face how much that means to me.

For lunch, we decide on a popular noodle house. To get there, we have to pass through a little park-like square where a bunch of acrobats are performing in front of a small crowd. I've never seen anything like it, so I'm glad when I'm not the only one who wants to stop and watch.

Rafael—who seems to know a lot about the mechanics of painting—explains to me that the reason the acrobats are able to stand in mid-air and fling each other unbelievable heights and distances is because they're playing with the density in the air particles around them.

Knowing something about how they do it, doesn't stop me from being totally enthralled with every flip the acrobats pull off. So, when the others decide to leave, I'm craning my neck to keep watching as I follow after them through the square. And that's when I notice that man with the professor sweater from the train, the fedora still covering most his face. He's several feet away from me, hidden partly from view by a small cluster of people enjoying the show, but, even though I can't see his eyes, I get the distinct impression he's watching me.

I falter in my steps a moment, and when I look around in front of me, I realize I've fallen behind the rest of the group. They're nearing the far edge of the square already, fully immersed in their conversations and obviously unaware I'm not with them. I shout out their names, but what with the acrobats' accompaniment music and the noise of the crowd, they can't hear me.

As I start after them again, I glance back at the fedora man, and see that he's started moving too. In the same direction I'm going. A glance behind me a few seconds later confirms he's still on my trail.

I try to remind myself that no one knows I'm the Way Reader and that it'd be foolish, anyway, for the takers to try to grab me in the middle of the afternoon in the middle of all these people, but the more aware I am that every face around me is the face of a stranger, the more vulnerable I feel. I hurry faster, but when the man picks up his own pace to keep up with me, I can feel the beginnings of a real panic coming on.

I'm almost to the street corner where the others disappeared, when I glance back again. This time the man's head is raised up, and our eyes meet. What I see makes my heart leap into my throat. He's got no real eyes at all. Just oval sockets of cold, slick silver.

The shock of it makes me stumble. Makes me twist around toward him in a mesmerized sort of fear. I'm on the verge of letting out a scream, when someone else grabs me from behind.

All the self-defense training Mom made me do must've been good for something because, at this point, my panic gives way to pure instinct and, before I can even process what my body's doing, I'm spinning around, swinging my hand up and back as I go.

Mostly by feel, I grab the second attacker just under their chin, all ready to shove them away from me as I'm coming around to face them, but then I actually see the person, and I freeze.

I mean, the woman standing there is so *not* a threat, it's almost shocking. She's crooked and ragged, with these eyes so wild and urgent and scared that even the idea that I was about to hurt her makes me let go of her fast, makes me start backing away.

She catches hold of both my hands, though. Grips them so tight with her bony fingers that it's alarming. Actually, everything about her is alarming, and not only because it's obvious she's not at all in her right mind.

"*Fix me,*" she practically hisses in this voice like rusted iron, and I can't tell if it's more a question or a command.

I glance around for that silver-eyed man, but he's gone. Completely vanished. Not even a sign of his sweater or hat in the crowd. Which I guess should be a relief, but it just makes me all the more uneasy.

"I'm sorry, ma'am," I say to the woman, trying to delicately release my hands from her grip while still scanning the square for any other danger. "I can't do anything for you."

"Yes." She lets go of my left hand but then takes my right hand in both of hers, pulling it up toward her head with deceptive strength and trying to press my palm against her skull while I try, in total dismay, to stop that from happening.

"You can," she insists.

I fight down an urge to just wrench my arm away from her. Despite the strength in her hands, she still looks to me like some fragile bird, and I don't want to hurt her.

In fact, it's dawning on me that I'm going to have to do something about her. I mean, someone in her state of mind and health probably shouldn't be left to roam the streets by themselves. But the question then is, what exactly *am* I supposed to do?

Several people have glanced at us as they've passed by, but not one of them seems inclined to get involved, and I'm aware of a new sort of panic setting in. The panic of feeling totally inadequate for this situation.

Finally, I get my hand out of her grasp, but she pounces in close to me, speaking in this grindy whisper that practically drenches me in the smell of her rotten breath.

"They broke me," she says, a disconcerting glint in her eye that's not at all helping to alleviate my panic. "They thought they erased the memories, but I will never forget."

I figure I should call for paramedics, which is another thing I don't have any idea how to do—maybe you just dial 911?—but obviously Dylan would know how to handle this situation.

"I'm going to call someone who can help," I tell the woman in a voice I hope sounds reassuring, but before I can expand my com, she grabs at my hands again, and this time her grip's painfully tight and extra desperate.

"Only you can help," she hisses right into my face, her blue eyes frightening and hypnotic. "*Please.* You have to make it work again."

My panic leaps straight into my throat at this point.

Neither of us are aware of a new person stepping up to us until he's put a hand real gentle on the woman's arm. There's something about his touch that instantly calms her, even if only a little.

"My apologies," he says to her. "But I do believe you're scaring the girl. Perhaps, if you let her go…"

He's got to be just a few years older than I am, but—whether it's the inherent sense of authority in his voice or the kindness in his face when she looks up at him—the woman does as he says. She drops my hands and pulls her own tight against herself in these rigid, knuckly balls, glancing between him and me.

"The girl—" she says, kind of faltering. "She can fix me."

The guy looks at me for the first time then. He's got dark brown eyes and dark hair, and light, cream-colored skin. A subtle sort of mockery tinges the kindness in his face, and there's something in that expression that strikes me as totally familiar, though I can't for the life of me name what it is.

"No, madam," he gives her a gentle smile. "No, I really don't think she can. Perhaps we can find someone a bit more likely to prove helpful?"

She looks like she's about to disagree, but then, from behind us, comes the voice of another woman.

"That won't be necessary. The poor dear is with me."

The three of us spin around to see who's talking, and this new woman is kind of a lot to take in.

She's nearly as tall as Leti, and she has what my friend Sylvia would refer to as an "ample bosom." There's something about her wide smile and intense, keen eyes that pretty much exudes *presence*. She's wearing a flowing dress of a thousand colors and her dark hair's wrapped up in a vibrant, purple scarf printed in little golden birds that are animated to flit around on the surface of the fabric.

"Hello, Sham," the brown-haired guy says, clearly familiar with her and not fazed at all. "What makes me think your statement's not entirely accurate? What are you up to now?"

The Sham woman's nose flares in a way that's sort of like a smile.

"Oh, I'll admit she didn't come into the park with me, but she's certainly under my protection. Elspeth," Sham says, looking at the tiny, broken woman with an authority that's altogether different from the brown-haired guy's. "Do you recognize me, dear?"

Sham holds her hand out like a peace offering, and the other woman perks her head up a bit as if maybe something about Sham is familiar.

"Elspeth," the troubled woman tries the name out. "Elspeth was my name once, I think. And you...you're Sham Haddad."

For just a second, there's this frantic relief that washes over Sham's face, but she gets it real quick under control.

"Yes. It's been a long time, dear. And I've been looking for you."

Elspeth takes a tentative step over to her, cautiously taking Sham's offered hand. Then Elspeth turns back toward me and points an emaciated, pale finger.

"That girl can fix me," she says, but this time it definitely sounds more like a question.

Sham's brown eyes turn toward me too, drilling into me as if she can see right into the fabric of my mind. I get this strange apprehension I'm about to be found out, but then she's wrapping her arm around Elspeth and turning away.

Giving the brown-haired guy and me a short nod in farewell, she gently pulls Elspeth along with her, and I can just barely hear her words as they walk off.

"For today, my dear, I doubt the girl would be of much use, but I will take good care of you until proper help is available."

There's a moment, right before they disappear into the crowd, when both Sham and Elspeth glance back at me at the same time, and the power of the scrutiny in their eyes is like a physical force against my chest.

The brown-haired guy has watched this whole exchange in a bemused sort of silence, and he turns a satirical smile on me now, his eyebrows raised and his head tilted in a way that reminds me of the Cheshire Cat. Or, more accurate, the Big Bad Wolf.

"I don't suppose *you* know what's just happened?" he asks, and I give a little shake of my head. He eyes me a few seconds longer and then says, "Dangerous people here in Deffro these days, you know. Best not to wander about by yourself."

Maybe it's his eyes that are so familiar, or something about the way he holds his mouth? Whatever it is, he puts me pretty immediately at ease. I take an exaggerated glance around us, as if I'm looking for something I just can't find.

"Yeah?" I say. "So, where's your protective entourage, then?"

His smile twitches. "Ah. Well. You see, I can take care of myself."

He clearly guesses this'll annoy me, but I can't think of an appropriate response. I mean, it's not like I was doing a great job of handling my situation before he showed up.

His smile gets even deeper, as if he knows exactly what I'm thinking, and then he does this quirk of a shrug and says, "I noticed a few academy-aged kids wandering down the street. I may be wrong, but it occurs to me you might like a hand in locating them."

He doesn't wait for an answer. Just starts walking off as if he's totally sure I'll follow. The sense of familiarity about him surges to the point of near revelation, but the answer still doesn't quite come. I feel like I can trust him, though. That same warm feeling in my chest I got when I met Dylan and Rishi. Taking a few skipping steps, I hurry to catch up to him, matching my stride with his.

"Who was that woman? Sham Haddad?"

He glances down at me. "A journalist. Rather respected, when she's not ruffling all the wrong feathers."

"Do you think her friend's going to be all right?"

His wry smile doesn't change much, but there's some unreadable emotion that passes over his face.

"What does it mean to be all right? Perhaps she's too far gone to fully comprehend her own suffering. Perhaps that's better than being sane enough to know it well."

I have no idea if he's joking or not.

"You're real cheery," I say, and I'm surprised when he lets out an involuntary laugh.

With that one laugh, though, I realize exactly who he is. I just can't believe it took me this long to figure it out.

"I know you." It comes out all crowing and childish, but I do feel like I just beat him at a game.

The guy glances at me again, quick and furtive. "Oh, I don't think we've met."

"You're Gwilim Lucas."

He stops dead in his tracks and looks right at me, considering. Like he's trying to decide what he's going to say next. There's a hint of sheepishness to his expression, and I can feel my smile growing more and more gloating. The family resemblance—the family good looks— it's so obvious, now I realize it's there.

"You are. Aren't you?"

He's saved from answering by Leti shouting my name from the far end of the street. She's standing there, a good head taller than most the other people walking by her, and she's waving her arms at me. Teresa's by her side, a sour expression on her face as her eyes lock on Gwilim, and the others are coming around the corner after them.

As soon as Gwilim sees them, something in his face shifts.

"That's my exit," he says, then dodges into a narrow alley between the buildings to our left, pausing just long enough to give me a jaunty little salute.

"Pleasure to meet you, Cousin Sophie," he calls, and then he's particle sailing away.

Seconds later, everyone else comes crowding around me, apologizing for leaving me behind. Wanting to know where I've been, what I was doing. Eilian's first concern, though—as soon as she can get a word in—is to ask, "Was that my cousin Gwilim?"

Her face is as unreadable as his was, but from her tone I'm guessing she's right on the verge of some real strong emotion. Anger or tears, I don't really know, but I feel like maybe I should tread lightly.

"Well, he took off before admitting what his name was," I offer, "but...yeah, I'm pretty sure it was him. By the way, isn't it illegal to particle sail in city limits?"

Leti and Min-suk burst out laughing at this, before Eilian can respond.

"Yeah," Leti says, "definitely Gwilim, then."

Apparently Eilian's in on the joke, though, because her face kind of relaxes and she gives a half-hearted eye roll as she lets out this quiet, exasperated sound.

"He's never truly happy unless he's breaking the law, just a bit," she says.

When we get home, we find Dylan reading in the den. He's on this love seat that's tucked into the big bay window, and Teresa immediately goes to sit with him, giving him a kiss and draping her long legs across his lap, tangling her fingers all up in his hair. Even though we all came in with her, the moment feels pretty private, and my instinct is to step right back out of the room again.

Eilian, though, goes charging forward, announcing that we saw Gwilim today. Teresa's expression, I notice, sours again at the mention of Gwilim's name, but Dylan sits forward, his eyes alert and hopeful as Eilian rushes on.

"Sophie was accosted by one of the people with disturbed minds," she says. "And Gwilim essentially rescued her."

She's summed up my whole dramatic experience in just a few dismissive words, but I guess they get the point across.

"Of course, as soon as the rest of us came back to find her, Gwilim made his escape. Trust him to be aggravating even while acting the hero."

I expect Dylan to laugh at this, but he doesn't. Instead, his eyebrows go down sort of disapproving, and he tilts his head in a way that feels like a warning.

"I'm sorry, but it sounded as though you said you weren't with Sophie when Gwilim found her."

Eilian glances at me, looking like she knows she's gotten herself into trouble but she's not entirely sure how. Leti and Min-suk and Rafael, who are all finding their own seats around the room, look immediately more alert too.

"Well," Eilian says, "we might've misplaced her for, say, a few minutes, but it's not as though she needs a babysitter—"

"You mis*placed* her?"

Dylan's half laughing, but I bet I'm not the only one that can see the apprehension in his face. Teresa, for instance, real quick shifts her gaze from him to me, and I have to try hard to act like I'm totally unaware of it.

"Eilian," Dylan says, kind of pleading, "I told her mum we'd take care of her. She's our guest here. We can't just go dumping her off in the middle of the city."

"I know, I *know*," Eilian throws her hands up. "I felt bad as soon as it happened." She looks over at me with a sheepish pout. "I truly am sorry, Sophie. I should've been watching out for you."

She looks so much like an impish pixie that I can't help laughing, and I'm about to say it's no worry, when Teresa speaks up instead.

"Seems like Gwilim took care of her for you, Ellie."

She says it with a bright little smile, but there's something about the look on her face that I do not like one bit.

Teresa and the others leave after dinner, and Dylan and I meet in his room for training. He greets me at the door and leads me over to the far corner, where there's a tidily arranged set of chairs surrounding a white coffee table. I flop down into the seat he indicates and curl my legs up under me. Then, on second thought, I carefully unfold my legs again and place my feet back on the floor because it occurs to me that maybe having people rub their shoes on his pristine furniture isn't exactly Dylan's favorite thing.

He doesn't seem to notice any of this. Just slides down into the chair across from me, leaning against the back of it and folding his arms behind his head like he's very much in his own territory. I don't know why, but there's something about him like that that kind of kills me.

"Well," he pins his eyes on me, and the way he drags the word out makes me wary despite his relaxed demeanor. "As Rishi and I warned may happen, you were added to a GIB watch list today."

"What?" I sit straight up, staring at him in dismay.

"On the list of possible Way Readers."

If my friend Logan were here, he'd probably say *everyone's* on some type of government watch list. Also, Dylan and Rishi did tell me this might happen but not that it'd happen so soon. I've already had more than enough scrutiny for one day.

"Remember," Dylan says, "it's common sense procedure for the GIB to attempt to suss out who the Way Reader may be before the takers do. Try to offer her some protection. Lucky thing is," he sits forward and leans his elbows on his knees, his voice taking on an understated sort of determination, "they made me head of the task force."

The look on his face then—real warm and confident—makes me feel like my lungs've turned upside down. I mean, he could give a person a seizure with a face like that. Still, I just can't get myself to match his optimism.

"We started with nearly thirty Way Reader candidates here in Deffro, a few others in other city-states," he says, in a reassuring tone, clearly picking up on the fact that I'm not super excited. "Narrowing down the list leaves us with over a dozen names, and narrowing down that dozen will be painstaking. The GIB is far from pinpointing you. Even if you remain on the list as we whittle it further, it'll mean you'll get added protection. And it's protection over which I'll now have control."

It is comforting, him acting so serious and competent like that, but there's still something bugging me. Something I can't quite figure out.

"Okay," I say, though, because I can't think of anything else. He can tell I'm not convinced.

"I can't take you off the list without causing suspicion," he's apologetic again. "I've already done what I could to make it sound like the idea of you as Way Reader was comical, and as I am leading the team, I can work to point their attention away from you."

That's when it comes to me. The thing that's been feeling wrong.

"Has the GIB already started watching me?" I ask, and something about my voice makes Dylan look at me a little closer.

"What makes you ask that?"

There's a clear picture in my mind now, of that man with the silver eyes. Just the memory of him gives me a cold feeling in the pit of my stomach.

"I was followed today. Before that lady grabbed me and I met Gwilim, there was a man following me. I first noticed him when we got on the Magnix to head downtown."

Dylan sits silent, staring at me with that inscrutable expression everyone in his family does so well.

"What did this man look like?" he asks finally. "It's best you tell me everything."

I describe the trip downtown and the silver-eyed man, and how he disappeared the second that Elspeth woman grabbed me. The whole time, Dylan's expression barely changes, but I'm pretty sure he's not pleased.

He settles back into his chair, but not in that comfortable way like before. Every muscle in his body is tensed, like some dangerous animal ready to pounce. He's staring me in the eye, but I'd be surprised if it's me he's seeing. He's somewhere in his own head, weighing the things I'm saying, calculating.

When I'm describing the strange man's metallic eyes, Dylan gets this weird, bitter smile. His own eyes are hard, and his hands are tight around the arm of his chair and, to be honest, he's kind of scaring me. When I finish talking, he doesn't say a word. Just shifts his gaze to the window behind me, where the moon's shining high and bright.

After a few minutes of a tense silence, I finally ask, "What *was* that man?"

Dylan's eyes come to my face for a split second before looking back out the window.

"A zoetic." He half-shrugs, like this detail's not all that important. "Modified steel face set to track you. Equipped with audial and visual recording, I'd wager."

The total lack of concern in his voice makes me want to reach across the coffee table and shake him. I mean, shouldn't he be a bit bothered by the possibility that, right this second, any number of taker creeps might be watching some video of me? Video of his sister and his girlfriend?

Before I can say anything, he shifts his eyes back to me again and lets out this tired sigh.

"Look, the fact that the takers are interested in you is no great surprise, but at this point their list of possible Way Readers should be unmanageably long. If they're using a humanized steel face—which is both illegal and possibly traceable, not to mention incredibly expensive —it means they've narrowed down their list enough to deem the risk worth it. They don't have the resources to have narrowed it down that much themselves. In fact, there's only one way I can imagine the takers could do it."

"You think someone from the GIB told them."

He gives this stiff nod, somehow managing to look both angry and kind of vulnerable.

"And for the zoetic to be trailing you by midmorning already, the takers had to be getting the information from us almost as we decided on it. I knew—or at least I suspected—there were double agents in the GIB, but this means it's someone I work with closely. Someone I think of as a friend, or perhaps even a mentor. Possibly one of my direct supervisors."

"So, is that it then? Do the takers know who I am?"

There's an odd sort of relief when I ask this, along with the dread. The appeal of being able to just be myself again. But Dylan shakes his head.

"I'll wager everyone on the GIB list was followed today, though probably not all using steel faces. The takers would be foolish to do anything more than that before they knew the Way Reader's identity with more certainty. However, you will need to be more careful, now that we know they're watching you so closely."

He runs his hand rough through his hair, which means, I'm guessing, he's not feeling quite as confident as he's letting on. Then he stands up, saying, "Well, all the more reason to train you further in self-defense."

He leads me to the gym outside his room, and we focus on effective defensive moves that don't require much skill in painting, so that I can protect myself without giving away my real identity too soon. I can't say it alleviates a lot of my fears, but I do feel at least a bit more ready to take on anyone—or any*thing*—that may trail me in the future.

After that, he gives me a beginner lesson in particle sailing so I can get away from an attacker quick if I need to. Tonight, I don't get going too fast, but I still cross that huge gym in only a few seconds. It's a strange sensation, doing the particle sailing myself instead of just being a passenger. It's like somehow getting slingshotted forward at the same time that I'm simply floating in space. Dylan has me do it over and over, until he thinks I'm really getting it. Then he moves us into his room for painting practice, where we're less likely to be seen.

As we sit at the coffee table again, I mention my sighting of Min-suk the day before. Dylan says he thought I'd seen something when I touched Min-suk's hand but hadn't had a chance to talk to me in private. He asks for details, digging for clues to the sighting's meaning, but neither of us can figure out what the universe is supposed to be trying to tell me with it. Dylan says there's been some trouble in Min-suk's family since his mom died, and maybe that's all it's about. He doesn't say what the trouble is, and I don't press because just having the sighting seems like enough of a breach of Min-suk's privacy.

After that, Dylan explains the painting principles of size manipulation. He has me work with a clay practice ball, like from the first training, and then an apple and a small potato he swiped from Uncle Uri's stash in the kitchen earlier.

Using the force of my own mind to make those things expand and shrink right there in my hands, feels awesome. So, when Dylan ruins the thrill by saying my technique, while functional, is lacking in finesse, it must show pretty obvious on my face.

He laughs out loud. "You simply need more practice. You're still learning faster than any average Painter would."

He tosses the clay ball to me.

"You can work on it when you have free time. Just don't do it where anyone can see you."

"Isn't this something the other kids my age already know?" I ask, thinking about Min-suk and Rafael playing with the water earlier today.

"Probably. But it'll likely not be long before you're much better at it than they are. In fact," he stands up, stretching his arms above his head for a second and then walking around the table toward me. "We can probably start on transforming material states tomorrow. Which means you need to focus on learning more particle patterns."

He slides down onto the arm of my chair and reaches for the helcom ring on my finger, taking my hand in his and doing that thing where he brings up the screen for me. Everything's been pretty businesslike up to now, but suddenly I'm all too aware of his body in my space.

"I'm downloading an index of particle patterns. You'll want to look over them, memorize them." He hands my screen back to me, pointing at a list that's showing there. "When you click on the names of things, it projects light matter diagrams so you can explore it from any angle."

I stare at the com, at the top of the screen where it says the index has over a million entries. Over a million different particle patterns Dylan expects me to memorize.

"You've got to be kidding me."

He just laughs.

"The more you know about what you're seeing, the more powerful your painting will be. And the more finesse you'll have," he adds with a smile. "A good Painter can tell when someone else's painting isn't up to scratch. I'm assuming you do wish to be a good painter."

"When you put it that way," I make a face at him, and he smiles again. "But still, you want me to memorize *all* of these?"

I flick my finger over the screen a couple times, scrolling down the seemingly unending list.

"Not all at once, of course. It's easier than you think, though. Especially with your mind. Here, let me show you."

He turns toward me a little more, which means we're so close we might as well be hugging. He wraps his fingers around my hand that's holding the clay practice ball, and this time I have to actually bite my lip when his skin touches mine.

"You know the pattern for an apple now," he says, as calm as if being this near me has no effect on him, because it probably doesn't. "So, to change this ball into an apple, all you need to do is to look at its particles and determine what the difference is between the two and what needs to happen for the clay pattern to look like the apple pattern. Then, in your mind, you will that change to happen."

With my particle sight, I see the shift in the patterns, from geometric spears of particles to bursting starlike clusters, as Dylan turns the clay ball into a shining, red apple in my hand. I obviously know it's nothing special, but it still feels magical to me, and in a sort of laughing surprise, I look straight up into Dylan's eyes.

It's a huge mistake. Because at the sight of my expression, an answering smile flashes across his face—like maybe, in just that moment at least, he finds *me* a little magical—and my heart thumps so hard, I think it's going to burst out of my chest.

Then his helcom ring, on his hand that's still wrapped around my fingers, vibrates to tell him someone's calling. And, whatever moment we may've been having, is immediately over. He lets go of me, standing up and pressing the button to answer the call.

"Hullo, Teresa," he says, real pleased. And as fast as my excitement had rushed in, it rushes right back out again, replaced with this achy sort of melancholy I'm surprised comes on so strong. As if hearing him say Teresa's name like that physically hurts.

Dylan looks back at me over his shoulder. "Sorry," he mouths, pointing at his com ring, and I know my training's done.

Standing up, I give him an awkward little wave. Then I book it out of his room so I don't have to hear him sounding so happy to be talking to her. By the time I make it back to my room, it's pretty obvious the melancholy's here to stay.

I do my best to practice on my own, but I'm not in the mood for painting. Finally, I give up and start getting ready for bed because I can't see there's much use in my staying awake any longer. Plus, tomorrow evening's supposed to be that fancy introduction party Nia and Uri are throwing for me, and I figure I could use some good rest.

When I'm climbing under the covers, I'm still feeling sorry for myself. Sorry and lonely and homesick. And pretending real hard that I'm only sad because I miss my mom and my friends back in Flemingsburg, and not at all because I'm jealous of the way Dylan feels about Teresa.

The blanket is already pulled way up to my chin when I remember my parents' locket, which I stashed in the back of one of the dresser drawers my first day here. I slide back out of the bed and shuffle through the dark over to the dresser, fumbling blind around in the folded clothes in the drawer until my hand slides over the metal of the necklace's chain.

The shape of the still beat up locket in my hand brings up the image of Mom standing in our kitchen, passing me that picture of my dad. I imagine his curly hair and his playful smile, and my heart feels somehow full and empty at the same time.

Taking the locket over to the bed, I slip under the covers, pressing the necklace one-handed, tight against my chest. I didn't realize how much of an emotional response I was going to have to the thing, but it's been a long day, and suddenly I feel on the verge of crying.

I think about what Rishi told me, about a person's essence moving over to another dimension when they die. It means my dad might still exist somewhere, and as I start to drift into sleep, I wonder if he ever thinks about me.

When something tickles at the back of my consciousness—something deep inside the locket—it's more on instinct that I reach my mind out to examine it. The sighting it unleashes brings me real shocking and sudden out of sleep. Though the state I'm in is not exactly what I'd call waking.

There's a hand around my throat, crushing me down to the ground as if it's going to press the air right out of me. I'm struggling against it, flailing in a frenzy and trying to make contact with whoever's got hold of me. I can't see anything. It's just pitch blackness all around, but somewhere near, I can hear the sounds of someone else in pain. Wheezing breaths that remind me of the death of that taker girl in the forest.

Suddenly, there's a voice hissing into my face, his breath full of a weird scent like chemical grass and cucumber.

"Did you really think you were special?" It feels like a knife thrust straight into my lungs. "Your gifts mean nothing with your witless brain directing them. Hear how your friend suffers for your foolhardiness. The universe made a mistake with you, but I will fix it."

He grips the top of my head with his free hand, his fingers driving hard down into my scalp, pushing my head backward.

"Don't worry. Though this will hurt quite a lot, you won't remember any of the pain afterward."

There's some *thing* in my mind now. Something foreign, as if my attacker's reaching his energy inside me. Pushing his own darkness right into my brain matter.

I'm petrified, trying to pull myself from his grasp but barely able to breathe. And that horrible gasping from the other person—some friend of mine dying beside me. Their breath is scratching like razorblades at my ears, and the panic's taking total hold of me. Pounding through my body and into the back of my throat, beating at my temples and threatening to overwhelm me.

Just as I'm sure I can't struggle any longer—that I'm experiencing my own death—the whole scene dissolves. I'm sitting upright in my bed in the Lucases' home. The lights are out, but moonlight's filling the room. There's no one there but me.

I burst into Dylan's room, shaking all over and calling his name, only vaguely remembering how I got up here. He's still on his com with Teresa, lounging in one of the chairs in the far corner, all bare-chested now and wearing those jersey pajama pants of his. At the sound of the door crashing open, he's up on his feet and spinning around toward me.

"Z—Sophie."

As soon as he registers the fear on my face, he says into the com, "Teresa, I'll call you back. Everything's fine. Yes, you too."

He's already moving across the floor, reaching me just as he's hanging up.

"What's wrong?" he says, gripping me by the arms real firm and bracing.

It's so bright in here. Such a startling white after the dark of the nightmare, the dark of the halls as I ran to his room.

"A sighting," I sort of stammer. "I—He—"

I don't even know where to start. The whole horrible thing's still real present in my mind, and I can't seem to stop shaking. I've gone all flimsy. Like any second, I might fall to the floor.

"Come here," Dylan tells me, and leads me back to the chair where I was sitting before.

He sits on the coffee table in front of me, leans his elbows on his legs and looks me sober in the face, waiting for me to calm down. When I start to stumble through my story he doesn't interrupt. Just listens, silent and still.

It's weird how describing it out loud helps the panic die down. Sure doesn't get rid of the fear, though. I mean, just minutes ago I could *feel* some man killing me, and there was nothing I could do to stop him. It may've only been a sighting, but it was pretty potent and real to me, and I don't know if the shock will go away anytime soon.

"Do sightings always come true?" I ask when I reach the end of my story, and Dylan hesitates before answering.

"Yes. Though not always in the way you expect. Rishi would explain it better, but while some sightings are merely hints or abstract interpretations of events, I believe a sighting as clear as yours is usually accurate. Did you recognize the voice of the man?"

"No."

"Do you know who the friend was? The one you could hear?"

For a second, I just study the straight line of Dylan's nose, count each perfect eyelash arcing off his eyelids.

"No." I say, instead of telling him I'm terrified the person I heard was actually him. That someday he might die because of me.

He's quiet, biting his lip and thinking. Then, "There's no conclusion," he says all of a sudden.

"What?"

Meeting my eye, his expression now edging somewhere near relief, he explains, "Your sighting had no conclusion. We don't know what happens to you or the other person. You can still determine the ending. Perhaps it's a blessing even, seeing it now, so you have something specific to train toward."

I try to picture it as a blessing, but all I can think about is the feel of that man's hand around my neck.

"When Rishi resurfaces," Dylan says, "he can help you put it all into perspective. That should be soon, but there's not much else we can do until then, except what we've been doing. Do you want me to come sit with you for a while?"

I shake my head, trying to be brave even though I'd actually love not to be alone right now.

"Do you want to sleep here with me?"

My heart kind of skips a beat. I mean, I know what he's actually asking, but I'm suddenly aware again of his half-naked body there in front of me, and of me in a lacy little camisole and pajama shorts combo I found in the wardrobe. And the fact that we're sitting so close to each other I can see the speckles in the color of his eyes.

All those feelings from earlier rise up again and, again, I'm aware that it'd be a disaster if I did any of the things I'm imagining. I think it's probably not a great idea for me to be one-on-one with him much longer.

"I'll be okay," I lie. "I was just kind of shocked."

"May I walk you to your room at least?"

Picturing the dark and winding halls out there, I give a nod, thinking I can probably control myself for that much longer.

The next day, I'm not feeling at all festive, but Nia and Eilian are. Before the sun's even fully up, they're running all over the house preparing stuff for the party, while Uncle Uri cooks unbelievable amounts of food in the kitchen.

After a quick breakfast, Dylan has to go to work for the morning, and Nia and Eilian and Uri head downtown to get some last-minute things for the party. Aunt Nia says there's no need to drag me all over the city for the sake of their errands, so I end up with a few hours at the house alone.

Considering last night's sighting and what Dylan said about preparing for it, I figure it's a great time to practice painting and self-defense. I make my way up to the gym outside Dylan's room, trying not to think about how eerie the house feels with everyone else gone. If that ghost thing wanted to really creep me out, now would be a good time for a haunting, but there's no sign of it this morning.

In the gym, I start out working on my particle sailing, then move on to some of the defensive moves Dylan showed me yesterday. There's a light matter screen meant for target practice along one wall. It can absorb the energy of anything that hits it, to avoid damaging the wall itself, so I use it to practice shooting fire. It's a repetitive enough activity that it's not long before I've lost myself in my imagination. Dramatically ducking and dodging attacks from invisible assailants, launching rounds of fireballs back at them while also, maybe, shouting things like, "Not today, cowboy!" or, "Try again, rawheel!" because in my head I'm fighting a band of takers in the Old West.

It's the sort of thing I would absolutely never do if I thought someone else might be watching, so I about jump out of my skin when I hear someone behind me clearing their throat.

Spinning around, I see Gwilim Lucas at the door to the gym, dressed all in black—which I can't deny looks real good with his dark hair and fair skin. He's leaning nonchalant against the doorframe, one eyebrow raised at me.

"No one else is here," I blurt out, my cheeks red hot and my mind racing over everything I was just doing in case it could reveal my real identity.

"You don't say." Gwilim sounds totally disinterested. "Fending off a band of outlaws, are we?"

"Um."

"If you're done obliterating them, I'm off for an early lunch, and you're welcome to join me."

He gives me a mocking smile, and then he disappears into the hall as if there's no question whether I'll follow. I consider making a point of not doing what he wants, but I am hungry and definitely curious. I doubt it's an accident that he showed up here when the rest the family's away. I don't know what's going on between all of them, but more time with Gwilim might give me a better clue.

A few minutes later, I'm in Gwilim's emvee—black all over just like his clothes—and we're headed downtown. He takes me to a restaurant that's real romantic inside. Not at all the mood he's giving off himself. There's low lighting and trickling water falling in sheets around each table, forming beautiful, sparkling walls.

My friend Sylvia would probably die in a place like this. In any other situation, I'd send her pictures. Of course, without hearing from me for so long now, she's probably already decided she hates my guts. Or she thinks I'm dead.

Almost as soon as we're seated, Gwilim gets a text message. He views it on his palm, resting his arm on the table as he reads. From my angle I can see the silver glow of the text even if I can't actually read it. From the way his brow creases, I'm willing to bet whatever the message says isn't great.

Muttering a distracted apology to me, he expands his screen and holds his thumb over the essensal energy sensor, composing what I'm guessing is a pretty careful response based on the time he takes in finishing it and the way he sits afterward, staring at his screen as if waiting for a reply.

It's hard not to lean forward and try to get a glimpse at what's happening on his com. And it gets harder and harder the longer he's absorbed in his text conversation.

When our food comes out, he's still lost in it. Barely looks up to say thanks to the waitress. When I mention that my food—some kind of marinated beef—is real good, he just nods and says, "Their signature dish."

I stare at his face, not knowing whether I'm more amused, annoyed, or just plain nosy.

"Eilian says you haven't been home in ages."

He gives a half shrug.

"I think they're pretty worried about you."

It's that shrug again. Then he runs one hand along the back of his neck in a sort of absent-minded discontent.

Resigning myself to a meal of total silence and wondering why it is Gwilim even brought me here in the first place, I turn toward the window beside us. It's a cold day and everyone on the streets is bundled up against the wind. It's interesting to me that here in Deffro —where the whole city could be temperature-controlled if they wanted —they've chosen to leave that up to mother nature for the most part.

I remember Dylan saying something about there being a vote on that a few decades back. On whether to heat the air in the whole city or only some of the parks here and there. If Dylan were here, I could ask him about it. If Rishi were here, I probably wouldn't even have to ask because he'd just tell me. Probably in excruciating detail.

I glance over at Gwilim, who's still engrossed in his com, a look of stony frustration on his face.

Down on the sidewalk below, I catch sight of a kid pushing this hovering stroller-like thing with a tiny white dog in it. The dog— sitting prim as a prince—is wearing a bright red bonnet with so many lacy ruffles at the front of it you can barely see the dog's face.

It may not be the most surprising thing I've encountered so far in Deffro, but it makes me smile. Glancing over at Gwilim, I say, "Some kid's got a dog in a stroller."

When he doesn't respond, I add, "The dog's wearing a lacy bonnet." And since it's pretty clear I'm going to have to provide my own entertainment, I keep going.

"I bet it's not even his own dog. I bet he lost a bet with his friend. Probably this is some sort of punishment for him. He looks real embarrassed about it."

I'm obviously making stuff up now. I can't actually even see the stroller kid's face. I still don't get any reaction from Gwilim, though, so I choose some other person walking along the sidewalk below, and I make up a story about them. This one's a former pickpocket who worked her way up to being a high-powered businesswoman, only she can't help but pinch a trinket from some unsuspecting victim now and again.

Still no response from Gwilim, so I start again, but this time, he does glance up. Gives me this sarcastic look that's just one crooked smile away from the frustration he was wearing seconds before.

"Your turn," I say, grinning back at him.

"Okay, *Farm Girl*," he says, in his usual, mocking tone, and I wonder how he knew that nickname. "I know I'm being a terrible host. Shall I prove I can do better?"

He places his elbows on the table and leans forward, resting his chin on top of one hand and looking me right in the eyes.

"So, what's my little Cousin Sophie's story? If you're such a good friend to my family, why haven't I ever heard of you?"

His question catches me totally off guard. I mean, it's not like I don't have an answer prepared for this, but it's the way he's asked it. Like maybe he knows something's fishy. The story Dylan told his family— that Gweneth and my mom simply lost touch for a while after my mom decided to go off the Painter grid—none of them even seem to have batted an eye at it. Gwilim on the other hand. Well, I can't tell if he's teasing or completely serious.

I open my mouth to answer, but just then someone calls out his name.

"Gwilim Lucas, you sly dog. You said you were busy."

This dark-haired guy with a round face and light brown skin strides toward our table. As he pulls a chair over and scoots in next to Gwilim, he looks me up and down, real obvious and bordering on gross.

"Looks like you are busy, after all."

"Yes," Gwilim says. "So go away."

"She can't *want* to be alone with you. Is he boring you with his childish sarcasm?"

"The opposite, actually." I wouldn't say I *dis*like the guy. It's just that, on first impressions, there's not much about him I do like.

He nudges Gwilim and says, "Going to introduce me?"

"Not likely."

"Do it for myself, then."

The guy leans over the table, offering me his palm. "Tom Cameron. Gwilim's mentor and best friend in the world."

The name sounds familiar, but I can't think why.

"I'm Sophie Warren."

His eyes narrow a little. "Gwilim's cousin, eh?"

"We're not actually cousins."

He lets out this annoying laugh and says, "Yeah, well, you do want to make sure to get that clear. Don't want people to get the wrong impression."

For just a second, there's a look on Gwilim's face that tells me he's not too keen on Tom Cameron right now either, but Tom's still yapping on.

"You don't look like a farm girl," he says to me. "You seem a lot more interesting than that."

"What are you doing here?" Gwilim says.

"Meeting Wotan Schmid, like I said in my text. Now that he's back in town he's decided to stay with us tonight."

I remember now where I heard Tom Cameron's name. This is the guy Gwilim's been hanging with lately? No wonder Dylan hadn't looked pleased by the news.

"You didn't mention that you were meeting him here." There's a strange expression on Gwilim's face. He turns his eyes on me, studies me with a look I can't read. Then he stands up. "I'll be sorry to miss him, but we'd best go."

"You're leaving already?"

"Cover my bill, and I'll pay you back tonight."

Gwilim's coming around to my side of the table, and I stand up, wondering what's going on.

"Where you two headed?" Cameron asks like it's some dirty secret.

"Do you think I'm going to spend our whole date staring at your ugly face? Nothing more calculated to ruin the mood."

Gwilim takes my hand and pulls me after him, giving Tom a brusque wave.

"Was this a date?" I tease as we're getting into the emvee a few minutes later.

"Sure." He shrugs. "Why not?"

While we're on our way home, I get a text from Dylan asking where I am. I tell him I went out to lunch and I'll be back soon, hoping I didn't worry him too much by disappearing and figuring that the detail of who I'm with is probably better relayed in person. Back at the house, I try to get Gwilim to come inside with me, but I'm not too surprised when he declines.

I'm also not surprised that, when Eilian hears what I've been up to, she gets this look on her face like she's just short of furious.

"What is going *on* with him? He's purposefully avoiding the rest of us, but then he goes off to lunch with you? I don't understand him at all."

I'm standing just inside the doors in the big ballroom where the party's going to be held, and Eilian and Aunt Nia are in the middle of putting up decorations with the help of a small horde of rented steel faces, who can apparently do some minor painting when they're programmed for it.

When I first came in the room, Dylan was helping too, but now he's leaning against the doorframe near me, and he's studying my face, kind of pensive and perplexed.

"I wonder what Gwilim's interest is in you?"

"Oh, come on, Dylan. That's obvious." Eilian gestures at me in a way I find embarrassing.

"Actually, I don't think he's too interested in me at all. He barely talked the whole time."

Eilian's not really listening. She gets down from the wooden step stool she was on and stands there, staring unfocused and stormy at the floor. Then she thrusts her leg out and kicks the foot of the stool real sharp.

"Why doesn't he come *home*?" she says in this little wail and goes stomping past me out of the room.

Dylan's eyes meet mine. Even though he hides it a whole lot better than Eilian, I'd be willing to bet he's as bothered by Gwilim's behavior as she is.

"She's not upset with you," Aunt Nia calls from her perch on her own step stool.

"Oh, I know. She's mad at Gwilim, and with what I've seen of him so far, I'd be surprised if anyone in Deffro wasn't."

Later, as everyone arrives for the party, Aunt Nia stations me and Eilian and Dylan by the ballroom door to greet guests. I don't know how many hands I touch in the first hour, how many names I hear and then immediately forget.

Last night, when we were talking about Min-suk, Dylan told me that the *pono* greeting is a common trigger for sightings. So, this evening, I was prepared to have a whole slew of them, but so far nothing's happened.

I don't know whether to be grateful or disappointed. I mean, the nightmare sighting is still painfully clear in my mind. Every time a stranger touches their palm to mine, I get washed over in the memory of that man's fingers digging into my skull. But having more information about him, or the Sons of Morning in general, would be nice.

Eilian wasn't lying about hundreds of people RSVPing. I guess since we're so close to that Gathering Day holiday their mom mentioned, there are extra people in the city right now, visiting their families. I guess, too, no one else in the Painter world has the same qualms Teresa's dad did about associating with the Lucases.

Even before the ballroom's full, the noise of all those people—the energy—hums through the air. I can feel it in my ignus, in the pumping of my blood. A rhythmic, off-time counterpart to the music playing from somewhere up near the ceiling.

At the last party I went to in Flemingsburg—a Valentine's Day thing in Sylvia's basement—there were maybe a dozen kids at most. The decorations, which I thought were real nice at the time, were things like fabric heart streamers and pink plastic cups that Sylvia's dad bought at the nearest Walmart.

There's no way you'd mistake any of the decorations today as being purchased at a department store. The ceiling is literally dripping with white wisteria, millions of snowy flower-cicles cascading around the already pretty impressive golden chandeliers. The sun-colored upholstered walls are marbled with the blue periwinkle plants Aunt Nia and Eilian convinced to grow vine-like from floor to ceiling. The air's filled with thousands of globe-shaped, glass lanterns that float above everyone's heads. And giant mirrors have been hung all over, reflecting each other across the room and making it feel like the whole world's contained in just this one huge, fantastical space.

Aunt Nia says the flowers have meaning. Wisteria for welcome, and periwinkle for new friendship. My body itself is practically drowning in lilies. Eilian wove them into my hair, they're embroidered into the bodice of my midnight purple ball gown her mom bought for me. Delicate lily earrings dangle from my ears.

Peace lilies for harmony, healing and balance, Aunt Nia told me. And I'm guessing Gweneth picked this whole outfit as a secret homage to my Way Reader duties.

It's a nice gesture. Especially since lilies are my mom's favorite flowers. Though I doubt Gweneth knew that. But one thought keeps popping into my head as the night wears on. I should be training right now. I should be preparing for that nightmare sighting to come true. I should be learning how to save lives. Dylan's, in particular. Mine too, if I can.

I can't seem to shake this lurking anxiety that something awful could happen at any minute and I'd just be totally useless when it came time to help.

It's a relief when the other kids start showing up. Rafael arrives first with his grandma and younger brother Gabriel. Mrs. Silva is a tiny, silver-haired lady with smiling eyes. She's pretty soft-spoken, but Gabriel is the opposite. As soon as Rafael's introduced him to me, that kid is pouring out words. He's probably only four or five, and he gives me a whole lecture, in an adorable little voice, about dinosaurs I've never heard of. He's about to launch into a different lecture on igneous rocks, when Mrs. Silva tells him not to use up all my time and drags him off to get refreshments.

After that, Leti comes in with what must be every person on the planet who's related to her in any way. Introducing them to me one after the other, so that their faces all kind of blur into each other in my mind.

If she didn't introduce her immediate family members last, there'd be no chance I'd remember them. Her older brother Tama's just as good-looking as she is, though his hair's cropped closer and he's got a narrower shape to his face. He's slightly shorter than Leti too, a thing Leti's sure to point out when she introduces him.

"As you can see," she says, "Tama didn't drink enough milk as a child," and she holds her hand over her brother's head to indicate the difference in their heights.

Her gloating ends, though, when Tama snatches her hand and twists her fingers back, so she has to bend down and sort of spin around to avoid the pain.

She cries out, mostly in annoyance, as Tama laughs. "Looks like I can still beat you in a fight, sister."

He moves a bit to keep his grip as Leti tries to dodge out of his hold, and neither of them sees their father stepping up between them.

Mr. Moeaki, who stands at least half a head taller than either of his kids—and whose shoulders span at least that much wider too—grabs Tama by the ear and pulls him back with so much force, he lets go of Leti immediately, letting out his own little whoops of pain until his dad releases him.

"Too hard! That's too hard!"

"I told you two, none of that tonight. You'll have your friends thinking our family has no manners."

Mr. Moeaki turns to me, his face shifting easy from faux disapproval to a wide smile.

"Allow me to apologize for these two. Sometimes I think they have trouble in their bones." He reaches over to flick Leti on the ear, but her mom, Ms. Huapaya, steps in now and bats his arm away.

"Just where do you think they get it from?" She demands, playful, as she moves around them to do *pono* with me. "They think because they're so much bigger than me, they can get away with anything, but I can always keep them in line. Because I'm smarter and meaner."

Her kids laugh, but her husband nods his agreement. "Everything she says is true."

She is smaller than they are, but I wouldn't say *much* smaller, and I certainly wouldn't want to cross her either. Just touching her palm, I can feel the strength in her arm.

I'm betting Leti's family creates a party atmosphere wherever they go, but when Min-suk shows up with his family, it's a whole different feeling. I mean, his sisters Ha-jun and Dan-bi are adorable little restless carbon copies of Min-suk himself. But they run off to talk to their friends pretty much as soon as they're done greeting us. It's their dad that unintentionally dampens the mood.

At first, there's nothing glaringly odd about Mr. Holm's behavior. I do notice that he barely looks me in the eye when we exchange *pono*, and also that there's a sheen of sweat across his forehead despite the comfortably cool temperature of the room. There's also the way he lingers by Min-suk's side, when Leti and Rafael's parents have already stepped away.

None of that would seem too notable to me, though, if it didn't become pretty obvious, pretty quick that the man's in a state of some distress. Like, the whole time us kids are talking, Mr. Holm can't seem to stay remotely still. His fingers are drumming on his legs, his feet are tapping on the floor, and his gaze is roving all over the room. A couple times, he blurts out these comments that only barely make sense in the context of the conversation, and it's clear he's having a hard time following what's going on.

But, other than Rafael shooting a few worried glances over at him and then up at Min-suk's face, no one else betrays any sign that they're aware something's amiss, so I try to pretend I don't notice it either. We all just carry on chatting with a forced cheer about who's at the party and what the Lucas family has done to transform the ballroom, or whatever other trivial thing comes to mind.

Min-suk himself is clearly less than cheery. While he definitely tries to appear like he's enjoying the conversation—plastering this half smile on his face and keeping his gaze pointedly directed at whoever's talking at the moment—I'm pretty sure the only thing he's actually paying attention to is his dad. Each time Mr. Holm makes one of his disconnected comments, I notice a tiny crease appear between Min-suk's eyebrows. And every few minutes, as Mr. Holm's repetitive tapping starts to get particularly noticeable, Min-suk quietly reaches his hand over to touch the man gentle on the arm as if trying to settle him down.

Then, out of nowhere, Mr. Holm announces that he'll be back in a moment.

"You have a nice time with your friends," he pats his son's shoulder real tender before wandering aimless away. And, as soon as the man is gone, Min-suk's relief is palpable. His face goes slack like every muscle in his jaw just released, and his chest rises kind of sharp as if he's finally able to breathe.

The relief doesn't last long, though. Only moments later, Mr. Holm is back, stepping in close to his son again and whispering intense in his ear. Whatever the man has to say, it has an immediate effect on Min-suk, who starts shaking his head in protest, twisting around to face his dad and insisting in an under voice, "No, *Pappa*. You promised. You said you'd stay with us tonight."

Now that Min-suk's turned away, a troubled glance passes between everyone else—so quick it seems involuntary—and from the expressions on all their faces, I'm guessing this isn't the first time they've seen this sort of thing with Mr. Holm.

I don't want to jump to conclusions, but I think I'm maybe starting to understand why Min-suk got so intense about that Stranger's Hollow place.

Observing Mr. Holm now, I can see that the sweat I noticed earlier has started beading on his face in earnest. The skin of his arms has gone all goosebumpy, and his breath as he whispers to his son sounds like it's building toward a panic.

Maybe Min-suk notices this stuff too, or maybe it's something Mr. Holm says, but Min-suk suddenly seems to relent. One minute, he's pleading hushed with his dad, and the next, he just stops. Shoulders sinking, he turns to us and says in this voice of resignation that something's come up and he'll be back in a little while.

Then he takes hold of his dad's arm and, with his other hand on his dad's back, guides Mr. Holm kind of somber and patient out through the ballroom door.

As we watch them go, I've got no idea what the others are thinking, but I feel like there's a stone lodged inside my chest. I don't have too much experience with addiction or people who are struggling with it, but I'm pretty sure it isn't something that can be cured by a simple matter of willpower or someone just caring about their kids enough to stop. I mean, it's obvious to me that the love in their family runs deep. And, if I am right in guessing that Mr. Holm is dealing with something substance-related or maybe even some sort of withdrawal, I can only imagine what life has been like for everyone involved.

Dylan's the first one to break his gaze away from the door. He turns and meets my eye real serious. Then Eilian and Leti and, lastly, Rafael, turn too. Looking at me like they're all wondering how to explain to the new girl what she's just witnessed play out with their friend.

I doubt any of them knows where to start, though, so it's probably a relief when Aunt Nia announces that it's time for dancing. She beckons us all toward the center of the ballroom, and, even though a touch of heaviness seems to trail after us, having something else to focus on does help dispel the tension a little bit.

It also helps that Painter dancing's like something out of a dream. Eilian and Nia took some time today to teach me some of the steps— similar to old-style waltzes and things—and Aunt Nia showed me a bit of an *ascensè* technique, where Painters add shallow pillows of less dense air beneath their feet as they move from one step to the other, which lengthens their stride and gives the illusion they're floating across the floor. Seeing Aunt Nia perform it around the family den and seeing it performed on the actual dance floor, though—well, those are two real different things.

With everyone dressed in their fancy clothes, gliding around each other in elegant, seamless twists—all of it backdropped by the already magical setting—it takes my breath away. Standing with Dylan at the edge of the dance floor, all I can do is stare.

"Do you like it?" he asks after we've been watching for a while, and there's a hint in his voice of that same sort of pride he had the first night I saw Deffro spreading out through the valley below us.

"It reminds me of the story of the twelve dancing princesses," I say, and he cocks an eyebrow at me.

"I don't believe I've heard that one."

I give him a teasing smile. "It's a story that reminds me of this."

"Fair enough," he laughs. "Want to try it?"

"Yes—no. I don't know," I falter, imagining myself stumbling around among all those highly coordinated people, but Dylan's already reaching for my hand, ready to lead me onto the dance floor anyway.

"I'll do most of it for you. Come on."

We swing into motion with everyone else, and with him guiding me along, it turns out I can perform most of the steps with an unembarrassing level of credibility. Then, once he's sure I've got the hang of the movements, he starts doing *ascensè*, and suddenly we're dancing on air.

"We're flying!" I laugh up at him, kind of afraid to look anywhere else in case I totally ruin this moment by losing my balance and falling on my face.

With his arm around me all warm and solid, our bodies close together, and his attention focused entirely on me—I think if there's going to be one truly happy moment the whole evening, this is probably it.

When the music stops and we're walking back across the room, I don't complain at all that he keeps hold of my hand as if it's just natural to him. But then we see Teresa waiting at the edge of the room, and Dylan lets go of me to wave at her. Picks up his pace a bit like it's instinct for him to close the distance between them as fast as possible.

Teresa's leaning languid against the wall, looking like a model in a midnight-colored dress, her hair straightened and in a chic, 20s style bob. Eilian's next to her, chatting away while picking at a plate piled high with cookies and custards and things. It's obvious Teresa's only half listening to Eilian, though. Mostly, she's watching Dylan and me, with that look in her eyes that makes me uncomfortable.

As we get closer, she pushes herself up from the wall, her body unfolding as graceful as if she were in some sort of ballet. Then, for just a second, she looks straight at me like she wants to be sure I'm watching, and she steps into Dylan's space, sliding her hand up and around the back of his neck to his ignus and pulling him into a kiss that's way more intimate than the occasion calls for.

I feel suddenly weird, standing right next to them while they're doing such a private thing. When I meet Eilian's eye, though, she seems to think it's hilarious.

"Get a room," she says when Teresa and Dylan pull away from each other. "There are children here. You could burn their eyes out."

Laughing, Teresa twines her fingers into Dylan's grip and leans her shoulder against his, smiling up at him. He smiles back, but I notice a tinge of a question in that look he gives her, like maybe he's not exactly sure what's just happened between them either.

She asks him to dance with her, and I'm relieved to see them go. Eilian and I join Leti and Rafael just as Min-suk returns.

"Did you send your dad home in a taxi?" I hear Rafael ask kind of quiet, and Min-suk gives a stiff shrug.

"He wouldn't let me take him myself. I just hope he actually makes it this time."

He glances toward his sisters and their friends, this heavy look in his eyes as if he's staring into the face of overwhelming responsibility.

The weight of it seems to hang over the rest of us too, until more people come over, wanting to talk or to ask one of us to dance. Bringing the party atmosphere with them again in a way that can't help being contagious.

I dance with Eilian, then Rafael, and then Min-suk. I'm on my way back from dancing with Leti's brother Tama when someone steps real purposeful into my path.

"You are Dylan Lucas's cousin Sophie, are you not?"

I look up in surprise. The woman's not exactly tall, but she sure gives off the impression of height. This feeling like, to see her properly, you'd have to shade your eyes.

"Yeah. I'm Sophie Warren." Using that name is feeling less and less like a lie.

"I'm Itsuko Laugadóttir," the woman says, her words coming out compact and to the point. "Dylan Lucas's supervisor at the GIB."

"Oh!" I say, trying not to show on my face that Dylan's ever suggested his supervisor might be a double agent.

"He's told me a lot about you," she says. "Quite a lot."

A tiny chill goes skittering down my spine, and I can't help thinking that everything about her is sharp. The tone of her voice, the angles of her face. I have a hard time imagining her ever smiling. I'm saved from having to respond to her by Dylan appearing miraculously at my side, Teresa right behind him.

"Director Laugadóttir," Dylan says. "I didn't realize you were coming."

"I thought I should pay my respects."

If Dylan thinks that's at all weird, he doesn't show it. Just says, "That's very kind of you," with this easy sort of sincerity I don't think I could muster myself. There's not much about the woman that suggests kindness.

"I cannot stay," she says to him. "There's something I must discuss with you privately."

Dylan's eyebrows rise a bit, but he gives her a nod. "I can speak to you now."

They excuse themselves—or rather, Dylan does the excusing. Then they walk off and leave me and Teresa standing there together, and compared to facing this Laugadóttir person, I'm definitely way more uncomfortable now.

Still, when Teresa's eyes shift to me, it's kind of a shock to see the full extent of her dislike there, finally wholly unveiled. I mean, this is the first time she's ever looked at me like she truly hates my guts.

"I heard you had a bad dream last night," she says like bad dreams are only for children. "It must've been so terrible, to bring you to Dylan's room like that."

She pauses as if she's waiting for me to respond, but I'm pretty sure nothing I could say would make this conversation go in a direction I'd appreciate.

"Did you know Uncle Uri brews a calming tea that helps people sleep?"

She pauses again, but I still wait to see what's coming.

"Seems to me it'd make much more sense to rush to *his* room the next time you have a bad dream." She flashes me one of her killer smiles. "Don't you think?"

Then she brings her hand up to my face and sort of pats my cheek, as if I really am just some kid. And with that one gesture she manages to make me feel real pointless and ridiculous and small.

It takes me a second after she's walked away before I can even breathe, and a second after that before I realize I'm totally furious. I'm not sure what makes me madder, the thing she just did or the fact I let her do it. Or maybe it's more than that. Maybe it's the reminder that, when there are people out there in danger because of me, I'm at this frivolous party, letting that petty princess treat me like I'm some sort of joke.

I mean, last night I had a sighting about Dylan dying right next to me, and by this evening I was already letting myself have fun.

There's a word they use in the Painter world—bisher—that means someone who's just a complete jerk, and I can't decide whether it's her or me it describes best right now.

I spin around on one foot and start pushing my way past people, heading toward the refreshment table as if it offers an escape. As I go, it occurs to me just how many strangers there are here and that, for all I know, any number of them could be takers. One of them could even be that nightmare man from my sighting. A thought that flares my anger even more.

When I reach the refreshment table, I grab a plate and start just shoveling Uncle Uri's carefully prepared food onto it like it's the end of the world and I'm gathering rations.

I don't notice Rafael until he's pretty much right by my side.

"Why the long face?" he asks, and my stomach practically jumps straight out through my chest.

As I spin around toward him, the jelly-filled pastry I'm currently holding slips out of my fingers and real nearly beans him in the stomach, grazing his shirt as he dodges out of the way. The look he gives me then is so full of laughing rebuke, you'd think I'd thrown the thing at him on purpose.

"Good aim," he says, painting away the powder trail the pastry left behind, then eyeing the pile of food on my plate. "Were you planning on eating all that tonight?"

"Yeah, actually," I answer kind of rueful. "I was probably going to shove every last bite down my throat while hiding by myself in a corner."

He's just bent down to pick up the pastry I accidentally threw at him, and he looks up at me in mild surprise, his bleached curls bouncing with the movement.

"Something's ruined your evening?" Standing, he hands the pastry to a passing steel face. "Am I allowed to ask?"

In normal circumstances, Rafael would be exactly the person I'd choose to confide in, but these aren't normal circumstances.

"It's nothing," I wave it away. "Just an annoying thing somebody said."

He opens his mouth—I'm guessing to ask for more details—when a burst of ear-piercing laughter makes both of us turn sharp toward the sound.

Not too far away, there's a man in the middle of a circle of people, apparently entertaining them by flailing his arms, swaying back and forth, and making babbling sounds through scrunched up, comical lips. He's maybe in his late forties with dark, shoulder-length hair slicked straight back, thick eyebrows and a gap between his front teeth. He's wearing a biker-style jacket that's printed with his own face on the front and back of it, the eyes in the face blinking and looking side to side as if watching the people around him.

He's definitely not someone I've met yet. I'm pretty sure I'd remember.

"That's the woman to a tee," one of his friends is crowing, and another one slaps the first on the back in agreement so hard it makes her snort.

"Oh! Oh!" a different friend shouts, like they're in a competition to prove who's enjoying themselves the most. "Do that weaselly fellow. The one that said Kepper's paintings were high art."

The group bursts out laughing again, and the man seems happy enough to perform some more.

I glance mystified over at Rafael, ready to make a joke, but the words stick in my mouth at the sight of the downright terror in his face.

"Rafael—?" I start, but he cuts in.

"I'll catch you later, Sophie." Then he takes off as fast as he can without breaking into an actual run, leaving me standing there by myself.

Turning back around, I'm surprised to find the jacketed man's eyes on me.

"Why, isn't this the guest of honor?" His voice is slick and false and bro-ish in a way that makes me immediately not like him.

He's taking a couple steps away from his friends, looking me up and down real critical as I eye him with a similar energy, wondering what was so scary about him it could send Rafael packing like that.

"The rumors do not lie," he says. "What's the word the youths are using these days?" He shoots an exaggerated look back toward his friends. "Alpha?"

Painters've got some strict rules about hospitality—Aunt Nia's been drilling them into me in preparation for the party—but I don't think they'd require me to fawn all over this guy when he's being pretty unquestionably annoying.

"I don't think we've met," is all I say.

He responds with, "No, indeed. I've just now arrived. Can't manage to be anything but fashionably late, unfortunately. I am José Anjo. Perhaps you've heard of me?"

I give a little shake of my head, and he clutches a hand to his heart like he's been wounded, looking back at his friends with this performative, cartoonish horror on his face. Then, when they laugh as if he's legitimately funny, the man straight up chortles.

I mean, I did not think chortling was a thing that actually existed in real life. I thought maybe it was reserved for old books and bad movies, but that man just went and did it right there in front of me.

At this point, I'm zero percent sure how Rafael could be afraid of him. Confused, yes. Irritated, definitely. But not afraid. And I've had just about enough.

"Well, it's real nice to meet you," I say, holding out my hand for *pono* and pasting on a smile so polite even Aunt Nia'd probably say I was overdoing it.

To my surprise, the guy just totally flips out. He does this wild backward leap away from me, holding his hands above his shoulders and practically shouting.

"My apologies," he says, as he makes a show of trying to recover, "but I have the most debilitating distaste for human touch."

I stare at him. I know there are people that do have phobias about touching other people, but it's the *way* he says it. Almost like, when it comes to humans, he sees himself as something else.

It's no small relief when Uncle Uri steps up beside me and says a friend of Aunt Nia's wants to meet me. I excuse myself as civil as I can, and I'm more than ready to turn away when Uri pauses like something's occurred to him, and he glances back at Anjo.

"Pardon me," he says. "But, don't I know you?"

Mere seconds ago, that Anjo guy was acting like he'd narrowly missed getting the plague, but now he slides easy enough into an oozing kind of condescension.

"Oh, I don't suppose you do," he says, lifting one real critical eyebrow and looking Uncle Uri up and down as if there's something glaringly wrong there. "I've lived in Refúgio all my life. A place I very much doubt you would appreciate."

I'm familiar enough with Uncle Uri's expressions to recognize the subtle glint of sarcastic humor in his face now, but I don't think Anjo could've caught it, or he wouldn't still be looking so smug.

"No, I've not had the pleasure of visiting that fine city," Uncle Uri says pleasant enough, and then he simply turns away from Anjo in a manner that couldn't possibly *not* make the man feel dismissed.

"Shall we, Sophie? Nia's friend would never admit it, but she's bad at waiting, and too much of it may cause her harm."

He's so cool about it, but for my part, there are major alarm bells going off in my mind. I mean, if Anjo's from Refúgio—the city Rafael's also from—odds are the man's not some random guy that just happened to scare the living daylights out of my friend. There must be something Rafael knows about Anjo. Something bad enough to terrify the kid practically to death.

And it occurs to me how convenient it is for Anjo to have a phobia that means not doing *pono* with anyone. Not giving any possible readers the chance to get a sighting into whatever hidden things there might be in his life.

As we walk away, I take one glance back at him, and I'm surprised to find him still watching us, such glittering hate in his eyes, it sends a chill down the back of my neck.

I hurry to walk closer to Uncle Uri, as if it offers some sort of protection, asking, "*Do* you know that man?"

Uri's lips turn down in a tiny, thoughtful frown.

"It would appear I don't," he says, and then he quirks one eyebrow at me. "But I'm not one to credit much to mere appearances."

It takes me a second to realize what he means by that, and then, without thinking how it might sound for me to act too curious, I ask, "How do you think you might know him?"

"The real question, Sophie, is who do I think he is? A puzzle that, at this moment, remains unanswerable."

Aunt Nia's friend is standing in a group of Painter politicians who are arguing about some bill called the Particle-Blocked Involvement Act that's coming up for a vote soon. It'd allow Painters to serve in political office in Particle-Blocked governments—a thing that's apparently been illegal up until now. The debate is heated.

All their security details are gathered against the wall behind them. Including a man named Jaap Jansen, who was introduced to me earlier as director of the GIB and, therefore, Dylan's boss's boss. So, another potential double agent.

Politics have never been my thing, and, with that Jansen man's stern eyes on me, I'm already a bit intimidated as Uncle Uri introduces me to a woman called Yvette Griffiths. She's wearing a long black gown with embroidery over the chest that depicts a brightly colored, rectangular face with two snakelike heads extending out of the sides of it and curving to meet just below her collar bone. Her shoes are black moccasins with detailed oak trees stitched in tiny beads over the toes, and she's got a small top hat perched at an angle on top of her long, intricately braided hair.

She's half Welsh and half 'Namgis—a Canadian First Nation that

Uri says is part of a group of tribes in British Columbia called Kwakwa̱ka'wakw—and she represents the Welsh people in the Painter Republic's parliament.

She's also Rishi's wife. A fact I realize as Uncle Uri's making introductions and I remember Rishi mentioning her name. If she knows who I really am, she doesn't show it. In fact, she doesn't say anything at first. Just smiles kind of subtle and studies me. Silent, like maybe she's not going to actually talk at all.

I can't figure out quite what I think of her. She's not much taller than I am, but there's a clear sense of authority to her, like she's spent most her life being in charge and she doesn't know anything different. At the same time, she gives off an inherent air of mischief. Like she's always on the verge of laughing. Probably the perfect match for Rishi.

"Well, I see in your eyes you've got intelligence as well as charm," she says finally. So blunt, it surprises a laugh out of me. "Your Nia is a dear friend of mine, and I'd like to count you as a friend too, if you'll allow it. You may call me by my first name, Yvette. Or Yvie. It's not a permission I grant to many."

I'm both wholly disconcerted and wholly pleased by this. I'm just explaining that she can call me Sophie—as if, under current circumstances, she'd call me anything else—when one of the other politicians in her circle, a man who I think is named Walter Brandeis, bursts out with this explosive, sarcastic laugh that immediately draws Yvette's attention.

The man looks exactly like Mark Twain, and he acts how I'd imagine Mark Twain acting, barking out his opinions over the top of everyone else and wielding a silver-plated cane like it's less for his support and more a tool for scolding. Right now, he's berating a lanky guy with beady eyes, whose name I don't remember.

"We don't interfere much in how they run things," Brandeis says, "And they don't learn we exist."

"But it infringes on the rights of Painters who feel allegiance to both the Painter Republic and the Particle-Blocked nations in which they live," the other man responds in this defensive grumble. "It's a matter of important freedoms."

"What you're proposing, Lamerding," Brandeis aims his cane at the man, "is meddling. Meddling in Particle-Blocked politics has never turned out well. Read your damn history books. Have you forgotten how we ended up with World War I?"

"On the contrary. We have always meddled in Particle-Blocked politics—we are doing it already—and it serves everyone quite well. Them included. We have been successful in staving off many wars between Particle-Blocked nations."

"We do it all out of the limelight," Brandeis retorts. "We get hired in supporting roles to the politicians, and we promote reasonable dialogue between countries. We don't make their laws for them. We can't have Painters taking on leadership positions in that world. It would be unfair to the Particle-Blockeds and dangerous for us."

"But we could do much more to promote peace had we more concrete power in Particle-Blocked nations. If we could *be* their politicians instead of simply their advisors."

"More likely we'd get some fool in office who gets himself caught, and our people would be exposed to the Particle-Blocked world. Or worse yet, some essence-thirsty takers get voted in and they don't stop wars, they start them."

"Should we limit the freedoms of everyone out of fear of the few?" Lamerding snaps, his face turning red with frustration.

"Aye, in this case we should."

Then, Yvette says, real amiable and composed, "Our policy toward the Particle-Blocked nations has always been to work toward peace through respectful persuasion but to leave them entirely autonomous. What you propose sounds benign, but what it will become is an infiltration. It is actually a question of preserving the freedom of the majority by limiting the few."

"Ha!" Brandeis shouts. "Griffiths is right, Lamerding, and you know it."

He's so triumphant about it, that I can't help kind of smiling. Which, it turns out, is a mistake.

Brandeis swings his cane around to point right at me, and he says in this gruff voice, "What do you think, girl? You've lived among the Particle-Blockeds your whole life. Think they'd appreciate us coming in and sneakily sitting in their governments while simultaneously pledging allegiance to another flag?"

"Oh, don't bully her into agreeing with you," Lamerding snorts.

"You're just mad because you know I'm right," Brandeis spits back.

His cane's still staring me in the face, and with everyone's eyes turned in my direction, I feel sort of foolish all of a sudden. I mean, what could I possibly add on a topic I know almost nothing about? I glance around at all of them, getting sympathetic and encouraging looks from Uncle Uri and Yvette, but it's obvious they're not going to bail me out.

"To be honest," I start, and my voice sounds to me like it's coming out of a six-year-old, "I can't say I understand everything you're talking about that well, but I think people—Particle-Blocked people— wouldn't be too happy if there were, um, other people messing with their governments."

Representative Brandeis bursts out with his booming laugh again and claps his hands together, which sends his cane dangerously close to hitting Lamerding in the face.

"*Well.*" Lamerding says, as if Brandeis was trying to assault him on purpose. "Don't be so sure of yourself, *Walter.* Just wait and see how your friends start coming over to our side. It won't take much to make them see the error in your arguments. Goodnight, Ms. Warren."

He gives me a curt nod and then does a pretty good job of storming off, despite all the people he's got to wade through and the way his security detail has to hustle after him. Jaap Jansen, the GIB director, follows along as well, his eyes locking with mine for a split second as he passes by. There's nothing friendly in his expression.

"Turn tail," Brandeis says as if to himself, though it's loud enough I'm betting Lamerding heard him.

Seems to me it's the perfect time to make my own escape. Half-laughing in an attempt to hide my discomfort, I say to Yvette and everyone else, "Well, it sure was nice to meet you," and I spin on my heel and hurry away too.

At this point, I'm pretty much done with strangers. So, I slip into the hall, and I'm headed toward a little study where I hope to get some privacy, when I hear Gwilim Lucas coming from the direction of the elevator.

"You must know you won't find welcome here," he's saying to someone in his lazy voice. "Your unpleasant face is bound to set up hackles."

I turn back toward him as much on instinct as any actual desire to talk. As he's coming around the bend, I see he's not alone, though. And there's something about the other man that immediately makes me wary.

He's older—stocky and smooth-headed—and there's a strange agitation to his body as he walks, as if all his muscles are in a constant state of flexing and unflexing. Even from here, I can tell there's something off about his eyes. His gaze is somehow intense and glassy at the same time, and when it locks onto me, it's obvious he's real aware of his surroundings. Almost too aware, with this disconcerting sort of hunger that makes me wonder if, actually, zombies might be real in the Painter world.

When Gwilim notices me standing there in the hall, he kind of falters for a second.

"Sophie," he says, as if it's a surprise to run into me at my own party.

At the sound of my name, the other man gets this look on his face like he thinks something's real funny. Like *I'm* real funny. Only his expression's a whole lot more like a snarl than a smile.

Trying not to stare too hard at him, I say to Gwilim, "Didn't think you'd come tonight."

"Have to keep you guessing," he answers, and I could swear there's a discomfort in his expression, underneath his flippant manner.

His eyes follow my gaze as it travels again to the other man's face, and, reluctant, Gwilim finally says, "This is Wotan Schmid," nodding over at the guy. "He's staying with Tom Cameron and me."

I try to imagine why Gwilim would have anything to do with the man, let alone stay under the same roof.

I know Aunt Nia told me I needed to be extra hospitable to everyone tonight, but this guy doesn't seem like the type you be hospitable *to*. Still, I try to sound sincere when I tell him, "Pleased to meet you," and step forward, offering my palm.

My politeness is totally wasted, though. He just stares me down for a long few seconds as if he's trying to intimidate me—which, by the way, totally works. Then, extra slow like he's making a point of it, he raises his own hand to mine, and it's about all I can do not to pull away.

I'm ready for the sighting this time. I'm expecting it. I'm even pretty sure what I'm gonna see when I feel my mind tipping down inside him, rushing toward the rancid, inky blackness that's writhing right in the center of his essence. What I'm not at all prepared for, though, is the searing pain. The way something about that dark thing inside him is so vicious my body actually feels it like a burst of fire in my bones.

It takes every ounce of strength I've got not to cry out with the burn of it. And, if it weren't for Dylan coming out into the hall right then—for his saying Gwilim's name in a sharp tone that makes all of us turn toward him—there's no way I could've hidden my sighting from either Gwilim or his alarming friend.

As it is, I can feel the strain showing in my expression as I come around to face Dylan. Even he doesn't seem to notice, though. All his attention is zeroed in on that Wotan guy.

"Mr. Schmid," Dylan says, and you could freeze a flying bullet with the chill in those two words.

Wotan just smiles deeper, his nostrils stretching wide as if he's actually breathing Dylan's anger in.

"Gwilim," Dylan says again, without looking away from Wotan's face. "Why have you brought that man into this house?"

For a second, Gwilim looks like he's been struck—like something in Dylan's tone has caused him legitimate harm—but then his own anger takes over so fast you'd think the hurt was never there in the first place.

"Oh, do I not have a right to bring whomever I choose into *this house?*" His voice is real cool even if the look on his face isn't. "This is still my home, is it not? Or have I only ever been a guest here?"

If he wanted to hurt Dylan back, he seems to have found the right words for it. You can feel the strain like a tangible thing in the air, and that Wotan guy—well, he looks like he couldn't be enjoying himself any better.

"Gwilim?" Aunt Nia's voice sounds out from behind us. "*Gwilim?*"

She's running from the door of the ballroom, and she crosses that distance so fast, you'd think she sprinted professionally. She's got her arms stretched out in front of her as if it'll help her get to her nephew quicker, but when she catches sight of Wotan, she just stops in the middle of the hall, her hands falling heavy to her sides.

When she turns her eyes on Gwilim again, her face is full of unpleasant questions, but he can't seem to meet her gaze.

"Mr. Schmid," Aunt Nia says real prim after several seconds of loaded silence, looking the man full in the face with the haughtiness of a queen. He just raises his eyebrows back at her in a gesture of pointed spite, his cruel smile twisting a little more cruel.

"He's staying with Tom," Gwilim chokes out in forced nonchalance, his eyes focused somewhere over Aunt Nia's shoulder. "While Tom's at work, I'm acting the role of host."

Her eyes travel over to Gwilim and then back to Wotan again, but she doesn't say a word in response. I'm hoping she's going to kick the man out of the house, even though I'm guessing that'd go against the rules of Painter hospitality. Once someone's invited in, you'd have to have a pretty clear reason to force them back out again so soon. But, even though I don't know exactly why Dylan and Aunt Nia are this upset about his being here, it seems like just the man himself is reason enough.

"Aunt Nia," Dylan says, dangerously quiet. "I'd like to talk to Gwilim alone. Is it too much to ask—"

He stops himself short, as if he's thought better of asking it.

Aunt Nia's face as she glances at him is nearly unreadable, so when she speaks to Wotan, I'm surprised to hear the hate that tinges her voice. I didn't even know that was an emotion she knew how to feel.

"There is no proof, as of yet," she manages to sound somehow both threatening and dignified at the same time, "for all the wrongs you've done, and so I would not be justified in treating you the way I would like to do. Under the circumstances, I will escort you into the ballroom with the rest of the guests, but have no doubt that I will watch you very carefully there."

She turns slightly, a silent command for Wotan to follow her. For a moment, I think he's not going to do it. That he's going to stand there and face off with her, but then he starts walking forward. Real slow, like he wants her to feel every step he takes.

Aunt Nia doesn't react. Just waits for him to pass by, and then she moves too, shooting one last cryptic glance back at her nephews before she and Wotan disappear through the ballroom door.

I'm about to go after her—to give Dylan and Gwilim their privacy—but Dylan doesn't wait for me to leave before he starts talking.

"That man is no good," he says, in a tense whisper. "Isn't that obvious?"

"And we've got a family reputation to uphold?"

Dylan's lips press together tight at this, and it's like whatever else he wanted to say doesn't matter anymore. Taking my hand, he spins around, muttering, "We'd best get you back to the party."

Then he's pulling me along like he's forgotten I need a chance to move my own legs. I'm about to tell him to stop or to slow down or something, when Gwilim jogs up on the other side of him, grabbing his arm and pulling him around to look him in the face.

"I'm sorry, Dylan. I never would have brought him here if I'd had a choice."

"What does that mean?" Dylan demands. "What have you gotten yourself into? Why are you chumming around with people like Tom and Wotan and their like?"

"Can't you guess?"

There's this long look between the two of them. I can't see Dylan's face too well, but I can see Gwilim's, and it's like he's begging Dylan to understand. I think Dylan's going to too. At least, I think maybe they're actually going to communicate instead of throwing useless spite at each other. But then, of course, that's the exact instant Teresa decides to step out into the hall.

"Dylan?" She looks at his hand around mine, at him and Gwilim staring each other down. "I just saw Wotan *Schmid* walk in with Aunt Nia. What is he doing here?"

Whatever moment of understanding Dylan and Gwilim might've had, Teresa's question makes Dylan's anger flare right up again.

He lets go of me and strides forward, saying, "That's what I'd like to know."

He takes her hand, gesturing to her that he wants to go back into the ballroom, but then he stops and turns to Gwilim again.

"I don't know what you're up to, but I should warn you that Itsuko Laugadóttir has become suspicious of the people you are giving your time to. You'd best be careful. And you'd best make sure that man doesn't do any damage here."

Then he and Teresa are gone, leaving behind that quality of quiet that comes after too much noise. And, in that quiet, I can hear Gwilim's breath, all quick and heavy.

"What was that about?" I ask, looking over at him with what I hope he sees is somewhat sympathetic curiosity. "What *is* going on with you?"

Before answering he takes in one more big breath, as if he's right on the edge of deflating. When he starts talking, though, he's very nearly like his usual self again.

"Long story. At the moment, I've got a slithering snake to watch, so the explanation will have to wait. Sorry about ruining your party, Cousin Sophie. I'll make it up to you sometime."

He walks past me toward the ballroom door, sort of touching my arm as he goes by and leaving me there with a hundred questions.

* * *

When I head back into the ballroom myself a few minutes later, it's with some pretty mixed emotions. I'm now even less in the mood to deal with all these strangers. The thought of seeing that Wotan Schmid guy again makes me feel sick to my stomach. But, on the other hand, the idea of him wandering around the house without my knowing exactly where he is and what he's doing is even less appealing.

I'm half expecting to see Gwilim and Dylan glowering at each other across the room, but, although they're definitely about as far from each other as they can manage, neither seems all that intent on the other person's whereabouts. Dylan's standing with Teresa and some of their friends not too far from the door, and Gwilim's leaning against the wall between two of the huge mirrors on the far side of the room. From these positions, the one thing they've got in common is that they both seem to be keeping tabs on Wotan Schmid.

That man's stalking slow and dangerous around the edges of the crowd, scanning everyone he passes with open and threatening malice. As if he's searching for someone specific, looking exactly like a predator on the prowl.

I pass Dylan, noticing the way Teresa looks up at his still stormy expression as if she's just dying to know more about what's wrong, and I move through the crowd over to Gwilim. Lean beside him against the wall, and glance up at him with an expression that's probably not too far from Teresa's.

"Your face," Gwilim says, without actually looking at me. "People might think someone's upset you."

"Seems like that someone's kind of a pro at upsetting people," I respond, and he gets a hint of a smile.

"I did say I was sorry."

I want to be annoyed with him, for bringing this trouble here tonight. For doing something he obviously had to know was going to upset his family, whatever their background is with Wotan Schmid. But I also feel a little sorry for him. When he said he had no choice about bringing that man here, I believed him. I can't guess at his reasons, but I believe what he said. I'm pretty sure Dylan would believe him too, if Gwilim would just stop being so mysterious about everything.

It looks like Aunt Nia's already told Uncle Uri something about what happened in the hall, because they're together now, against the wall by the refreshment table. Uri's got hold of Nia's hand, and the two of them are also tracking Wotan's every move, so stony-faced they look downright dangerous.

Not far from them, I see that José Anjo man again. He's in the middle of telling some new, overly-acted anecdote to his friends while they laugh and laugh. No one can possibly be as funny as that, and I wonder if they're all afraid of him like Rafael. If they only laugh because they have to, because they know some dark secret he's got hiding underneath that annoying act.

I check for Rafael and find him standing beside Min-suk and the other friends at the far end of the ballroom. Min-suk and Eilian are caught up in whatever story Leti's telling, but Rafael's eyes are riveted on Anjo, and it's clear his fear from earlier is just as present now. His grandma and brother Gabriel are with a group of young kids and their accompanying adults only a little ways away from Rafael, and I notice that Mrs. Silva keeps glancing over at Anjo too, this look of trepidation on her face, her body angled as if to block Gabriel from the man's view.

Whatever Rafael fears in Anjo, it seems like Mrs. Silva fears it too, and I can't say I love the fact that there is both a Wotan and an Anjo at this party right now. Maybe not every suspicious character in the Painter world is out to get me or anyone I care about, but I can definitely feel my sense of unease growing.

"What's up with that guy?" I ask Gwilim, indicating José Anjo with a nod of my head. When Gwilim sees who I mean, he gets this weird look on his face.

"Anjo? A paper doll. All decoration and poses with nothing on the inside. Everyone says he's an artist, though I've never seen any of his work, so I couldn't say. Came to Deffro about a year ago and grew enormously popular within a mere few months. Probably because he's a pompous little flatterer, and I don't doubt he only makes friends to use them."

If that were all there was to the man, I don't think Rafael and his grandma would be so afraid, but I keep that thought to myself.

"You should try flattery, you know," I tell Gwilim. "You could probably be as popular as José Anjo if you worked a little harder. Your own family might even like you."

He lets out this crack of laughter, and I think maybe there is a chance I could get him to tell me something about what's going on with him. But then he cuts himself off short, his eyes fixed suddenly straight at the ballroom door. When I follow his gaze, I see a security detail there, surrounding a dark-haired, handsome man—all perfectly styled clothes and a movie star sense of poise—who's making his way through the crowd, stopping every few steps to shake hands and grace party guests with his impressive smile.

I don't need the sudden tension in Gwilim's body to tell me the identity of the man. He's definitely much older than Gwilim is and, I'm thinking, a whole lot more arrogant. But, other than that, the resemblance is uncanny.

Gwilim's dad. The one who abandoned him. The president of the Painter Republic.

At the moment, the man's bending over a little elderly woman, holding her hand in both of his and looking into her eyes with a practiced air of attentiveness as she talks. Off to the side, a photographer's snapping photos of the two of them, the flash of her camera somehow exploding in the air instead of on the camera itself.

President Lucas nods his agreement to whatever it is the elderly lady's saying, and he pats her hand all comforting before moving on to the next person waiting for a chat. The whole vibe he puts out is like he just can't get enough of listening to these people. Like they're doing him real big favors by taking up his time.

When he notices Gwilim and me standing against the wall, though, this odd little smile pulls at the corners of his mouth. He excuses himself from the woman he's currently talking to and starts moving purposeful toward us through the crowd.

Glancing up at Gwilim, I take in the expression on his face—anger, maybe some sort of disgust even—and I'm suddenly sure I don't want anything to do with whatever's about to go down.

I start to step out of the line of fire, but Gwilim slips his arm around my shoulders and, gentle but firm, pulls me even closer to his side.

"Oh, don't abandon me now," he says with dark humor, his eyes never leaving his dad's face. "You'll have to meet the man eventually, Cousin."

As if by some pre-arranged cue, Dylan and Eilian materialize out of the crowd then, lining themselves up on either side of Gwilim and me like a couple fancily dressed bodyguards. Clearly there for moral support despite Dylan and Gwilim's quarrel in the hall.

Just as Gwilim's dad reaches us, the photographer darts out ahead of the president's own security detail and starts snapping photos of the five of us together.

"An unexpected family reunion," the president says to Gwilim in a voice not meant for the rest of the ballroom to hear. "I'd not thought to see you tonight. My sources tell me you've been avoiding most of your family ties of late."

The security guards have lined themselves up in a perimeter around us. I'm sure they're just protecting the president from any threat that might try to get through from the outside, but I can't help feeling more like they're trapping us in.

"I've been visiting friends," Gwilim responds, cool and unwelcoming. "You should teach your sources not to exaggerate."

President Lucas accepts this with a nod of his head, this look on his face like he's mildly amused by it.

"Odd choice in friend who's been getting so much of your attention, though. Son of the man who put your uncle in jail?"

My reaction to this little bombshell about Tom Cameron is probably pretty visible on my face, but at this point nobody's paying attention to me.

"How is my brother, by the way?" the president asks Dylan and Eilian. "I believe you still visit him dutifully."

When Dylan answers, you don't have to look too hard to see the irritation on his face.

"He's as well as could be hoped," he says, "under the circumstances."

"Yes, it must be quite hard on him, to have been caught in such a hypocrisy."

The effect of those words is like the shock of a thunderclap. I feel it in the tension of Gwilim's arm, see it in the expression on Dylan's face.

But it's Eilian, who's mostly been feigning boredom up until now, that can't help responding.

"He didn't do it," she spits out, and she looks ready to say a whole lot more, but then something happens that makes it pretty much a moot point.

"*You*," a voice hisses from behind the president, and he turns sharp to see who it is.

Gwilim recognizes the person before I do, and he's already stepping around to block me from view by the time I realize it's that Elspeth woman standing there. The one Gwilim rescued me from yesterday. She's just outside the ring of bodyguards, staring President Lucas down like she'd love nothing more than to break his neck. I thought the way she acted toward me was intense, but right now she looks downright terrifying.

"*You did this to me.*"

"Excuse me?" President Lucas asks, sounding truly confused, if curious.

His guards are barring Elspeth's way, though they haven't made a move to do anything else yet. They're waiting for the president to give them some sort of signal, but at this point he doesn't seem too inclined to.

"What is it you imagine I did?" he asks, and that strange little smile is playing on his lips again.

I'm wondering where in the world Elspeth came from. I mean, she's all dressed up for the party—and she actually looks almost healthy even—but if she'd been here the whole time, I'm pretty sure I'd have noticed.

"You think," she snaps at him, "that your conscience can remain clean because you never laid a hand on me yourself?"

By this point, everyone even sort of near us has noticed something's going on. Anjo and Wotan, for instance, are both observing this exchange with what seems like a special interest. I can't be the only one that hears the sudden bite in the president's voice when he responds now.

"I don't know you, woman."

He towers over her with his authoritative, athletic body, but even still, when she takes the teeniest, tiniest step forward, there's something so menacing about it I'm surprised he doesn't react.

"They may have tinkered with my memory," she says, chilling and calm, "but my painting is still very much intact."

Then all at once, with a sudden tensing of her muscles and a guttural, hair-raising sort of scream, she erupts into a pillar of electricity and flame.

Screams sound out through the room, and I start toward Elspeth, but both Dylan and Gwilim grab my arms to hold me still. The president's bodyguards have sprung into motion. Some of them falling back to act as a second line of defense and some of them trying to catch hold of Elspeth. But, even though the electricity flaring around her doesn't seem to be doing her any harm, the sparks she sends out at the guards make them jump away again, shouting in pain.

Some of the people in the crowd are trying to back away from her, while others are pushing forward to get a better view. The president himself is just standing there, facing Elspeth's wildness down with an angry sort of calm, despite the fact she's moving toward him tiny step by tiny step through the lines of his security.

Then, one of the female guards that's been trying to get her hands on Elspeth, steps away from the rest of her team and pulls out a weapon that looks like something from a sci-fi movie, all rippling from the inside with light matter and energy, as if the thing itself is somehow alive.

At the sight of it, it's like everything else in the room slows down. I'm crying out, lunging against Dylan and Gwilim's hold as the guard raises her arm to aim. Then, with a bright flash, her weapon goes off, and Elspeth just crumples to the ground.

My scream escapes at the same time as others in the room. Then there are more shouts as more people realize what's just happened.

I'm staring dumbfounded at Elspeth's motionless body, barely aware of the way the noise of the crowd is threatening to build into total chaos. Then President Lucas holds his hand up for silence, and with just that one authoritative gesture the commotion stops.

"Please don't be alarmed," he says, his voice carrying easy across the room. "It was simply a tranquilizing shot, am I right?"

"Yes," says the guard, holstering her weapon and hurrying to help her colleagues lift Elspeth off of the ground. "She'll be conscious again in roughly a half hour."

"That woman is unwell," one of the onlookers calls. "She needs help."

"Obviously." President Lucas turns his head toward the speaker. "My team will transport her safely to the hospital."

The guards are already starting toward the door when a familiar voice comes from the crowd.

"I will take her."

Sham Haddad, the journalist who claimed responsibility for Elspeth the other day, steps out into the open space in front of the president, this barely controlled fury in her eyes.

President Lucas considers her for a long minute with a satiric smile curling the edges of his lips.

"Ms. Haddad," he says finally.

"Elspeth is in my care. I'll take her to the hospital," she says again.

Her gaze flicks over the president's half dozen security guards and then, just for a second, her eyes lock on mine. Even though it's barely long enough to count as a glance, I'm left feeling—just like with that first time I encountered her—that she's looked inside me. Seen something about me that I don't even know.

"I might've guessed you had something to do with this," the president says to her. "Were you aware, when you brought her out in public, that your friend's mind was so troubled?"

Sham glances at Elspeth, hanging limp in the security guards' arms, and a bitter smile passes over her face. "Not like this, no. I'll be finding her some help now."

She steps forward, but with a slight signal from the president, a couple of the guards move to block her path.

"I hardly think it's reasonable for you to transport her anywhere by yourself," President Lucas says. "My team will do it, as I indicated.

You're welcome to accompany them."

I'm watching Sham's face, and I'm wondering how she's going to deal with this situation without actually fighting her way through it. Then Gwilim lets go of my arm and strides forward.

"I'll help Sham," he announces, moving easy through the circle of guards while they try to figure out what they're supposed to do about the president's own son. "Between the two of us, we'll manage fine, so no need to diminish your security detail."

If President Lucas was angry before, I'm pretty sure he's downright livid now, though he tries not to show it. He's staring hard at Gwilim, and Gwilim's staring hard right back, this glint of defiance in his face. It's a battle of wills, and watching the two of them, it's wild to me how different they can be while looking so much alike at the same time.

Just when it seems like one of them has got to break, Aunt Nia comes bustling forward with Uncle Uri.

"Oh, Gwilim, what a wonderful idea," she's pouring out words in that way she does. "The poor dear needs friendly faces around her when she wakes. Not the mugs of these brutes."

She swats at the guards' shoulders all affectionate and playful. Then she just lifts Elspeth right out of their hands with that gentle firmness only she can manage.

They glance toward the president for guidance, but it's clear that with his sister in charge now, there's nothing more to do. From the look on his face, I don't know if he's ready to wring her neck or laugh out loud.

Gwilim's quick to help her, the two of them slinging Elspeth's arms over their shoulders while Uncle Uri and Sham Haddad paint a sort of light matter hammock below her body.

"Well," President Lucas says, in wry resignation. "I suppose she couldn't ask for a better escort. Would it be too much to expect a full report once you get her to the hospital? I am, you see, sincerely concerned for her well-being."

"Of course, Hiarwar," Aunt Nia throws over her shoulder as they move Elspeth out of the room. "I never would've thought otherwise."

A smile flashes over his face, and, as if to hide it from view of the watching crowd, he spins back around to Dylan and Eilian and me.

"It had been my intention," he says, and to my total consternation, it's me he's staring at. "To pay proper respects to the farm girl staying at our ancestral home, but, after what's just transpired, I find I'm not terribly interested in remaining here any longer. Please believe that I have quite pressing presidential matters to which I must attend and allow me to bid you adieu. Your servant, Ms. Warren."

He gives me this dismissive nod and holds out his hand for *pono*. It takes me a minute to figure out what he's doing, but then I hurry to press my palm against his.

I feel the sighting before it hits me, that sense of being dragged suddenly straight inside his skin. Though, while I'm able to react better than I have before, I'm afraid I don't keep the shock completely off my face.

I mean, I'd already guessed the president was a dangerous person, but I definitely was not expecting to see the dark thing purring inside his essence, its inky tentacles curled around itself almost catlike and restless. A monster waiting for its next meal, patient but not at all calm.

I can feel my whole body tense with the surprise of it, and I'm sure the president notices. Or maybe he doesn't. For just a second, at least, I think he's looking at me a little closer—more curious and careful—and then that impression's gone. He's turning to say his goodbyes to Eilian and Dylan and sending a curt nod in my direction. Then he's striding toward the door without another look back, his security guards and that photographer trailing behind him with a bit less sense of order than before.

Everything else is practically pandemonium. Voices are raised in fear as people wonder to each other what just happened, how it connects to the Sons of Morning. Because everything these days does.

"What was that about?" Eilian turns toward me and Dylan. "Obviously, it's no surprise that someone should want to kill Uncle Hiarwar, but what did that woman say about him *tinkering* with her mind?"

Dylan's received some sort of message on his helcom, though, and he's not paying attention. As he reads it, his face goes real grim, and he raises his head and locks his gaze on the ballroom door where President Lucas just exited.

Two uniformed women are stepping in, looking sober as they scan the room. I've never seen an actual GIB uniform before, but I'm guessing that's who they are, because, when they catch sight of Dylan, they seem to recognize him. Without a word to Eilian or me, he starts to make his way through the crowd toward them, and they move to meet him.

"What's going on?" Eilian asks, but she says it like she's got a pretty good idea what it means to have people in uniform show up at your door.

I don't answer because my eyes have locked on Wotan Schmid. He's watching Dylan talk to the agents, that vicious smile of his playing on his lips, and, not too far off, I notice that Anjo man watching Wotan with an expression like a father ready to scold his mischievous son.

When Dylan turns away from the agents, his face is even whiter than before, his eyes unfocused. He starts back through the crowd like someone in a trance as he weaves between the guests. And when I realize where he's headed, I feel as if my heart's grown suddenly two tons heavier.

Like most everyone else here, mine and Eilian's friends are totally unaware of this new development. They're standing together in the middle of the room, talking. Probably still about the uproar between Elspeth and the president. They greet Dylan with curiosity clear on their faces. Then, when he places his hand on Min-suk's shoulder and says something quiet in his ear, Min-suk looks so suddenly broken I think he might actually fall to the ground.

On reflex, my gaze cuts to Wotan again, and I catch him watching this exchange with an arrested expression on his face like this is exactly what he's been waiting for.

Beside me I hear Eilian breathe out, "*No*," in the voice of someone who knows.

Min-suk's following Dylan back toward the ballroom doors, and now other people are starting to become aware of the officers waiting there. Min-suk's sisters break away from their group of friends and hurry to his side, their eyes wide and full of apprehension, and Teresa joins the procession just before they slip out into the hall.

My gaze meets Rafael's and then Leti's. Both of them are standing totally silent against the backdrop of the rest of the room's whispers.

As if by some unspoken understanding, the four of us start moving at the exact same time. Eilian and me meet Leti and Rafael halfway across the room, and then we all make our way toward the door.

Around us, we can hear the hum of more party guests questioning what may be wrong, and I'm wondering if this is that moment I've been dreading. The one where my Way Reader skills are needed and I've got absolutely nothing of worth to give.

Out in the hall, Dylan's waiting, as if he had no doubt the four of us would come.

"Min-suk is speaking with the agents in the library," he says as he strides toward us, and even though he's doing his best to project a sense of calm, his voice is tight with agitation.

"What's happened?" Eilian asks, quiet, and it seems to me that Dylan nearly loses it completely.

"It's his da, Ellie," he says after a pause, using her pet name that I've only ever heard Aunt Nia or Uncle Uri use. "Loui Holm has been killed."

Thirty minutes later, sprawled on my bed in the privacy of my own room, I look up Min-suk's dad's death on the helix. I find one, cold mention of it—*Loui Holm, once highly-sought Deffron reader, dies tonight, aged 49*—before Dylan knocks on the door and comes striding in.

"What did you see when you met Wotan Schmid?" he asks, barely waiting for the door to close.

Geez.

Obviously, Dylan and I need to discuss everything that happened tonight, but I'm still in the emotional space surrounding Min-suk's grief. Dylan had asked the four of us friends to wait while he emptied the house of the rest of the guests. Asked us to be there outside the study, so Min-suk wouldn't feel so alone when it was time to go to GIB headquarters and deal more directly with the morbid details of his dad's death.

I'm still picturing Min-suk as he said goodbye. The way he looked totally disoriented. Destroyed. The way he held onto his sisters like they'd float away if he let them go for even a second. The way he buried his head in Rafael's shoulder like he was on the verge of collapse.

Then there was Teresa, trailing silent behind them, her whole body vibrating with such fury, I swear I could feel it radiating off her as she passed me by.

It would've been nice to take just a minute, maybe, to talk with Dylan about these things, but he obviously didn't come for that sort of chat.

"Do you think Wotan realized I had a sighting?" I ask, resigning myself to the inevitability of this conversation.

Dylan gives a sharp shake of his head.

"He wasn't here for you."

There's still a residue of his own disquiet in his face, but there's something else there too. Determination. A restless energy that, even when he's staring right at me, makes me feel like he's barely aware I'm there.

"I saw inside him, into his essence," I say. "There was a darkness there."

"Darkness?"

"I've seen it before. The night we got to Deffro and we had to hide from those takers in the woods? I saw this same sort of tentacled dark thing inside both of them too."

"That's all?"

He's obviously disappointed, and when I give a short nod of my head, he spins sudden away from me, saying, "*Dammit,*" under his breath in a way that makes me kind of flinch.

"I'm sorry," he turns back to me quick, sincere. "That wasn't about you."

"You were hoping for some other type of sighting?"

He nods, and then, bringing one hand to his face, he rubs at the bridge of his nose, closing his eyes for a long couple seconds. Then he says, "And my uncle? Did you see anything when you exchanged *pono* with him?"

I'm a little hesitant to respond. I mean, it doesn't seem like there's a whole lot of love lost between the president and pretty much any of his family except for Nia, but still, I'm not sure how Dylan's going to react.

"Same thing," I answer after a pause. "Not as bad, but, yeah. That same darkness."

Dylan just stands there real quiet, and I don't know how to read the expression on his face. Kind of angry? He's facing toward me, but he's looking at a spot somewhere behind my head. When his eyes do focus on me again, it's even harder to read the look in them.

"It's called the stain or the spot. I've only read about it in history books. No normal Painter can sense it. Not even most Way Readers can."

"What is it?"

"I don't know if it's a truly physical thing, or perhaps merely something intangible that the Way Reader's brain interprets in that particular way. But people are said to develop stains when they participate in takings."

Even though he's being careful not to give much emotion away, I know what he's getting at, and I'm guessing on the spectrum of good and bad news, this one leans pretty far toward bad.

"Your uncle's a taker?"

He waits a second to respond.

"I don't know. There may be other reasons for someone to have a stain like that."

He doesn't seem too convinced.

"The woman at the party tonight," I say. "She's the same one that grabbed me yesterday. I don't think all the stuff she was saying is totally irrational."

Dylan's eyes narrow. "What do you mean?"

"I don't know. She just seems real coherent about certain things. Things you wouldn't think someone in her state should be. And, I mean, she *knows* her brain's not working right. Isn't that supposed to be a sign of sanity or something? She kept telling me someone broke her and that only I could fix it."

"You think someone *has* been messing about with her mind?"

The feel of that nightmare man reaching into my head flashes up again, and I give this little nod. The possibility that maybe he wasn't trying to kill me should be reassuring, but it's actually not. Not when I consider the alternative.

"I think maybe it's the Sons of Morning. Didn't Eilian say, the other night in the den, that people've been turning up with their brains like that?"

Dylan's quiet, but he seems pretty struck by my idea. I watch him, study the hint of grief that's been hidden just under the surface of every expression he's had since the GIB agents showed up.

"Do you think maybe your uncle's in on it all somehow?" I ask, a bit more tentative. "With the Sons of Morning, I mean. With ruining people's minds?"

It's a long while still before he answers, standing there and staring off into the far corner of my room again.

Finally, he says, "I don't know. If my uncle is involved, he'd be in some position of power within the Sons of Morning organization."

"Yeah, doesn't seem like he'd be too eager to answer to anyone else."

Dylan shoots me this sarcastic almost-smile. "No, he's not what I'd call a team player. Even the thinnest connection between Hiarwar and the Sons of Morning would mean disaster. The things they'd be able to do with his help—" There's this sudden flash of bitterness over his features. A stinging realization. "Or, of course. The things he's already done."

Just as abrupt as he came, Dylan says, "I've got to go."

He's nearly to the door before I manage to get my own question out.

"Dylan, who is that Wotan man?"

The look he gives me then is dark and hard.

"An assassin for the Sons of Morning, though he doesn't kill for the energy. He simply kills to kill."

Before I can say anything else, he wrenches open the door and he's gone from the room. I didn't even get a chance to talk to him about Anjo. About the rest of the muddle of things running through my head.

I feel suddenly vulnerable. Awash in a situation where there are too many unknown variables. In a world where a man like Wotan Schmid can even exist.

I want to cling to my mom. Talk to calm, sensible Rishi and have him tell me everything's going to be okay. I pull out my com, look for news on Loui Holm's death again. This time there are a few more articles, but I only get through part of one before I can't read any more.

Loui Holm was found dead this evening in the alley behind Marrow's Tavern in Stranger's Hollow an hour after attending a party at Lucas House, the article says. *Officials report that he had been tied to a lamppost and his organs slowly heated to boiling point, likely while he was still alive. The victim had been overheard in the tavern earlier, claiming an apparently false mentoring relationship with the Way Reader. It is believed that his groundless claims may have been a contributing factor in the attacker's motivation to kill.*

With a snap, I shrink my com back into my ring and then just sit there on my bed, staring into the shadows at the other end of the room.

I think of that sighting I had when Min-suk and I met. Of him weeping alone in the dark somewhere. I can guess now what the sighting was about, and I'm suddenly furious it was given to me at all. I mean, what good does it do me, to know the exact dimensions of Min-suk's grief? I could've guessed it on my own. Why wasn't I given a sighting that was worth something? That could've made it possible for me to stop this from happening in the first place?

I jump up from my bed, practically fling myself out of my bedroom. I need some fresh air, and I know just the place to get it.

A few minutes later, as I storm out of the elevator on the aerie level and through the outer doors onto the balcony, I've got Wotan's face real clear in my mind. That hungry look in his eyes as he watched Min-suk's world fall to pieces. I feel sick. In my stomach, my heart, my head.

Bracing myself against the railing, I stare out at all the twinkling lights of the city. Try to find some comfort by telling myself that each light represents someone who's still alive and well. Someone who the takers and their cruelty haven't touched.

"It's all a lie," I hear, sardonic, from behind me and, at the sound of Gwilim's voice, I feel my anger explode.

I spin around, ready to lash out at him for bringing even a small part of tonight's trouble, but once I get a good look at him, most of that anger drops away.

He's leaning against the wall of the house, flicking tiny sparks off his fingers, and, though at first glance he appears about as careless as a person could be, I notice in his eyes how he's staring at the city like he's never hated anything more in his life.

"From up here everything appears serene." He doesn't look at me as he talks. "We all like to imagine we're safe, that bad things only happen to other people, but not one of us lives without catastrophe hovering one heartbeat away."

"I thought you left."

It's not even close to what I'm really wanting to say.

"I came back."

I stand there, watching him send those sparks out into the night sky, letting the cold seep through my skin even though I know, now, how to make the air warm around me.

"Why did you bring that man here tonight?" It sounds angrier than I meant it, and a wave of frustration and disquiet washes over Gwilim's face.

"I can't tell you that, Sophie. I know it sounds trite, but it really is safer for you the less you know."

"Do you work for the GIB too?" I ask. "Like, in secret?"

He just looks at me, and I get the impression the answer's no.

When it's clear he's not going to say anything else, I turn back around and stare over the balcony's edge where the moonlight's catching on each crystal of the frozen snow in the garden below, as if everything's been covered in a dusting of tiny stars. In the shape of each snow-covered tree or bush, the transition from light to shadow's so gentle it's almost like there's no real darkness at all.

Glaring down at it, the threat of tears comes on so fast I have to bite my lip to make sure I don't cry. I don't understand how the world can still be so lovely when the things happening in it are so definitely not.

"How is Dylan?" Gwilim's voice cuts through the silence.

I glance around at him, where he's still just flick-flicking those sparks off his fingertips. His expression hasn't changed, but it's strange to me, his asking about Dylan like that. I mean, Dylan wasn't the only one upset tonight.

Gwilim can see my confusion, and there's a sudden edge to his voice when he says, "Didn't you know? Loui Holm was killed the same way Dylan's brother was. Boiled alive from the inside, and Dylan was the one who found Padrig like that."

I feel my heart sink down the whole length of my spine.

"No one's told you about this." An incredulous realization passes over Gwilim's face, and he gives this bitter laugh. "Well, the family hasn't been much for talking these days."

"Did Wotan Schmid do it?"

It comes out in a rush, my own voice harsh in a way that surprises me, and at first Gwilim doesn't respond. Just stares at me like he's trying to decide how much to say.

"Look it up for yourself," he answers finally, brusque but not exactly unkind. He flicks one last, enormous spark off his fingers and thrusts himself up off the wall. "But don't read the regular news outlets. They only have part of the story. Read whatever you can find that comes from Sham Haddad."

Then, touching his fingers to his forehead in some sort of sour-faced military salute, he disappears back into the house.

I don't know why I haven't thought to look up the death of Dylan and Eilian's brother before. Or even their dad's incarceration. I guess it felt intrusive. Like, if the Lucases wanted me to know about it, they'd tell me. But when I do look it up, back in my room, it's not too hard to see why they might avoid the subject entirely.

Turns out the two events are basically one and the same thing. Their dad wasn't just framed for treason, but also for murdering his own son. As if the one wasn't bad enough.

In the standard news sources, the story reported was that Cadfan Lucas—Dylan and Eilian's dad—was alleged to secretly have been a member of the Sons of Morning all along, and he was only using his journalism as a cover while he worked covertly to help the takers infiltrate the Republic government. In this version of the story, Cadfan's trouble came when his secret was discovered by Padrig, who was an agent for the GIB just like Dylan. Because apparently, the Lucases don't know how to do anything normal with their lives.

Cadfan, in an effort to keep his criminal dealings hidden, was supposed to have lured Padrig to their family cottage in the mountains outside of the Deffron valley, where he tied Padrig to a chair, broke every one of his toes and fingers so he'd be in too much pain to use his painting to fight back, and then heated Padrig's insides until they seared right through his skin.

After that, he used Padrig's own blood to write words like "gindge" —that term for a dead body that Dylan hated so much—and all sorts of other awful things all over the walls inside the cottage, in an attempt to make it seem like a revenge killing and point the blame on one of the other takers Padrig had been chasing down in the course of his investigations. Then, after taking care of all that awful business, Cadfan is supposed to have pushed it even one awful step further and left Padrig there for Dylan to find.

As far as I can tell, not a single one of Sham Haddad's articles on Padrig's death are still published on the helix. So, at first this is the only version of the story I can dig up. It makes me sick to think what Padrig went through before he died, to think of Dylan finding his brother's body in a state like that. To think what it must've been like for the Lucases to have to deal with their dad being thrown straight into a murder trial after all of this, and then sent to prison.

When I do find references to Sham Haddad's reports, it's like some grim scavenger hunt. All the information is in bits and pieces. Mostly posted on conspiracy theory sites, and I can't help thinking how pleased to death my friend Logan would be about the fact I'm having to take those seriously.

Apparently, no mainstream news outlet would publish any of Sham's work on the subject—on the grounds they couldn't verify the facts themselves—and when she started posting her articles on her own website, the GIB came in and forced her to take them down. They said it was libel against government officials and that it threatened the security of the Republic.

By then, though, other people had already copied her articles for themselves, and they've kept her version of the story alive. Based on what I'm able to scramble together with the things they quote from her, Sham's version of the story goes like this:

Almost two years ago, when his parents' research on the Sons of Morning seemed to be hitting some snags, Padrig launched an investigation of his own through the GIB. He suspected there might be a double agent or two on the force, so he did most his work in secret, enlisting help from Dylan, who'd been working at the GIB for about a year himself.

To get around any possible double agents that might try to hinder their investigation, they decided to set up some added leverage and approached Sham with an offer of a big story, on the condition that she help them gather information.

Sham says the day he died, Padrig had hinted to her that he'd discovered something crucial to bringing the Sons of Morning down, and that he'd need her to be ready to write a piece on it to be published the next morning. He never contacted her again.

He and Dylan were supposed to meet at the family cottage that evening to go and get one last bit of proof that Sham's article would need, but when Dylan got there, Padrig was already dead.

No one knew for sure what information Padrig had gathered—he'd been vague about it even to Dylan, in the hopes it'd keep his brother safe—but Dylan told Sham he had reason to believe it was, at least in part, about Wotan Schmid, who Padrig suspected was one of the main killers for the Sons of Morning.

And, in fact, once Padrig's death was made public there was a witness that came forward saying he'd seen a man leaving the woods by the Lucas cottage that night, and the description he gave exactly matched Wotan Schmid. Unfortunately, only two days later, the witness went on a streaking fit, running stark naked through the streets of downtown Deffro. It was determined he was mentally unsound, and his testimony never made it to the actual trial.

That's when everything started pointing toward Cadfan as the killer. Like how, originally, the records for the city's illusion barrier—the energy barrier that keeps Deffro hidden from the Particle-Blocked world—showed an unidentified essensal code passing through on the night of Padrig's death. "Unidentified" meaning it didn't match anyone who was already in the barrier's system. But then, twenty-four hours later, the system suddenly showed that the code was a direct match to Cadfan Lucas.

Also, at least three takers who were already in GIB custody came forward to testify that they'd seen Cadfan regularly at Sons of Morning gatherings. Though, after his trial, they all mysteriously disappeared from the detention centers where they were being held. A com—which no one close to Padrig had ever seen in his possession—was discovered on his body, and a text message was found to have been sent from it to Cadfan stating that Padrig had discovered his father's secret and was going to bring him to justice.

And then there was Cadfan's best friend, John Cameron, who also worked at the GIB and had been influential in Padrig getting his job there. John had sworn at first that Cadfan was with him the whole evening as part of some games night they held on a regular basis. But, at the trial itself, he said instead that Cadfan hadn't been with him at all. That Cadfan had threatened the life of his son Tom if John didn't act as an alibi.

Even the regular news outlets reported that it was Cameron's switch in testimony that really clinched the case against Cadfan. The other evidence might've been dismissed in the face of Cadfan's spotless reputation, but John Cameron—who was a Kwakwaka'wakw elder and whose family line, like Cadfan's, also ran all the way back to the start of the Republic—was respected as well. In the end, the jurors trusted him.

It's hard not to see President Lucas's hand in all this, both in the corruption of evidence for the trial and in the way none of that corruption got reported with any credence in the news. I mean, there had to be someone with a lot of power doing this stuff, and if the president's a taker, it makes sense it'd be him.

Dylan must've realized it when I told him about his uncle's stain, but I wonder if Gwilim knows yet. Wonder if that has anything to do with the anger that's so evident in his face sometimes. I can't even begin to comprehend what all this has been like for the Lucases, what things are going to be like for Min-suk. It seems like the pain of it would be overwhelming. Just numbingly, impossibly big.

I lie there on top of my covers for a while, my com expanded in my hand, showing a picture of Padrig that was featured in the news. He looks young and happy and vibrant, and so much, in his own way, like Dylan and Eilian and Gwilim that it feels like it might literally break my heart.

I don't know exactly when it is that I fade into something like sleep. Or how long after that before consciousness starts coming back to me, but, as I become aware of my surroundings again, I also notice a familiar feeling. That certainty, like a tickle in my ignus and in my chest, that someone else is in the room.

It sends me shooting straight up in my bed, as wide awake as if I'd never been sleeping. The lights are all out—even though I know I didn't turn them off myself—and the room's in total darkness, but I can still tell he's here, standing at the foot of my bed. My skin's crawling with the knowledge of it.

The ghost thing takes a step sideways, as if he's going to come around the corner of the bed toward me, and I suck in a breath, all sharp and gasping. Spring to my knees, ready to launch myself onto the floor and make a run for the door.

He stops at that, though, as if my fear's the thing that's stopped him. And then he retreats. One step. Two. Away from the bed completely. Then, he's just gone. The same way he faded away before, only this time the room's real crowded with his absence, as if the air particles are rushing to refill the space where he was just standing.

That's when I notice my com screen, hovering at the foot of the bed where there's no way I could've accidentally pushed it in my sleep. It's facing away from me and the screen's bright, though it's just this mess of frenetic, static buzzing.

I reach out real tentative to touch the thing, and nearly pull back again when I encounter waves of excess electricity pulsing off it. A type of electricity that—based on what I've experienced of the Painter world so far—I'm pretty sure should not be inside my com in the first place. Electricity that looks and acts almost exactly like a person's essensal energy.

I sit, staring at the frizzing screen of my com. Then, real careful, I slide away from it off the edge of my bed and walk out of the room. I'm definitely spooked by what just happened, but mostly it's given me a lot to think about, and I figure I'm not going to get much more sleep at this point anyway.

I make my way up to the balcony, part of me hoping I'll run into Gwilim again, but no one else is there. The air is brisk, and this time I take the time to create a bubble of warm air around me as I stare at the still dark sky.

I think I know what that ghost thing is now. Other than frightening me half to death several times, it's been pretty non-threatening. And, after sensing that essensal-type energy in my com, I remembered what Rishi said about people's shadows and essences being split sometimes when they're killed violently. About the shadow being left in this world while the essence passes on to the next.

How'd he describe it? Not being fully one place or the other? Basically, being aware of everything your life used to be—probably longing for it—but not actually being able to live in it. It makes me angry that takers just carelessly allow this to happen to people. Destroy them in multiple ways just to feed their own cravings.

I'm pretty sure I can guess whose shadow's been haunting me. That picture of him from the news is real clear in my mind, and I feel my anger growing stronger the more I think about him being left in that state. I don't understand why it'd be me he'd choose instead of someone in his family, but I figure it must have something to do with my being the Way Reader.

Just another way I'm probably supposed to help someone, but I've got no idea how.

I should head back to my room. Get at least a couple hours sleep before breakfast, but I'm not at all tired now, and my hands are itching to be doing something.

Copying out some of the particles in the balcony railing, I multiply them in my hand until I've got a small sphere of wood. After a couple tries, I manage to transform it into clay, pretty convincingly close to the particle pattern in my practice ball downstairs.

Then I sit cross-legged on the floor of the balcony, adjusting my bubble of warmth so it's centered on me. Dylan had been planning to train me on color transformation after my introduction party. That obviously didn't happen, so I figure I'll try to study it out myself.

Before the party, I'd read a bit about painting in colors. So, I know that, in order to change the color of something, you've got to take into account a mess of factors. Surface properties and light wavelengths and a bunch of other things.

To get started, I form the clay ball into my best version of a dragonfly, and then set to work trying to make it look as much like my com ring as possible. Just to give myself something interesting to work with. After a couple dozen failed attempts, though, the dragonfly in front of me looks pretty splotchy and gross, covered all over in different hues of a murky, unsanitary brown.

My mostly sleepless night is starting to catch up to me, and the painting concepts I'm trying to apply are feeling maddeningly out of reach for my tired brain. After another half dozen tries at it, I'm so frustrated, I'm near ready to tear my hair out of my head.

Slumping backward against the rungs of the wooden balcony rail, I shove the clay insect away from me with the toe of my shoe, as if the dragonfly itself is the problem.

The first haze of sunlight has started to brush the tops of the mountains, but the wind is going strong and, with where I'm sitting now, my shoulders and head are outside of my bubble of warmth. I'm too worn out to do anything about it, though. The cool air hitting my neck sends goosebumps marching down the surface of my arms and legs. Strands of my hair keep flying across my face, tickling at the skin of my cheeks and under my chin.

I try to tuck the hair behind my ears a couple times, but the wind pulls it right back out again. Admitting defeat, I finally just lean my head back against the railings with a sigh. Close my eyes and give in to the feel of the wind rushing over me.

I tell myself that I need to go back to my room before I fall asleep out here and freeze to death, but I can't make myself move. I stay there, leaning against the balcony rails. Using my particle sight to absent-mindedly track my hair as it goes flying around my face in earnest now, whipping wild against my closed eyelids.

After a while, my brain starts working despite itself, and I find myself noticing how the bare light of dawn interacts with the particles in my hair. Opening my eyes again, I watch with both my particle sight and my actual sight as the effects of the light on the hair particles also affect the way the hair color appears to my eyes.

And, as I'm watching, the principles of color painting finally click into place in my mind. Not, honestly, like I actually understand the science of it, but it's like I can see the recipe. I can imagine what ingredients I've got to add to get what I want, and with that realization a flood of renewed energy hits me.

I grab the clay dragonfly and hunker over it again. And this time, a trickle of some pretty impressive, shimmering blues and greens starts across the surface of one of its wings, and I can't help letting out a delighted little crow of laughter. I mean, after so much struggle I *did it*. I figured it out, on my own.

"This likely isn't the best place to be doing that," I hear Dylan's voice from the door of the aerie.

I practically jump into the air, shoving the dragonfly under my body to hide it from view as if Dylan doesn't already know I'm the Way Reader.

"When'd you get here?" I demand, with a lot more shock than accusation.

"My point exactly."

He's leaning against the frame of the door, his hands in his pockets and a hint of a smile on his face.

"What if I'd been someone else? After only a few days, you're already getting into territory many of the others at your stage haven't begun to touch."

He comes around in front of me, and crouches down, pulling at my hands to get a glimpse of the dragonfly, and I notice now with a little embarrassment that the wings on the thing are pretty wonky.

"You're doing quite well," he says, the approval in his voice reigniting some of that pride I had a few minutes earlier. But then he adds, "I've got something to tell you." And he looks at me with one of his unreadable expressions that makes me sure he's come to give me bad news.

"Is it Min-suk?" I ask. Then, with more worry, "My mom?"

His eyebrows shoot up in surprise.

"No, not at all. Rishi's back. He's ready to begin training you. You start this morning, after breakfast."

"*Serious?*"

"Don't get too thrilled," Dylan says, kind of wry. "As a cover, we're telling everybody you're taking tai chi."

Of course. Because tai chi lessons are a thing Painters say you need if you're totally awful at painting.

I make a face at Dylan, and he laughs. Somehow, though, it strikes me as one of the most exhausted sounds I've ever heard, and I look closer at him.

"I've a few minutes before I'm expected back at the office," he says, shifting his eyes away as if he can tell I've noticed something's off. "Shall I help you with your color-changing technique?"

He sits in front of me, and, as I pull myself up into a cross-legged position, he takes the clay dragonfly in his hand, looking it over.

"Of course, it appears you've essentially sussed it out. I can teach you some helpful tricks, though."

"You're going back to work this morning?"

He nods.

"You were gone all night. Have you even had any sleep?"

Throwing a masked glance at me, he shrugs. "We've got to strike before the takers cover up anything."

I think about what I know of his dad's trial, and I understand his sense of urgency. Still, there's only so much he can do before he's going to need a rest. And, honestly, it's hard not to think about the fact that Padrig lost his life going after this Wotan guy. Seems like Dylan would be facing just as much risk.

"The shimmer you've used here is quite good," he says to me, ignoring the clear concern in my face. "However, since you've created only one reflective layer on the surface, it can't offer as much brilliance as is possible. If you think of it more like a diamond, which contains many planes that reflect light at different angles, then you can achieve a fuller and more complex shine. Let me demonstrate."

He scoots closer to take hold of my hand and place it on the dragonfly with his so I can see what he's doing in the particles. There's a long list of other things we should probably discuss right now, but I give in. Let him continue on with his lesson. And, when he suggests teaching me a bit more self-defense, I let him do that too because, as long as he's talking to me about the finer points of painting, he seems at least a little more like his usual self.

When we're taking the elevator downstairs half an hour later, though, and he leans against the wall and closes his eyes, it's not just that he looks exhausted. It's like he's taut. Brittle. As if he's being stretched so far from absolutely every possible direction that he might just snap.

I feel bad bringing anything up that could add more strain, but there are some things he's got to know, and I don't think I can hold off any longer.

"You should look into José Anjo," I say, and one of Dylan's eyes comes open in a mild sort of curiosity.

"The artist?"

"He—" I'm not exactly sure where to start. "Rafael Silva—when he saw Anjo he looked downright terrified. And the man wouldn't do *pono* with me. As in, when I tried to touch his palm, he totally flipped out. And then, I caught him watching Wotan last night, and Anjo *knows* that man. I mean, when the agents got here, it was like he knew exactly what Wotan had done."

Dylan has slid up straighter against the wall and he's got both eyes fully open now, looking at me all serious and attentive.

"Did you notice anything else? Did he smell at all like that man from your sighting, perhaps? Sound like him?"

I can't believe that's not a thing I'd even thought to check.

"I don't know. His whole vibe seemed like some sort of act or something, and we were never close enough for me to pick up any scent."

Dylan goes quiet for a minute, stares thoughtful at the elevator wall. Then he turns his eyes on me again, and I don't know how to describe the way that look makes me feel.

"That's good work, Zanny," he says, kind of grateful, of all things. Sincere. "It's—Well, I think it's something that could prove very useful."

The elevator comes to a stop at my floor, and Dylan gets off and starts walking with me down the hall. Looking up into his face, I ask him how the Loui Holm case is going, and I notice it takes him a second to respond.

"It's hard to know at this point," he finally says, watching his feet as he walks. "There's still the problem of the double agent—or agents—at the GIB."

"Have you found anything that could point to Wotan?"

Dylan shoots me a dismal smile. "Nothing conclusive."

There's more I'd like to ask, but we're almost to my room and there's one thing in particular I want to clear up this morning.

"Do takers have the ability to make themselves invisible?"

He quirks one questioning eyebrow at me like he's trying to figure out why this topic is coming so out of the blue.

"They've got the same abilities as any other Painter," he answers. "Though, technically yes, it is possible to play with the particles in the air around you and make it look as if you aren't actually there. Some of the GIB vehicles have that capability, but you'd have to be highly skilled to do it for yourself. Especially if you were in motion in any manner at all."

"What about getting into the house? Would it be possible for one of them to sneak in here?"

I don't think I sound scared—I'm just trying to rule out the possibility that my invisible visitor's anything other than a Painter's shadow—but Dylan looks full on at me now, as if I've just confessed to having another nightmare.

"Why do you ask that?" he wants to know, but for some reason I don't really want to tell him.

I was considering it, when it first occurred to me who the ghost thing probably was, but now it seems like it'd be pretty cruel to offer something like that to Dylan before I'm absolutely certain.

"It's just—" I give a little shrug. "It's just something I've been thinking about."

I must not be too convincing, though, because Dylan searches my face, his own expression hinting at a careful kind of concern.

"Our house has an essensal barrier set up. We're the only people that can get inside unless one of us brings someone in, and you'd need a small army to produce enough energy to break that barrier down, so no. No one could sneak in, invisible or otherwise."

We've reached my door, and when I turn to face him before stepping inside, he surprises me by leaning one hand against the doorframe and looking me steady in the eyes.

"You're safe here," he says. "As long as Gwilim doesn't bring any more takers, at least, no one can hurt you while you're in our home."

It's not what I was expecting, that type of response from him. I have to admit I don't dislike it. I mean, it's nice when he puts on that reassuring air, but I don't actually need reassurance right now. At least, not about that.

"I know I'm safe," I tell Dylan, trying to show still that I'm grateful for his concern. "I'm not worried about myself."

He searches my face a little longer.

"We're going to beat them," he says finally, in a different tone, standing straight and looking down at me with a sort of confidence that's meant to be shared. "We can't stop anyone from ever having to feel pain, but Zanny, it won't be long before you're a force to be reckoned with."

I stare back at him for a minute, kind of surprised at how much I needed to hear that.

"Thank you," I murmur.

"I'll meet you in the emvee hangar after breakfast, to take you to tai chi. Get some rest now, if you can."

He turns to walk off toward the marble stairs, and I stand looking after him, thinking how someday I want to be able to make everything right for him, in the same way he manages—at least for little moments like this—to make everything right for me.

The static's gone from my com when I step back into my room. Instead, the screen is full of a bunch of news notifications reporting that Representative Brandeis—that Mark Twain-ish man from my introduction party, who's some sort of leader in the Painter Republic's parliament—has moved the vote on the Particle-Blocked Involvement Act up, so it's now only three days away. It doesn't mean much to me, but apparently, it's such a big deal it's almost completely shut the Loui Holm story out of the headlines.

Still, when I get to breakfast, it's obvious Nia and Uri and Eilian have learned exactly how Mr. Holm died, and I'm guessing it's brought back pretty horrible memories.

Elian's totally silent. Poking at her food with her fork and staring blank into the floral centerpiece. At the other end of the table, though, Aunt Nia's like some human white noise machine. Drumming her fingers on the tabletop, scraping her spoon along her plate without actually scooping up any food. After a restless few minutes, she leans over to Uncle Uri and starts talking in this low whisper, as if Eilian and I can't still hear pretty much perfectly from where we're sitting.

"If it is the self-same method in nearly every way, does that not call my brother's conviction into question?"

Uri glances at us, like he's well aware we can hear every word.

"Cadfan certainly can't have done this one too, not under the circumstances," he replies, his own voice carefully quiet. "I'm sure Dylan won't miss the opportunity to make that obvious."

I look over to see what Eilian thinks of this, and even though she's not giving much away, it'd be hard to miss the tension in her muscles. The tightness to her lips.

"When that man was at the party last night, he must've come straight from killing Loui," Aunt Nia's still whispering. "He came here to *our* house to gloat. To watch Loui's poor boy get the news, and to stare us in the eyes as we relived what he did to Padrig, what my brother has suffered in his place."

Aunt Nia may not be saying any of this for our benefit, but the effect on Eilian is immediate and intense. She sits up straighter, her face going real alert.

"Wotan Schmid was at our *house* last night?" Her voice cuts through the air all dangerous and raw, and Aunt Nia snaps her head around toward us, as if she honestly hadn't realized we were listening.

"He came *here*," Eilian says again, thudding her pointer finger down on the table for emphasis. "To Zanny's party, after what he'd done to Min-suk's da?"

"I'm so sorry," Aunt Nia says, and I don't know if she's apologizing for Wotan's presence in the house or for blurting out everything. "I thought you must've seen him here, dear. There was little we could do about it. We couldn't force him to leave, not with nothing actually proved against him."

I notice she doesn't mention that Gwilim was the one who brought the man in the first place.

"*Calon tân,*" Eilian breathes out. "Don't the rules of hospitality have *limits*?"

She pushes her chair quick away from the table and stands up.

"I don't feel well. I'm going to my room."

Stalking to the door, she flings it open so hard, it comes flying back and slams itself shut behind her. Aunt Nia rises to go after her, but Uncle Uri touches her arm to hold her back.

"She'll need some time alone," he murmurs. "Words aren't going to help her right now."

It's obvious Aunt Nia doesn't quite believe him, but she sits down anyway. And, even though I think Uncle Uri's probably right about this one, I've also got to admit it does feel kind of lousy to just hunker down here after Eilian's stormed away.

Aunt Nia starts pushing food around her plate again. After a few minutes, I ask, tentative, if that Elspeth woman's all right.

"Oh yes," Aunt Nia glances at me with the sparest smile. "The hospital could do little for her poor mind, so they very wisely sent her home with Sham Haddad again, to allow her the comforts of companionship and familiar surroundings."

More likely, the hospital didn't have much choice, once Aunt Nia and Sham decided on it. It is nice to think Elspeth's with Sham for now, but I doubt the president would just let her get away with making a scene like she did, so it's not what I'd call one hundred percent reassuring.

The three of us barely say four sentences to each other for the rest of breakfast, and I doubt any of us actually eats. We stare at our food in silence, and, every once in a while, when I do look up at Nia and Uri, it sort of hurts to see the lines of worry etched so deep on their faces. See the sadness they wear in the slope of their shoulders as they sit quiet in their chairs.

When I stop by Eilian's room to check on her after breakfast, there's a sign on the door that says, *Yes, I do actually want to be alone right now.*

I can hear her in there crying, big, gut-wrenching sobs. So, I just stand there, staring at that sign and listening to her, thinking of the look on Dylan's face last night when he told us about Min-suk's dad. Thinking of Min-suk and his sisters. Of Padrig and Mr. Holm dying in so much pain. Of Gwilim hiding out on the balcony, alone with his own anger.

Kind of like scratching an itch, I reach my mind into Eilian's room and find it's easy enough to pinpoint her essence, to sense that the energy inside her seems all fractured and broken somehow. And, at the sight of it, a sudden, pressing fury surges through my muscles, my bones.

Somebody has to do something about all this. I mean, *I'm* supposed to be doing something, and I just hate—*hate*—that I can't conjure up a single idea. Isn't the universe supposed to be guiding me? Or am I a dud, after all?

After a few minutes, I head back down to the hangar to meet Dylan, telling myself I'm respecting Eilian's privacy by not bothering her, while really just feeling like the ultimate worst friend.

Dylan says I need to know how to get to training on my own, so, instead of going in his emvee, we take the Magnix. The friend group was supposed to meet at a park called The Menagerie this afternoon for some sort of Gathering Day-themed scavenger hunt Deffron kids do every year. After what happened last night, I'm pretty doubtful any of the friends are even going to show, but Dylan says they may want the distraction.

So, in the station, he points out on a map how I'll get to The Menagerie after training, warning me to always be on the lookout for anything suspicious or out of the ordinary, and to call him immediately if I need help.

Thanks to Mom's focus games, being on the lookout is something I've practiced my whole life. But, when the station is all crowded with morning commuters and the train itself is even worse, it does feel kind of daunting to imagine doing this without Dylan as a guide.

When we're finally above ground again at the end of our ride, it seems like pretty much everything in this new neighborhood is under construction. Steel faces of all shapes and sizes are climbing over the buildings, tending to basic tasks while artisan builders see to the more complicated work.

Where there's not construction, everything looks like it's been years since it's seen real care. Each side of the street is lined with one long, rectangular building, like any boring old strip mall back home. Which Dylan says was the point.

"It was meant to offer a Particle-Blocked shopping experience," he explains. "Another instance where Painters thought it would be amusing to mimic the Particle-Blocked world. Used to be fairly popular, until the novelty wore off. City's working to revitalize it now. But, as it's currently an area of little interest and it's near Rishi and Aunt Yvie's home, Rishi thought it perfect for the entrance to your hidden lair. Only a few new shops have been established here so far, so the foot traffic will be minimal."

We head to the third door on the right side of the road, which opens on a long hall lined with glass-fronted shops. The lights are off in all of the ones we pass except for a starkly lit travel agency where an elderly couple's talking to someone at a tall counter. None of them notice as we walk by.

At the end of the hall, there's a shop with no windows and with a wooden door instead of glass. A brass plaque says, *Ms. Miranda's School of Energy Flow: Specializing in dance and tai chi.* Another plaque under that says, *By appointment only*, with a number to call, which, Dylan tells me in an undervoice, goes directly to a fake voicemail message that says Ms. Miranda's currently not taking new students.

The door opens at the touch of Dylan's hand. Programmed for either of our essensal codes, he says. As he steps aside to let me in, I notice he tucks his hand against his body to check a message lit in dark purple on his palm. As soon as he reads it, there's a change in his face, a tension to his jawline that I think could either be anger or fear. He doesn't say anything, though. Just shuts the door and leads me down the hall.

Everything in the shop's set up like a legitimate dance studio, complete with a lobby at the front and a mirrored room in back. I guess in case someone manages to get through the front door. There's no one there, though, and our footsteps echo kind of hollow and muffled as we walk.

In the back studio, Dylan heads for the furthest corner on the right, stopping before he reaches the wall.

"Take care," he holds his hand out in warning. "The floor here is an illusion barrier. Anyone else walking across it would feel solid ground beneath their feet, but for us—"

He takes another step, and his foot disappears into the floor about halfway up his calf.

"We could find ourselves tumbling down a long set of stone stairs. Careful now," he says, heading downward and beckoning for me to do the same.

It's strange to watch myself disappear into the ground. Strange to feel the tickle of the barrier's energy as it swallows more of my body with every step. Rising above my elbows, my shoulders, my chin, my eyes.

The passage is narrow, the rocky walls dotted with lights that buzz to life as we approach, and Dylan was not exaggerating when he said the stairs were long. They go on and on, and it's starting to feel like we're headed to the center of the earth itself when we finally step out into the huge cavern at the bottom, where it looks less like the center of the earth and more like the middle of outer space.

First off, it's huge. Way bigger than any rooms in Lucas House. But, more than that, it *looks* like something out of this world. With all these neony lights etching out sweeping patterns in the ceiling, the walls, even the floor. As if the lights were spread with a giant brush full of fireworks.

All across the cavern, there are stalactites and stalagmites reaching toward each other from floor to ceiling, covered in their own swirls of light just like everything else in the room. And hanging from the top of the cavern between the stalactites, vines drape down in graceful tendrils of living curtain, falling all the way to the ground in one corner of the cavern and creating a sort of room, near an arch of light in the wall that Dylan says is the entrance from Rishi and Yvette's house.

"They live a couple of streets over, so they created a passage from their basement. They'll be here any minute."

In the room-like space formed by the hanging vines, there's a table and chairs set up. A bunch of benches line the edge, and a raised platform sits against the far wall, littered in vivid-colored, embroidered pillows. Off to one side, there's a pool of water too, with floating flowers bordered in their own share of neon bright lights.

"Yvette designed everything," Dylan says, as I bend down to touch a finger to the glowing line of one of the lilies. "She's an architect and interior designer as well as a politician. Did the orca and bird buildings downtown, for instance."

"It's organic!" I say, probing the plant-like particle pattern of the neon lights. "As in, *alive*."

Dylan smiles. "The lights are bioluminescent. They stop the air from growing stale."

Standing straight again and looking around me, I can't help wondering what kind of mind Yvette must have.

When she and Rishi step through the hanging vines a minute later, my stomach does a nervous flip flop. Rishi's face is shaved now, which makes him seem at least a couple decades younger. And with him in a well-tailored, dusty gray suit and Yvette with her dark hair loose and the skirt of her long dress fluttering dreamlike around her ankles, the two of them look like the leads in some moody art film. And, for a second, it feels like maybe it's been years since I last talked to Rishi rather than just a few days.

When he sees me and Dylan standing there, though, his face breaks into a grin—that same grandfather smile I remember from before. He comes bounding forward to give Dylan *ramu*, and I'm surprised when he does *ramu* with me too, his forehead pressing against mine and his palm sending reassuring energy through my ignus at the back of my neck.

Yvette also gives us both *ramu*, a thing that's both gratifying and totally disarming. I mean, even Aunt Nia didn't give me *ramu* until, like, the second day in their house. And last night at the party, Yvette was a little intimidating.

Today, though, away from all those other politicians, it's easy to see how she and Nia could be good friends. In fact, she reminds me a lot of Nia. The way she takes my hands and steps back to look me over with this whole bounty of affection in her face, as if I'm a kid she's known and loved for ages.

"I'm so *pleased* to see you again," she says, and pulls me into another hug, enveloping me in a pleasant scent of fresh-cut lumber and unfamiliar spices.

"The place is stunning," Dylan says, and I agree wholeheartedly, swearing that I couldn't imagine anything better.

Yvette's eyes light up with that momentary playfulness I noticed last night. "Charmers," she says with a smile that shines, and I catch Rishi watching her like he's never seen anything he liked so much in all his days. He gets right to business, though.

"We have much to discuss," he says, pulling his eyes away from Yvette and gesturing toward the table in the center of the room. "Shall we debrief?"

As we move to sit down, Dylan gets another text, which he seems to like even less than the one earlier. Again, he says nothing about it. Just turns his attention to Rishi, who's asking how the Loui Holm case is coming. The question adds a renewed sense of exhaustion to Dylan's voice.

"Quite honestly, it's proving hard to find anything concrete. The best we've got is a witness who remembers that, a few minutes before he disappeared, Loui was talking to a bald, German-sounding man at the bar."

"Wotan Schmid?"

"Certainly." Dylan gives a slow nod. "But we can't bring Wotan in based on a description that could apply to any number of men walking the streets of Deffro on a given day."

Another message springs to life on his palm, and this one seems to make him even more tense. But still, when he looks back up at the rest of us, he tries to act like nothing's wrong.

"I told you that Zanny noticed something odd about José Anjo—"

"I've never liked that man," Yvette interjects real cheerful, and Dylan can't help flashing a bit of a smile.

"No, nor probably should you, though I can't say I've found anything concrete on him either. A search on the helix turned up very little. Only his personal pages, some social media accounts, a few articles that discuss his art. The worst anyone can say about him is that he's a bit narcissistic, which we already knew. But I did find something concerning. He lives alone in a flat in the older section of the Arts District, and he's surprisingly hermitic for someone with so many friends. He's been known to stay shut in his house for days at a time with no one else coming or going."

"Not entirely uncommon for some people," Yvette interjects again, and Dylan gives a slight nod.

"True. Only, his neighbors say he always reappears looking much, much refreshed. Even hyperactive."

My mind flashes back to that jittery, hungry look in Wotan's eyes. That's probably not quite what Dylan's describing, but Yvette clearly knows what he means.

"He's performing takings," she says, suddenly serious.

"That would be my guess." Dylan looks pretty grim himself, and Rishi's watching him close. Waiting to see what he'll say next. "But he's doing so without anyone appearing to enter or leave his house. So, the question is, how is he managing it?"

He looks around at us.

"And there's another thing I found. His name, Anjo. In Portuguese it means 'angel.'"

We all stare at him.

"As in, *The* Angel," I say, my voice flat.

"It seems rather on the nose for someone trying to hide their identity," Rishi says.

"No one could accuse him of being subtle."

"What will you do?" Yvette asks.

"What can we do?" Dylan gives a bitter sort of shrug. "We can't toss Zanny at him, unprepared. And, without the Way Reader leading them yet, the Keepers of the Way don't have the legal jurisdiction to go after Anjo within city limits unless they get a warrant from a Deffron judge. As far as the GIB goes—"

He rubs hard at the bridge of his nose.

"With possible double agents still in the mix, I must be careful how I move forward. We need proof. I'm working on a method of surveillance that wouldn't make it obvious to the agents implementing it that Anjo's the target but that somehow still gets us the information we require. It's complicated and will take extra time, but it will ensure that no one can tip him off."

The number of things Dylan's having to juggle seems totally unmanageable, and, as if to prove my point, he gets another text message right then. This time, he looks like he might feel physically ill, and I'm not the only one who notices.

"What's wrong?" Rishi asks, and Dylan's quick to say it's nothing.

"Only work," he offers, trying to sound unconcerned, but then he changes his mind. "No. It's—The GIB has, in my absence, decided to call Loui Holm's death a copycat murder. Not an exoneration of my da, but an homage to what Da is supposed to have done to Padrig." His mouth twists, as if anger's sparking on his tongue. "Director Laugadóttir has just warned me against openly pursuing the investigation as anything else."

There's silence in the cave as we all process what this news must mean for him and his family.

"Is that Laugadóttir woman the double agent?" I ask, remembering her terrifying demeanor last night.

"Don't know." Dylan gives a sharp shake of his head. "Perhaps she believes she truly is looking out for me, like she implies. Could be anyone higher up than me. Maybe it's even the director, Jaap Jansen. My uncle's president of the Republic and he's a taker, so why not the head of the GIB?"

He leans against the table, his head hanging in a momentary show of defeat. Then he looks up at Yvette, slow like he's about to say something he thinks he maybe shouldn't.

"Perhaps the Gwylwyr could…"

I've got no idea what the word is he just said, but Yvette clearly knows it. Her expression twitches with something near a smile, and when she responds to him there's a note in her voice like she's admitting to a secret.

"A couple Gwylwyr agents *have* recently managed to infiltrate the Sons of Morning inner circle. They've not yet been allowed in the presence of Beelzebub or The Angel himself—though, we did have some suspicion of Anjo being involved with the organization to a certain degree. All that is to say, yes. Gwylwyr agents may be able to uncover helpful information."

I'm now more than a bit lost, and I open my mouth to ask what exactly they're talking about, when Rishi beats me to it.

"The Gwylwyr, as I can tell you're wondering, Zanny," he starts, a little twinkle in his eye, "are the Welsh elite security force. Every city-state has one, and the Gwylwyr is Deffro's. The identity of the director of the Gwylwyr is generally kept a secret. Though, perhaps not such a great secret if Dylan knew it was Yvie."

"A hopeful guess, merely," Dylan says, a bit sheepish, and Yvette offers another hint of a smile.

"I'm sure you realize that this information cannot leave this room," she cautions, and Dylan and I both assure her we understand. Though, to be honest, I'm still struggling to process this additional dimension of Yvette's personality.

Dylan gets another text, then, and his expression darkens again.

"I'd best get going soon," he says. "Which means," he looks at me real pointed, "it's time."

"Time for what?" I ask, suddenly wary.

Instead of answering, Dylan pulls a black, plastic-looking card from his pocket. On the front it says, *Yokio's Frozen Delicacies*, with a picture of some sort of ice cream dish and the word *Rewards*. He offers it to me, and as soon as it touches my skin, the thing shudders into the shape of a Particle-Blocked cell phone right there in my hand. I just about drop it out of surprise, which makes Yvette let out a little chime of laughter, and even Dylan smiles.

"It's attuned only to your essensal code," he says. "In case anyone finds it in my possession. I've planned everything so that I'm sure it's entirely safe to make a call now without it being tracked, but I can only give you five minutes."

I stare at that phone, sort of scared to acknowledge what I think it means in case I'm wrong, while also thinking that, with everything else Dylan's got on his shoulders, it's incredible he took the time to arrange this for me as well.

"She's waiting," he says. "All you need to do is hit send."

He doesn't have to tell me again. I stand and walk a few feet away to give myself some privacy, flicking my thumb over the send button as I go. Even though it's probably only a couple rings before Mom answers, it feels like an eternity, and as soon as I hear her say my name, the tears just erupt out of my face. I mean, it's like full-on Mount Alexandra.

When I try saying something back to her, it comes out cramped and choking. She does this quick intake of breath, and I hear the tears fill her own voice.

"Are you all right, honey? Have they kept you safe?"

"Yeah," I say, but it's more a croak than a word.

"You haven't encountered any of those—those takers?"

I've got no idea how to answer this. I don't want to worry her, but, also, I don't want to lie.

"It's been close a couple times," I say finally, managing to sound slightly less like a frog who's being choked to death. "But Dylan and Rishi've protected me real well."

"Oh, Zanny."

The pain in her voice—I feel it in my chest.

"I'm okay, Mom. Really."

I glance around at the others and catch Rishi and Yvette sitting with their hands clasped across the table and their eyes pointed down like they're both saying some silent prayer. I wonder what's going on with them, but then I notice the look on Dylan's face as he's watching me. This troubled empathy so clear in his eyes that my tears suddenly threaten to burst out again.

"Three minutes," he mouths, apologetic, and I turn quick away.

There are so many things I've been wanting to tell Mom—so many things I've been wanting to ask her—but it's looking like most of it's going to stay unsaid.

"How've you been?" I take a few more steps from the table, wanting my last minutes with her to be as private as possible. Wanting to pretend like everything's actually normal right now. "What've you been doing?"

"A lot of little nothings. I'm just trying to keep myself busy, really. I'm enjoying spending time with your cousins, McKenna and Calum. They're several years younger than you, but I think you'd like them a lot."

Cousins. It's still strange to think I have family out there who I've never met.

"If you like them," I offer, "I'm sure I would."

When Mom and I say our goodbyes a couple minutes later, it takes a lot to fight back a fresh flow of tears, and I stand with the phone still up to my ear and my back to the others until I feel like I've got ahold of myself. When I do turn around, I make sure not to look any of them in the eye.

Dylan stands and comes to meet me, taking the phone from my hand and sliding it into his pocket as it turns back into the Yokio's rewards card.

"I'd best be off," he says. "It'll look suspicious if I stay away any longer. Are you sure you can find your way to the scavenger hunt from here? You remember how to read the Magnix map?"

I'd nearly forgotten about the scavenger hunt. I'm not exactly eager to go at this point, but I nod anyway.

"All right," he says, taking this little breath. "If anything seems remotely suspicious, you'll call me, yes? We'll meet tonight for training, as usual. Now that Rishi's helping you with painting and reading, we can focus on self-defense."

There's something in his eyes that still looks kind of concerned, and as he turns to leave, I surprise myself by reaching out and grabbing his hand.

He turns back to look at me, curious.

"Good luck," I say, and for a second, he just stares like he doesn't know how to respond. Then, with the tiniest hint of a smile, he nods his head and turns and strides away through the vines.

When I look over at Rishi and Yvette, they're watching me, still holding each other's hands, with a weird touch of sadness in their faces. I can't tell if it's sympathy or something more personal to them.

"Are you ready for some tai chi?" Rishi asks with a gentle smile, and I laugh.

"Born ready."

"You'll want to remove your shoes. It'll be hard to do it in boots like those."

I look down at my red combat boots—the same ones I wore my first day in Deffro—and, even though I'm confused as to how they'd affect my painting, I bend down to take them off.

Rishi removes his shoes as well, and his suit jacket, and then moves over to the open space between the table and the cushion-covered platform. I watch him crouch down in a sort of lunge, spreading his arms out and swinging his torso around like he's warming up for some physical activity.

"Wait a second," I say, "are we really doing tai chi?"

Yvette bursts out laughing, and Rishi throws a smile over at her.

"Of course. Exercise of any sort—be it tai chi, running, swimming—are, in actuality, quite helpful in improving a Painter's particle manipulation. It strengthens the connections between your body, essence, and shadow, and it assists in the flow of essensal energy. Tai chi just happens to be my favorite method. Come, let's start."

He directs me to copy his stance, so I crouch in a squatting lunge beside him, holding my arms out and feeling like some strange scarecrow thing. Yvette's watching with a smile on her face, and when I shoot her an uncomfortable glance, she gives another bubbling laugh.

"Don't mind me. I'll be doing my own thing."

She touches her thumb to her com ring to project some light matter, waving her hand at the ball of dark green light like she's displaying a prize on a gameshow.

"I've a new building design in mind, so I'll barely be aware of you."

"You will need to learn not to be distracted by your surroundings," Rishi calls my attention back to him. "You're doing fine. Just put your hands like this."

I try copying him, pinching the fingers of my right hand together and pointing down, holding my left hand tall and thin, palm forward.

"Yes," he says, "now swing your arms around—nice and slow—and step this way like so."

I manage to do it—barely—but with the next motion I feel myself tilting off balance, and I'm sure I'm about to fall on my face. My arms flail on either side of me, and I have to take an extra step just to keep on my feet.

"It requires some practice," Rishi says with a smile as he twists his own body around again, so smooth it's almost uncanny.

His tai chi's real graceful, but for me the motions are so unnatural it's hard to imagine ever doing them with anything close to grace.

"Think less about *what* you're doing," he instructs, "and focus on your essence and your ignus. Feel the energy in each and feel how they're connected to each other. Feel how the energy flows out from them and into your arms, out through your fingers as your hands pass by each other like this. Yes. Now feel the energy flowing down your legs and out through your toes as you slowly move your foot around to the other side."

I *can* feel the energy, like he says, as if it's gliding through my veins, rooting through every layer of my body right down to the tiniest particles. Filling me with a sense of power and potential, similar to how I felt that moment I first decided to come to Deffro.

As Rishi's voice continues, quiet and steady, the movements themselves begin to feel more comfortable too. When he finally stands up straight and says it's time to tackle particle reading, I'm actually kind of disappointed. He assures me the energy will stay with me as we read, though.

"Flow work is simply a warmup for the real thing."

We sit among the cushions on the raised platform, cross-legged and facing each other. And Rishi's right, at least, that the energy doesn't seem to leave. It buzzes through my body still, eager to be used for something.

After plumping some pillows behind his back, Rishi looks at me and says, "As you've found, sometimes sightings come to you of their own accord, but it's also possible to seek them out. In fact, that is what many readers do for a living, search out sightings about others' lives, on their behalf. You simply need to look for sighting triggers, or tangles of accumulated particles that hold what you could call particle memory. Of course, calling it memory is not entirely accurate, as the triggers do hold information about events happening in all directions of time, not only the past."

He's fully into lecture mode, and I can't help smiling at the familiarity of it.

"Sighting triggers tend to gather in objects of significance to a person. A favorite book, a treasured memento. For today, we will use something of mine. Since you are important to me yourself, my possessions may offer you sightings that apply to both of us."

Rishi pulls his wedding ring off his finger and hands it to me. It's mostly made of metal—gold, I'd say, by its particle structure—but it doesn't look like metal on the outside. Instead, it's this deep, rich brown with soft graining on it like wood. The surface is veined with carvings that reveal the gold underneath, spelling out an unfamiliar word, *ne'nagwą'nakwąla*.

"This is an object of the greatest significance to me," Rishi says. "Yvette made it for me herself, as is tradition in many Painter cultures. The word you see there means 'going home' in Kwak̓wala, the language of her mother's people. Her wedding ring has the word *bāṛi* on it, or 'home' in my language of Bangla, because home is what we are to each other."

The way the light of the cavern reflects off the ring, it's like the grooves of the letters themselves are glowing.

I look at Yvette, where she's still sitting at the table, her legs tucked up on the chair and her lip pinched into her teeth as she fiddles with her light matter. She's shaped it into a tall flower, its petals bursting out the top and cascading to the table surface like an exploding star.

It's like everything that woman touches exudes an effortless beauty.

"There should be myriad triggers to find in the ring. Shall we try?"

I'm surprised at the strength of the fear that surges so sudden inside me—at the way my whole body seems to seize at the mere thought of having another sighting.

Rishi notices, studies my face, his own expression full of empathy.

"Dylan told me what you saw the other night," he says. "The sighting in which someone is harming you. It can be hard, after experiencing something fearful like that, to welcome any sightings again. However, sightings—even the fearful ones—are gifts from the universe, offering you a chance to prepare, or to give you important insight. A sighting is, in fact, the safest way to have your first encounters with the dangerous things of life, because nothing can hurt you there."

He's got a point. Even if my pulse doesn't seem to believe it.

"And I will be with you," he adds. "Sitting here in person, for one, but also, I will accompany you through your sightings. It is possible for us, as readers, to see the exact same thing, if we stay connected like so," he presses his palms against mine in a sort of double *pono*, "Shall we try?"

I give a nod, still much less confident than I'm letting on. Though, in the brief silence between us, I can hear Yvette murmuring something to herself as she works, and her voice is a strange kind of comfort.

"Close your eyes," Rishi says. "It will be easier to focus. Now, breathe in and feel your body and your mind strengthen. As you exhale, let yourself spread away from your core. Find a path from one particle to another—one bundle of particles to another—deep into the recesses of the ring."

It's a strange sensation. That awareness of movement without actually moving.

"Look for a disturbance in the particle patterns. A cluster or a knot—yes, there's one. Now reach your mind out to touch it."

I see it, a bunch of shimmering particles stuck together, rolling over each other like a tangle of tadpoles.

The transition into the sighting is almost instantaneous. One second, I'm in the cavern, still vaguely aware of the cool stone of the platform against my crossed feet and legs. Then, the next moment, everything around me is bright and sun-filled.

We're standing on a vast stretch of green grass. In the distance, I see a huge white obelisk that I recognize right away even if I've never seen it in person. A circle of American flags surrounds it, and there are people everywhere, running away from the place where we're standing. On the lawn below the monument, sitting at a haphazard angle, is my Chevy truck. There's someone inside it, but the light of the sun is hitting the window and creating a glare that makes it impossible to see them clearly.

Then the sighting's over. My mind's fully back in the cavern again, my eyes wide open and staring at Rishi's curious face.

"What was that?" I ask, but he just raises an eyebrow and gives a wry shrug.

"I thought perhaps you would know. You received no direction nor sense of purpose for the sighting?"

"Nope." Just like usual. "I mean, I'm pretty certain that's the Washington Monument, and that's definitely my truck, and that's a whole load of real terrified people. But neither I or my truck've ever been even close to that place, so my mind's drawing a total blank on helpful information."

Except for the thought that, whoever's in the truck is probably someone I know, and I do not love the idea of them being in whatever situation that seems to be.

"Well," Rishi presses his lips together, considering, and apparently unaware that a small sense of panic is starting up inside me again. "We'll simply tuck this sighting away for future reference. Shall we try once more—?"

But the decision's already made. I feel my mind hit another sighting trigger and, without my doing anything, I'm spiraling down into a darkness so heavy it's almost a shock. Then I'm shooting out again into a dreary light that reminds me of the fluorescent bulbs in my high school back home. I hear Rishi say my name, feel him grabbing for renewed hold on my hands, sending his mind in after me.

I see a cave-like room, the walls covered in faded, medieval-style tapestries and other ancient-looking artifacts. It's unclear where the light's coming from, but it's spare and too bright at the same time, casting everything in stark contrast between light and shadow. In each of the back corners, there's a sarcophagus with double encasements, as if they're meant to hold the remains of conjoined twins.

There are two men in the place. The first, at the head of the room behind an imposing black desk, and the second looming over it from the opposite side, his manner bristling with obvious anger. I can see the general shapes of them, but I can't really make many details out about them beyond an impression of their facial expressions as they interact.

The second man, though—he's speaking in taut, low tones, with his hands pressed tense against the top of the desk as he leans over it, and his voice is easy enough to recognize, especially with the barely controlled fury in it.

"You said this would never be traced back to me, Anjo," President Lucas is saying. "And yet there was so very public a display. How was it, again, that so many of your specimens escaped their holding cells at the lab? How did such a number of them have a chance to roam the city freely and turn public attention on me, just when you swore your efforts were beginning to come to fruition? And bloody *marw*, how did that woman possibly reverse your process?"

Behind the desk, Anjo seems relaxed despite the president's anger. Almost too relaxed. Sitting confident and commanding, like he believes he's very much in control of this situation. When Anjo speaks, the sighting offers me a hint of that scent of his, and I feel like I could choke on it.

"Perhaps she was a reader," he says. "We still don't know everything about the functioning or power of readers' minds. I might ask you, Mr. President, why it is we cannot seem to locate this Elspeth woman now? She appears to have vacated Ms. Haddad's residence almost immediately on returning to it."

"You would prefer I'd prevented her from going with Sham Haddad at all, I suppose?" says President Lucas. "And risked revealing a too-pointed interest in the woman after the things she'd just alleged? There are enough conspiracy theories already, and our plan relies on utmost secrecy. There can't be any public suspicions surrounding Parliament's vote."

"Let me assure you that we are as invested in success as you are." Anjo's voice is entirely different than it was at my introduction party. Smug, but with an obvious threat in it. "We are the ones that came to you, you might remember."

When the president responds, I can hear his expression in his tone. That cruel twist of his smile, the subtle clenching of his jaw.

"Then perhaps you could keep your wild bulldog in check," he snaps. "It was quite a business for me covering up his previous aberration."

With that, the president spins on his heel and storms out of the room, leaving a heavy silence to linger behind him.

As I come out of the sighting, Rishi's ready for it. He's watching me with his eyes narrowed, kind of intense. Yvette's there too, hovering by the platform and studying my face with just as much worry, as if somehow, she knows something's happened.

"Did you see that too?" I ask Rishi, feeling my heart pumping a few beats too fast even though I'm well aware I'm not currently in any danger.

Rishi raises one speculative eyebrow.

"It appears the universe has decided to make our Sons of Morning mystery a measure clearer at last."

It's not hard to put two and two together as we discuss the sighting afterward, Yvette sitting on the platform with us now. The vote President Lucas mentioned has got to be the Particle-Blocked Involvement Act. It's the only bill anyone's really talking about in Deffro these days, and, when you think about it, it makes sense how it'd help the takers. Even I can figure out that if they had more leeway to serve as political leaders in Particle-Blocked governments, it'd make it a whole lot easier for them to instigate wars and feed on all the essensal energy.

From there, it's not too big a stretch to imagine how Anjo messing with people's brains might come in handy too. I had thought maybe he just liked hurting people, but Hiarwar talked about a lab, and referred to Anjo's victims as "specimens," and it occurs to me that Elspeth and the others may have only been practice, leading up to the real prize. And the more I think about it, the more my nightmare sighting takes on new meaning too.

"Anjo's turning people into his puppets," I blurt out.

Rishi and Yvette were just talking about how impossible it'd be for the takers to get the bill passed. How the number of politicians who oppose it is way bigger than the number who support it.

My words stop them mid-sentence, though, and they turn toward me.

"Or, at least," I feel suddenly uncomfortable under their scrutiny. "I think that's what he's been trying to figure out. Like, how to rewire people's minds."

Neither of them responds at first, and I think maybe I've totally missed the mark. Then Rishi says, "In other words, Anjo could reshape a politician's brain to make them vote for the Particle-Blocked Involvement Act against their will."

It wasn't exactly what I was getting at, but it sounds pretty obvious once he's said it out loud. Yvette isn't so sure, though.

"Even if Anjo can perform such a profanity, how could he possibly hope to alter so many minds in time for the vote? Accessing anyone's internal organs—let alone their brain—would require most of the stores of his essensal energy. Even with takings."

"They may only need to alter one mind." Rishi looks at Yvette real steady and serious, and if I don't understand what he's getting at, she does.

"It wouldn't be me," she shakes her head, though she's clearly struck by his idea. "We've been careful to mask how much sway I have within our coalition. If that is their plan, it would be Brandeis. Anjo might believe there's a fair chance that, if Walter changed his position, others would follow."

"By moving the vote up, Brandeis has put a target on his back, then."

Yvette's quiet for a moment, and when she speaks again, there's a heaviness in her tone that borders on dismay.

"If Anjo truly is able to do this, it would mean he has *such* power."

I think of my nightmare sighting again. Think of Anjo's energy forcing its way into my mind.

"How much power?" I ask, real wary, and I'm not reassured by the sober looks they give me or by the way, when Rishi responds, he's extra deliberate about his wording.

"I imagine it would rival that of a Way Reader's."

"As in," I say, "a fully functioning Way Reader."

Rishi isn't the type to sugar coat anything. He just stares back at me, and his lack of answer is answer enough.

I brace my hands against my legs, trying to keep my expression passive while, in my head, I'm wondering what exactly the universe was thinking, pitting me—some barely competent kid without even close to enough training—against a man like Anjo?

"He's not actually a Way Reader, though," Rishi says, quiet but firm, as if he's guessed exactly what I'm thinking. "Whatever skills he may possess, the universe will make you strong enough to beat him."

Rishi believes it. I can tell in his voice he buys in wholeheartedly to this concept of me and "the universe" that's supposed to be guiding me. But so far, the universe hasn't seemed to consider me of much use.

"Has a Way Reader ever failed before?"

Rishi's not expecting this question. I see the way his body sort of sways back like he's been physically off-balanced by the surprise of it. I notice, too, the way Yvette looks quick at him like she wonders what answer he'll be able to conjure up.

"That is," Rishi says, real careful, "somewhat up for debate."

"Meaning?"

He presses his lips together.

"There have been Way Readers who died before their work was complete. However, the things they'd already set in motion—the people working with them—were able, eventually, to complete that work in their place. So, in that way, they did not fail."

"Even though they died."

"Yes," he says. "Even though that."

Yvette turns to look at me, and it's like I can actually feel the weight of her sympathy. I, on the other hand, appear to have gone totally numb.

The idea that I was putting my life on the line with this whole Way Reader thing has always, I realize, been safely abstract until now. And then, there's the question of what harm Anjo could do with me, if he got control of my mind. Assuming he could make my Way Reader skills actually work.

"What do we do, then?" I ask, my voice about as emotionless as I feel. "How do we—I guess—set my work in motion? Seems like it's time we came up with some sort of plan."

Rishi studies my face for a good long minute, like he doesn't totally trust my sudden reserve.

"Until you're ready to face the man," he says finally, as if it's a given that someday I will be, "I suppose we simply take one step at a time."

"And the next step?"

"Brandeis," Yvette brings us neatly back to the problem at hand.

"Yes." Rishi stands up, smoothing out the lines of his trousers and looking at Yvette and me. "We should offer him the protection of the Keepers of the Way."

When I leave the training cave twenty minutes later, I'm full of a complicated mix of emotions. Yvette and Rishi are headed off to see Brandeis by themselves. Which means the two of them are busy "putting the work of the Way Reader into motion." Meanwhile, they told me to go to the scavenger hunt still. Try to act normal and keep to my expected schedule.

"Perhaps you can find a subtle way to acquire more information about Anjo from your friend who seems to know him," Rishi says, which I guess means I'm not completely useless.

When I step out of the tai chi studio into the main hallway, the travel agency is empty and there's no one else around. The building feels eerily quiet, and I'm suddenly aware of how alone I am. Making my way kind of wary to the front door, I pause in the shadows and peer out at the street. From what Dylan said, probably both the GIB and Sons of Morning are keeping tabs on me now, but I don't see anyone suspicious.

I reach my mind out, searching along the street and through the buildings for any essences with stains. Reading practice seems to have honed my skills, and it's easy enough for my mind to cover some distance. There are more people out than there were this morning, but I don't sense any stains. Which means I'm probably not likely to be facing a full-on taker ambush, at least.

I do notice an essence that feels familiar, though. Someone moving down the sidewalk on this side of the street. My mind pinpoints them, tracking them as they approach. And then, right before I actually see them, I recognize who it is.

Leti comes into view, walking along easy as you please with her gold-streaked curls glistening in the sun. I think she's going to go right on past me, but she glances in through the glass door and sees me there despite the shadows. The surprise on her own face is so subtle it's more like mere realization, and before I can think what to do, she's already changing course.

I can't just keep lurking in here. So, I push through the door to meet her, trying not to act like I was in any way hiding.

"Sophie." Leti's usual exuberance seems subdued today. "What brings you here?"

"Tai chi," I grimace. "You?"

"Gift for a friend." She raises a canvas bag she's got hanging at one side. "You headed to the scavenger hunt?"

I hesitate for a second, and Leti says, "I don't know if Min-suk or Teresa will make it, but Rafael and Eilian have already said they're on their way."

Which means Dylan was right about them wanting the distraction.

It's eleven Magnix stops to The Menagerie, the park where the scavenger hunt is held, and Leti seems to have about as much on her mind as I do, so neither of us talks much.

When we come up out of the station, the long, ironwork fence of the park stretches along the street across from us. A forest of dense evergreen trees makes up most of what we can see of the park itself, and, as we step up on the sidewalk in front of it, I'm washed over in the too familiar scent of mountain pines.

A pang of homesickness shoots through me so fast it's almost physically painful. I haven't seen this many evergreens all together since I got to Deffro, and it floods me with memories of Mom and our little mountain farm.

I'm not ready for it when Leti suddenly breaks in on my thoughts.

"I lost my sister too."

It's a strange sort of confession coming so out of the blue, but when I look up at Leti, nothing much about her expression has changed. Except for her eyes. They seem to bore into mine even keener than usual.

"You what—?" I stammer out.

"Not like Padrig Lucas. Or Min-suk's dad. But it was by the takers nonetheless."

I'm staring at her, struggling to comprehend what's even happening right now. Is there anyone I know here who the takers haven't hurt in some way? Whose lives they haven't destroyed?

"It was a year ago today," she says, her chin tilting up, making her look like some angry goddess. "I just wanted to tell someone that."

Then she spins on her heel and strides away from me, down the sidewalk and through The Menagerie's front gate, leaving me standing there stunned, wondering why I was the one she chose to tell.

The Menagerie is a mostly forested park that gets its name from its scattering of dioramas of mini zoetic animals that wear clothes and walk upright. There's one of them just before the park entrance, under the pines on the other side of the iron fence. A whole village of tiny, Swiss-looking houses decorated in Gathering Day purple and blue and gold. Interlaced with cobbled streets, where at least a few dozen small animals are going about their day as if they were real people with real responsibilities.

Any other time, I'd probably stop and watch them, but I'm not in the mood today.

The entrance to the park leads to a plaza that's shaped like a long rectangle framed by evergreen trees, with a giant white gazebo at the far end. There are all sorts of garlands and baubles and other blue, gold, and purple decorations everywhere. Hanging off the trees. Tucked into patches of flowers and blossoming hedges that technically shouldn't be thriving at this time of year.

A long line of kids wait for their turn at the gazebo, to be assigned to teams of two or three and issued little golf cart-sized, open-top emvees called pods. There's a sort of hum in the air, the collective restlessness of a hundred kids hyped on holiday cheer.

Leti's standing near the back of the line with Eilian and Rafael, looking as composed as if she hadn't just confided in me that today is the memorial of one of the worst events of her life.

When I join the group, stepping into place between Eilian and Leti, Eilian's in the middle of relaying details about a call she made to Min-suk this morning, while I was gone. She's explaining, in a strained monotone that, since Min-suk's mom is already dead, he's the one who had to officially identify his dad's body.

Min-suk's absence today feels like it's got a presence of its own. Like the particles are heavier around the space he'd normally be, and I find myself staring at Rafael. Wondering what he's feeling, considering what Min-suk's going through.

He looks pretty awful, honestly. Like he didn't get a wink of sleep. I'm guessing he's not going to be too eager to talk about anything that happened last night, let alone feed me details about a man who clearly terrified him as much as Anjo did.

Rishi told me to be subtle—as though I really needed that warning —but I think it's going to be tricky to figure out how to bring the subject up at all.

As if he can sense my attention, Rafael looks over at me, and when his eyes meet mine, I swear I see a flash of fear there again. A hint of uneasiness and dismay. He looks quick away, and I try to shift my attention back to Eilian, but I'm left feeling weirdly unsettled.

Eilian explains the details for Loui Holm's memorial service, which will be held after Gathering Day. There's a slight breeze that's blowing her curls across her face, but she doesn't bother to brush them away. It's like she's on autopilot, and I wonder what actually brought her out today. Why she feels the need to pretend she's even a little okay.

Looking around our circle, it occurs to me we've all got things we're trying to hide. Only, watching Eilian, I think it's mostly herself she's lying to.

Then Rafael glances in my direction again, but his eyes focus on something in the distance, over my right shoulder. His jaw goes slack, and his brows snap together.

"Min-suk."

The name comes out of him almost as quiet as a breath, but it makes Eilian stop mid-sentence, and all of us turn to follow his gaze.

Min-suk's standing there at the entrance to the park, at the foot of the huge iron gate. He seems frozen in place, like he's already sure he shouldn't have come. His hands are in his pockets, and his shoulders are slumped. Instead of one of his usual, carefully styled outfits, he's just wearing jeans and a faded old sweatshirt, the hood pulled up over his head so it shadows his eyes.

He looks smaller somehow today. Tired and brittle. He's not crying right this minute, but even from here I can see that the skin of his face is swollen with the remnants of tears. At the sight of him like that, I feel my heart break into a million pieces.

"Oh, *Min-suk*," Eilian breathes out, and rushes forward to wrap him in a giant hug.

A few minutes later, Min-suk's explaining to us that today, after Teresa left on some unnamed errand, he sent his sisters to their friend's place so he could work out the logistical mess left after his dad's death. But, once he had the house to himself, he realized he couldn't handle being alone. That he needed a break from grief for a while.

Everyone's sympathetic. We're all glad he's here. Even kids I've never met before step from their place in line to give him their condolences. Rafael keeps hold of Min-suk's hand, gripping it tight in both of his own while Min-suk tries to smile and thank people for their well wishes. Leti and Eilian take it on themselves to help keep the mood up, joking lightly with each other, recalling stories of funny things from their shared past.

By the time we're getting close to the gazebo where they're assigning emvee pods, the five of us are all at least pretending to be cheery.

Until Eilian says, in a tone of mock authority, "All right, you lumps. How're we going to split these teams?"

And Rafael chooses that moment to totally destroy the cheerful illusion. With this odd look on his face, he lets go of Min-suk's hand, turns to me, and asks in a strained voice if I'd like to be on his team.

I'm not the only one who's taken off guard. Eilian's eyebrows go up, and she and Leti shoot glances at Min-suk, who—it's easy enough to see—is more than a little nonplussed.

We can have groups of three, so it would've made sense for Rafael to invite me to be on a team with him and Min-suk. But it sure didn't sound like that's what Rafael meant.

As if to prove that point, Rafael takes a step closer to me, his back now turned toward everyone else. He does not seem happy. His shoulders are hunched forward, and his jaw's real tight, and there's something about his expression that makes me think it wouldn't take much for him to break into tears.

I wanted to talk to him alone, but this does not feel like the way to do it. I'm trying to figure out how to respond, when Min-suk decides, I guess, to let Rafael off the hook.

Plastering on a fake smile, he drapes his arms all nonchalant over Leti and Eilian's shoulders and says to them, "Team Good Old Days, then? Just like when we were ten?"

And with that, the decision's made.

Rafael's shoulders seem to drop about half an inch, and I'm pretty sure he doesn't look at Min-suk again—or any of us, really—until we've reached the front of the line. Everyone carries on talking as if nothing happened, but Leti and Eilian keep meeting my eye like they're wondering what exactly is going on, and, despite pretending like he's cool with the situation, Min-suk looks like any energy he had left for the day has been knocked clean out of him. Though, from the expression on his face every time he glances at Rafael, I'd say he's more confused by the kid's behavior than hurt by it.

We receive our pod assignments in silence. Listen to instructions on how to use the scavenger hunt list, which we can view on the light matter dashboards of the pods. Rafael asks real stiff if I have a preference as to who drives. When I say no, he claims that responsibility.

As the other three climb into their pod—Leti and Eilian in front, and Min-suk in back—Rafael forces on a bright smile and calls over to them, "May the best team win!"

As if everything's totally fine. As if he hadn't made things unbearably awkward.

Then he sets the pod into motion before the others have even properly settled in. As we go gliding away, I meet Eilian's gaze. She raises her eyebrows again as if to say, *What gives*? But I don't understand what's happening any better than she does.

The Menagerie's enormous, the forest laced all over with pathways for the pods and more of those zoetic villages. Sometimes, breaks in the trees reveal fields filled with wildflowers. There's a big avenue that heads into the park and then splits off into smaller pathways, and when Rafael sends us off to the right, the densely packed trees block us from the other pod's view pretty much immediately.

This may not be how I'd have arranged a private conversation with Rafael, but now the opportunity's presented itself, I figure I better not waste it.

"So," I turn to him, hoping my voice conveys a friendly curiosity. "What happened last night? With that man Anjo."

It's like I've uttered magic words. Only the spell they cast is not a good one.

Rafael snaps his head around, his eyes somehow both terrified and accusing.

"What do you mean?" he demands in the most un-Rafael voice, and I find myself stammering.

"I just—I mean—When you saw him, you acted scared."

"Oh."

He turns back toward the front, that sudden aggression fading.

"It was nothing. He's just some man my parents know."

It was definitely not nothing, and after the way he reacted just now, I have a ton more questions. Before I can say anything, though, the air rings out with the sound of Eilian whooping like a banshee. Their pod, with Leti at the controls, comes zipping around in front of us and then slows down so Rafael has to go slower too to avoid bumping into them.

"We decided it'd be more fun to scavenge all together," Eilian announces, twisting around to lean over the back seat and smile at us real big. "One jolly family. You'll never be rid of us now."

She and Leti laugh, and I catch Min-suk sort of shaking his head like he was not on board with this, his gaze finding Rafael as if he can't help but look at him.

Rafael forces his expression into something like his usual smile, and he even manages a laugh, but I think you'd have to be obtuse not to see the kid's definitely not happy.

He drives in near silence for the next while, following our friends as they seek out scavenger hunt items, Eilian sometimes leaping out of their pod before it's totally stopped. Whenever she finds something on the list, Leti commands us to mark it down.

Min-suk tries to get into the spirit of it with them, and I do my best to join in too, but the longer the hunt goes on, the more tense Rafael seems. A couple times I catch him checking something on his helcom, and it makes me worry more about what's up with him.

We're over halfway through the list when Leti and Eilian spot another zoetic village, shouting that they've hit the jackpot even before they can properly see what's there. They speed around the bend to pull into the clearing, and Eilian's already climbing out of their pod to look closer at something Min-suk's pointing at. But this time, Rafael doesn't follow them. Doesn't even slow down. Just drives right by the clearing.

Before the trees of the forest have shut them off from view again, I have just enough time to see Leti turn in her seat to watch us zoom past, her eyes wide and intense as they lock on me.

"Hey," I say, pointing my thumb back in their direction as I turn toward Rafael. "What's that about—?"

Then I see the expression on his face.

His jaw's clenched so hard the muscles in his neck actually stand out. His skin's looking almost pale, and I think I see a sheen of sweat starting on his forehead.

"Rafael?" I demand as we go zooming around another bend. "What're you doing?"

In response, he just increases our speed.

"Stop it," I say, my voice rising. "Stop the pod."

But he doesn't, and I throw my mind into his essence for a clue as to what's going on. It's a mass of anxiety and guilt and panic.

"Rafael," I say, quieter now, but he doesn't even glance at me. My hands are gripping the front of my seat real tight.

The sun's getting low in the sky now, and its light shines stark across his face, casting his features in elongated shadows that make him look almost like a stranger. My stomach turns sick with fear.

We're going too fast for me to jump out safely. Not without using some intense painting I'm not even sure I could pull off. Whatever part of the park we're in looks wilder. The snow's thicker and the edges of the path are more overgrown, and I get the impression we're far away from any sort of help.

We take a fast turn, and then another. There's still a part of me that's finding it hard to process the idea that Rafael could actually be a threat. Then, straight ahead of us about a mile or two, I suddenly sense half a dozen spots of inky blackness. Takers' stains, eager and hungry like horses chomping at their bits. So, this is what Rafael really is.

Without waiting to think it through anymore, I launch myself up out of my seat and kick my foot sideways to slam against Rafael's side, throwing him hard against the other edge of the pod and freeing the dashboard from his control.

He cries out as the pod veers off the path into the underbrush, but I've got only one objective right now. I slap my hands against the light matter controls to force the pod into a near immediate stop, which sends both Rafael and me plunging forward and smashing into some kind of emergency energy barrier that explodes in front of us and stops us from bowling out of the pod completely.

Scrambling for hold on the dash or the floor, I feel myself sliding topsy-turvy back toward my seat. But then my feet hit the bottom of the pod, and I don't wait to see if Rafael's okay. I catapult myself out the door and start running back toward the main part of the park, cursing my legs for being so inconveniently unsteady.

My heart's pounding like there's a hundred pumping pistons in there, and when I hear the sound of Rafael's footsteps behind me, I throw myself so hard forward, I think my veins might actually burst.

"Stop!" he's shouting, his voice raw with something that may be animosity or may be fear. "*Please.*"

I can feel him gaining on me, and I'm just remembering I could try to particle sail, when Rafael surprises me by suddenly appearing at my side. Clearly having particle sailed himself.

"I said, *stop!*" His voice is a crack of desperation in my ear as he wrenches me by the arm.

With the combination of Mom and Dylan's defense training, I should find it easy enough to get out of Rafael's hold, but the instant he touches me, I'm thrown completely off balance by the shock of a sighting that's unlike anything I've experienced so far.

I'm really *in* the sighting this time. As in, inside Rafael himself, seeing through his eyes and feeling everything he's feeling.

At first, it's all just a chaos of sounds and figures, a tornado of panic through his body. Then I'm aware of somebody holding him back by his arms. Of Rafael struggling to get away—to get *to* somebody.

There's a figure sprawled on the ground several feet in front of us. Rafael's grandma, all burned and bloody and motionless. But, while I can tell Rafael's definitely distraught over her, she's not the one he's struggling toward.

Beyond her, other figures come into focus. A hulking man and woman, almost identical, dragging between them this writhing, lashing little boy. Gabriel. Trying to twist around to look at Rafael, screaming with every molecule in his body, over and over.

"Rafa! Rafa!"

And at the sound of his terror-bitten child's voice—the sight of his tiny, flailing body—my panic surges, my heart breaks.

Rafael's panic, I mean. Rafael's heart. Everything in him is trying to pull his strength to the aid of Gabriel, who means so much to him, but the hands gripping him hold fast, and he can barely move.

Then a voice comes from behind, right near Rafael's shoulder. Full of a familiar, oh-so menacing chill.

"I really thought threatening your parents' business would be enough. If you had simply agreed to assist me in the first place, none of this would have been required. Now, I believe, you might find it in your heart to cooperate."

That scent of Anjo's may not be present, but I'd recognize his nightmare voice anywhere. It fills my head with the pounding warning of danger and brings me sliding back into myself.

Back into an awareness of Rafael's hand wrapped hard around my own arm, of the way he's dragging me down the path again. Back in the direction of the pod, heedless of the way I keep tripping over rocks and plants and other debris hidden under the snow. My toes and shins and knees taking a beating even through my Painter-made clothes.

"Sophie," he's saying in a frantic voice. "Sophie, I'm so, so, sorry, but I have to do this."

I'm disarmed, off-kilter. After having just been inside his thoughts, understood his panic, I can't picture him as the bad guy. Still, no matter what the universe has decided to show me about him, I can't just let him sacrifice me.

I wrench my arm backward, trying to pull it free, but his grip's so tight now, I just end up rebounding and falling to the ground, my arm still firm in his grasp.

The force of my fall spins Rafael around, and he stands over me, trying to yank me to my feet again, a look of terrible pleading in his amber eyes. His face is covered with tears.

"Please," he's practically shouting. "*Please.*"

I can see how much he doesn't want to do this, and I can see how completely he also believes this is his only option. And, for just a second as I'm dangling there in his grip, I don't even know what to do. I mean, isn't my job as Way Reader to help Rafael?

Then comes Leti's voice.

"There you two are."

Rafael practically drops me to the ground, and we both jerk our heads around toward her. She's standing at the bend in the road beside their pod, where Eilian and Min-suk are still sitting, staring wide-eyed at Rafael and me. The sun's starting to dip behind the mountains now, but there's still enough light to see the expressions on their faces.

"Eilian thought you might be cheating at the game," Leti says, too much cheer in her voice. "Doesn't look like the scavenger hunt extends this far, though."

The look in Rafael's eyes when I glance back at him now. Wild. Reckless. With a jolt of warning, I realize I don't know what he's going to do.

Then there's another sound. Shouts from all over in the woods. Lights flashing in the dark like some disorganized disco under the trees. And a moment later, Dylan's by my side, his eyes so fierce and fiery it's almost a shock to think they're his at all.

He thrusts Rafael away from me with a force that sends the kid stumbling backward.

"Take him to the GIB," Dylan barks at a group of human-shaped shadows that are materializing out of the forest, lights shining in their hands and around their heads. "And search the woods for his collaborators."

Then Dylan's leaning over me, holding out his hand.

"Sophie," he says, and with just that word, I feel an intense relief rush all the way down my spine.

Dylan pulls me through the outskirts of The Menagerie so fast I can barely catch my breath. His hand's tight around mine, in a way that makes me unsure if we're running from something or to something. The look on his face, when I catch a glimpse of it, is stark. Scarily grim.

My own heart's beating in staccato double-time, threatening to pound right out of my chest.

For some reason, I keep thinking of Leti's expression right before Dylan sped off with me in tow. When he instructed her and Eilian and Min-suk to go home, and then took off with me without giving any explanation. Eilian sure looked like she had something to say about it, and Min-suk was in shock. But Leti just stood there and nodded. Real stoic and unfazed. I don't know if I'm impressed with her or kind of unreasonably annoyed.

Dylan's emvee is parked at a remote edge of the forest where there's no ironwork fence marking the end of the trees. If this were a Particle-Blocked movie, the emvee would squeal all dramatic as we spun out into the street. But it's silent as ever as Dylan dodges past other emvees and around corners like some raging animal on the attack, his eyes bright and dangerous while the rest of his face is set as stone.

I'm gripping the edges of my seat, thinking how this is still a much less terrifying ride than the one Rafael just took me on.

I've been in my own sort of shock, I think, but now I finally find my voice.

"What's happening, Dylan?" I ask, and his answer is tinged with something a lot like fury.

"Attempt on the Way Reader. Tried for all the girls on the list at the same time. If we'd taken any longer getting to you—What were you doing alone with Silva anyway?"

I flinch at the force of his question, but after a minute I say, "Just sort of happened, I guess. I wanted to ask him about Anjo."

Dylan's eyebrows snap together and, if anything, he looks even more furious than before.

"Have you talked to Rishi today?" I ask, wondering if he knows about this morning's sighting. "Did Brandeis agree to the Keepers' protection?"

Dylan doesn't answer until we've gone tearing around another corner, but then he shoots a glance at me, and when he speaks, his voice isn't as harsh.

"The Keepers were too late. The Sons of Morning have had a busy day."

My breath stills.

"Have they—? Has Anjo already worked on him?"

I picture Brandeis, so full of blustering confidence. Now reduced, maybe forever, to mental captivity for a man I'm certain he'd thoroughly hate.

"Can't say," Dylan answers, bleak. "We still don't know where he is."

We're pulling into the emvee hangar below what I assume is GIB headquarters. It's probably the least inviting place I've been in Deffro. All cement bricks and thick metals like some post-apocalyptic fortress. Even most the emvees hovering in their stalls seem severe. Giant things reeking of military might.

As we drive down the aisles looking for an empty spot, I stare out the emvee windows and think how, after what's just happened, this is definitely not high on my list of places I want to be. It occurs to me Rafael's probably being brought here too, in a much less pleasant manner, and I can't help feeling distressed about that.

"I had another sighting." I wish my voice didn't sound so spare.

Dylan pulls into a parking space and shuts the emvee off, looking over at me.

"I think," I say, as the emvee settles in, rocking gentle side-to-side,

"Rafael did this thing tonight because Anjo's making him."

The corners of Dylan's lips twitch down, but he doesn't speak.

"Last night, Anjo and his people killed Rafael's grandma, and they took his little brother. We should—" I sort of hesitate. "We need to find Gabriel."

As if Dylan doesn't have enough going on right now. I can't just let the takers hurt the kid, though. Plus, the universe finally gifted me with a concrete sighting—with information we can actually use—and that's got to mean we're supposed to do something about it.

After a second, Dylan says, "I'll see to it." But it's hard to miss the weary strain that stretches across his features. "In the meantime, we've got to focus on getting you through this next step. Inside, people from my team will ask you questions. We can't avoid it. You should give them every detail you safely can without revealing yourself. Tell them you've only now discovered you were on any list. Act baffled, confused by all of this."

I let out a half-sarcastic sigh. "That shouldn't be too hard."

The inside of the GIB's like one huge maze, with every wall lined ceiling-to-floor in constantly changing 3D light matter maps. We move through corridor after corridor, one essensal coded door after another. The further we go, the more trapped I feel.

Finally, we step into a huge room full of what seems like an army of GIB workers. All moving in and out of aisles between rows of glowing, translucent cubicles.

We move brisk along the edge of the room, Dylan nodding at people we pass but not stopping. There's an agitation to the air. A sense of urgency. A couple times agents break away from their cubicles to move into step beside Dylan, updating him on the situations with other suspected Way Readers, shooting veiled glances over at me.

I can't help wondering what these other girls are like. What it is about them that put them on the Way Reader list. But there's no chance to ask. We just keep moving along, at a pace that makes me a little breathless.

We're nearly to the far corner of the room when two agents I recognize—the ones who gave Min-suk the news about his dad—step out of the last row of cubicles, and something in their demeanor makes Dylan finally stop.

"Mickering, Suto," he greets them. "What do you have to report?"

"We've lost contact with Agents Chahal and Ndosi."

Dylan's jaw muscles tighten, but he just stands there staring at the agent I think must be Mickering. She's a tall woman with a long face and a permanent-looking furrow to her brow.

"It's been over six minutes," she says.

Dylan lets out a breath but shows no other reaction. "Backup?"

"Entered the scene approximately three minutes ago," Agent Suto answers now. A muscular woman, whose head twitches birdlike to the side when she speaks. "Found signs of engagement but no one there. They're searching the area."

I'm not exactly sure what any of this means, but, based on Dylan's expression, I figure it can't be good. He's quiet another few seconds, then gives a quick nod of his head.

"I'll escort Ms. Warren to a secure room and be back with you directly. Continue attempting contact with Chahal and Ndosi."

He's already striding off again, barely checking to see if I'm following, and as we head into a hallway lined with a series of heavy-looking metal doors, he's definitely distracted. Disturbed.

The room he takes me to is bare. Bare walls, bare white floor. Even the table and chairs set in the middle have a sense of bareness. I stop just inside the door and stare.

"Someone should be with you in a few minutes." Dylan pauses in the doorway, looking in my general direction but not quite at me. "I'll come for you when I'm finished."

When he turns to leave, starting to pull the door closed behind him, suddenly the idea of being left alone in this room feels scarier than anything else that's happened today.

"Dylan," my voice comes out like a plea, and he stops and looks back at me. "How long do you think you'll be?"

For just a moment, there's the tiniest hint of a smile on his face. The smallest sense of reassurance.

"Not forever," he says. "Don't worry. Nobody will eat you."

Then, he closes the door between us, and I hear the muffled sound of his footsteps as he strides away.

I stay standing there for a minute, considering the layout of the room. The stark lighting. The metallic table with two chairs on one side and only one on the other. Like the set for an interrogation scene in a movie, where they'd take criminals to shine bright lights in their eyes and shout threats.

Not sure what else to do, I sit down in that lonely chair on the nearest side of the table, and I feel immediately how the chair's too tall, the frame too stiff. My feet can't quite rest on the floor. Sitting with my back to the door like I am, it seems like the whole arrangement is specifically calculated to make any occupants feel on edge and vulnerable.

I find myself turning every couple seconds to check if anyone's standing behind me. Maybe with a knife.

Dylan's right about it not being long before someone comes, but I'm not sure he's right about them not eating me. It's that Itsuko Laugadóttir woman first, bursting through the door with her alarming face and abrupt manner.

"Ms. Warren," she says, more by statement of fact than by greeting, then she stalks toward the other side of the table without another word.

She's followed by her boss Jaap Jansen, the director of the GIB. When he was at my introduction party last night, I don't remember him towering so big as he does now. If he were shorter, the man'd probably be called stout, but he's not short. He seems to fill up the entire room, with too-broad shoulders and a neck so thick his head ends up looking like an egg perched on a stump.

I also don't remember him being so leering-eyed, his gaze landing on me with an unnerving sort of hungriness. Like, given the chance, he really might gobble me up and every last piece of the world along with me.

He looms his way over to sit next to Itsuko Laugadóttir.

"Ms. Warren," he pins his greedy eyes on me. "I believe we've met before."

No way Dylan knew these two were coming to do the interview or he would've warned me. And if his supervisor and the director of the whole GIB feel the need to conduct my interview themselves, I can't help thinking something's gone wrong here.

I check both their essences, to be safe, but there's not a stain in either one of them.

"We understand that Mr. Rafael Silva tried to abduct you today, on behalf of the Sons of Morning," Jaap Jansen says.

It's an assertion, not a question. And maybe if it were coming from someone like Agent Suto or Mickering—or if I weren't so on edge already that I'm clearly not able to think too straight—I might just say, "Yes, but it didn't seem like he wanted to do it," and then hope Dylan can sort it all out before Rafael's had to spend too much time locked up in the GIB. But for some reason, staring into this Jansen man's eyes, I can't serve Rafael up to him so easy.

On pure reflex and without any sort of a plan, I find myself saying, in an extra Farm Girl-like voice, "That's what I've been told, sir. Though I just thought the kid was trying to, like, get me alone or something. I don't know about any takers."

It's not what Jaap Jansen's expecting. He raises one real precise, obviously skeptical eyebrow.

"You believe the boy had merely amorous intentions? You think it likely he would go to such lengths for a purpose such as that?"

The Laugadóttir woman doesn't say anything, but her sharp eyes are so steady on me, it's hard not to squirm.

"Boys do some pretty irrational stuff sometimes," I say, but as the words are coming out of my mouth, I'm thinking that, no, actually, I do irrational things. I mean, what exactly do I think I'm going to accomplish with this? All Dylan said was to act confused. Not try to exonerate Rafael for something he really tried to do to me. Whatever his reasons for doing it.

Jaap Jansen, for one, clearly doesn't think my comment is funny.

The glare he gives me is so cold, I swear I can feel the temperature of the room drop. But, for just a second, I'm near certain I catch the flash of a smile on Laugadóttir's face.

My eyes fix on her in surprise as Jansen says, in a voice full of accusatory irritation, "You were discovered by our agents in, what they described as, considerable distress."

I pull my eyes away from Director Laugadóttir and look back at Jansen.

"Never said the guy didn't step over the line."

My palms are sweaty against the metal arms of my chair. I've definitely made a huge mistake with this Rafael thing, but now I've started down that road, I think I'd probably better stick to it.

"I mean, you don't have to think someone's a taker to be pretty upset when they drag you off to some remote location against your will."

From the flare of Jaap Jansen's nostrils, I'd say he's probably well beyond not pleased, but his voice is steady, if biting, when he asks, "You want us to believe this Silva boy was not trying to offer you up to the Sons of Morning? Are you trying to *protect* the young man?"

The fact that he's hit on exactly what I'm trying to do, makes my guts curl tight around each other, but I force myself not to break my cool.

"Not asking you to believe anything, sir. Just explaining that I didn't know until half an hour ago there might be any sort of takers involved in this, and I just don't want to tell you that, yes, Rafael was taking me to those Sons of Morning when I don't know for sure he was. If the GIB says that's what he was up to, well, I'm sure you're right. I just don't know that myself."

I give him a pointed, perfectly polite smile, channeling my friend Logan's special brand of sincere dopiness like my life depends on it.

"Happy to give any information I can, though, about what I do know."

"All right," Jansen's sarcasm splutters off his lips as he leans, menacing, over the edge of the table toward me. "Let us assume for the purposes of this interview that this Silva boy was taking you to the Sons of Morning. Perhaps you could tell us why he thought you might be the Way Reader."

So *that's* why Jansen's here. The realization that he's just trying— pretty clumsy—to figure out if I'm the real Way Reader starts an imbecilic bubble of laughter inside me that I have to work hard to clamp down.

"Well," I start, trying to play like I'm considering the man's question real careful instead of about to give in to a totally irrational moment of hilarity, "that's a thing I also don't know. Just now, Dylan Lucas said it's something to do with my growing up on a farm in the Western United States, though that seems like a pretty broad category to me."

"*No*, Ms. Warren. What I want for you to tell me is if there's anything special about you. Something your friend Rafael might have noticed."

This time I take it too far. I know it even as the words are slipping out of my mouth, but by then, I'm already committed.

"I'm a bit double jointed in my right hand," I say, showing him how I can curl down just the tips of a couple of my fingers, making them look like witchy claws. "But I'm pretty sure Rafael didn't know that."

Jaap Jansen springs out of his chair, slamming his hands down so hard on the table my heart nearly explodes out of my chest.

"Agents have *died* today, Ms. Warren. You think we're playing *games*?"

He's bent over the table, as if he might actually lunge across it at me, and now that Laugadóttir woman really is smiling. Sliding her eyes between Jansen and me with a delighted expression so lacking in warmth I wish she'd kept that smile to herself.

But that's not what's made me feel suddenly so sick to my stomach. I didn't realize anyone had died. Somehow that hadn't even occurred to me.

"No, sir," I stammer, dismayed. "I didn't know—"

Was it those agents Chahal and Ndosi? It'd make it worse if I knew their names.

"There's nothing special about me, sir. That's what point I was trying to make. Nothing special at all."

He stares hard at me with his glowering eyes, then straightens up, kicking his chair backward.

"That'll be all," he snaps, turning and marching to the door before Director Laugadóttir's even stood up. "If you think of anything in the least *helpful*, Ms. Warren, do let us know."

He yanks the door open hard, and I think it's a surprise to all three of us to see Dylan standing there, frozen in the act of reaching for the handle. For Dylan, though, it seems less a surprise to have the door wrenched out of his grasp than to see who's the one wrenching it.

"Director Jansen." Dylan's voice is as collected as ever despite the startled rise of his eyebrows. "Director Laugadóttir. I came to see if Sophie had finished her interview."

Jaap Jansen doesn't even look back at me when he says, "Well, *I've* finished with it. Get the girl out of here. She's become an unnecessary and vexing distraction."

He pushes past Dylan, and Itsuko Laugadóttir follows behind, stopping to say to Dylan in her abrupt way, "I'm assuming you're the girl's ride home. You've got thirty minutes while I cover your team."

Then she's gone too, and as Dylan turns back toward me, I can't help feeling again like I've done something wrong. Like, in typical Farm Girl fashion, I've bungled things up pretty royally.

Dylan leads me back through the GIB even faster than when we came. At a few points I have to actually jog to keep up with him. As we pass the cubicles where we met Agents Mickering and Suto, there's a difference to the energy in the air. Everyone's still busy, but it's like someone's put a trance on them. There's an extra sluggishness to their movements, a solemnity to their faces that sends a strange sort of chill through my chest. When I catch a glimpse of Agent Mickering's face, the furrow in her brow looks a lot more severe.

Dylan doesn't pause until we're in his emvee and pulling out of the garage into the blue light of evening, and then he drives with the same fury that got us to the GIB an hour or more before.

There's a difference with him now, though. I don't even have to peek into his essence to recognize the way his every movement's underlain with a special sort of pain. I find myself staring at him as we careen around corners. Watching that pain grow in all the lines of his face.

We're stopped at an otherwise empty intersection, when, so sudden it makes me wince, Dylan just erupts.

"Dammit!" he shouts, slamming his hands against the dashboard. "Dammit! Dammit! *Damn. It!*"

His hands slam down again with each outburst, the light matter controls stuttering with the impact. Until, just as sudden as he started, he stops.

With this rough noise like a gasp, he sends the emvee drifting off to the side of the road, under an archway between two buildings, where a mass of willowy tree branches hangs down over our windows and blocks us from view. He slumps forward with his head on the dashboard and his hands slipping down to his sides in a sign of utter defeat.

I'm paralyzed in my seat. Totally unsure what to do, so I just sit there watching him, instinctively trying to quiet the sound of my own breath.

"The takers abducted one of the girls we're supposed to be protecting," his voice comes finally, a confessional kind of whisper. "I was too focused on getting Wotan. I left my team unprepared, and now we've lost some of them too."

It takes a second for me to recognize the choke in his voice for what it really is. I've never seen him even close to tears, and the effect it has on me…

I've touched Dylan's hand before, but never quite like this. As my fingers go sliding around his, I feel energy—warm and earnest—slip from my essence almost without my willing it, down through my arm and into the place where our palms connect.

His breath seems to go still at the surprise of it, and then, with the barest sort of pressure, I feel his hand grip mine back.

Back in my room, I bring the helix up on my com and search all the social media sites for the girl the Sons of Morning abducted today. Dylan said her name was Rebecca Arnold, and it's simple enough to find her.

Her features are daintier than mine and she's got dark brown eyes instead of my grayish blue ones, but they're the same oval shape, and there's the same dark, curly hair. There's even one picture—she's sort of mock-scowling at a friend—where her expression strikes me as so much like mine that I think it'd be easy for someone to mistake us, if they caught only a glimpse.

She posts a lot on the helix about how she wants to be a journalist someday, and she's got a website where she's gathered probably a whole book's worth of information about the Sons of Morning. Names of the known and suspected takers. Events that could, by even the tiniest coincidence, be connected to the Sons of Morning. She's even got a list of all missing persons whose disappearances haven't absolutely been proven *not* to be at the takers' hands because, "odds are, it's probably the takers' fault."

Her site has 8,983 followers, which is maybe not the most ever, but it definitely counts as a solid platform.

No wonder she's on the potential Way Reader list. On the surface, she looks a whole lot more qualified for the job than I do. And with a blog like hers, even if the takers realize she's not the real Way Reader, they might hurt her just to prove a point.

Crouching on my bed, I stare at her words—her face. I think again of

Gabriel Silva, the fear in his voice and his flailing little body as he was dragged away from Rafael. I have to do something. I can't leave it all up to Dylan.

Going to my dresser, I pull my parents' locket out of the back of my underwear drawer. Training with Rishi this morning feels like years ago, but he said sighting triggers tend to congregate in objects of significance, and this is what I've got.

Sitting cross-legged on my bed, I try to calm my mind and reach into the particles in the locket, even though there's still part of me that's nervous about what I'll find.

Rishi made it sound like it should be easy to pinpoint sighting triggers when I'm looking for them, but I search for a full thirty minutes without so much as a hint of a disturbance in the patterns there. My head starts hurting with the effort, and finally, in frustration, I shove the locket away from me and flop down on top of my bed. My com screen is still floating in the air, with pictures of Rebecca plastered all over it, staring back at me.

She looks disappointed.

I move to swipe the screen away but pause when a breaking news alert pops up. And then another, and another. Sitting up straight, I pull the screen down toward my lap to get a better look.

The notifications say Walter Brandeis is holding a press conference with President Lucas. At this very moment, Brandeis is coming out in favor of the Particle-Blocked Involvement Act.

So, it's done. Anjo has successfully reshaped Walter Brandeis's mind.

It's almost too much. I thrust myself off my bed and stomp to the nearest window seat, slumping down there and pressing my forehead against the cold glass.

It must be pretty late by now. The moon is high and bright, but it looks warped through the haze of whispery winter clouds that fill the sky. Its chill light falls on the yard in misty patches, so it hides more of the world than it actually illuminates. For once, the scenery matches my mood.

I press my finger firm against the window, poking at the particles in the cold outside air, until tiny ice crystals begin to form along the surface on the outer side of the glass. Moving my finger up and around, I shape a crystalline image of a flower bent over itself, a bad copy of the thing Yvette designed in the training cave.

It takes me a moment to notice the atmosphere of the room begin to change. The slightest sense of an added chill in the air and the growing awareness that I'm no longer alone.

"Padrig—" I say with a jolt of realization, and I'm up and out of my seat, scanning the room for a sense of him.

As quick as I pinpoint his location between me and my bed, he's moving. Faster than I would've thought he could. Rushing forward and passing straight through me in this shock of impossible cold, making the hair on my body stand straight on end and pulling a rough gasp out of my lungs.

"*My hell,*" I spin around after him as the curtains at the side of the window go exploding out like they've been hit by an enormous wind.

It throws me stumbling back a few steps, so I end up half sitting on my bed, my heart pounding and my breath sharp.

"Padrig—" I say again, but stop real sudden, staring at the window as what looks like hot breath brushes across the darkened glass— across the drooping image of my frosty flower—and his invisible finger begins to write something in the condensation there.

S, he scrawls. And, even though I'm now one hundred percent certain he doesn't mean me harm, I still feel a shiver crawl up my spine at the unnaturalness of it.

H. A. M.

Another burst of condensation. And below Sham's name, he writes the digits of a Deffron helcom number.

I consider waiting for Dylan, but this is the first actually doable task I've been offered, and I enter Sham's number into my com with a sense of determination that lasts right up until the moment I hear her voice.

"Ms. Monroe," she says, and I freeze at the sound of my real last name.

"Oh, I'm not—" I start, ludicrously thinking that I can somehow pretend she's wrong, but she has no time for that nonsense.

"I must see you this morning," she says, in a tone of someone used to giving commands. "9:00. Don't tell anyone. Do you have a pen and paper? This is a secure line, but for your safety we'd best not risk you having my address recorded on your com."

I go scrambling for a notepad and a pen as she launches into the directions to her house. I'm about to ask her to repeat them, to make sure I got them right, when she says, "I'll be waiting," and hangs up. Just like that. Without me even saying a word.

For a while, I sit on my bed, wondering what it is I've just silently agreed to. I only meant to call the woman, to find out why Padrig wanted me to contact her. Not go sneaking off to see her all by myself.

It's a long couple hours until dawn. When breakfast time's looming and there's still no sign of Dylan, I try calling him on his own secure line even though Sham said not to tell anyone, but he doesn't answer. So, I figure I'll go down to breakfast, and try him again after that. And if he still doesn't answer, I think I already know I'm going to see Sham anyway.

I've got a giddy nervousness building in my stomach as I pull on my boots and stand up, surveying my room like it's the whole world and I'm about to step bravely into it. When I catch sight of my parents' locket still on the corner of my bed where I left it last night, I scoop it up and fasten it around my neck. After not getting any sighting's from it, it's lost most its connotations of fear for me. And today, I wouldn't mind a little reminder of my parents as I start on my first real mission.

Grabbing a coat so I can leave straight after breakfast, I step into the hall and just about jump out of my skin at the sight of Eilian waiting there.

She's leaning against the wall, browsing on her com with the practiced boredom she does so well. At the sound of my surprise, she looks up and raises her eyebrow, as if I'm the person who's out of place in this hallway right now.

In a rush of memory, I see her again last night, sitting with Min-suk in the emvee, eyes gaping at Rafael's hand tight around my wrist. The expression on her face when Dylan told them essentially to go home and forget about it.

Of course she's going to want answers.

"Hey," I say, real unconvincing. Behind me, the door clicks shut, trapping me out here with her.

"Hey," she mimics, standing up slow from the wall. "Had a nice night?"

I really didn't.

"I guess," I say. I have no idea how I'm going to explain anything to her.

Her smile is dangerous.

"Heading to breakfast?" I ask, starting down the hall, as if I actually have any chance of escape.

She steps in close beside me and keeps her eyes steady on my face as we walk.

"Is this you playacting nothing happened?"

"No," I say. "It's just—"

If I want to have any chance of getting out of the house to see Sham, I'm going to have to offer Eilian something. We're coming up on the top of the marble stairs, and I make a decision as we head down.

"I'm not supposed to say anything," I start, and she raises an eyebrow again. "But, if you promise not to tell anyone else…"

I'm hoping if she thinks she's supposed to get no information, the little bit I'm about to share will be enough.

"You probably won't believe it," I throw in, partly because I think she won't, and partly just to annoy her.

"Get to the point, Sophie."

We're coming to the bottom of the stairs. It should give me just enough time to explain about being on the Way Reader list. To laugh about what a ridiculous idea it is, and, if she presses for more, give her basically the same story I played off at the GIB last night. But before I can say anything, the doorbell rings, followed by an urgent, pounding knock, and Eilian's interest in my story is gone in an instant. Moving as fast as if someone's life depends on it, she leaps off the last step and launches herself at the door.

It's Min-suk there. His cheeks bright with cold, a look of panic on his face and his hair wet with either sweat or rain.

"Teresa's missing," he gasps before either of us can say anything. "I think the Sons of Morning have her."

"Get Nia and Uri," Eilian says to me with an authority I've never seen from her before, and I turn to run for the dining room. But the two of them must have heard the doorbell because they're already rushing toward us across the great hall.

"What's wrong?" Nia calls, like she's bracing for the worst. Like she's been in this moment before and she knows exactly what's happening.

"Teresa's missing." It doesn't sound real, coming out of my mouth. Why Teresa? Why target her?

Eilian pulls Min-suk into the house and slams the door shut behind him.

"What do you mean the Sons of Morning have got her?" she demands, worry making her sound angry.

Min-suk's upset too.

"She never returned from her errand last night. I called her. Tried any means I could imagine to get hold of her, and just—nothing."

He's shivering, standing there like he's lost, his hair as wild as if a blizzard attacked it and the bottom of his pants soaked almost to the knees.

"By the time I realized she really wasn't coming home, it was late and I couldn't leave my sisters alone. Not with—Not with everything. So, I had to wait until I could get our Auntie Lena to come stay with them. I tried calling Dylan, but I haven't been able to get through to him. Tried anyone else who might've seen her. Went anywhere I thought she might be. Far as I can tell, she hasn't been home since yesterday morning."

Min-suk's normally so in control of his emotions, it's strange to see his eyes so wide, his voice breaking like he's trying not to cry.

"I went to Safety Services. They said they're overwhelmed with missing person cases. Can't do anything for her until she's been gone a full 24 hours. That's when I remembered—it's so *inexcusable* that it took me so long."

He grits his teeth, frustration shuddering down his frame, and Eilian moves like she's going to give him a supportive touch on the arm, but then seems to second guess herself and lets her hand drop to her side again.

"Teresa gave me a code to track her com. Said she was nervous being here without her parents. Asked me to use it if she ever—if she ever—"

He stops, looks around at each of us, his hands coming out in front of him like a sort of plea.

"Her com went offline at 2:35 yesterday afternoon. In a back alley in Strangers Hollow."

"What in bishering hell was Teresa doing in Strangers Hollow?" Eilian demands, and Min-suk looks like he's about to sink to the floor.

"Who knows? It has to be the Sons of Morning, though, doesn't it? If I'd just remembered to track her sooner. But I—She's gone."

Nia, who's been listening with her eyes hard on him, crosses the floor and wraps him in her strong arms.

"No, dear," she says, pressing his head tight against her shoulder and speaking into his hair as if he were her own child. "You've done well. You've come to the right place. Haven't we got Dylan at the GIB? And Gweneth, with her connections to the Keepers of the Way? We'll find Teresa." Aunt Nia glances at all of us with a gentle affirmation that nearly makes it fact, but Eilian looks sick to her stomach. Sick and angry. This is a nightmare she's lived before too.

"You should contact your other friends," Uncle Uri says in his quiet, steady voice. "See if anyone else has heard from her."

Eilian nods, kind of scrambling to expand her com and looking grateful just to have something to do.

"I'll try Dylan," Uri says, and expands his com too.

Watching them, it feels like gravity's stopped working in the room. Like we're all floating in space with nothing to anchor anyone.

I may not like Teresa much, but I wouldn't wish this on her. And I wonder why, yet again, the universe didn't bother to warn me. Why it never seems to help me save anyone you'd think it was my job to save. Then I remember that the universe did offer me something today. Or, at least, Padrig did.

"I have to go to the bathroom," I say, in case anyone's paying attention, but no one acknowledges me at all.

Aunt Nia's asking Min-suk questions, Eilian's on her com, and Uncle Uri's calling Dylan again with no answer. I think for the third time.

"I'll try the GIB directly," he announces when Dylan still doesn't pick up.

None of them notice when I turn and walk down the length of the wall by the marble stairs, past the elevator and to a door in the corner of the great hall that Eilian told me leads to her parents' room. She also mentioned there's a hallway that goes to the back garden.

In a matter of minutes, I'm out of the house, stepping through the secret gate into the alley, and on my way to Sham Haddad's.

Sham's place is in a neighborhood of wide row houses that, all connected, form a sort of miniature mountain range, with each sharp-angled gable marking one of its peaks.

Her front yard's so covered in snow that its two huge willow trees remind me of looming monsters rising out of the earth. I hesitate on the sidewalk, not sure now that I've done the wisest thing in coming here. But Padrig sent me to her, and it can't really be a coincidence, can it? Even if there's only the barest chance Sham can help, I have to trust in that right now.

I reach for the wrought iron gate that leads to the front walk, but stop when my dragonfly ring starts buzzing, announcing the number for Dylan's secure line.

"Did Uncle Uri get hold of you?" I ask as soon as I've answered the call.

"Sophie," Dylan starts, but I cut in. Afraid, I guess, of hearing how upset he must be right now.

"Teresa's com went offline in Strangers Hollow. You've probably already thought of this, but we could find clues there to where she actually is."

"Sophie—"

"Is it possible they're keeping her in the same place as Rebecca Arnold? We could rescue them both at the same time."

"Sophie," he says again, this time with a weight to his voice that makes me stop short. "We've just found Rebecca Arnold."

I grip the latch on Sham's gate, staring into the total white of her garden, and will Dylan not to mean what I think he means.

Life doesn't work that way, though.

"She's—?"

"She's dead."

It's like something inside me bursts. Something vital and unbelievably painful.

"How?" I ask.

"Can't be certain yet. Looks like a ritual killing. I believe her body was left specifically for our agents to find. And—there's something else." He pauses for a spare second. "All the Sons of Morning who were taken into custody last night—they were killed too. In their cells, in what looks like the same ritual."

My heartbeat jumps into my eardrums.

"Rafael?"

"No," Dylan breathes out with a hint of relief. "We didn't have enough proof to keep him. You may have saved his life by not giving in to Jansen's interrogation last night."

I should feel happier about that, but all I feel is numb.

"Sophie," he says again, low this time, like he's revealing one of his most private secrets. "Some of those takers were barely more than kids."

I think of how I felt when those first two takers died beside me in the forest. How horrified I was and how calm Dylan seemed at the time. Maybe, though, seeing death never gets easy. Maybe you just train yourself to pretend it doesn't hurt.

I have no response for him. What do you say to something as awful as that?

But Dylan has more.

"I'm unable to help find Teresa." His voice now—I didn't think he could sound so shattered. "The GIB is in chaos trying to suss out how the killings happened here despite locked cells. Everyone is under scrutiny. I'm taking a risk just being on the com with you. Uncle Uri's calling my mum. Along with her status in the Keepers of the Way, she has contacts with Deffro's Safety Services, our equivalent to the police. They may be able to help. If, by some chance, I can see a way to doing something on my end—" He breaks off. "But for now, I'll simply have to trust in them."

Again, I have nothing to say. The Sons of Morning are always too many steps ahead. What are the odds Teresa's even in a state to be saved by now? The takers certainly made short work of Rebecca.

After Dylan hangs up, I just stand there in front of Sham's house, letting snowflakes fall cold against my face and thinking that I hadn't even noticed it start snowing.

Sham opens her door wearing a full-length, deep gray dress with loose sleeves that run all the way to her wrists. Compared to the flamboyance of the clothes she's worn before, she looks like she could almost be in mourning.

"Come in," she says, and stands back in a way that feels more like an imperative than an invitation.

The inside of her place is stunning. It's like an enormous greenhouse, open all the way up to a glass roof at least two-stories high, with a curving wall in the center that runs around the circumference of a circular inner courtyard.

The entrance is one long, narrow hallway formed by giant, intricately carved bookcases with mother of pearl insets in dynamic floral patterns. Hand woven rugs stretch across the floor leading to the central courtyard, and the floor itself is made up of tiny pieces of blue and green tile set in a repeating, circular design.

Above us, in between giant swaths of vibrantly colored fabric that swoop from the top of the center wall down to the floor, zoetic birds soar around the ceiling, filling the air with their soft, twittering voices.

And, down around eye level, there are little flying monster-type things the size of butterflies, with horns, and leathery wings, and sparkling eyes, and wide, mischievous smiles.

One of the monsters comes flittering close to my face as Sham leads me through the entrance hall toward the courtyard. It looks at me with its tiny head at a tilt, as if its zoetic brain is actually taking me in. And, for a second, I almost believe it is.

Sham glances over her shoulder, like she can feel my awe.

"That's a jinn," she says in a voice that should include a smile but doesn't. "Or, at least, my idea of one. This is all a bit over the top, isn't it? My grandparents are from Syria, and, growing up, I loved the beauty of their homes. However, my parents had unique spiritual views. They hated what they thought of as the extravagance of their parents, and they rejected anything to do with painting. It always seemed such a terrible waste to me, to possess these abilities and not to infuse our lives with fantasy."

She lifts her right hand up to another one of those jinn things as she passes, so that it grabs onto her fingers and holds on for the ride. I dodge careful around the jinn in front of me and hurry to catch up with her, wondering what level of skill Sham must have, if she can make zoetics as lifelike as these.

"Where's your friend Elspeth?" I squint through the space between a couple bookcases as we pass, searching with my mind for extra essences.

"Somewhere else. Safe. You'll see her when the time is right."

There's something about Sham today. Not that she struck me as real warm before, but she seems almost as on edge as I feel. There's a tightness to the movements of her body, a crispness to every word she says.

She leads me to the huge transparent wall at the center of her house and brushes away some of the ceiling-high swaths of fabric to reveal an arched, glass door that leads out to a wonderland of a garden. An explosion of citrus and white-blossomed trees fills the space, as well as rose bushes with neon pink flowers and a variety of other flowering shrubs. Fireflies dance through the air, bright enough to be seen in the morning light. There's a tiled fountain in the middle of the yard, and huge Poplar trees line the edges. Though there's no ceiling over the garden, the air is the perfect balance between cool and warm, and, when I look up, I can see the falling snow melting above us as if it's hitting an invisible energy barrier.

Sham points me to a tiled patio, where she has me take a seat in one of two enormous, cushioned Versailles chairs made out of the same dark wood as her bookcases and inlaid with more mother-of-pearl floral designs. A small, eight-sided pedestal table stands beside my chair, where an offering of hot tea and jelly-filled cookies are laid out. Sham sits in the chair across from me, releasing the tiny zoetic jinn from her finger and back into the air with a gentle twitch of her hand.

The setup of this space seems to lend itself to cozy chats, but that's obviously not what Sham has in mind. Almost as soon as I've settled into the depths of my seat, she pins her eyes on me.

"How did you acquire my number?"

It comes as a surprise. I mean, she seemed so certain about everything on the com that I think I sort of believed she and Padrig had somehow arranged this together.

"There's only one person who knew how to reach me that way," she says.

"Padrig." It comes out with a stammer. "It *was* Padrig who told me."

Sham's eyebrows go up, her shoulders shift back a little, but it's not real surprise.

"So, Padrig's shadow is roaming the house, then," she says as simple as if Padrig's merely returned from visiting friends. "Are the Lucases aware?"

I shake my head, and Sham gives one, short nod in return.

"Well, you'd be more attuned to his presence than they would, being the Way Reader that you are."

There's a strange bite to this last part, something almost like bitterness. She's looked away from me, back toward the glass wall of her house, and her right hand's pulling at a crescent-shaped pendant that's hanging on a chain around her neck, the copper tones of the necklace standing out against the cool tones of her skin.

Something's wrong. After what happened with Rafael yesterday, I'm not taking any chances. I dip my mind into her essence, where the energy's pulsing with so much wild anxiety, I almost flinch.

It's not the same as Rafael, but, still, I'm immediately on high alert.

"How'd you know I was the Way Reader?" I ask, my voice maybe sounding sharper than I meant it. "How'd you know my real name?"

A flash of dark humor crosses Sham's face.

"I'm a reader, Ms. Monroe." She taps one finger against her temple and turns her eyes back toward me. "Thought that would've been obvious."

Nothing's obvious to me these days, but that's not what bothers me. Rishi thought he was the only reader who was given my actual name —who saw my face—so if Sham did too, who else is out there with that knowledge rattling around in their heads? How many people in this city even *are* readers?

"Does that worry you?" A softer smile pulls at one corner of her mouth, but then it's gone. She sits up a little straighter, grander. Stares at me with a strange, heavy sort of significance. "The universe gave me your identity for two reasons. One," she holds up an authoritative finger, "I can be trusted with that information. And two," and again there's that subtle sense of hardness to her voice, "you are going to have a very interesting impact on my life."

I get an odd twitch in my stomach. A pang of dread that I have no way to understand, but she doesn't give me time to think about it.

"I knew you would contact me. I simply didn't know by what means. But now, Alexandra Monroe, I have a question for you. And, as we have limited time, I hope you don't mind if I jump right in. Have you heard from Teresa Maphanga?"

"Teresa?" I repeat, as if that wasn't my exact reason for coming here.

"Teresa Maphanga has been working for me."

It's not what I expected her to say. At all. I gape at her. Wide-eyed and totally dumbfounded.

"Teresa has undoubtedly not told anyone that her stepfather, Beau Millers, is part of the Sons of Morning," she explains. "She discovered it herself shortly after Padrig's death. In fact, it might serve you to know that her mother and stepfather are responsible for the knowledge that has allowed The Angel to mold people's minds. Only, Teresa's mother didn't realize that's what it was being used for. When she found out—when she learned who Beau was working with—she was killed. In the act of trying to get Teresa and herself away from him. Since then, Teresa has been held captive in Beau's home. Until last week, when she escaped."

I feel my whole understanding of Teresa shifting with every word Sham says. Is *anyone* in Deffro what they seem?

"Her mother was my best friend, and one of the truest people I have ever known," Sham continues, seemingly unaware she's entirely blowing my mind. "Teresa came to me as soon as she was back in Deffro and insisted on helping me bring the Sons of Morning down, having been told by her mother that I'd been privately working with a small team to gather information against the takers. Once I had a solid set of tamper-proof evidence, I intended to share it with you, Ms. Monroe, though Teresa and my other operatives were unaware of your part in any of this. Teresa was covering someone else's shift last minute yesterday, gathering the final pieces of the puzzle. I expected her back early this morning. Expected to have that evidence for you now."

Sham leans forward, looking me even harder in the eye.

"I'm worried something may have happened to her. Do you have any information?"

My heart sinks. I was hoping Sham could help *us*. Plus, I can guess now why she has that anxiety in her essence, and the news I've got is not going to help. I take a note out of Rishi's book, though.

"Teresa's gone," I say, straight to the point. "Her com went offline yesterday afternoon in Strangers Hollow, and she hasn't been seen since."

The muscles of Sham's face go slack.

"*Khara*," she hisses, and I don't have to know the meaning of her word to feel her dread.

If Teresa's been taken in the act of spying on the Sons of Morning, her chances of surviving are pretty much none.

Then Sham shoots real sudden out of her chair, as if she's a coiled spring that's been waiting to burst. Without a word, she strides across the patio, back into her house, and I scramble to follow. She heads through more corridors of bookshelves to a space filled with a desk and a couple worn, leather-type chairs. She swipes her hand over the bare desktop, and a large light matter screen takes shape above it.

"You said her com went offline in Strangers Hollow?" she asks as she brings up a window on the screen that looks like some type of map program. "Normally Teresa should have had one of my trackers on her, but, as she was called in last minute, she didn't come for it first."

Sham types some numbers onto the screen, and the map spins and slides, refocuses. She bends in to look closer. It takes her barely a second to find what she's looking for, and then she's in motion again.

"I hadn't wanted to risk pointing any taker suspicion toward Teresa in case everything was truly all right, but now I must go do what I can to find her."

She twirls around and grabs at a cloak and a knit hat that are hanging on a hook on one of the bookshelves, then stops and does a half-turn back toward me, pinning me down with her piercing gaze.

"Alexandra Monroe," she says, like my name's some kind of incantation, "the man Teresa was tracking was Wotan Schmid."

Everything inside me goes still.

"I'm going to trace him myself," she says, "and do everything in my power to find her. If he had killed her, someone probably would have discovered her body by now."

It's the smallest comfort.

Sham's hand is gripping that pendant of hers again, and I find my own hand reaching up to touch my parents' locket, searching for some sort of grounding. I keep picturing Dylan, his world destroyed again by Wotan Schmid.

When I sense a sighting trigger deep inside the locket, I don't hesitate before touching my mind to it. Whatever the universe is offering right now, I'm ready to receive it.

In an instant, I find myself in a stone room again, just like Anjo's office. It's bigger, though. Not quite cavernous, but close. The ground is covered with dozens of human bodies. All of them too thin. All of them too filthy and packed in too close. They're groaning. Repeating strange phrases over and over in voices bent with pain. A part of me believes for one second that the universe has dropped me into an actual hell, but then I see Teresa. She's sitting against one wall, and though her face is smudged with dirt and her hair's a mess, she's the cleanest of the people here. The newest addition.

At first, the comparison between her and them makes me think she's okay, but then the sighting brings me in closer. There's something wrong about her eyes. She's staring straight ahead of her and up a little, toward the opposite wall, and she doesn't blink. Just stares, totally motionless except for the slight rise and fall of her chest that shows she's breathing.

When the sighting twists my perspective around to where she's staring, I see, at the top of the opposite wall, a thin sliver of a window set at a sloping angle in the stone. It's not much more than a drain, really, with something wet sludging down the bottom surface of it. But it offers Teresa a small rectangular view of the outside world. And in that view, I can see the top portion of a fountain, with three stone bears sculpted to look like they're playing in the water. Far behind that, is the shimmery glass wall of one of Deffro's downtown buildings.

I don't recognize the place, but it's unique enough, I'm certain it wouldn't be hard to figure out where it is. And, as if the universe senses the purpose of the sighting has been served, I feel myself being pulled back to the real world. I try to crane my mind around to get one last glance at Teresa, but before I know it, I'm staring at the interior of Sham's house again. Staring at Sham.

She's still standing where she was, watching me like she's well aware I was having a sighting. There's a hope in her expression. All taut and fragile, though, like she's too scared to let it have free reign.

"I know how to find Teresa," I say, absolute surety ballooning in my chest. "She's still alive."

I flick out my com screen to call Dylan's secure line.

Dylan's near silent as I explain what I've seen. Then he tells me real businesslike to hold on and just hangs up. Doesn't call back until fifteen minutes later, and the whole time Sham and I are sitting in those leather chairs in her office, waiting. Neither of us talking.

I'm consumed with anxiety, tapping my heel against the floor. Scratching at a crack in the leather of the chair I'm sitting in. Dipping my mind down into the particles to repair it, and then quick un-repairing it again because it occurs to me Sham may have left it like that on purpose.

I don't know what's on her mind, but she's perfectly still, staring ahead and sitting so straight she could almost be a mannequin. A couple of her jinn things take up residence on her shoulders and one of the zoetic birds roosts on the top of her head, and still, she doesn't move.

She doesn't move when Dylan calls back, either, except to shift her eyes to watch me talking to him. But as soon as I've shut down my com and confirmed to her that Dylan has located the building where Teresa's being kept, and he's on his way to get her, Sham's out of her chair so fast all her zoetics explode off her into the air.

"Where're you going?" I jump to my feet too, my heart doing its own leap at the suddenness of it, but she's already out of her office and moving down the entrance hall to the front of her house. I have to practically sprint to catch up with her.

"Sham?"

She stops at her front door and turns back to me. One of the jinns is still clinging to her hair, and she brushes it off as she looks me real foreceful in the eye.

"Zanny, I have a duty to fulfill for you, and I have to do it by myself. So, I'm going to leave here now, and you're going to go back to Lucas House and stay there until you hear otherwise from Dylan or me."

There's no room for negotiation. Which just makes my anxiety stronger.

"What're you—?" I start, but Sham holds up her finger in such a clear command to stop that I actually do.

"You'll know when the time comes. Now, go home."

She starts to turn, and then looks back at me again.

"By the way, you should know that Gwilim Lucas and Tom Cameron are working for the Gwylwyr," she says. Then, she yanks open her door and disappears.

I don't know what to do with myself after that. Obviously, first thing is to try and process Sham's parting news. I remember what Yvette said about two Gwylwyr agents infiltrating the Sons of Morning. And from there, it's not a huge leap to figure out why Gwilim and Tom were chumming around with Wotan Schmid.

Of course Gwilim couldn't just have been a normal spy like the rest of his family. He had to be part of some elite group and put himself in the most danger possible.

I'm left with a whole lot more questions than answers still, and the idea of going home holds zero appeal. Watching the others fret over Teresa, waiting around while Dylan and Sham are out there probably risking their lives—I just don't think I can do it.

So, when Eilian calls as I'm leaving Sham's, I let it go to voicemail. And when I reach the Magnix station, I walk right by it, telling myself I'll get on at the next station.

After I avoid picking up another call from Eilian, she texts demanding to know where I am, and I tell her I went to check on something. That I'll be back soon. She asks what in bishering hell I'm doing, but since I've got no idea how to answer that, I don't.

I pass the next Magnix station, and the next. Until, before I know it, I've walked almost halfway back to Lucas House. When I check my com again and finally register just how many calls and texts I've got from Eilian—from Nia and Uncle Uri and Min-suk too—I realize how unkind I'm being by letting them worry.

Stopping to rest against the rocky base of an office building, I go to text them that I really am on my way, when a call from Sham pops up on my screen. And then, a split second later, a call from Dylan comes up too. On reflex, I answer his first.

"We've got her," he says without preface, his voice spare and totally lacking any sense of triumph. "Her and the others. They're on their way to the hospital now."

Hospital. I figured from the sighting that most those people weren't doing great, but somehow that word sounds extra stark.

"How bad is she?"

"Bad. She's in shock, and The Angel took away her painting."

The bluntness of it stops my breath for a second. It hadn't occurred to me this was something Anjo would have the power to do. I've known about painting for less than two weeks, but already I can't imagine life without it.

"Does she remember it?" I ask. "Did he leave her memories of what painting was like?"

"Yes," Dylan answers, grim. "That's one thing Anjo made sure to leave."

I know Anjo's done way worse than this, but it seems like such a calculated, hateful way to be cruel. I can't imagine what Teresa must be feeling. What this all must be like for Dylan. When he ends the call, I just stand there, like I'm in a trance. I don't know if Dylan's called his family, but they probably ought to know what's happened, and I should probably get home to tell them.

Before I can look up the location of the next Magnix station, though, I get a voice message alert from Sham. When I accept it, her words come gasping through the com, her breath heavy like she's running or particle sailing.

"Wotan caught me in his flat."

The urgency in her voice is unlike anything I've heard before, and I feel it spring up in my own body too.

"I got the proof, but he found me. You must come now. To my

house. It's the only place I can hope to keep this information secure. It must be you who finds it there."

Then there's a crashing sound and Sham lets out a shout. The line goes dead, but it doesn't matter because I'm already running. Tearing down the street and dodging around people on the sidewalk. A moment later, not caring who notices, I break into a particle sail.

Please, universe. Please let me make it there in time.

My rational self breaks through quick enough and reminds me I won't be doing Sham any favors if I get arrested for particle sailing. I veer off the main road and keep to back alleys, too panicked to appreciate that I'm managing a full-on sail for the first time. When I reach the end of an alley that leads to Sham's street, I force myself to hold up a minute, to take stock of the situation before bursting into the road.

My heart's beating so hard, I'm surprised the ground beneath me isn't shaking with the force of it, but as I peer around the corner of the nearest building, I realize I'm too late.

Who knows how Wotan got into her house—you'd think Sham would have some sort of security barrier in place—but there he is. Him and his writhing, noxious stain, stepping out of her gate as if he owned the place. Even from across the street, there's no mistaking that look in his eye. That jittering tautness of his body that I remember like some terrible deja vu from the night he killed Min-suk's dad.

"No." This cannot be reality. "No, no, no."

I wait only long enough for Wotan to move out of sight, then I explode out of my hiding spot and charge across the road in some wild hope things will turn out different than I already know they are.

Sham's door is ajar, hanging from only two of its hinges. The place is a total mess. The bookshelves that shaped her hallways have been toppled over. The swaths of fabric hanging from the ceiling have been burnt, in parts, to a crisp, and some of them are still smoldering.

Zoetic birds and horned jinns lie scattered on the ground, looking like dozens of dead things even though they were never alive.

"No."

I throw my mind out for some sign of her essence as I pick my way over the debris. A few of her still functioning zoetics hover in the air watching me, and I can't tell if it's just my imagination that reads their expressions as full of grief.

Then, there it is, the barest hint of essensal energy out in her back garden.

Stumbling fast over the mess left of her house, I swipe aside the tattered fabric covering the door, urgent to get to her, even though I know well enough what I'm going to find.

It's worse than I could've imagined.

She's in the same Versailles chair she sat in this morning, only now she's slumped into the depths of it. Held there by thick vines that look like they've crawled out of her garden and attacked her. They pierce through her shoulders, her arms, her hands, straight into the upholstery of the chair, which must be how Wotan kept her still while he tortured her.

Blood oozes around the wounds from the vines, but they're barely the worst of her hurts. Her fingers are all broken, her hands, a mangled mess. There are burns across most of her skin—or at least what's left of it. And her torso's melted open to reveal an oozing, steaming wreckage of what used to be the organs that gave her life.

The smell of it. Burnt blood and flesh and fear. The strange dampness to the air, as if Sham's garden itself is sweating.

All of it is awful, but it's Sham's face that really does me in. Her head's hanging at a terrible angle, her mouth gaping open and her expression frozen in the middle of a pang of agony.

I fall to a crouch beside her chair, fist in my mouth, pressed sharp against my teeth as if pain will possibly wake me from this nightmare. Huddled there looking up at her, it's like my whole self splits. I'm aware of my thumb pressing the back of my dragonfly ring, hear my voice instructing my com to call Dylan, but it doesn't actually feel like me.

It's some other girl who waits, trembling, for him to answer. Some other girl who tells him in a monotone that Sham Haddad is dead. That Wotan Schmid's the one who did it.

"What in *nefsakes*—?" Dylan bursts out, but it's some other girl that responds to him. The real me can't move, can't breathe.

"I'm at Sham's house now," that other me says, and Dylan cuts in.

"Who's there with you?"

"No one. Wotan's gone. He didn't see me."

"Sophie," Dylan says, and it's a command. "I want you out of that house. Now. Before any of the Sons of Morning come to clean up Wotan's mess. Kolus Park is around the corner to the north. It should be empty this time of year. I'll meet you at the large oak at the center of the park."

"Okay," the other me agrees in a voice like everything's normal. Like Dylan's just arranging a time to meet for lunch.

But when that other me gets off the com, and stands and turns to follow Dylan's instructions, finally the real me takes hold again.

The me who has, this whole time, been too, too aware of the dregs of Sham's essensal energy draining useless away. I do need to get out of here like Dylan said, but I won't let Sham meet the same fate as Padrig. I won't allow Wotan's evil to leave another shadow behind.

I've got no idea how to perform a rite of crossing, and it takes pretty much all my will just to get close enough to her ruined body to do it. With her slumped so deep in the chair, I have to bend in to get to her, and the heat of her insides washes over me so strong and pungent I pull quick back, gagging.

Burying my nose in the sleeve of my other arm, I force myself to lean in again and hover one hand over her chest above where I sense the last of her essence. Probably I'm supposed to actually touch her to do the ceremony properly, but there's no way I'm going to be able to handle that.

Closing my eyes, I try to center all my focus inside the shell of Sham's essence, and then I simply will her energy to move toward me, slow and steady, to give both her essence and shadow time to pass over and avoid turning this into a taking.

It works. I'm kind of surprised that it works. And I'm surprised at the way I can *feel* Sham in her energy, as if it's the purest form of Sham herself. I'm surprised, too, by the sheer intensity of the power. It's like drinking in a promise, or the secret of creation itself. The things I could do with this energy. The worlds I could form.

I'm almost giddy with it. No wonder the takers get addicted. Who wouldn't want to feel like this all the time? But there's something else there too. A warning. A reverence. Burning in my chest with that sense of knowing that I've felt before. Telling me this power isn't mine to use. That it'd be sacrilege to claim it for my own needs.

When the last of her energy seeps into my essence, I can feel—more in my gut than anything—that her essence and shadow are both gone. That somewhere, in some unknown dimension, I've managed to make sure Sham's whole.

I step away, almost trembling with relief at being able to complete this one task, at least, and I look down at her body again.

It's a mistake. Even though I know for certain now that Sham isn't just this body, and that, in some meaningful if hard to understand way, Sham's still with me in the form of her energy—after experiencing what I just did, the sight of her so broken and tortured again is almost too much to bear.

It's time to go.

I turn and take a couple steps toward her house, but then—

"Alexandra."

Spinning back around, I stare at her body in surprise, but it hasn't moved a muscle. It can't. Every ounce of life is definitely gone.

"Alexandra," her voice comes again, barely more than a whisper, and I spin back toward her house, thinking that I failed after all. That I'm going to see her shadow standing there.

But it's not her shadow.

It's one of her jinns, hovering in the air in front of me. Sham's pendant necklace—that delicate copper moon hanging off an equally delicate copper chain—draped across its outstretched tiny hands like an offering.

"Alexandra," it whispers quieter than before, its horned little head tilted at an angle.

"Alexandra," her voice comes out of its mouth even quieter still, and I feel a spooked sort of chill run down my spine.

The thing holds the necklace out further, saying my name again, this time so quiet it's barely a word. However Sham managed to program her voice into the jinn, it's obviously wearing off.

Kind of tentative, I reach out and take the necklace between my thumb and forefinger. Lift it gentle out of the tiny creature's hands and slide it into my coat pocket.

Then, mostly as an experiment and purely on a whim, I hold my left hand up in front of where the zoetic is floating in the air, and, after a second of staring at me with its head still tilted to the side, it climbs onto my palm and sits itself down.

Not sure what exactly I think I'm doing—or why—I paint a little pocket into the inside of my coat, then slip the zoetic in, where it twists around until it can poke its head up out of the pouch. I don't know if it can actually think or feel anything, but it looks happy enough.

Now it's really time to go.

Sham's essensal energy is like a perfect late summer evening, or the first scent of spring flowers in the air. Or that feeling in your chest when nostalgia hits you. All those things wrapped into one. And it's disconcerting to be aware of something so pleasant inside myself at the same time that what I'm actually feeling is closer to desperation.

A lot has happened in the last couple days. The takers have hurt a lot of people. If this power called "the universe" is really in control, I don't understand why it doesn't help. Doesn't show me more clear what I'm supposed to do. To be. And I worry, for the hundredth time, that the reason the universe hasn't done more is because there's a problem with me.

I slog through the snow on my way to Kolus Park, not bothering to stop the cold wind from freezing my cheeks. Every terrible event that's occurred since I got to Deffro plays over in my head. I grip Sham's necklace and keep track of her jinn's movements in its pocket against my heart, and, by the time I reach the park, I'm a wreck of warring emotions. Few of them good.

I find the big oak Dylan mentioned, and I take refuge under the shadows of its bowing branches. Press my back hard against the gnarled bark of the trunk, tracing its winding particle patterns with my mind and wishing it'd swallow me inside.

I get a few more texts from Eilian that I can't think how to answer, along with a wave of news notifications saying that today's session of Parliament was abruptly adjourned after Walter Brandeis tried to physically attack Yvette Griffiths. Apparently, he flew into a rage when she held their coalition firm against the Particle-Blocked Involvement Act despite his change in opinion. Or, more accurate, despite Anjo changing it for him.

I swipe quick through the articles until I find something saying Yvette, luckily, seems to be unharmed. Then I catch sight of Dylan sprinting across the park. Cutting straight through the snow-dusted lawns and trailing a line of dark footprints behind him.

I'm expecting him to be frustrated, like last night after The Menagerie. I expect him to demand to know why I was even at Sham's house. But instead, he runs full speed to me, takes me by the shoulders, and pulls me in toward him so hard I feel the zoetic in my pocket jump.

Dylan presses his forehead against mine, his nose to my nose, and his hand moves, reflexive, from my shoulder toward the back of my neck like he's going to give me *ramu*. But, just as I can feel energy sparking between his fingertips and my ignus—just as that familiar tingle starts to ripple over my body at the relief of his touch—he lets go again. Steps away and looks me up and down.

"*Calon tân*, are you all right?"

I've managed not to cry through this whole thing, but with that one question, all my outward calm dissolves, and I burst into tears.

Dylan's arms are around me again in an instant. His hand on the crown of my head this time, my face tucked in against his shoulder.

"I know, Zanny," he says, quiet but kind of raw. "I know."

And even though it's pretty awful if I think about it, there is a comfort in the fact that he, of all people, really does understand.

It seems like ages that he lets me stand there soaking his coat with snot and tears. He barely moves a muscle until my crying has stopped, and even then, he only pulls back enough to look into my face.

"Uncle Uri's going to take you home," he says. "He'll refrain from asking questions, but, Zanny—I need to know why you were at Sham's."

He says it with such a soft sort of apology, with his eyes staring so sympathetic into mine, I almost start crying again.

Swiping my hand hard across my face, I paint away the tears. Then, kind of self-conscious and maybe stalling for time to compose myself, I reach over and paint away the mess I left on Dylan's coat too.

Trying to keep my voice steady, I say, "Padrig sent me there."

"Padrig."

"Padrig's shadow."

It's all I can get out just now, especially seeing Dylan's face as my words sink in. The sudden mix of hope and grief and something even more complicated.

"I should've known," he says after a minute, and there's a tautness to his voice like it's taking everything in him to keep his cool. "He's— he's at the house, then?"

I nod, solemn. "I think something about my being Way Reader lets me sense him."

He stands there frozen, looking lost, his hands heavy on my shoulders and his gaze tracking across the trunk of the tree behind me. When I feel the buzz of his com through my coat, he blinks like he's pulling himself out of a dream.

"Uncle Uri's here," he says after checking the text on his palm, then looks down at me with another apology.

"Clearly there's more to discuss, and I'll meet you at home as soon as possible, but I'd best join my team at Sham's. I'll tell them you were looking into Padrig's death on Eilian's behalf. And that's why you were there."

Apparently, he's not ready to share whatever feelings he's having over the news about Padrig's shadow, and I'm not going to press him on it. He starts to shift like he's going to leave, but there is one more thing I need him to know before something else happens and I don't have a chance to tell him.

"Dylan," I grab his hand as it's slipping off my shoulder, and he turns to look at me, already a step away. "Teresa was working for Sham, to track Wotan Schmid."

"What?" I've got his full attention again.

"Teresa's stepdad is with the Sons of Morning," I start spilling out everything Sham told me, as best I can remember. "Her parents are the ones who figured out how to reshape people's minds, but when her mom realized what it was being used for, she and Teresa tried to get away. Teresa's mom, she—she got killed. And Teresa's stepdad kept

Teresa captive. She's not in Deffro because he let her come. She escaped."

Dylan's staring at me like I just stole the air from his lungs. Like he's on the verge of drowning. I try not to think about the fact that it hurts every time I'm reminded how much he cares about Teresa.

"Teresa got caught trying to gather what Sham thought'd be the last piece of evidence we'd need for a solid case against the Sons of Morning. So then, once we knew Teresa was safe, Sham went for that information herself, and Wotan found her. Instead of going for help, she went back to her own house so she could make sure I got this."

I pull out the necklace and hold it up, letting the moon pendant dangle at the bottom of the chain.

"I've got no idea how exactly, but I figure this gets us the information we need."

I expect Dylan to have a lot of questions—especially considering the expression on his face the entire time I was laying everything out—but he just stares at the pendant. Takes a tiny step closer to me and lifts the moon in his hand.

"This was Padrig's," he says. "It's a data storage device he created. I didn't know he'd gotten it to Sham before—before everything."

Dylan's fingers close around it for a second like he's about to take it, but then he puts the thing back into my hand.

"I don't dare bring this near anyone from the GIB. We can access the files tonight, at home." He looks me direct in the eyes again, a dawning flare of conviction brightening all his features. "Zanny, Sham is—was —one of the best investigators I've known. If she's been gathering evidence—"

He does this little twitch of his head, a brief flash of some spare emotion.

"This could change everything."

It's not exactly a full-blown hope, but I sense Sham's energy move in response to it. A sort of humming confirmation that this is what she died for. To stop the takers and save lives.

The ride home with Uncle Uri is near silent. I mean, it's not like he's ever a big talker, but even his breath seems quieter this afternoon. As if the air in the emvee's limited, and he's doing his best to leave most of it for me. I can feel him glance over every few seconds, though, so I'm guessing he'd really like to know what's going on.

When we get home, and we're stepping through the door leading from the hangar to the house, he says, "Nia and Eilian are with Minsuk in the blue salon."

It's an invitation. A request, even. I'm sure they're all worried sick, but I just don't think I can handle seeing them right now. Uncle Uri doesn't try to stop me when all I do is nod a sort of thank you and turn the other way.

Safe in my room, I close the door behind me, lean against it and, almost involuntary, slide down to sit on the floor. A movement against my chest reminds me about the zoetic jinn, and I fold back the lapel of my coat to let it climb out. As soon as it's free of its pocket, it goes fluttering to land on the nearest pillar of the four-poster bed. It looks down at me from there for a second before turning to explore the rest of the room.

With a sigh, I lean my head back against the door, and bring my knees up to act as a rest for my arms. That's when I notice the blood.

Down the side of my knee, a splash of dark, reddish brown on my leg.

I'm scrambling off the floor so fast. Shedding my coat and trying to yank my pants off me. They get stuck on my boots, and, in my sheer panic, I end up just tearing the pants apart. Shredding them off my legs on the particle level and disintegrating them mid-air even as I'm trying to fling them away from my body.

The jinn stares from where it's now perched on top of one of the wardrobes, but I barely register it. I'm gasping, dry heaving. Shaking so hard I almost bite my own tongue.

It's not enough to get rid of the pants. I manage to get my boots off by just searing through the laces, kicking them across the floor. Claw my sweater and shirt over my head and hurl them away from me too.

I don't come out of my panic until I've made it into the bathroom and I feel the warm shower water pouring over me. Until it's been pouring over me long enough I can be sure it's washed away any possible residue I could've tracked from Sham's house. Then I huddle on the floor of the shower and cry, sure this day has redefined me in ways I still don't comprehend.

I can't be in my room after that. The horror of Sham's death is too present. I stay only long enough to get dressed and extricate Sham's necklace from my outer coat pocket, praying I don't accidentally touch anything unpleasant on the coat too.

My plan is to take the necklace to the aerie and try for a sighting, but I'm barely ten feet from my door, when Dylan comes striding around the bend in the hall. At the sight of me, he falters in his steps. Takes in my still wet hair and my change of clothes, and it's like he just knows.

"Zanny," he says, almost under his breath, and he comes toward me in a way that makes me think he's going to wrap me in his arms again. But just before he reaches me, he stops. Drops his hands awkward to his sides.

His eyes as they search mine look about as haunted as I feel. He's probably come straight from Sham's. I try to imagine what it must've been like for him, walking into that scene after what happened to Padrig. We stand staring at each other for a minute, not knowing what to do or say.

"The pendant—" I speak up finally, and I reach toward where I hung it around my neck, but I stop when I hear the sound of hurried footsteps on the marble stairs.

A second later, Gwilim sprints into view, his breath coming hard and a shimmer of sweat covering his face. When he sees us standing there, he pulls up short.

"Sophie—" he says, his voice brimming with a very un-Gwilim-like urgency. "Sophie, we need your help—"

Before he can get anything else out, though, Dylan steps forward. Swiping his hand through the air like he's marking a line that can't be crossed, and saying, "You cannot be here, Gwilim."

Even I'm surprised by the sharpness in his voice. Gwilim's eyes go wide, his lips tightening and his chin lifting in defiance. Based on past experience, I can tell exactly where this is going, and today is really not the day.

"He's working with the Gwylwyr, Dylan," I cut in before they can find more ways to rile each other up. "That's why he was with Wotan Schmid."

Dylan freezes where he stands, his eyes locked on his cousin. Gwilim stares back, still with defiance, like he's fully ready for Dylan to accuse him of some other thing. Instead, Dylan deflates.

"Oh," he breathes, in a voice of revelation. "Oh," he says again, like he definitely should've guessed.

He seems suddenly a little less substantial. Like the only thing holding him upright was adrenaline, and it all just got sucked out of him.

"Appears I've bishered things pretty thoroughly this time, haven't I, Gwil?" he asks, and the sheer amount of chagrin in his voice would thaw anyone, I think. At least, it seems to work on Gwilim.

With something almost like a smile touching his lips, Gwilim says, "Wouldn't be the first time. But bloody *marw*, Dylan, I'm not here to hash things out with you. I've come for the Way Reader. And yes, Sophie," he turns to me, "I know what you are, and if you don't come with me now, Auntie Yvie's at risk of becoming Anjo's next puppet."

"What?" The word almost rips out of me. Last I knew, Yvette was safe in her parliamentary chambers, recovering from Brandeis's attack.

"What do you mean becoming Anjo's puppet?" Dylan demands. "Does he already have hold of her?"

But before Gwilim can answer, Eilian's voice comes from behind him, explosive and harsh.

"What did you just say?"

Gwilim spins around, revealing Min-suk and Eilian standing in the hallway on the other side of him, near the top of the marble stairs.

"What did you just call Sophie?"

"You've *got* to be joking." Gwilim throws his head back in exasperation.

"No more lies." Eilian starts forward, her gaze so on fire with fury I'm surprised the three of us don't go up in flames. "This family's become so bishering good at them, and I'm done. Last night, Rafael and Sophie were dragged away by the GIB. Today Teresa's had— what?—part of her *brain* removed? And we've been scared *witless*," she stops in front of me and jabs me in the chest, "wondering where in the hell Sophie's been all day."

Over her shoulder, I'm staring at Min-suk still standing at the top of the stairs, his eyes intense on me. I have no idea what to say. Dylan, who looks near as dumbfounded as I feel, opens his mouth to offer who knows what, but Gwilim jumps in instead.

"Did you not just hear me, Ellie? We don't have time for this. Auntie Yvie's been caught by the Sons of Morning, the Gwylwyr and the Keepers are gathering as we speak, and the only person who has a chance of stopping The Angel from destroying Yvette's mind is Sophie here. Your questions can wait."

If Eilian's thrown by anything Gwilim said, she doesn't show it. Just shrugs, still glaring hard at me.

"All right, then. You can explain everything on the way."

There doesn't seem any point in denying I'm the Way Reader now. And, even if we had time to attempt to talk Eilian and Min-suk out of coming with us, I think we all know it'd end the same. Dylan does try to protest that it'll be too dangerous, but Eilian says Padrig used to train her in self-defense and she can handle herself. Then Min-suk adds, in a voice that's absolutely unyielding, that we can go ahead and try to stop him from coming along. And that's basically that.

At least, I'm not interested in standing around debating about it. I've already failed to save enough people for one day.

"Let's go then," I say, and head for the stairs, avoiding meeting Min-suk's eye as I pass him and not waiting to see if anyone else follows.

Everyone does, though. A moment later, Dylan's falling into step at my side, and I hear the others behind him.

There's no more debate about who's coming. Gwilim asks after Nia and Uri, and Eilian says they left to see Teresa at the hospital. Then Dylan starts grilling Gwilim on logistics. Where's everyone gathering, how many people are supposed to be there, do we need any further support.

"We can use all the help we can get," Gwilim responds, so Dylan starts calling a handful of GIB agents he says he's sure he can trust, telling them to join us at the training space Yvette made for me, and giving them directions.

A minute later, we're all crammed in Dylan's emvee—Gwilim in front on the passenger side and me squeezed between Eilian and Min-suk in back—and Dylan's pulling us out of the hangar so fast it throws our bodies against the backs of our seats.

If I'm honest, I can't say I'm feeling great about this rescue mission. I mean, I don't even know exactly what we're rushing toward, beyond the fact that I'm about to be pitted against a man who's more powerful, maybe, than any Painter ever. While the most complicated painting I've managed is color manipulation.

Plus, after everything with Sham, I could probably use more time to breathe. To wrap my thoughts around what's even happening right now. I keep searching my mind for guidance. Waiting for that warmth in my chest to tell me I'm doing the right thing by rushing to Yvette unprepared, but nothing comes.

"Are you truly the Way Reader?" Eilian demands as we careen out of their driveway.

"Guess so," is all I can manage as a response.

Eilian doesn't seem so furious anymore, but, on my other side, Min-suk's staring at me just as intense as before.

Now that he knows I'm the Way Reader, I'm betting he hates me for not saving his dad. Probably he'd hate me even more if he knew I'd had a sighting about it but wasn't clever enough to figure out what it meant.

"And you've been the Way Reader this entire time?" Eilian asks.

"Guess so," I say again, and silently thank the universe when Dylan takes hold of the conversation by pressing Gwilim for more details on Yvette.

First, Gwilim explains that this afternoon, once it became obvious that Yvette had more influence than Brandeis over the politicians who oppose the Particle-Blocked Involvement Act, the higher ups in the Sons of Morning were in a panic trying to figure out how to guarantee the passing of the bill in only two days. Anjo apparently hadn't thought to put it into Brandeis's brain to just change the day of the vote in the first place, so they were left to fret over their options.

It reminds me of President Lucas yelling at Anjo in my sighting yesterday, and I wonder again if Gwilim knows about his dad's involvement in all this. I'm betting the president's not too pleased with Anjo right now, and I guess it should be reassuring, knowing The Angel makes his fair share of mistakes. But everything's moving so fast, and, no matter Anjo's faults, the man is still way more powerful than I am. I doubt we're going to be able to just waltz in and grab Yvette.

Beside me, I notice Min-suk expand his helcom screen and bring up a text chain between him and Rafael. He scrolls up the display of messages and then back to the bottom like he's scratching some sort of itch. He's tried to nonchalantly angle his screen away from me and Eilian, but there's not enough room in the emvee for him to block it fully from view without making it obvious that's what he's doing. I can't help seeing the last few messages on the chain, all of them from Min-suk to Rafael, timestamped yesterday starting right after the GIB agents dragged Rafael away.

What just happened? The first one says. *What were you trying to do with Sophie?*

Then, a couple hours later, *No one's answering the door at your house, and I'm worried about you.*

At least let me know you're all right.

The last message was sent at 11:55pm, and there's been no reply. If Rafael wasn't kept overnight at the GIB, I worry what his lack of response to Min-suk could mean. I doubt Dylan's had a chance to look into the whereabouts of Rafael's brother Gabriel, and I hate to think what Anjo might've done when Rafael failed to bring me in last night.

I wonder, too, what Min-suk must've been feeling all this time, with his dad being killed, and then Teresa getting kidnapped by the Sons of Morning, and then radio silence from Rafael.

As if he can feel me reading over his shoulder, Min-suk suddenly closes his fist to dissolve his com screen and snaps his gaze over to me. The look in his eyes, all hopeless and angry—I feel it like a punch in my gut.

I open my mouth to say something—as if I've even got any idea what to say—but Min-suk apparently doesn't want to hear anything from me. He looks quick away again. Slumps his head against the emvee window and pinches the bridge of his nose with his fingers like he's forcing himself not to cry.

I didn't think I could feel any more terrible, but, staring at the back of Min-suk's head, I suspect I haven't even begun to understand the amount of misery one person can hold.

Gwilim's in the middle of describing how he and Tom Cameron were at Tom's flat today when Wotan showed up with a team of takers, demanding that Tom go with them. Wotan was on his com with the Sons of Morning leader Beelzebub, getting thoroughly chewed out for having killed Sham and causing a mess today, when the Sons of Morning were in the midst of another giant mess. As penance, Wotan was supposed to abduct Yvette so Anjo could do to her what he'd done to Brandeis.

Tom Cameron—being Kwakwaka'wakw like Yvette and also a friend to one of her nephews—had been chosen to serve as bait. Get her to meet him in the stairwell of her building on the pretense of having some secret information to share, where Wotan and the rest of their team would nab her.

Tom didn't have time to think up a way out of it without blowing his cover, and, when Gwilim called Yvette to ask what exactly they were supposed to do about it, she "went rogue," as he puts it. She decided this was an opportunity to locate The Angel's hideout and maybe even ambush the guy. She had just enough time to set a tracker on herself, instruct Gwilim on the seeds of a plan, and give him a message for Rishi before Tom and the Sons of Morning showed up. Then she let herself be taken.

Per her instructions, Gwilim called Rishi—I can only imagine what that conversation was like—and, while Rishi took off to gather who he could of the Gwylwyr and the Keepers of the Way, Gwilim came to get me. Having been told by Yvette that I was the Way Reader and that the only way this plan would work was with my help.

At this point, with a wry glance back at me, Gwilim interrupts his story to say that he'd had his own suspicions about my identity since the day we met. That he'd been on Gwylwyr duty—trailing the steel face that was following me—and he'd started to wonder who I really was after that Elspeth woman kept insisting I could fix her brain.

"Well, I still can hardly swallow it," Eilian interjects. "No offense, Sophie, but the idea of you as Way Reader is bloody unbelievable."

I one hundred percent agree with her. Which makes it all the more baffling that Yvette trusted me enough to put her life on the line like this, believing I could save her. I can't think what about the two times I've interacted with her made her think that trust was warranted. Maybe I should see it as a compliment, but mostly I just feel exhaustion and dread.

Unlike last time, the training cave neighborhood is bustling. There are emvees parked all up and down the street, barely leaving room for Dylan to find us a spot. He and I get everyone past the tai chi studio illusion barriers by holding onto their hands or arms and walking them through. Then we're all hurrying down the long stone stairway, and I start to become aware of a horde of essences waiting for us below, giving me a pretty good guess as to where all the emvees on the street came from.

I'm not ready for it when Rishi's essensal energy hits my mind with such a pulsing ache I almost choke on it. The surprise sends me stumbling over the lip of one of the steps, and I throw my hand out to try and catch myself against the wall. My fingers only graze the stone, though, and I keep on going.

I think I'm about to tumble headfirst into Eilian and send us all flying down the stairs, but then Min-suk's there. Coming in from behind me and grabbing hold of my elbow to keep me upright.

"You okay?" He asks after he's steadied me on the step.

I look stunned around at him, my heart pounding in my chest, and I find he's looking back at me with a level of concern and understanding I'm not expecting. Especially considering I spent the whole ride here imagining he hates my guts.

I recognize in his eyes a heaviness that mirrors my own, though. The worry over his two little sisters, left with only him as caretaker now. Worry over his cousin Teresa lying broken in some hospital bed. Worry over Rafael disappearing, possibly in danger somewhere.

And, whoever Min-suk blames for his losses, I realize maybe it's not me after all.

For a second, I almost can't breathe from the relief of it, but Rishi's energy is still real present in my mind, full of an anxiety that could turn easy to grief if things don't go well today. And I feel, so concrete and clear in this moment, everything that's really at stake right now. Everything that could be lost when it turns out I'm not powerful enough to beat Anjo.

I open my mouth to say something to Min-suk—to try and get out any of the hundred things running through my head—but again I can't find the right words.

"I don't know what I'm doing," is what I blurt out, unable to stop it from sounding like an apology.

Min-suk surprises me by letting out this tired, sympathetic laugh. "Honestly, Sophie," he says. "Does anybody?" Then, giving my arm a light squeeze, he turns to continue after the rest of our group.

When we reach the bottom of the stairs and step into the training cave, the sheer number of people there does nothing to ease my anxiety. The Gwylwyr agents are wearing dark uniforms with the shoulders and lapels embroidered in a pattern of repeating, vertical rectangles and lattice-like horizontal lines. Others—Keepers of the Way I'm guessing—are wearing all black, unmarked tactical gear.

There have to be near a hundred people. One hundred people who, according to Gwilim and Yvette, don't have a chance against Anjo without my help.

My first instinct is to spin on my heel and run straight back up the stairs again. My second instinct is to just disintegrate myself to dust. Instead, I grit my teeth and try to ignore all the eyes that track us as we make our way across the luminescent floor to where Rishi's talking to several authoritative-seeming figures.

They're standing around a 3D light matter model of a large building that's formed out of several giant evergreen trees grown so close together they've been fused into one. When Rishi sees us, there's no sign of his grandfather smile. No move to greet us with *ramu* or offer his usual warmth. The most he manages is a spare nod. An attempt at assurance, I think, though I'm guessing he doesn't have a whole lot of that to spare.

Real brusque, he names the Gwylwyr and Keeper team leads at his sides and then introduces the five of us to them. If he's surprised to see Eilian and Min-suk in tow, he doesn't mention it. And when he introduces me as Zanny Monroe instead of Sophie Warren, I know it means my days of hiding really are over. It's a moment that wasn't supposed to come until I was ready to face the takers. Instead, I feel like it's blown in like a whirlwind and thrown me clean off my feet.

At the use of my real name, Eilian gives me a sharp side-eye and Min-suk raises a brow, but neither of them seems to feel that now is the time to say anything.

Dylan mentions that he's expecting some GIB agents, and Rishi sends someone upstairs to meet them and help them through the illusion barriers.

When Rishi starts detailing the plan for Yvette's rescue, I listen, silent and increasingly numb. The tracker Yvette put on herself shows she's been taken to the building in the 3D model. It's an old, derelict museum that sits in the forest on the west end of the city. We're going to head there by emvee—Dylan says his GIB friends are bringing enough vans to transport everyone—but we'll stop far enough from the museum to hopefully not be detected. Everyone will then particle sail the rest of the way through the forest, still avoiding detection by using some devices the Gwylwyr have that can cloak the essensal energy of anyone wearing them.

Once we're at the museum, I'm supposed to try and sense where Yvette is in the building. Then, Rishi will go in first, with what he calls a "forward team," to neutralize guards. My team—led by Gwilim, and including Dylan, Eilian, Min-suk, and a bunch of Gwylwyr, Keepers, and GIB—will go in next, heading straight for Yvette, while the remaining teams scour the rest of the building for Sons of Morning and any clues that could shed light on what the takers have been up to.

After Rishi gives these instructions, he has Gwilim explain what he's heard about The Angel's process for altering minds.

Gwilim makes sure to emphasize just how unbelievably powerful The Angel is rumored to be, though that's information that I, at least, have already had emphasized plenty. But then he says that, even with Anjo's power, before he can properly manipulate someone's mind, the man has to perform multiple takings and a series of energy flow exercises. Probably, Gwilim says, the takings were already in progress by the time Wotan showed up at Tom's door, so there's nothing we can do about them, but Anjo's energy flow exercises should give us a little time before Yvette is really in trouble. Still, we'd better be on our way soon.

The Gwylwyr and Keeper team leads disperse to pass out essence blockers and give instructions while Rishi, Gwilim, and Dylan wrap up some finer points of the plan. I try to listen to the things they're saying, but I keep thinking about the fact that we're discussing Yvette's fate here, in the middle of a space she created. At the same time that Anjo's preparing to deconstruct her mind that imagined it.

I can't stop picturing his hands on Yvette's head. His energy reaching down into her brain like he did to me in my nightmare sighting. And I keep remembering the part of that sighting where some friend of mine was dying beside me. I'd assumed before that it must be Dylan, but now, looking around me, I realize there are several people here in Deffro I've come to care about.

Eilian and Min-suk have been listening to everything in near as solemn a silence as I have, and I wonder if maybe they're starting to regret coming now. If the details of Anjo's power and the reality of what he can do has made them second guess their choice at all. Especially considering this whole plan hinges on me.

As if she can feel me watching her, Eilian glances over and meets my eye, and for once, she doesn't crack a joke or fall back on sarcasm. She just takes this long breath in through her nose and gives me a grim sort of smile.

Then she catches sight of something off to my left, across the cave, and her eyes narrow in a snap.

"What in bishering hell is Leti Moeaki doing here?" She demands, and Rishi breaks off talking as we all turn to look.

Sure enough, there Leti is. At the entrance to the training cave, in a group of uniformed GIB agents that includes Mickering and Suto from last night, as well as Leti's brother Tama. Leti is standing smack in the middle, in full uniform too, as if it's the most natural thing in the world to her.

Her eyes meet ours over the top of the crowd, and she gets a sheepish smile on her face as she offers a little wave.

It really shouldn't be a surprise to find out Leti's working for the GIB. I mean, most our other friends have ended up being more than what they seemed. Leti's brother Tama has apparently been part of the Bureau as long as Dylan, and around six months ago, he was tasked with starting a highly secretive, early recruitment program. Leti was one of his first recruits, and it turns out she's been spying on me on Dylan's behalf pretty much ever since I first met her. Though Dylan says he wouldn't call it spying.

"I simply asked her to keep an eye on you whenever I couldn't be around."

Several of my past interactions with her have come into sharp focus. Her just happening to meet me outside the training cave, for instance. Her dragging the others to my rescue at the Menagerie last night. The sheer lack of shock on her face when Rafael and I were carted off to the GIB.

Another day, I might've feigned indignation over Dylan and Leti working together behind my back, but today I just say, "A lot makes sense," and leave the indignation to Eilian, who demands to know why she wasn't early recruited too.

The whole conversation is happening on the way to get Yvette. We're packed into the back of one of the emvee vans brought by the GIB agents, most of us strapped into bench seats that run along each side. Agent Mickering's at the controls with Gwilim giving instructions from the passenger seat.

Rishi and half the forward team are in a van ahead of us, and a string of nearly a dozen other vans follow behind, all driving through Deffro at a near chaotic pace. Though, no one else in the city would know we're passing through, since the vans all have that invisibility feature Dylan told me about the other day.

The mood in our emvee isn't what I'd call cheerful, but there's definitely a heightened sense of energy. Everyone's hyped on adrenaline now we're actually on the move. I think I'm the only one who's feeling progressively worse every second closer we get to Anjo. Me, and maybe Dylan, whose gaze I keep catching on me real searching and serious like he's trying to read the state of my mind in the lines of my face.

Discussion of Leti being in the GIB leads pretty natural into a discussion about the things that happened at The Menagerie last night, and it only takes a moment for Eilian to realize what it all might mean about Rafael.

"Was he taking you to the Sons of Morning?" She turns to me, her eyes wide and disbelieving. "He can't really be—" she starts, and I find I've got just as much instinct to defend Rafael against the question in her voice as I did with Jaap Jansen and Itsuko Laugadóttir.

"The thing is—" I try to head her off, but Min-suk cuts in instead.

"He'd have a good reason," he rushes out. "Rafael would never hurt anyone if he could help it. He hates the Sons of Morning. It's the whole reason his grandma brought him and Gabriel here. His parents were working hand-in-hand with the takers down in Refúgio, and Rafael and Mrs. Silva wanted to get Gabriel away from it."

That adds some layers to the sighting I had and begs for follow up questions we don't have time for. It also makes me extra angry that Anjo targeted Rafael after he'd already tried to get the takers out of his life.

"The Sons of Morning killed Rafael's grandma and kidnapped his little brother," I say, meeting Min-suk's eye with as much commiseration as I can muster, though there's no amount of commiseration that makes this news okay. "Rafael was doing what he thought he had to do to get his brother back."

Min-suk looks like he just got hit in the gut. Eilian and Leti, too. I'm guessing the three of them are about ready to burn the world down on Rafael's behalf right now.

"They took Gabriel?" Min-suk says, but it's not a question. It's an expression of dismay.

My eyes meet Dylan's for the slightest second, and it's obvious he's pinpointed what he was searching for in my face. Obvious that he understands exactly what I'm feeling as I report this information to my friends, as we head toward my first real fight—my first real test. Because Dylan's probably felt it all himself. The uncertainty. The fear. The need to be more than you're pretty sure you are.

We've hit the outskirts of the city, and we're moving down narrow lanes lined by moss-covered trees. It's only a few minutes before we pull into a large clearing in the middle of a densely forested area. The vans are still invisible, but I can sense everyone's essences as each emvee pulls in and parks along one side of the clearing. It's wave after wave of all these people's apprehension and impatience and fear, and it's a lot like how I imagine drowning.

Gwilim shows us how to activate our essence blockers, and then he gets out of the van to join Rishi and the other team leads at the other side of the clearing. The blockers are small, button-sized pins we snap into the inside of our shirts, and I can tell when everyone else in the clearing activates theirs, because their essences drop out of view. Only a couple at first, and then everyone is suddenly gone. I'm surprised at how bare my mind feels without the awareness of them.

After that, Agent Mickering starts passing out tactical vests and guns. The vests are made from a lightweight material that she assures us should provide protection from things like fire or electricity or impaling, but I can't say I feel too protected once it's on. I'm guessing anyone who wanted to kill me could find a way around the vest, if they were skilled enough. And I'm guessing Anjo definitely is.

The guns offer a little more reassurance, once Mickering explains how they work. Though I notice the ones given to Eilian and Min-suk and me are smaller than everyone else's. Probably because we're not officially combat trained. The guns look a lot like the one the president's security officer used on Elspeth at my introduction party. I can feel the electricity inside it, waiting to be released, and I wonder how much of that electricity it'd take to actually kill a person.

The sun's low in the sky already as everyone piles out of the vans. Other than the faint sound of lowered voices and the scuffing of feet on the ground, the only other noises are the ones you'd expect in a forest. Leaves rustling in the breeze, bird calls. I can't help thinking that at home, on a quiet winter evening like this, Mom and I would probably be cozying into blankets on the porch swing with our electric space heater pointed at our feet.

Next to me, Eilian is staring around the clearing at everyone in their tactical gear and their holstered guns around their waists, all of them looking real official and intimidating. She lets out this quiet whistle through her teeth.

"*Calon tân*, Sophie," she says under her breath. "You sure you're ready for this?"

The fact that she's absolutely serious and not teasing even a little is not what I'd call a vote of confidence, but I can't blame her for having doubts.

No, I want to tell her. *No, the universe hasn't prepared me for any of this.*

What I say instead is, "Going to have to be ready, I guess," and I avoid looking at Dylan because I don't want to see how easy he reads me this time.

Gwilim comes over, saying it's time to be on our way and giving me the slightest nod of acknowledgement like he actually thinks I've got a chance of pulling this thing off tonight. Then he tells us all to follow him back across the clearing to get into position. As we start after him, Dylan falls into step beside me.

"For the record, my bets have been on you since day one," he says, quiet enough only I can hear.

I snap my gaze up to his face and find him looking sidelong down at me.

His words are like a blessing, like the casting of a spell. I feel the warmth of them move through me with a tremor of something that feels like strength. Then, ahead of us, Rishi raises his hand in a signal to the team leads, and Gwilim gives the command for us to move out.

Particle sailing full speed through the forest with the cool wind bracing against my cheeks and Dylan's words still bouncing around my head, I almost dare for a second to indulge in a little hope. But this isn't a day for that sort of thing, and we're not even halfway to the museum, when Anjo's essence sears sudden through my mind. Hits me with his stain so poisonous that I drop straight out of my particle sail. Slam face down in the snow, where I start writhing, keening with the pain of it like a wounded animal.

I hear my friends calling out. Hear the alarm in their voices. I feel someone trying to grab hold of my shoulders as I flail around, trying to calm me down, and I know that Dylan's here with me, but I can't focus on anything beyond the pain of Anjo's stain. It's like being eaten from the inside out. It's bloodthirsty and insatiable, as if it's had generations to grow its hunger.

"Bloody *marw*, what's wrong with her?" Gwilim asks, and I'm aware that he's beside me too. That Eilian and Leti and Min-suk are crowding near, as well as most the rest of our team.

"A sighting, I think," Dylan answers. "It's never been this bad before. Zanny," he says to me. "Zanny, you know how to channel this. You know what to do."

With the state I'm in, I'd be lucky to remember even one of the meditations he taught me, but, thankfully, the pain's already fading. The initial shock of Anjo's stain must be done working through me, and, as it dims, the world begins to right itself in my mind, and I can see the man's essence more clear. See the sheer strength of it, like he's running off nuclear power when the rest the world's still using batteries.

There are three other energies in his essence too. Three more takings, three more deaths.

I can sense everyone else there with him. Wotan Schmid, along with a load of other stained essences. Tom Cameron. Yvette, whose essensal energy is such a tangle of determination and trepidation, it's almost painful in its own way. Then I sense someone I didn't expect, and I force my awareness back to my own surroundings. Force myself trembling to my hands and knees.

"They've got Rafael and his brother Gabriel too," I announce, ignoring Dylan and Gwilim's offers of help as I push myself shaky to my feet. Our whole team's circled around now, all of them staring at me in a way I try to ignore. "Not far from Yvette, I think. And from what I can feel of their essensal energy, they're terrified."

Leti and Eilian are clearly appalled by this news and Min-suk looks like he's about to be sick.

"You can sense them from this far away?" Leti asks, a barely hidden awe in her voice.

At the same time, Dylan says, "You can see what they're feeling?"

"What did you sense of Yvette?" Gwilim's question gets right to the point, and I meet his eye with a grim expression.

"I don't think Anjo's touched her yet. But I'm guessing she'd be real happy if we showed up soon."

The museum is an ancient looking thing, with ladders of ivy crawling up near every inch of the giant evergreens that form it. There's something imposing and gothic about it and, in the increasing darkness of evening, it'd be hard to find a more fitting setting for the evil things Anjo's apparently been doing in there.

We meet everyone else far enough inside the tree line that we can't be seen from the museum itself. As I update Rishi and the other team leads on my sighting, I've never seen Rishi's face look so bleak. My little meltdown in the woods only cost us a few minutes, but we didn't have any to spare in the first place. Rishi waits only long enough for me to check my mind again for a better idea of where exactly everyone is in the building before he leads his team in.

There are taker sentries walking the perimeter, but they must not be expecting visitors because there are only a few of them, and the forward team has no trouble taking them out. In almost no time at all, the rest of us are following Rishi's team stealthy and silent through the giant front doors.

The inside of the museum is run down and dimly lit. The paint on the walls and ceiling is cracked and peeling, and the same vines from outside are crawling their way through window frames and across the walls. Doors hang off hinges and huge brown spots dot the splintering marble floors, marking places where muddy water must've sat stagnant long enough to leave stains. Whatever the takers have been doing here, they don't seem to have improved the place much.

Off to the sides, I catch glimpses of rooms that've clearly been used as storage spaces of some sort, with large crates stacked on top of each other in somewhat organized rows. I had sensed probably two dozen takers on this main level, but Rishi's team makes quick work of them too, so that all we see of them is their bodies sprawled on the floors in the rooms and along the edges of the hallways.

Back at the training cave, I wasn't sure what Rishi meant when he talked about neutralizing people, but when I check the takers' essences, I see they're still alive and unharmed. Rishi's team has just put them into some sort of sleep. How, I'm not sure, since no one seems to be using their guns.

What I do know, is that moving near silent through this half-rotted building dotted with unconscious bodies feels like we're caught in a bad dream. As we make our way through what used to be the lobby and down the main hall, our guns out and at the ready, I'm holding my breath. Waiting for something horrible to happen.

Thanks to the forward team, though, we're able to make it to the main stairs without any problems, and then our group follows Rishi's people downward while the other teams move to the top floors to deal with the few dozen takers I sensed up there.

The museum basement is a series of rooms filled with crumbling shelves holding crumbling artifacts. Here and there I think I recognize objects you might find in a Particle-Blocked museum—old pottery and things like that—but the lighting's so bad and everything's so covered in dust, it's hard to be sure what we're actually seeing.

Just like outside, it doesn't seem like the takers are too worried about intruders. There aren't even any guards stationed down here. Anjo and Yvette and all the other essences on this level are crowded at the far end of the building. Still, out of extra caution, each time we come to a new door, Gwilim signals for us to stop and wait, to allow the forward team to double check for Sons of Morning in the next room.

The closer we get to the other end of the building, the more oppressive Anjo's essence becomes. He's got so much power in him that it's like walking straight toward a giant furnace, and I'm starting to sweat as if that's exactly what I'm doing. My stomach's boiling with nerves too. I feel like I could easily throw up, and, when I sense

Yvette's essensal energy suddenly start spiking with pain, it's all I can do not to scream at everyone to hurry up.

When we do finally reach the area where I sensed essences, Rishi stops his team and waits for us before going through the next door. He brings up a smaller version of the 3D museum model on his palm so I can use it as a reference point for figuring out everyone's locations. There are two large, rectangular rooms left. In the first, I sense a couple dozen takers spread out, but there's no one in there I recognize. Anjo and Yvette are in the room after that, along with Wotan Schmid, another handful of takers, Tom, Rafael and Gabriel.

There's little chance even Rishi's super-skilled team is going to make it through that first room undetected, so Rishi gives new instructions, all terse and concise. His team will go in and engage the takers in that room. They'll keep them occupied while my team moves around the room's circumference to the door in the far corner. Then, once we're through that door, Leti, Eilian and Min-suk are supposed to get Rafael and Gabriel the hell out of here, while the rest of us deal with Anjo and the other takers and try to save Yvette.

There's no time to ask questions or to even wonder what the odds are of this plan working. As soon as Rishi's done giving his commands, the forward team heads into the next room. Shouts of alarm come from the takers inside, and then there's a series of small explosions marking the first actual exchange of fire tonight. After that, everything moves so fast, it's a blur.

With Gwilim and Dylan in the lead, our team pushes through the door and along the wall to the left. The room is filled with low, transparent cubicles defining the boundaries between metal-tabled workstations covered in vials and glass tubes and a bunch of other things that give the place the air of a lab from a cheap sci-fi movie.

The room is in total chaos. People are everywhere, fighting like I've never seen before. Fire and ice and arcs of electricity are flying, from people's hands and their guns. Lighting up the room at almost rhythmic intervals, like some deadly dance party.

I catch sight of Rishi in the middle of it all, diving and dodging and leaping into the air as he avoids taker attacks while letting loose his own barrage. Seeing him like that, I wonder how I ever thought of him as grandfatherly.

Meanwhile, Yvette's rising pain and panic is throbbing at the front of my mind, so strong now it's almost as staggering as Anjo's poison energy. As I follow Gwilim and Dylan along the length of the wall, running in a half crouch with my gun held out in front of me like I actually know how to use it, I try to comfort myself with the fact that I'm also feeling a rising frustration in Anjo. Which tells me that, whatever is going on in the next room, even that man's not too happy about it. I just hope that means Yvette's managing to fight him off for the time being.

The forward team is doing a good job of keeping the takers occupied, and, other than having to dodge a couple stray bursts of fire or electricity, we make it around the room without much incident. I'm even starting to think maybe there's a chance our plan really will work. But, with all the noise happening out here, I guess we've already lost our element of surprise.

Just as we're coming up on the door to the next room, it bursts open, and a raging wall of flame explodes out of it. The heat hits us first, sucking my breath clean out of my lungs. I gag, throwing up my arms on reflex, as if that's going to stop the flames. Thankfully, Dylan and Gwilim have better instincts, and they extinguish the fire before it melts us all away.

What they're not ready for, though, is Wotan and a bunch of other takers to come charging out right after it. There's a moment of realization on Wotan's face when he sees Gwilim and Dylan here together. Then his expression shifts into a cruel smile, and he ploughs straight into them, leaving the other takers to go for the rest of our team.

Wotan's momentum bowls Gwilim and Dylan into me, and I'm thrown, stumbling backward. I land hard on my hands and knees, and the gun gets knocked out of my grasp and goes skittering across the floor, far out of my reach.

I'm about to go after it, when someone's suddenly grabbing me by the collar of my tactical vest and yanking me upward like a rag doll. I find myself staring into the menacing eyes of a giant of a man, and I realize he's one of the two takers that helped kidnap Rafael's brother.

Over his shoulder, I see the other one, who looks like she could be his twin. She's grappling with Leti, Tama, Eilian and Min-suk, and I can't say it's reassuring that it's taking all four of them to deal with one of her.

The man holding me grins real wide, and I don't wait to see what he's planning. I slap my hand to his face and ignite a ball of flame right over his eyes. He screams and drops me, and I use what I know of that ascensé dancing technique to balloon a pillow of air below me and cushion my fall.

I manage to land on my feet, only stumbling a little, but before I can do anything else, Dylan's at my side, grabbing hold of my shoulders and steering me toward the door to the next room.

"Go!" He shouts. "Get to Yvette! We'll back you up as soon as we can."

Everyone else from our team is caught in the fight now, and I hesitate on the reflex to try and help, but Dylan shouts again for me to go as he dodges a blow from the giant taker man's heavy fist. I feel a pang of terror and pain from Yvette so intense it takes my breath, and I don't wait any longer.

I duck around Gwilim, where he's scuffling with Wotan Schmid, and I take off toward the door. When I get to it, though, it's locked, and I have this moment of panic, yanking at the handle as hard as I can several times before thinking to use my painting to try and open it. I'm just reaching my mind inside the door, looking for some sort of lock mechanism, when I sense Tom Cameron's essence on the other side and the door flies open, near clipping me as I hurry to back away.

Behind him, in the middle of a stark white room, I see Yvette on a hospital-like bed, struggling against straps that are lined in a red light that seems to be hurting her. Causing her so much pain, I'm guessing, that she can't paint properly. Doing, essentially, what Wotan achieves when he breaks his victim's fingers.

Anjo is bent over her, his hands gripping her head tight and all his attention so trained on trying to get into her brain that he barely seems aware of the fight going on in the other room.

"Close that door!" He snaps at Tom without bothering to look over his shoulder. "It's breaking my focus."

But Tom doesn't move. He takes in the chaos happening in the lab behind me, and then his dark eyes lock on my face. He's barring my way with an unreadable expression frozen on his features, and I think maybe Gwilim was wrong. Maybe Tom has double crossed the Gwylwyr and he's going to swing that door closed again, shutting me and everyone else out. Then he steps away and motions me quick inside.

I don't wait for any further prompting. I dash into the room and find myself staring past Anjo's torture table straight into the stunned eyes of Rafael Silva. He's huddled against the far wall, his arms clasped around his little brother, keeping Gabriel's face tucked tight into his shoulder to block him from seeing what's happening to Yvette.

Beside them looms another double set of those conjoined twin sarcophagi I saw in Anjo's office in my sighting yesterday morning, and between those there's a rough-hewn stone altar with a bloodied, inert body of a boy about my age lain across it. One of Anjo's takings.

I rip my eyes away, trying not to be sick.

Now that I'm in the room, I can't seem to make myself move. I'm staring at Anjo's back, and I've got zero idea what to do next. Because, faced with the full, unbelievable power of his essence, it's obvious that, once he turns that power against me, I won't have much of a chance. And neither will anyone else here.

Tom Cameron is still at the door, holding it open and watching the fighting in the lab. Practically dancing on the balls of his feet with the antsy urgency of a person waiting for someone else—anyone other than just me—to come to the rescue.

You have to fight a super-powered sociopath, I try one of Mom's thought exercises, *armed only with your body and your brain. What do you do?*

But I don't get a chance to answer that because, just then, a few things happen at once. Tom glances back at me and we lock eyes, acknowledging together that it looks like saving Yvette has come down to the two of us. Then Wotan Schmid, apparently having freed himself from his skirmish with Gwilim, comes smashing into Tom from the side, knocking him away from the door and fully into the other room at the exact same moment that Anjo, oblivious to what's really happening behind him, twists around to bite out another command to

318

Tom to close the gindging door. Only, instead of seeing Tom there, his gaze falls on me.

I expect him to rush me or attack in some way, but he just goes still, his eyes lighting up and a spiteful grin stretching across his features.

"Well," he says, in the voice of my worst nightmare. "If it isn't the little farm girl, after all."

I was supposed to face Anjo with a whole team as backup. I was supposed to have a gun, and the element of surprise. But I've got none of that. It's just him, me, the two terrified Silva boys, and Yvette, who's still writhing against the pain of the glowing red straps.

I have enough time to register the thought that Anjo's probably going to be the only one to make it out of this room alive, and then he attacks.

With a sudden movement of his arm, he sends a lash of fire toward my face that I barely manage to dodge, the heat of it burning the air near my cheeks and filling my vision. I stumble back a few steps just as a shard of ice comes at me too, and I'm not fast enough to dodge that one. The ice slashes my arm and I gasp, clapping my hand against the wound as Anjo lets out a low laugh.

"Did you really think yourself a match for me?" He laughs again and sends another round of fire and ice, one right after the other.

Dodging them is a little easier this time, and it shakes me out of my paralysis. At least, I'm starting to think clear enough to try for some sort of plan.

I know I'll never beat Anjo with skill or strength. Pretty sure my own energy will be used up long before he even makes a dent in his. In fact, I doubt I can beat him at all. What I maybe can do—what is probably the only thing I have even a chance of doing—is keep the man distracted long enough to allow Yvette and the Silvas to escape, and maybe deplete his energy to a point that Rishi and Dylan and the others can subdue him with all their strength combined.

When Anjo sends the fire and ice again in the exact same pattern as before, I figure he's toying with me, but it offers me a chance to lock eyes with Rafael and give him a meaningful look in Yvette's direction, in what I hope is a clear enough message he'll know what I need him to do.

"Is this what you trained for, Farm Girl?" Anjo shoots some more fire. Real halfhearted, like he wants me to notice exactly how little effort he's putting in.

To my relief, out of the corner of my eye, I see Rafael leave his brother by the wall and move quiet and quick toward Yvette.

"Or maybe this?" Anjo sends another shard of ice. Only this time when I step out of the way, he turns the floor beneath my foot soft as quicksand, and I sink into it up to my shin, my whole body nearly falling to the ground. Anjo barks out another malicious laugh, and I yank my foot up, keeping my gaze fierce on his smug face.

Behind him, Rafael's using his painting to slash through Yvette's straps. As soon as those things are gone, her writhing stops, but then she just goes limp on the table, her head lolling to one side. For one horrible second, I think maybe we were too late. Maybe the strain of fighting Anjo was too much for her. But then, as I dodge another attack —a ball of fire and another spot of quicksanded floor—I see Yvette rolling herself slow off the opposite side of the table.

Rafael moves to catch her, but she slips through his arms and lands on her hands and knees with a loud thump.

Anjo turns toward the noise, but I move quick to pull his attention back. I was hoping to preserve my own essensal energy longer, but now I make my first attack.

"Is this what you're playing at?" I shout, and send fire and ice straight at his face. I've never actually formed ice before, but it's easy enough to do, and it nearly catches him off guard.

He has to step backwards to dissolve the ice and fire before they hit him in the eye, and he lets out a growl of frustration that he turns into a caustic laugh. Twisting back toward me, he advances a few steps with a flourish that calls attention to the fact that the man is wearing a full-on, actual cloak, as if he's trying to look like a cartoon villain. Though I've got to admit, it is pretty menacing the way it billows out behind him when he moves.

"You like little games?" I say, shooting off another round at him and moving slightly to the right to keep his focus away from where Rafael's now helping Yvette move back toward the wall and his brother. "This make you feel like a real tough guy?" I launch another round, too on edge right now to taunt him with anything legitimately clever.

Anjo looks more irritated by the things I'm saying than by my actual attacks, which he bats away as easy as if they were bits of fluff.

"Are we exchanging playground insults now?" he scoffs, but he does shift his body to keep me in his sights.

When I send a succession of fireballs his way, though, he dissolves them almost as they leave my hand, and then he levels his gaze on me with a bored sigh.

"Most Painters lack any real imagination," he says. "So, I doubt you've trained for something like this."

Then he attacks my heart. Clenches his fist all theatric in the air, and I feel it in my chest as if his hand really is crushing my heart inward.

Gasping at the pain, I plunge my mind into the particles there and push back just in time to stop him from killing me in that one move.

It's not supposed to be so easy to damage the inside of a body. That's what Dylan and Rishi said. Wasn't that why Wotan had to break all Sham's fingers and stake her to her chair? Why Anjo had to use those torture straps on Yvette? But maybe Anjo only needs extra help when he's trying for precision. Maybe when his only goal is destruction, it's as easy for him as taking a breath.

I knew I'd be out of my depth fighting Anjo, but I'm starting to understand just how much it's going to hurt. He stares me down, his eyes gleeful and wild, and I try not to show on my face that I feel more afraid now than ever before in my life.

When Anjo attacks my liver, the pain is somehow worse than in my heart, and I almost drop to my knees. Groaning through the ache of it, I force myself to stumble back from him, to draw him further into the room as Yvette and the Silvas move along the far wall toward the door.

At the first sound of my pain, Rafael had stopped and looked over at me in distress, but Yvette urged him to keep moving. Which means that, whatever Anjo did to her, she at least still seems in control of her own mind.

Anjo goes for my lungs next, letting out a laugh when, this time, I do end up falling to my knees, clutching at my chest. I'm trying to make myself stay calm. Trying to remember the techniques Dylan taught me, but sparring with Dylan is a lot different than fighting someone who actually wants to do me harm.

My brain is flying through ways to attack Anjo back—to at least make him stop hurting me long enough for me to catch a breath—but it's taking everything I've got just to stay alive right now. Luckily, the others are nearly to the door, which means I only have to hold on a bit longer.

"I could do this," I grunt at Anjo through gritted teeth, "for, like, a whole three more minutes."

It surprises a genuine laugh out of the man, but then he punishes me for it by going for my stomach, my esophagus, my kidneys, my lungs again. All one right after the other.

At the back of my mind, I'm aware that Anjo's using a lot more of his essensal energy with these moves than he was with the fire and ice. I can sense it draining more quick out of him. But fighting him off is taking even more than that out of me, and I wonder with a pang of anxiety if, with my essence still intact, he can see how much energy I've got left too or if that's only a Way Reader thing.

I'm bent over now, clenching my fists and just about every other part of me against the pain. And when I glance toward the corner to gauge how much longer I have to take this, I see that Rafael and Yvette are struggling to open the door just like I struggled before. Because of course they can't get through. Anjo's a sadist. In a room meant for takings and torture, of course he'd have it programmed so no one except his own people could leave. And, of course, even my meager hope of allowing Yvette and the Silvas to save themselves was doomed from the start.

When Anjo goes for my heart again, I nearly don't catch it in time. For a split second, it seems to implode in on itself before the force of my will puts it right. The pain this time is so sharp, it sends me slumping all the way to the ground, my face slapping onto the cold, hard floor.

Anjo starts toward me, and I feel the elation bubbling in his essence like he knows he's already won.

Then there's the sound of something hitting the door hard from the other side. Of yelling and a couple small explosions along the doorframe. I hear Dylan's voice there, along with Gwilim and Rishi.

Everything that's happened in here has played out over the background noise of the fighting in the other room, but now I notice that something has shifted in the chaos out there. It sounds less like a battle and more like the sounds of an agitated crowd. I sense several dozen unblocked, unstained essences in the building and fewer takers by far, and it strikes me that somehow our side has acquired backup.

There are a couple more explosions at the door and then frantic shouts for Tom Cameron, which is when Anjo finally stops attacking me. Because he's probably having the same epiphany I am. That Tom Cameron's essensal code can open that door, and that there are a whole lot more people out there who, at the very least, are going to make it harder for him to keep torturing me.

With an exaggerated sigh, Anjo turns to deal with the situation, leaving me gasping and trembly on the floor. For a moment, I'm relieved he's not hurting me anymore, but then two thoughts surge to the forefront of my mind and wipe away any relief.

The first thought is that Yvette, Rafael, and Gabriel are still between Anjo and the door. And the second is, that even if Anjo doesn't hurt them, as soon as he decides he's not messing around anymore, he could kill any of my friends by simply reaching his mind inside them and crushing something vital like he's been playing at doing to me.

I'm moving before I've even formulated a plan, pushing myself up off the floor, throwing my mind into the lights in the ceiling and grabbing hold of the electricity there. Then, as I launch into a wobbly run, I picture all that electricity just raining down on Anjo.

I've never done painting at that distance before, and I don't expect it to work. So, it's almost a surprise when streams of white, hot lightning really do come bursting out of the ceiling and fly straight into Anjo's back and chest.

He must've been so sure he'd already beaten me, because he's not ready for it at all. The sound he makes is almost a wail as he spins around to try and meet the attack, but it's coming from all directions, and it doesn't stop. As if I somehow accidentally commanded all the electricity in the museum to surge to this spot—to him—and, as I blow past him, I'm almost transfixed by it. My mouth gaping at the way his whole body actually lights up from inside.

I don't hang back to see what else might happen. The door is swinging open, and I can see Tom and Dylan and Gwilim and all my friends on the other side. Most of them are covered in burns and cuts and bruises, but they're very much alive. Gwilim grabs for Yvette, pulling her past him and into Rishi's arms as Rafael picks up Gabriel and runs out after them. Min-suk folds the two Silva boys into a quick hug, then carts them off with the help of Eilian and Leti.

Dylan waits by the door, reaching his hand toward me as if he might physically pull me out of the room too, but there's only one thought in my mind now.

"Go, go, go!" I shout at him, waving my hand in a command. "He's too strong! Get everyone out of here!"

Because whatever I did with the electricity just now, I've got no confidence it'll hold Anjo for long, and my stores of essensal energy are already dangerously depleted. Anjo, on the other hand, still has so much energy left, that we'd need a much bigger army to withstand him.

Whatever Yvette thought her plan could achieve, our only option at this point is to get everyone to safety and wait to face Anjo again some other day, after the universe decides to finally grace me with my real Way Reader powers.

Dylan shouts for everyone to fall back, and anyone still left in the lab starts pushing toward the exit. But there are too many people, and too many cubicles and tables still in the way.

Our group of friends barely has time to make it partway across the room when, at the back of my mind, I sense an intense pressure on the particles of the wall behind us. I scream at the top of my lungs for everyone to get down, but I'm not fast enough. The wall explodes. Pieces the size of giant boulders fly outward, and I fling my hand up instinctive, picture all of it turning to dust in the air. And, without my understanding how it's happened, it works.

A cloud of grit rolls over the room. It stings as it plasters my skin and pours into my lungs. I choke on it, hear other people coughing, but as far as I can tell, no one's been crushed to death.

Then I hear Anjo's laughter. Full-bodied and cruel. Everyone stops in their tracks, and we all turn toward the sound like we're in a trance. He emerges from the dust, out of the hole he blasted in the wall. Floating through the air with his eyes wild and his cloak rippling behind him.

"So, this is it," he says, his voice carrying through the room as he points at me with a sweep of his arm. "*THIS* is what the universe sent to stop me?"

He looks slow around at all the eyes transfixed on him.

"This *child* is all the universe can muster? After being taught your whole lives to bow to the whims of the universe, this is the hero it gave you. You were promised an all-powerful Way Reader, but what you received is a clumsy little girl."

The floor beneath me goes soft again, and I lurch sideways, my arms flailing for balance for a second before I manage to solidify the earth and regain my footing. Dylan comes in behind me as if to help, but I shake my head at him, my cheeks hot.

Anjo sneers to the crowd, "If you wish to see something truly powerful, I will happily demonstrate."

In all that's happened today, I guess my mind's been opened up in some new way, because, yet again, I sense a thing that I shouldn't be able to sense. There's a change in Anjo's essence that coincides with the barest shift in his expression. The slightest warning of what's about to come. Then, with a tick of his hand, he flings a near invisible thing at me. A dagger made, somehow, of his own essenal energy. So dense and sharp and thin it can't be seen by the naked eye, and I'm guessing probably most people in the room don't even know what's happening.

I thrust my mind out to meet it—to dissolve it in the air before it reaches me—but the bonds in its particles are too strong. I brace myself to get hit and realize too late it's not me he was aiming for.

The dagger sails past me, grazing my shoulder and sinking straight into Dylan's chest, passing through his tactical vest like it isn't even there. He cries out in pain and falls, thudding to the hard floor with an awful sound.

"*Dylan!*" I spin toward him at the same time that I sense everyone around me start moving too. Swelling forward to try and help. But before anyone can reach us, Anjo's on me.

He grabs my head and lifts me up by it, slamming me down to the ground so hard it takes my breath and sends ringing pain through my skull. With a motion of his hands, everyone that was coming to our aid just goes flying away as easy as if they were bits of debris. Then Anjo flings up an energy barrier to keep them all out and wraps his other hand around my throat so tight all the world around us goes black, leaving just Anjo above me, painfully clear.

I'm flailing against his hold. I can hear Dylan gasping a few feet away, and I realize this is it. This is the nightmare I've been dreading.

As if to prove me right, Anjo's grassy breath comes hissing into my face.

"Did you really think you were so special?" he demands, and it's worse than the nightmare, because now I can see the hatred on his face. The rabid jealousy that fills the man so full he can't hide it. And now, I know for sure it's Dylan dying beside me.

"Your gifts mean nothing with your witless brain directing them."

Even though I've only heard Anjo's words once before, I know what he's going to say almost as if I'd memorized it.

"Hear how your friend suffers for your foolhardiness. The universe made a mistake with you, but I will fix it."

His fingers digging into my scalp drive my head into the hard ground. No matter how much I kick against him, I can't get him off me, and I know what's coming. Fixating on a point below his face—a silver, wing-shaped clasp that's holding his cloak together—I tell myself I'm ready for the feel of his mind entering mine, but then it's there and I know I never could've prepared myself for the violation of it.

"Don't worry," he says. "Though this will hurt quite a lot, you won't remember any of the pain afterward."

This is where the sighting ended. This is where I'm supposed to perform some act of self-determination and make real life events go my way. But I'm so, so tired. This day has been too much, from start to finish. With so little sleep, and Teresa missing, and Sham's death. With all my poor attempts at fighting Anjo, which have already drained me to my core.

As he burrows into my mind, searching for whatever information he's looking for, I'm aware of people attacking the energy barrier, trying to get in.

I throw my will against Anjo's again, like I did when he was targeting my other internal organs, but it's no use. I don't have the energy left to stop him. At least, not enough of my own.

Deep inside my essence, where it's been tucked out of sight through this whole ordeal, I become aware of Sham's calming energy again. A wave of hope washes over me, but when I call on the energy, it doesn't budge. *Not for this*, it seems to say, and I want to scream back, *If not now, then when?*

I'm still struggling against Anjo, but I feel the end of my fight coming and there's part of me that just wants to give in.

Then, as if it has a life of its own, my parents' locket goes skittering on its chain across my chest, dragging Sham's necklace with it. Until they both come to rest in the nook between my collarbones, and I'm washed over real sudden with the memory of Mom pressing that locket into my hands the night we said goodbye. Of her holding my face and telling me how proud she was. Telling me that I was already all I needed to be to fulfill my Way Reader role.

A pang of guilt shoots through me. Shame, at how easily I failed her —failed everyone—but it's hard to remember the love of your mom without feeling at least a little worthy of it, and I know I can't give up. Maybe I'm not as powerful as The Angel, but maybe just being Zanny really is enough.

You're trapped in the grip of a raging madman, I try Mom's thought exercise again, *and you've got about zero of your own energy left to give. What do you do?*

Slowing my breath and trying to ignore Anjo as he pokes and prods at the inner workings of my brain, I focus on my energy flow like Rishi taught me during tai chi. I let go of my worry that I'm not powerful enough, that I don't know what to do, and I call on what I think has probably always been the best part of me—what I suspect has probably been the thing helping me all night—my imagination.

Pulling from another memory back in Flemingsburg—that moment when I decided to be the Way Reader—I imagine myself tapping into the energy of the universe again. Imagine that energy collecting in the veins of my toes and fingers, fizzing up my legs, my arms, through my abdomen. Flooding into my essence, swirling up the back of my neck, then into my brain.

Anjo senses something, and starts to pull away, but he's too late.

I let the energy erupt out of me. Straight out of my essence in a torrential beam of light. It hits Anjo in the chest and throws him backward so fast I only have time to see his eyes go wide with surprise and pain before he's out of my sight. I hear the sound of his body hitting against the barrier he created, and a second later, I'm aware of the barrier itself starting to dissolve.

I rise to my feet, slow, but strong. I'm on fire with energy. I can feel it pulsing through me. Touching every particle, charging through my bones. I'm the sun itself. The brightest star.

Rishi and Gwilim and several of our other friends scramble over the last of the energy barrier and then stop to stare at me. There are loads of other people behind them staring as well. I see the awe in their faces, and I realize I'm radiating light. My whole body glowing as if I really am a sun.

Anjo's lying ten feet away. If it'd been anyone else but him, I'm sure what I did would've killed them, but Anjo isn't anyone else. He starts to push himself shaky off the ground, one hand held hard to his chest as he turns around to face me.

Whatever he did to withstand my beam of energy, has definitely used up a lot of his reserves, but with the takings he did, he still has more than enough. I, on the other hand, am near fully drained. What I'm doing right now—channeling the energy of the universe—it still requires something of me, and I don't know how much longer I can manage it. Anjo could probably beat me and everyone else here if he was smart about it, but there's something else that's changed for him now.

The man's afraid. I can see it shuddering through his essence and tensing up his face. His eyes dart around the crowd of people watching us, then lock on me. He thinks he's trapped.

"Do you surrender?" I ask him in my most authoritative voice. "Do you agree to give yourself up to the GIB?"

He sneers. Let's out this bitter breath of a laugh. "So, you're a believer in the moral high ground, are you? I suppose I shouldn't be surprised."

He takes a slow step toward me, and I push my glow a little brighter, trying to warn him off. Trying not to show my own fear.

Near me, Dylan's breath has gone quieter. Out of the corner of my eye, I see Gwilim kneel down beside him, start to do what he can to keep him alive. Dylan's energy blocker must've gotten knocked off at some point because I can see his essence, and I can tell he's draining fast. I worry if I don't end this thing with Anjo soon, Dylan really will die.

"You're outnumbered," I tell Anjo, sliding as nonchalant as possible into a defensive position, hoping the move is at least a little intimidating.

Around me, I see other people taking up defensive stances as well, their faces illuminated by the light pouring off me.

"Anjo," I say in another bluff attempt, "you don't know what I'm capable of—"

Before I can finish, he's springing toward me.

Pushing himself off the particles of the air so that he reaches me in almost an instant. He grabs for my throat again, digging in his fingers, and what I do next is pure instinct.

I explode.

Energy erupts out of me more wild than before. Not just out of my essence, but all down the front of me. A light so bright it blinds even me. I hear Anjo bellow in pain. Hear shouts as everyone else dives for cover. Feel the sensation of all that energy expanding and then suddenly collapsing back into me like I'm a supernova. And then, like a supernova, I black out.

When I come to, my head's swimming and I feel like just about every inch of my body's been bruised, inside and out. The whole room is in chaos, with people running here and there, and at first I can't figure out what's going on. There are only two things I'm sure of.

One is that I can't sense Anjo's essence anywhere. Which means, either he's dead, or he's gone.

The second is that Dylan's still dying.

Grunting in pain, I roll onto my side, blinking away my dizziness and looking to where Dylan is sprawled on the ground a few feet away. Eilian's kneeling at his head looking grim, and Gwilim's bent over him, his hands on Dylan's chest and desperation in his face and his essensal energy.

I push up to my hands and knees. Force myself to start scoot-crawling over to them. Around us, I notice Gwylwyr and Keepers and GIB making floating light matter cots for the injured so they can transport them out of the room. Someone in a Gwylwyr uniform shouts to Gwilim that the medic vans will be here any second, and Gwilim shouts back that he needs help now.

The rest of our friends are nowhere to be seen, and, along with Anjo, I can't sense Wotan Schmid or any other takers here. Which means, whatever else is going on right now, I can give my whole focus to Dylan.

When Gwilim notices me lurching toward them, he lets out this awful, anguishing sound.

"His energy's draining," he says to me. "But I can't locate the wound. I can't fix what I can't see."

Eilian doesn't say a word. Just locks her eyes on mine in a kind of plea.

I pull myself up on the opposite side of Dylan and start checking him over as if I even know what I'm looking for. Gwilim's right. There's no blood. No actual sign of entry.

"I'll see what I can do," I say with more confidence than I feel, considering I'm definitely no medic and my own essensal energy hasn't replenished much.

When I lay my palm on Dylan's chest, all that tells me he's still alive is the bit of warmth left in his body, the slight rise and fall of his lungs, and the presence of the very last dregs of his essensal energy. At first glance, his essence itself seems to be intact, but I know that can't actually be the case or his energy wouldn't be near gone. Whatever damage Anjo did to him, I think it was meant to be hard to find.

Closing my eyes and forcing my breath to slow down, I try to tap into my imagination again. I picture Anjo's energy dagger. Picture the moment when it entered Dylan's chest. Then I imagine the wound pulling me in, drawing me to it like a magnet.

And there it is. Way down, on a particle level so deep, I wouldn't be surprised if there isn't even a name for it yet, I can see the place where Anjo's weapon pierced Dylan right through the shell of his essence itself. The tiniest injury, as far as size goes, but now I can see that the whole particle structure of his essence is compromised by it. Somehow, I know fixing it is going to require a lot more energy than I've got, and I don't think my body has the strength to try channeling the universe a second time.

Which means, yet again, I'm left with only one other option. This time, though, as soon as I reach my mind for it, Sham's energy responds. That hint of spring flowers and summer rain shifts inside my essence as if it's eager to be used.

It's almost easy after that. I open a path from my essence to Dylan's, and Sham's energy moves down my arm, through my fingers and into his chest. Wraps itself around his wound and weaves the particles of his essence back together like threads of light being stitched on a translucent loom.

It's beautiful. But also, I can't help feeling a touch of regret as Sham's energy leaves me. Maybe in reality I did barely know her, but having had so clear a sense of her inside my essence for even a few hours makes this moment feel like I'm saying goodbye to a cherished friend.

When it's done, there's no fanfare. No fireworks. No gasp of breath from Dylan to indicate he's been miraculously stolen from the grips of death, but I know right away he's going to be all right. And I know, too, that I've given all I can give for one day.

I slump sideways so fast, Gwilim lunges to catch me.

"Sophie," he says like a question, his body stretched awkward over the top of Dylan's still motionless frame.

"At some point you're going to have to start calling me Zanny," I say, waving him away and pushing myself back up to sitting. "Dylan's okay. I fixed him with my Way Reader powers."

I wiggle my fingers to demonstrate, and Eilian lets out something between a sob and a laugh.

I can't seem to focus proper on her or Gwilim's faces, but I feel their essences filling with relief.

"Where's Rishi and everyone else?" I ask, noting that my words are slurring like I'm drunk and that I seem to be swaying again. My eyes close of their own accord. "Did that bisher Anjo die?"

Eilian's laugh this time has a tinge of bitterness to it.

"Unfortunately, he got away," Gwilim answers. "Along with Wotan and a few others. But Anjo seemed pretty badly off. Rishi and Tom and that Laugadóttir woman led some teams after them. Leti and Min-suk took Yvette and the Silva lads to the hospital. Medic vans are on the way."

My eyes snap open, focusing as best they can on Gwilim. "Laugadóttir was here?"

"Don't know how she knew what was happening, but she came with backup."

A wave of anxiety washes over me at the thought that we don't know what that woman's true loyalties are. If she's on Anjo's side, she could be leading them into a trap.

"We gotta go after them," I try to stand up, but Eilian leans over now and grabs my arm real firm.

"No, you don't," she says with surprising authority. "What you've *got* to do is rest until those medics arrive."

I try to protest, but I'm way too tired.

"They've got it well in hand," Gwilim assures me. "Rishi and Tom won't trust that woman too easily. And they've oodles of Gwylwyr and Keepers to watch their backs." He stands up and starts toward me. "In the meantime, you'd best lie down before you fall over. I'll use my com energy to make cots for you and Dylan."

I've got loads of questions that need answering, but I also want very much to not be upright anymore. I ease myself to the ground again to wait while Gwilim pulls the light matter from his com, but as soon as my head touches the debris-covered floor, I'm already drifting off.

I wake up in the back of a large emvee ambulance, aching all over and lying in a floating cot that sways gentle in the air with each turn the ambulance takes. It almost rocks me straight back into sleep, but then I see Dylan in another cot beside me, still unconscious and looking about as near death as he did before.

For a second, I panic, thinking I managed to botch his healing after all. A quick check in his essence tells me his energy is slowly building up, though. There's a medic in the back of the ambulance with us, and when I ask her how Dylan's doing, she assures me he really is all right.

"He may sleep for another day or so, yet," she says. "It's part of the body's natural response when it's healing a wound on the essensal level."

She tells me about my own injuries too, saying I've got a whole lot of external and internal bruising, and that I'm being taken to the hospital to make sure there isn't anything worse.

"It's as much a precaution as anything. With treatment, you should be fine soon enough."

Which is about as much information as my brain can handle, I guess, because I drift off again after that. The next few hours are a haze of brief, half-waking episodes stretched between anxiety-filled replays of all the worst moments of the day. Sham's ruined body. Anjo attacking my heart, my lungs. Dylan falling to the ground.

You'd think making it through the real-life version of my nightmare sighting would've offered some relief, but instead my mind's just hoarding even more nightmares.

I'm vaguely aware of being brought inside the hospital and moved into a room that's so nice it feels like it belongs in a hotel. Of seeing Dylan being pushed past me into the room next door. Aware of a couple nurses changing me into a beige hospital gown and placing light matter sensors all over me before inputting information into light matter panels on the side of my unbelievably comfortable bed.

I'm not entirely sure it's not a dream when Rishi visits to tell me they weren't able to catch Anjo, and to assure me that Yvette's going to be fine. That the doctors found bruising across her brain and burn marks on her skin from where the straps hurt her, but that, like me, she should be pretty much good as new after a few days of care.

Then I'm lost to the nightmares again, and when I finally, really do wake up, I'm alone in my room. The sun's pouring through a huge window, and most my aching is gone. At first, I think maybe several days have passed, but when I check my com, it says it's only the next morning.

While I was asleep, the news of my real identity seems to have gotten out. I have a flood of news notifications with headlines like, *Way Reader Revealed!* or *Lucas Family Friend More than She Appears*, with a picture of me that Eilian apparently posted on the helix during my introduction party.

In the photo, I'm all done up in that dress Eilian's mom got me, and, while I do look totally amazing, I also look completely and utterly overwhelmed. Which is fitting, I guess. I haven't stopped feeling overwhelmed since this whole thing started.

I only skim through a couple articles before turning off my news notifications altogether. Yesterday, I realized my secret was on its way out, but I hadn't considered what it'd be like to have everyone in the Painter world knowing I'm the Way Reader and having their own thoughts and feelings about it.

So, I ignore the news, and I check my text messages. There are several from Gwilim, asking me to tell him how I'm doing and updating me on everything that's happened since I came to the hospital. He confirms, like Rishi did, that Anjo and Wotan got away. He says he and Tom and a team of Gwylwyr are searching the museum for any more clues to where Anjo might've headed. He also says that, thanks to information he and Tom gathered while they were infiltrating the Sons of Morning, the GIB and Keepers are partnering to run a bunch of raids on taker hideouts in Deffro today.

Eilian must've already told Uncle Uri and Aunt Nia everything that's happened because there's a message from Uri saying he hopes I'm doing well and that they plan to come see me later, as well as a series of messages from Nia that are exactly what I'd expect. She should've guessed I was the Way Reader. It was obvious to her from the start that I was special. She can only imagine the burden that must've been on my shoulders this whole time. And then a message pouring out her gratitude to me for saving Dylan and Yvette's lives and keeping Gwilim and Eilian safe, which fills me with a confusing mix of emotions.

There's still a huge part of me that struggles to believe yesterday was anything more than luck. I mean, I barely stumbled my way through it, and I've got zero idea how reliably I can recreate the imagination-powered moves that helped me win in the end. I don't feel like a hero, and I'm absolutely terrified by the thought of having to face Anjo again. At the same time, I can't help being a little proud of myself too for what I managed to do. A little relieved I didn't fail.

Luckily, my Deffro friends aren't as sentimental as Aunt Nia. There's a bunch of messages from them on a text chain Eilian's jokingly named, *These Bishers*. It starts last night, and at first, it's all them just checking in with each other and confirming everyone's all right.

Eilian says she made it home, and Leti says she's with her brother Tama at the GIB. Min-suk lets everyone know Rafael and Gabriel are physically unharmed and that they'll be staying with him and his sisters for the foreseeable future. Rafael tries to apologize for attempting to kidnap me, but the others tell him in no uncertain terms that he has no reason to apologize to them. They tell him that I explained his situation and that they all understand. If he wonders how I knew about what happened, he doesn't ask, and I figure he and I will have to chat sometime.

He does ask if anyone knows how I'm doing, and Eilian says Nia and Uri stopped by my room at the hospital while I was sleeping and were told I'd be okay. She mentions, too, that I instructed her and

Gwilim to call me Zanny, and adds, *as if that's even a real name.*

Then, as the night wears on and I still haven't communicated, Eilian starts texting things like, *Do you suppose that Zanny person will ever wake up?* And, *She thinks because she saved my brother's life, she can laze about.* After a few more like that, Leti joins in on the joke too.

"*I'm Zanny, and I'm a real-life superhero,*" she writes as if imitating me. "*I no longer have time for my normie friends.*"

I grin as I read through their messages, wondering how it is that, in just the few days I've been here in Deffro, these people have come to mean so much to me.

When I text, saying, *I'm sorry. Who's this? Are you some of the people I saved yesterday?* I get a rapid series of laughing gifs and animated stickers in response.

It all seems so natural and everyday, and I'm surprised by a sudden rush of homesickness for Sylvia and Logan back in Flemingsburg. This twisting pain in my chest and gut and an overwhelming craving to know what they're doing right now. What they'd think about everything that's happened to me. What they'd say about my new friends.

I'm just about to test if I can access their Particle-Blocked social media accounts through the Painter helix, when a blond-haired nurse comes through my door saying he's here to check on me.

He's probably only ten years older than I am and, at first, when he keeps stealing glimpses of my face as he's checking my vitals and pulling the data from the light matter sensors stuck to me, I figure maybe he thinks I'm cute. Then I remember all the articles about my being the Way Reader, and I realize his less than covert glances are actually just brazen curiosity.

Then, as he runs a scanner over my torso to get images of the bruising in there, he says all astounded that he's never seen anyone heal so fast. Going on and on about how I was only admitted twelve hours before and the bruising's already halfway to being gone, like I'm some sort of aberration. A thing to study or stare at through glass. And the more he exclaims, the more I wish he'd just hurry and be done.

He redeems himself a little when he finally tells me I'm free to get out of bed, as long as I don't leave the hospital and I don't remove my sensors before my doctor gives her okay. He also says I can take a shower and get dressed, pointing out a Painter-style cleaning machine in the bathroom that can wash and mend yesterday's clothes in only a few minutes. Things I do as soon as he leaves my room.

A mental check next door tells me Dylan's essensal energy is nearly renewed, but there's such a peace to it I figure he's still sleeping. Another check tells me Yvette's just down the hall and that, while she's clearly in some pain, she's probably awake.

I find her sitting upright in her hospital bed in a room that looks exactly like mine. She's busy with something on her com, but as soon as I step through her door, she closes it down and says without preamble, "You want to know why I did it."

Which, of course, is true.

She leans against the upraised back of her bed and locks her gaze on me with the look of someone who has a doozy of a story to tell. Her hair is pulled into a no-fuss bun at the nape of her neck, and she's still wearing one of the hospital's beige gowns, but I think it'd be hard for Yvette to look anything but regal.

"The answer is, I did it to save Gwilim and Tom, and you'd best sit down because I have some things to get off my chest."

She flashes a very Yvette-type smile—one that says, *I'm using my joking voice, but trust you'll do exactly as I've suggested*—and I drag one of the room's cushioned chairs over to her bed, only wincing a little with the pain the effort sends through my insides.

"The only reason either Tom or Gwilim was involved with the Gwylwyr is because of me," she explains as soon as I'm seated. "After Tom's dad betrayed Cadfan Lucas, the fury in those two young men was obvious for everyone to see. Both had already, in the past, shown tendencies for a certain amount of self-sabotage, and it occurred to me that, where none of my current Gwylwyr agents had yet had much luck infiltrating the Sons of Morning, these two might manage it simply by seeming reckless enough.

"I didn't think much beyond that. I approached Tom, and Nia's precious Gwilim—who are both like family to me and trust me as such —and I asked them to do something that I have not, if I'm quite honest with myself, at any point been fully certain was a wise or fair course of action. I made Gwilim pretend openly to believe Cadfan was corrupt. Tom didn't have to pretend to hate his father for selling Cadfan out. He just had to pretend at different reasons behind his anger. Ones that made it more believable he might turn to the takers himself. Then I made them keep the truth secret from their families and closest friends, even to the point of doing harm to some of their most treasured relationships. Even knowing it could harm my relationships with some of my closest friends, when it finally came out."

I think about her friendship with Nia. About the tension between Gwilim and pretty much the whole Lucas family, and I understand the guilt in her voice.

"I'd convinced myself our goals were more important than anything else. That I wasn't asking them to risk anything more than what I would risk myself. But when Gwilim called me yesterday saying Tom was on his way with Wotan Schmid, my only thought was that I needed to do whatever it took not to lay suspicion at either of their doors before I could ensure their safety."

"You were willing to sacrifice yourself to The Angel to keep Tom and Gwilim safe?" No matter how I look at it, I can't imagine Yvette making that decision without accepting on some level that she was going to come out of it with her brain a mush.

"I'm not the hero you're imagining, Zanny. I believed you wouldn't let us down."

This is the part that's still so baffling to me. I mean, what about me could possibly have made her so confident? "Are you a reader?"

Her smile then is tired and tinged with melancholy. "No. But I trust my instincts, and I'm good at reading people. I saw in you someone who'd do what was needed, when the time came."

I'm quiet for a minute, looking up at her. Trying to comprehend the fact that her belief in me hadn't stemmed from my being the Way Reader but from something she'd seen in me myself.

I only stay with her a little longer after that. I can tell talking is wearing her out, so, once it's clear she's said all she needed to, I make an excuse to leave and let her rest.

I'm planning on tracking down some sort of breakfast but, as I'm stepping into the hall, I get a message from Eilian saying that Dylan's awake and she and Nia and Uri are coming to see him now. I've barely read her whole message before I'm beelining it straight for his room.

It may be the case that Eilian also mentioned that, since Teresa's staying in this very same hospital, her doctor said she could come see Dylan too. And it may be the case that, as much as my opinion of Teresa has shifted, I'm not exactly eager to have a chat with Dylan while under her careful scrutiny.

But mostly, if I'm being honest, the reason I go rushing to his room is probably because something changed for me the moment I watched Anjo's impossible dagger hit Dylan in the chest. Something I'm not about to examine right now but that makes it feel absolutely imperative I see him this instant and confirm he's okay.

Dylan sounds tired when he answers my knock on the door. When I step inside, he's leaning against the upraised back of his bed with his expanded com screen floating above his lap. Instead of looking at the screen, though, he's staring out the window at the cloud-dotted sky. And, the way the morning sunlight falls across him, he looks like the subject of some classic painting. A wounded soldier, contemplating all he's lost.

That little something that I'm not examining tries to make me feel things about seeing him like that, but I force myself to focus on other details. Like the fact that, other than seeming a bit fatigued and strained, his color's mostly back to normal and his essensal energy is fully refilled.

Then he turns and sees it's me, and a smile erupts across his face— all soft and warm, and unabashedly pleased. I feel it like a slug in the heart, and the thought flies through my head that I don't know what I'd have done if he'd died.

Suddenly self-conscious, I say, "Hey," real eloquent and offer him an awkward wave.

"Hey," he says back, his smile deepening. "You're all right, then? Gwilim said you took a beating."

"Well," I move kind of tentative toward the side of his bed, motioning at myself with my hands. "As you can see, I'm doing just fine. According to my nurse, I'm a medical oddity who's got spooky fast healing powers."

Dylan laughs, and I feel like warmth's just spilled through my insides.

"What about you?" I ask. "Feeling like someone who nearly died?"

He leans his head back against his pillow and considers me, still smiling. "I'm doing all right, thanks to someone."

I really cannot handle him looking at me like that.

"I'm guessing you heard Anjo and Wotan got away?" I blurt out, and Dylan's immediately more sober.

"Yes." He nods. "About that. It's occurred to me that we don't know what Anjo is able to see when he goes into someone's brain to alter it. How much detail he might have been able to obtain while he was in your mind. We also know that, outside of Anjo and Wotan, there's still Beelzebub to contend with. So, to be safe, I think we'd best bring your mum to Deffro now and put your uncle and cousins in protective custody."

I've never felt such a thrill of excitement and apprehension at the same time. Apprehension at the idea that Anjo might be able to find my mom, and excitement at the thought of seeing her.

"The doctor wants to keep monitoring me here for another day at least," Dylan continues, "but Rishi and Tama can help you make the necessary arrangements. The Yokio's card is in my trousers' pocket."

He points to where his clothes are neatly folded on top of a dresser against the near wall.

It's probably a reflection of my current state of mind that it feels weirdly intimate to dig through his pockets, even though the pants aren't even on him. I hold them kind of ginger while trying not to look like I'm being awkward about it, and as soon as I feel the rewards card shiver into the shape of a cell phone at the touch of my fingers, I'm quick to grab it out and slide it into my own pocket.

"We've still got Sham's files to go through," I say as I turn back to Dylan, reaching up and busying myself with unclasping the chain from around the back of my neck. "We've also got a lot more people on our team now." I pull the necklace out from under my shirt as I move back to the side of his bed, dangling it toward him like an offering. "Maybe, if there's some way to copy whatever's on this, we could have Eilian and everybody help us sort through it all."

He sits upright, reaching for the necklace at the same time that I move to drop it into his hand, and my fingers brush against his on accident. I make an embarrassingly audible sound at the essensal energy that sparks between our skin. But, for once, I could swear it affects Dylan too, because he goes real still for a second, and when he pulls his hand back from mine, I see his chest rise like he'd been holding his breath.

"It shouldn't be too hard to suss that out," he says, and if he actually was affected by my touch, he doesn't show it in his voice. Just tips the necklace from his right hand into his left and looks back up at me all matter-of-fact.

"Well, then." I tap a finger reflexive on the sideboard of his bed, not sure what to do or say now. "I don't want to wear you out before your family gets here. Think I'll go hunt down some breakfast, and then try getting hold of Rishi and Gwilim."

I start to turn away, but before I can take a step, his hand's around my left wrist, holding me in place.

"Zanny—"

I turn back toward him, trying to keep my expression neutral even though my pulse is suddenly hammering so hard I'm sure he can feel it in his fingers.

"I should've been there," he says, once my eyes have locked on his. "You shouldn't have had to face Anjo alone."

I'm not sure whether he means when I was stuck with Yvette and the Silvas in Anjo's torture chamber or when Anjo was trying to mess up my brain. But, as bad as those moments were, nothing Anjo did to me was actually the scariest part about yesterday.

"Until I'm more a match for his power, I don't want anyone I care about anywhere near that man." It comes out of me real raw, and I'm not even embarrassed that Dylan might pick up on the implication that I care about him. "The best thing you can do is keep yourself alive."

We stare at each other, his fingers still around my wrist and my breath short. This time I'm almost certain there's something in the way he looks at me, but then my com buzzes with an incoming message and the automated voice says in my ear it's from Gwilim. I pull my gaze away from Dylan's and turn my com hand palm-up to see the message.

I figure Gwilim's just sending another update or checking in on me, but when I register what I'm actually seeing there, I freeze.

"What's wrong?" Dylan asks, immediately on alert.

"Nothing. It's just—"

I turn my hand so Dylan can see the picture of the silver-winged clasp Gwilim found in the museum rubble. A part of me is there again, Anjo's hand around my throat and his energy inside my mind, but Dylan just looks up at me, questioning.

"Anjo was using this to hold his cloak together. I had a real clear view of it when he was attacking me."

I see the understanding glimmer in Dylan's eyes. His hand has slipped down my left arm so that our palms are near touching, and now he folds his fingers full around mine so the sparks of our energies pulse against each other. He doesn't say anything, but he doesn't need to. He's probably familiar with the sort of fear my body holds now. The knowledge of pain and violence that it's learned from firsthand experience.

I'm betting he'd also recognize how determined I am to do anything in my power to stop Anjo from hurting anyone else like that.

"There's a chance I can get a sighting from this thing," I say, quiet. "Something that might lead us to where Anjo is. I think, the sooner I get started on that the better."

Even though I'm dreading what that clasp might show me. Dreading actually finding Anjo again.

I pull my hand soft out of Dylan's, and he doesn't stop me. But as I turn to go, he says, "Just remember you're not alone in this, Zanny. We all care about you too. We're here to help."

I glance back at him as I start to pull on the handle of his door, offering him a crooked attempt at a smile.

"You know what's the mark of the greatest superheroes?" I ask, trying to make my voice playful and light.

Dylan raises an eyebrow.

"The sort of people they count as friends."

Touching my fingers to my forehead as if tipping a cap to him, I open his door the rest of the way and step out of his room.

GLOSSARY OF TERMS

Note that pronunciations reflect how words are said in the world of the Painters and not necessarily in the root languages from which the words are derived.

Alpha [AL-fuh] – *slang*. Trendsetter. An original.

Ascensè [ah-sen-SAY] – a technique used in Painter dancing, where the density of the air beneath the feet is manipulated to cause the dancer to momentarily float between each step they take.

Aykar [AY-kar] – ceremony where the Way Reader is presented to the Seven Elders of the original seven city-states of the Painter Republic.

Bāṛi [BAH-ree] – Bangla word meaning "home."

Bisher [BISH-ur] – *slang*. A highly unlikeable person. Someone belonging in a rubbish bin.

Calon tân [KAH-lohn TAHN] – *slang*. Welsh Painter expletive. Directly translates as "heart of fire."

Emvee [EM-vee] – transportation vehicle that moves using electro-magnetism.

Essence [ES-suhns] – internal organ that is both made of essensal energy and stores an individual's essensal energy.

Essensal code [es-SENS-uhl kohd] – essensal energy pattern that is unique to each individual.

Essensal energy [es-SENS-uhl EN-ur-jee] – energy found in a person's essence. A core part of an individual's sense of self. Energy used by Painters to fuel particle manipulation.

Flaring [FLER-eeng] – the act of shedding energy while a Painter is undergoing their transfiguring.

Gindge [Gihnj] – *slang*. Offensive term referring to a dead body once its essence and shadow have passed on to the next dimension.

Gwylwyr [gwihl-WEE-ur] – Welsh word meaning "watchers." Name of Deffro city's elite security force.

Helcom, com [HEL-cahm, cahm] – smart device similar to a smartphone but worn as a ring on the finger.

Helix [HEE-lihks] – term for the Painter version of the internet.

Ignus [IHG-nuhs] – part of a Painter's brain near the base of their skull that regulates particle manipulation.

Ionic [ai-AHN-ihk] – *slang.* Unpredictable. Chaotic. Usually used to describe a person.

Keepers of the Way [KEE-purz uhv thuh WAY] – ancient organization that champions the forces of good. Protects and supports the Way Reader.

Kwakwaka'wakw [KWAHK-wahk-kay-WAHK] – meaning, "the people who speak Kwak´wala." Referring to the eighteen First Nations of British Columbia who speak the Kwak´wala language.

Kwak´wala [KWAHK-wuh-luh] – a Wakashan language spoken by eighteen First Nations in Western Canada.

Light matter [lait MAT-tur] – a form of highly energetic matter that produces little heat.

Magnix [MAG-nihks] – Deffro city's underground train that moves using electro-magnetism.

Marw [MAH-roo] – Welsh word meaning "death." Used by Painters as an expletive, often preceded by the English word "bloody."

'Namgis [NAHM-gees] – a Kwakwaka'wakw tribe in the northern Vancouver Island area.

Nefsakes [nev-SAYKS] – *slang.* Expletive. Amalgam of the Welsh word "*nef*," meaning "heaven," and the English word "sakes."

Ne'nagwa'nakwala [NET-nah-kwuht-NAH-kwuh-lah] – Kwak´wala word meaning "going home."

O, hridoy jole [OH, HUH-REE-doy JOH-lee] – *slang.* Bangla phrase translating to "Oh, my heart is burning."

Painter [PAYN-tur] – an individual who can alter matter with their minds.

Particle manipulation [PAHR-tik-uhl man-IH-pyoo-lay-shuhn] – the act of altering matter with one's mind.

Particle sailing [PAHR-tik-uhl SAY-leeng] – mode of travel used by Painters. The act of moving through space by pushing one's mind or willpower against nearby particles.

Particle-Blocked [PAHR-tik-uhl blahkt] – someone who is not a Painter. Someone who cannot alter matter with their mind.

Particular pattern [Pahr-TIK-yool-lahr PAT-urn] – the unique makeup or structure of connected particles that shape a given form of matter.

Pono [POH-noh] – derived from the Maori word meaning "honest." A Painter greeting used when first meeting someone. The act of placing one's palms flat against another person's palms.

Ramu [RAH-moo] – derived from the ancient Akkadian word meaning "to love." A Painter greeting used between close friends and family. The act of placing one's hand across the back of another Painter's neck, near their ignus.

Reader [REE-dur] – a Painter who can use sighting triggers to receive visions.

Rite of Crossing [rait uhv CRAHS-seeng] – ritual performed in the event of someone's violent death. The act of slowly pulling a dead or dying individual's essensal energy into your own essence in order to give their essence and shadow time to pass over to the next dimension.

Seven Elders [SEV-uhn EL-durz] – elected representatives for the seven original Painter Republic city states. Largely symbolic.

Shadow [SHAD-oh] – what Particle-Blocked people refer to as an aura.

Sighting [SAIT-eeng] – a vision.

Sighting trigger [SAIT-eeng TRIG-gur] – a cluster of particles that can trigger a vision for a reader.

Sons of Morning [suhnz uhv MOHR-neeng] – secret society/cult centered on the practice of harvesting essensal energy from people who have been killed violently.

Steel face [steel fays] – a zoetic that is typically somewhat humanoid and has a face made of silver metal.

Taker [TAY-kur] – colloquial term referring to a Painter who preys on other people in order to harvest essensal energy.

Transfiguring [tranz-FIHG-yur-eeng] – process a Painter's body goes through as it develops the proper organs to facilitate particle manipulation. Usually takes place in late teenage years.

Way Reader [way REE-dur] – a particularly powerful reader, said to be chosen by the universe every century or so and tasked with the responsibility of defeating the greatest evil of their time.

Zoetic [zoh-E-tihk] – a machine made from biological materials.

CAST OF CHARACTERS

In order of appearance. Pronunciations are best approximations.

Alexandra (Zanny) Monroe [a-leks-ZAN-druh (ZAN-nee) mahn-ROH] – Daydreamer living a quiet life in her small mountain town.

Rishi Mitra [RIH-shee MEE-trah] – First of Zanny's two guardians. Married to Yvette Griffiths.

Dylan Lucas [DIH-lahn LOO-kahs] – Second of Zanny's two guardians. Considered by some to be annoyingly good looking.

Logan Jacobsen [LOH-guhn JAY-kuhb-suhn] – One of Zanny Monroe's childhood best friends.

Riona Monroe [ree-OH-nuh mahn-ROH] – Zanny's mother.

Nia Lucas [NEE-uh LOO-kahs] – Dylan Lucas's aunt on his father's side. Married to Uri Jacoby.

Uri Jacoby [YOO-ree JAY-kuhb-ee] – Dylan Lucas's uncle by law. Married to Nia Lucas.

Eilian Lucas [AI–lee-ahn LOO-kahs] – Dylan Lucas's younger sister.

Gweneth Dela Torre [GWEN-eth DAY-lah TOH-ray] – Mother of Dylan, Padrig, and Eilian Lucas. Married to Cadfan Lucas.

Leti Moeaki [LEH-tee moh-EE-ah-KEE] – One of Eilian Lucas's best friends.

Min-suk Holm [mihn-SUHK hohlm] – Another of Eilian Lucas's best friends.

Rafael Silva [hah-fah-E-OO SEE-oo-vah] – Min-suk Holm's boyfriend.

Teresa Maphanga [tuh-REE-suh muh-FAYN-guh] – Min-suk Holm's cousin.

Elspeth [EL-spuhth] – Woman Zanny encounters on the street.

Sham Haddad [sham ha-DAHD] – A journalist.

Gwilim Lucas [GWIHL-lihm LOO-kahs] – Dylan, Eilian, and Padrig Lucas's cousin. Son of Hiarwar Lucas.

Tom Cameron [tahm KAM-ruhn] – Gwilim Lucas's friend.

Mrs. Silva [SEE-oo-vah] – Grandma to Rafael and Gabriel Silva.

Gabriel Silva [gah-bree-E-OO SEE-oo-vah] – Rafael Silva's little brother.

Mr. Moeaki [moh-EE-ah-KEE] – Father to Leti and Tama Moeaki.

Tama Moeaki [TAH-mah moh-EE-ah-KEE] – Leti Moeaki's older brother.

Ms. Huapaya [wah-PAH-yuh] – Mother to Leti and Tama Moeaki.

Ha-yun Holm [hah-YOON hohlm] – One of Min-suk's little sisters.

Dan-bi Holm [dahn-BEE hohlm] – Another of Min-suk's little sisters.

Loui Holm – [LOO-ee hohlm] Min-suk's father.

Itsuko Laugadóttir [EET-suh-koh LOY-yuh-DOH-teerh] – Dylan Lucas's direct supervisor at the Global Intelligence Bureau.

José Anjo [joh-ZAY AHN-joo] – A popular artist Zanny meets at a party.

Jaap Jansen [yahp YAHN-suhn] – Director of the Global Intelligence Bureau

Yvette Griffiths [ee-VET GRIH-fiths] – representative for the Welsh people in the Painter Republic's parliament. Married to Rishi Mitra. Nia Lucas's good friend.

Walter Brandeis [WAHL-tur BRAN-dais] – Representative of Central Canada in the Painter Republic's parliament.

Lamerding [LAM-ur-deeng] – Irish representative in the Painter Republic's parliament.

Wotan Schmid [VOH-tahn shmiht] – An unfriendly man Gwilim brings to a party.

Hiarwar Lucas [HYAHR-wahr LOO-kahs] – President of the Painter Republic. Brother to Nia and Cadfan Lucas. Gwilim's father.

Agent Mickering [MIHK-ur-eeng] – Agent at the Global Intelligence Bureau

Agent Suto [SOO-toh] – Agent at the Global Intelligence Bureau

Notable characters who are mentioned but not seen

Sylvia Álvarez [SIHL-vee-ah AL-vuh-rez] – One of Zanny Monroe's childhood best friends.

Cadfan Lucas [KAHD-vahn LOO-kahs] – Father to Dylan, Eilian, and Padrig Lucas.

Cerian Lucas [KEHR-ee-ahn LOO-kahs] – Mother to Gwilim Lucas.

Padrig Lucas [PAH-drihg LOO-kahs] – Dylan and Eilian Lucas's older brother.

John Cameron [jahn KAM-ruhn] – Tom Cameron's father.

Beau Millers [boh MIHL-urz] – Teresa Maphanga's stepfather

ACKNOWLEDGEMENTS

From conception to publication, *LESSER DEMONS* took over twelve years to become a reality. This is the book that helped me figure out what kind of writer I wanted to be and what kind of stories I wanted to tell. As with most accomplishments in life, I could not have done it on my own.

My first thanks go to Jordan, who kept believing in my writing dreams even when I forgot. Big thanks to Bethany, for reading and re-reading and being excited about every turn this journey took. Thank you to Kathy, Kathy and Mitzi, who helped make my story stronger. And thanks to all my sensitivity readers and cultural consultants, Meghalee, Samiat, Alex, Areej, Nicole and Sia. You helped make the characters more true and vibrant on the page.

Thank you to Gega for bringing Zanny so vividly to life. To Mitzi, again, for lending me your design skills. And thank you to my parents for making stories such an integral part of our family life. I wouldn't have grown into the writer I am without the seeds you planted.